Dark mist shrouds the entire Apothakery in a creeping plume and the sunlight disappears.

Everything yellow turns a dull purple in the changing light and it suddenly feels like midnight, not noon. Folks squirm to the perimeter of the small shop to avoid the mysterious mist. The fog hovers, not quite reaching my patrons or the corners of the room. Finally, it stops spreading.

Ominous, but I'm more concerned the obsidian smoke will change the flavor of any exposed baked goods. I really hope Gertha Fudge isn't right about troublesome Witches and Warlocks. She'd never let anyone live it down.

As I am a *reads the menu ahead of time* kind of girl, surprise is not my favorite feeling. Do I have a recipe for shock? Probably involves ashwagandha and some moonlight.

I swing around the counter, grab an empty sheet pan for defense, and face the fog. Is it just me, or does the mass seem . . . cranky? I hesitate momentarily but Momaw and my mom wouldn't tolerate a threat like this, so I won't, either. I'm not going to be the Frost who loses the family shop to a *cloud*.

But then the mist dissipates with a *POP* before I can swing at it. Shock dusts every face in my periphery when a black envelope falls to the floor at my feet.

Surely this isn't for me . . . And yet, curious, I reach down—

"Don't touch it, child!" Ms. Buchanan fans herself with an empty cupcake liner. "That's higher magic there, that is. I'd recognize the foul stuff anywhere."

My hand pauses. Farmer Kelsey nods. "*Warlock* magic."

THE FAREWITCH OF FOXE HOLLER

ELLEN PAULEY GOFF

SAGA PRESS

LONDON NEW YORK TORONTO
AMSTERDAM/ANTWERP NEW DELHI SYDNEY/MELBOURNE

SAGA PRESS
AN IMPRINT OF SIMON & SCHUSTER, LLC
1230 AVENUE OF THE AMERICAS, NEW YORK, NEW YORK 10020

First Saga Press trade paperback edition July 2026

Interior design by Milly McKinnish

Manufactured in the United States of America

1 3 5 7 9 10 8 6 4 2

Library of Congress Control Number has been applied for.

ISBN 978-1-6680-9917-9 (pbk)
ISBN 978-1-6680-9918-6 (ebook)

To Betty Jo Wickline, Donna Nevaline Vibbert, and Chuyi Leong—
for the grandmothers, witches, and other gritty women

PART ONE

honey

Chapter One

FRIDAY, APRIL 1

Honey's Helpful Hint, from
Honey Frost's Southern Cookbook for Recipes Gone Wrong:

The first thing you need to know about making cornbread is that food is magic.

A holler is best at just that: hollering.

If the folks of Foxe Holler—a crumb of a town way down on a forgotten, lonesome shelf in the pantry of the South—are good at anything, it's making a fuss.

From behind the safety of the counter, I absorb the chaos of the hunger-fueled Friday-morning rush at the Frost Apothakery, the town's only bakery and apothecary of culinary cures. Family run, of course. *Epicures*, Momaw Frost used to call them, despite our efforts to gag her stubborn wordplay.

Your Apothakery now, girl. Momaw's voice chimes in my head from beyond the living world. Not literally. We Frosts don't have that kind of magic. You'd have to trek miles over to a larger town for a Tombwitch.

Right. *Mine.* Honey Frost's Apothakery. My insides squelch.

But I don't have time to dwell on how my twenties didn't go according to plan, because Ms. Buchanan is on one helluva tear this morning.

"And if I have to listen to that woman tell me about her canned pineapple one more time, so help me—Gertha, I said, you would think angels blessed you the way you carry on, but I know the good Lord does not care a lick about your church luncheons . . ."

I mumble a quick *Is that the truth?* and bite my tongue. Any polite nodding—ingrained in my DNA like a *Yes, ma'am*—is only encouragement for a hurricane like Ms. Buchanan. I pass a still-warm honey bourbon bread pudding over the head of the chatty old woman to the man behind her, for his insomnia.

"Thank you kindly," he says, already sniffing the bag.

"Sure thing, Mr. Earl," I answer, hoping my eyes say *Please save me from this conversation*. No luck. He's already munching on his remedy as he walks out the door, and I'm grateful he's got a short drive home 'cause my bread pudding works *fast*.

"—but between you and me, the only thing she yammers on about more is her grandbabies. I told her, Gertha, I said, the only reason you got a litter of grandbabies is because your children are trying to distract you so you quit bothering them—"

"Ms. Buchanan—" I try, but she's been chugging along for five minutes, oblivious to the line that's now ten deep. And I've still got to rescue the cornbread from the oven. The Apothakery is not meant to stop. It operates as quickly and efficiently as the Frost women who've been running it for decades. And I'm pretty sure one of Gertha's prolific children in question is just out of earshot by the door, perusing the apple butter I jar myself. My mom calls it the curse of small towns; Momaw Frost would've gleefully declared *karma*.

I stretch around Ms. Buchanan to hand Eva Mae a fresh Louisville Benedictine sandwich, for her pregnancy fatigue. The young woman doesn't wait to take a bite as she cedes her place in line to the next customer, her dark eyes already clawing back some sparkle as the cucumber hits her tongue.

Inheriting the Apothakery way earlier than I was supposed to—or wanted to—makes me a battlefield-promoted Farewitch. But seeing someone's expression after the first bite of something I made never gets old. It's as addictive as any sweet.

Ms. Buchanan, however, does get old.

"Ma'am, please . . ."

"Oh, you should have seen Gertha when we were younger, a real hellcat that one, and now all she's got time for is grandbabies, canning, and spewing that nonsense about magic and the downfall of the Holler. She won't even buy from you and I know she needs something for her arthritis. So I told her, Gertha, I said, you quit what you're on about, bad apples stirring up trouble don't make the magic itself bad, and no Witch's magic is gonna hurt you worse than the cigarette I know you sneak when you think no one's looking—"

"Ms. Buchanan!" I exclaim. The customers behind Foxe Holler's self-proclaimed most-informed church lady (but don't say that in front of Gertha Fudge) take a collective step back.

The old woman eyes me, her wrinkled cheeks swelling with a *hmph*. "No need to shout, sugar. I'm old, not underwater."

With tired fingers that spent hours kneading this morning, I push a large yellow box across the counter. Enough for a week. "Yes, ma'am. It's just your jam cake is ready."

"My jam cake?" Her silver hair glimmers in the late-morning haze peeking through the windows. Gossip and sunshine, a typical Southern spring day.

"Yes, jam cake. Every week." *For six years.*

"Well, whatever for? I ordered apple dumplings."

"For your memory. Ma'am."

A pause. Then a bark. "Oh, hush, Beauregard," Ms. Buchanan snips.

I peer over the counter and see shiny dark eyes and a wet nose.

Beauregard Buchanan is a beauty of a standard poodle, his midnight fur like licorice cotton candy and as glossy as the glaze on my jam cake. I wish my own hair looked that groomed, but when I hit twenty-five and trudged home to Foxe Holler, I cut myself some feral bangs like any self-respecting quarter-life-crisis victim.

"Beauregard's fussy because he hasn't had his morning nap yet. Gertha was up mowing her lawn at Satan's hour this morning. Wasn't she?" Ms. Buchanan coos at the poodle, then waves a knobby hand at the cake box. "Thank you, sugar. I know it won't be as good as your mama's, but it'll do, such as it is."

Because I grew up with Southern politeness baked into my bones, I don't point out that the old woman didn't know what the hell her order was thirty seconds ago. Instead, I ignore the insult and sneak a few dog treats into a to-go bag. And I definitely don't hope she thinks they're cookies by accident. "Believe me, ma'am, she's still the Holler's Farewitch in my mind, too."

"Mmm-hmm. How is mayoral life treating that mama of yours?"

"Just fine." *Not fine.*

"Guess we all got jobs to do. You tell that Mayor Frost I say hey, you hear?"

A timer dings from the back.

I startle with relief. Lord, I love that sound, and not just because it rescues me from countless awkward conversations. My customers protest when I head for the kitchen.

"Two minutes!" I promise, slipping into the back before someone catches me. Old Blanche, the choir director, is looking particularly hangry.

The smell of butter hugs me the moment I slide into the peace of the kitchen. I inhale, nostrils greedy. Our neighbors and customers are important, sure. Our town has relied on the Frost family's food and baking magic for decades, ever since the Holler was no more than a whisper. And a Farewitch is nothing without a town, without the folks who depend on her culinary cures.

But the kitchen . . . I might not be the Farewitch my mom is, but the kitchen is home.

Tension seeps from my shoulders and stomach. The only sounds are my deep breaths and the massive churning oven. An only child of a single mom and one grandma, I made that oven my best friend growing up.

If I had kept up with friends more instead of work, someone

would be here to laugh at that joke. Or would've at least warned me about the bangs.

But there's no time for reminiscing or dawdling in a Farewitch's kitchen.

I free two cast-iron skillets of cornbread from the oven just in time and leave them to cool. Frost women do not burn their cornbread. With a pastry brush, I Van Gogh some honeysuckle butter onto the perfectly golden full moons.

Then my stomach shrieks—when was the last time I ate? That banana before sunrise? Can't remember. I'll scarf down some reject scraps of something later. The cornbread sells better fresh out of the oven and I have a full shop waiting. A full town depending on me.

Every town has a Farewitch, sometimes several for big cities. But as the official Farewitch for this Holler, I'm responsible for upholding the reputation of generations of Frost women, of protecting our legacy for curing all manner of ailments with the right recipe and ingredients, the right intention, and the right dash of my own unique magical flavor.

It's a Michelin Star honor.

With Michelin Star pressure.

Self-taught chefs and bakers, my mom, her mom Momaw Frost, and all the Frost Farewitches before them were experts at managing oven temperatures just as well as neighbors with too much flavor. It's part of the job, and six years into it now, I follow my duties like I follow the family recipes: precisely.

Because if I don't . . .

Momaw Frost appears in my mind. Not her seasoned scratchy voice this time, but her skeletal frame fighting a wasting disease that no recipe could cure. As a girl, I watched my mom bend over kitchen grimoires all night long; as Farewitches, they're our bibles. Other Witches, from Hearthwitches to Greenwitches—even the elusive Tombwitches—traveled to help, asking for nothing in return. Finally, Warlocks passed through the Holler at the idea of a good challenge. They promised a whole spice drawer of magical solutions and exclusive potions, *higher* magic much stronger than the *lower* practical magic of Witches.

For a price, of course.

But after the Frost family bank account was dry as a sawdust biscuit, the Warlocks disappeared and the only ingredient Momaw Frost ever needed was time. More time for us to find the solution.

Her death hung on us like a lead apron. It still does. But if I do this Farewitch thing right, the Holler can depend on me. Which means Mom can depend on me.

I glance at the vaulted brick wall next to the oven, where hangs the Frost family's vast collection of cast iron. Skillets and grill pans and cornbread molds in the shape of whole ears of corn dangle from the chipped brick, seasoned under generations of strong butter, stronger magic, and the strongest women. Despite the delightful floral aroma of the honeysuckle butter cooling over the nutty cornbread, my heart clenches.

I'd trade one of these priceless, magic-imbued skillets for my mom to be here with me right now. If only to see this batch of cornbread, which looks perfect, humility be damned. Rich gold crust to match everything else in this place.

Once, I looked forward to becoming a Farewitch. But at forty-five, not twenty-five.

I studied and organized and routined my way through college. Graduated and tucked in to the usual tasting menu of odd jobs and sporadic travel until my savings grew crumb dry and I hunted for the next job. But in a chaotic layering of events I can only picture as shoddy croissant laminating, Foxe Holler's long-standing mayor died and my one and only mother, Marigold Frost, somehow got herself appointed the next.

When I came home for the funeral, I first remember feeling glad (stunned) my mom was close enough friends with someone to attend their funeral. Because of our workload, Farewitches just don't end up with close relationships. Second came unease. I found the Apothakery was barely afloat. Typical Frost, my mom deluded herself into thinking she could conjure up the time and energy for a hundred-hour workweek. The third feeling was . . . I realized something was *wrong* wrong when my mom could no longer lift her own skillet.

A Farewitch's cast iron is her ancestors', seasoned with generations of flavor and literal magic that seeps into every new morsel of food. It's the foundation of our altars and the Sisyphus boulder we haul again and again from a hot oven, year after year, decade after decade.

So the only heir in the Frost Farewitch line—me—donned an apron, filled the vacancy, and stayed. But this was the job. A holler needs a Farewitch. *This* Holler needs *this* Farewitch.

Like I said, no pressure.

At the farmhouse sink, I splash cold water on my neck and avoid looking at the old Frost family kitchen grimoires strewn across the table in the center of the room. That mess is for later. One step in a recipe at a time. Folks are hungry.

I cut the cornbread into plump golden bricks on a tray. In the hands of a Farewitch, cornbread can cure the common cold or general under-the-weather malaise. Mom has a stunning recipe with an old incantation to go along with it that makes the bread particularly buttery and makes it work faster than unregulated Sudafed.

A breeze, awfully cold for April, slithers into the kitchen through the back door I left open for air. I shiver.

True to Ms. Buchanan's gossip, Gertha Fudge is on a tear lately, claiming the unusual season of spring colds is the work of bad magic, specifically that of the frightful old Warlock living alone up at the edge of the Holler. She's got the other church ladies echoing her, too. Although folks tend to blame him for all of the Holler's bad weather, now that I think about it. Rain? Angry Warlock. Hail? Warlock with a migraine. Tornado? Warlock with a vendetta.

Not that I'm complaining—more colds mean more cornbread. Better for business. I should give him a discount on snickerdoodles. That is, if he ever left his tomb of a house.

This is the one oddity I've not been able to figure out in my thirty-one years, even having grown up here: Not once, with eyes or scrying mirror, have I ever seen this Warlock. Not at the farmers' market, the post office, or even the courthouse, where a person must theoretically have to renew a driver's license once in a while. Or, most importantly, in my shop.

Everyone shops here. If it weren't for the other rumors—about his extensive archive of magical tomes—I'm not sure I'd believe he exists. Sometimes, I hope those whispers are true, since the Holler's one library burned down when I was little. But no matter what Gertha Fudge tries to make the Holler believe, I'm more frightened one of my long blonde hairs will wind up in the banana pudding than of some stuffy old loner Warlock who may or may not be tampering with seasonal allergy patterns.

I steel my nerves, take a few breaths, grounding myself in the comforting buttery atmosphere. Strong as cast iron. I let the peace and quiet of the kitchen work its own charm. Food is magic, and so is alone time. Hunger pangs tickle my belly button, but I ignore them. Brain on, stomach off. I need to remember: Everything I do is for my mom.

I glance at the mountain of recipe books again. Everything is for her.

Into the fire again, then.

As I carry out the steaming cornbread, my famished customers are exactly where I left them. I spend the next hour stuck in the looping cul-de-sac of Southern small talk. Ms. Buchanan doesn't leave, but she at least moves to a table where her poodle is safe from heavy boots and sharp church heels. I sell ambrosia salad for cravings, coconut cake for allergies—plant, not pet; that's coconut cream pie—and chocolate chess pie for a dose of randy spirit in the bedroom.

Farmer Kelsey pays for his chess pie in wrinkled bills that smell loamy. He's been with his missus for thirty years, as he reminds me every time he visits, like I could forget. "How's that cookbook you're writing coming along?" he asks today.

I cringe on the inside. That. Right. "Oh, it's going. Going somewhere." Another project I don't have time for. I tie his box with a saucy silk red ribbon. "You two eat this together now, you hear? Date night."

Sometimes I fantasize about what it would be like to have what these two have. It doesn't even have to be now. I'm only thirty-one. I could wait five years, ten . . .

"You know," he begins, and I feel my stomach drop. "My nephew is single—"

Oh no.

"—and you don't have to *marry* him, by any means, but—"

No no no. I know the nephew he means, and . . . no thank you. Anything but this.

Then to my surprise and to the shock of everyone in the Apothakery that morning, *anything* happens.

The shop door blows open on another chilly gust of wind, hinges squealing.

Dark mist shrouds the entire Apothakery in a creeping plume and the sunlight disappears. Everything yellow turns a dull purple in the changing light and it suddenly feels like midnight, not noon. Folks squirm to the perimeter of the small shop to avoid the mysterious mist. The fog hovers, not quite reaching my patrons or the corners of the room. Finally, it stops spreading.

Ominous, but I'm more concerned the obsidian smoke will change the flavor of any exposed baked goods. I really hope Gertha Fudge isn't right about troublesome Witches and Warlocks. She'd never let anyone live it down.

As I am a *reads the menu ahead of time* kind of girl, surprise is not my favorite feeling. Do I have a recipe for shock? Probably involves ashwagandha and some moonlight.

I swing around the counter, grab an empty sheet pan for defense, and face the fog. Is it just me, or does the mass seem . . . cranky? I hesitate momentarily but Momaw and my mom wouldn't tolerate a threat like this, so I won't, either. I'm not going to be the Frost who loses the family shop to a *cloud*.

But then the mist dissipates with a *POP* before I can swing at it. Shock dusts every face in my periphery when a black envelope falls to the floor at my feet.

Surely this isn't for me . . . And yet, curious, I reach down—

"Don't touch it, child!" Ms. Buchanan fans herself with an empty cupcake liner. "That's higher magic there, that is. I'd recognize the foul stuff anywhere."

My hand pauses. Farmer Kelsey nods. "*Warlock* magic."

Everyone leans back, like just whispering *Warlock* ensures a pox. Beauregard the poodle barks and, I'm pretty sure, pees a little.

"Now you all sound just like Gertha Fudge," I say, eyebrow raised, trying my best to appear relaxed. They're perfectly safe in the Apothakery. Whether pests or mold or bad weather, nothing dangerous—not even nefarious mail posted by curmudgeonly cumulonimbus—can make it past the warding a Farewitch's magic bakes into her kitchen over the years.

"What if Gertha's right?" Farmer Kelsey asks, eyes wide. Folks nod with him. "The Widow Witch is bad enough. Now the Warlock is knocking at our doors?"

By their reaction, you'd think we have an infestation of them. But the Holler only has one, as far as I know. I'd like to point out that no one my age has even seen the man, but I can't over the escalating sounds of my customers growing frantic.

"The Warlock ruined my tomato crop last summer—"

"My chickens won't lay eggs because of him!"

"He's why we don't have a library, burned it right to the ground . . ."

"I heard he did it so he could steal the books."

"People *died* in that library, you know."

"It's not him. This has to be the Widow Witch—"

"Don't be silly. It's too early in the season yet."

I ignore the warnings and reach for the envelope a second time. My fingers tingle with that just-scraped-by feeling that comes with remembering to grab an oven mitt just in time before touching a hot baking sheet.

But the tiny constellations of oven-burn scars on my hands are one of the undeniable things I have in common with my mom and Momaw. Like the blonde hair, I inherited that urge to reach into the heat. Momaw always said there's no such thing as foul magic, only foul intention.

I snatch up the envelope.

Folks gasp, then seem almost underwhelmed when I don't immediately burst into flames. A prickling sensation kisses my neck. My fingernails turn blue. The envelope *does* burn, oddly. Not painfully, though. A good burn. The first bite of something hot yet delicious.

When I open it, I find glittering silver scrawl on thick black paper.

Dear Ms. Frost the Younger,

I am in need of a Farewitch. The situation is advanced and beyond my efforts.

Report to Knight Manor on Monday morning. You will be compensated handsomely.

Regretfully,
Mr. Knight
The Warlock of Foxe Holler

I look up to find everyone's eyes on me. Waiting. Perhaps for the inevitable *kaboom*.

This has to be an April Fool's joke. Folks have seen the Widow Witch more than the infamous Warlock, and she plagues the Holler once a year.

But my stomach growls with fear, not hunger, and I know this isn't a game. At one point or another, I've healed everyone in Foxe Holler of something.

Nearly everyone.

But folks come to me for everyday ailments. Not problems too complicated even for a Warlock's magic. So why me, now? Why a second-rate, stand-in Farewitch?

A gnarled knot of worry twists in my gut, dampening the fear.

What the Warlock of Foxe Holler doesn't know is that I can't heal him.

What everyone *else* doesn't know is that I'm a fraud.

Chapter Two

SATURDAY, APRIL 2

Honey's Helpful Hint, from
Honey Frost's Southern Cookbook for Recipes Gone Wrong:

Butter is a sensitive soul. It will melt under heat and pressure and soon you'll be peeling sticky, gloppy biscuit dough off your fingers. Cold hands—and a cold heart—can keep it strong.

The next evening, after I close up the Apothakery, I head into town and deliberately bypass the courthouse on the main square, where my mom's mayoral offices are.

Marigold Frost won't be there.

Instead, I stroll into Foxe Holler Hospital at precisely the moment visiting hours begin. The Warlock's letter weighs heavy in the front pocket of my overalls.

Antiseptic floods my nostrils the moment I pass through the sliding doors. I'm armed with a tray of the Frosts' signature deviled eggs (for energy levels) and a slew of other curative baked goods to dole out to staff and families hunkered down in the waiting room, even to patients, whoever needs a pick-me-up. Before women and Farewitches could own their shops, we had a long history of operating out of tiny home kitchens or making house calls. In a small town with a small hospital, sometimes it's easier for me to come to the customer.

A nurse with long silver-brown hair swoops in before I even make it to the front desk, kind face beaming. "Saturday already, Honey?"

"Despite my best efforts to decipher the pandemonium of my Momaw's kitchen grimoire, there is still no spell for stopping time." I hold up my offering. "Hope y'all like deviled eggs."

Nurse Carolina Vázquez smiles, taking the tray. "Why do you think I let you keep visiting?" She drops her voice to a conspiratorial rasp. "I hear the Warlock passed you a note."

I try not to give myself away by patting my pocket. The hospital is frigid, but today my cheeks are warm with guilt. I swear I can feel harsh eyes on me, like everyone in the waiting room knows I haven't yet refused the Warlock's offer like a good Witch should. The Warlock is rumored to be ancient, even immortal, so I was expecting the letter to dissolve into dust. Go out with a bang.

But if I really thought that, would I have kept it in my pocket the last twenty-four hours?

I don't answer that. What would my neighbors think, knowing I'd kept a probably cursed item from a Warlock whom everyone despises?

Carolina raises a perfectly threaded, graying eyebrow. "I heard there were fireworks. Or lightning? I can never understand old Beulah; she carries on too fast."

I snort in a way Ms. Buchanan would surely frown at. "Greedy gossips. It's been a literal *day*." Folks have made it clear I'm a poor replacement for Marigold Frost, yet my name on their tongue is their favorite flavor.

She smirks like a best friend would, even though we're on opposite ends of the millennial spectrum. "Did he really sign his letter *ex-oh-ex-oh*?"

"You're terrible. All of you."

Then her teasing expression falls like a bad soufflé. "I'm serious, though. *He's* serious. He makes the Widow Witch look like a Halloween costume."

It's barely April, and the Holler is more anxious than ever. Each spring, the Widow Witch earns her name and leaves behind one widow before the summer solstice. My gut says some of these vanishings are just the nastier pieces of work fleeing the altar or the old marriage bed—and town—the minute the weather turns nice and they get bored. She's always felt like an old wives' tale used to scare young women. I can hear the church ladies now:

The Widow Witch was once a young woman who remained unmarried and childless, so for bitter revenge, she preys on a loving couple each wedding season.

But the lore isn't only hysterics.

One person *always* disappears.

Last spring, it was Sonny Cumberland. Younger than me, and newly married, too. Although gossip says he and his new wife already had words in the middle of church on account of whatever happened at his bachelor party.

"The town hasn't seen this man's face in twenty-five years. And to think, that big old mansion used to hold parties. With real people!"

"Maybe he likes his alone time." It's *my* go-to excuse to get out of social commitments. "Shoot, if I lived in a mansion, I wouldn't leave, either."

"No one likes themselves that much. You can't be a recluse in a reclusive town. They cancel each other out. That just makes him suspicious."

I lower my voice. "He's only asked for a Farewitch, like any other customer." So why am I sticking up for him so quickly? "Can anyone tell me exactly what is so terrible about this man? Give me a list of his crimes?"

"He's a Warlock. That's everything you need to know. They spread plagues, conjure storms, ruin crops—"

"Mess with hen egg-laying patterns?"

"Exactly! You and I know better than anyone they're just elitist hoarders of powerful magic." Her eyes catch me with memories we share of my mom's futile hunt to cure Momaw's fatal illness with all the magic and money we had. Where was the Warlock of Foxe Holler, this Mr. Knight, fifteen years ago when his town's Farewitch was dying?

I intend to find out. Given I'm here and not at the shop preparing tomorrow's dough, it's obvious I could do with a bit of *elite powerful magic.*

"Warlock or not, he's a resident of this Holler. Which means he's entitled to the help of the Farewitch."

The nurse's face softens. "What are you going to do?"

That's the headline of the day, isn't it?

FAREWITCH FROST FACES FIASCO OR FATE?

Another odd thought takes over. A silly one, really. If no one has seen this Warlock in decades . . . how old is he, exactly?

"Does anyone *actually* know what the Warlock did twenty-five years ago that sent him into isolation? Beyond speculation and making him the devil in every farmer's almanac?"

Carolina shrugs. Her dark eyes gloss over for a second, then refocus. "Something terrible." She shakes her head. "I'll take you down the hall."

Like every other Saturday, I follow Carolina down a hallway that reminds me of egg whites. The chemical smell, abrasive overhead fluorescent lighting, and the fridge-cold air are all a well-known ritual at this point, but that doesn't make this comfortable. Though I'm partial to rituals. What's a recipe if not a brief, previous ritual?

This is our ritual. And it's a lie.

Well, a *partial* lie. More a half-truth? Mom always told me I should've studied law.

I *do* visit to be friendly, to make sure the evening staff don't run out of snacks because the day staff get first dibs on the treats folks bring in. It's not odd to see a Farewitch visit a hospital so often, but the patients here are mostly dealing with severe illnesses I can't cure. Cancer, lupus, Alzheimer's . . . I respect a Farewitch's limits. All magic has its ceiling.

No Witch or Warlock can create life or conjure extra time where there is none.

The Frosts have always worked alongside modern medicine. A chamomile and lavender cookie can brighten someone's day, but with a Farewitch's spell, it can literally help a patient get some calm rest to help their recovery. Lemon and olive oil cake distracts a fussy baby whose tired parents have been up all night, but with one of my sigils baked into the bottom, it can deliver a little boost of anxiety-fighting goodness.

Other types of Witches do spellwork, too. As a Hearthwitch, Carolina is leagues better than me at serious defensive warding. Even someone without any magic can craft medicinal tinctures and homeopathic cures. But without the inherited Farewitch magic, the intention and family affinities, those cures are just like any other over-the-counter fix at a drugstore.

Exhibit A: the truth. I do provide the magical sustenance.

But Nurse Carolina provides the discretion. When we reach the wing for longer-term residents, we stop outside the usual room. No name on this door.

Exhibit B: the lie.

Carolina nods at the door. "You should get in there. Rough day for her."

Then I'm alone, one hand pressed against my overalls pocket with the letter, the other on the doorknob.

Don't get me wrong. I'm grateful for Carolina keeping an eye on things. The emotional debt I owe rivals the hospital bills. She took care of Momaw Frost those last few months and understood the grim situation then, just as she understands the same . . . sensitive situation we're in now. Maybe it makes me ungrateful, but a delicate tablespoon-of-vanilla-sized part of me wishes I never needed to get to know her in the first place.

The Warlock's invitation—demand?—gnaws at the back of my brain matter. What could plague a Warlock that he can't cure himself? Especially if the rumors are true about his archives and he has endless magical texts and spell books at his disposal. I'm not sure whether to be highly suspicious and afraid . . . or intrigued. Or all three.

A voice comes through the door. "I know you're out there. Stop overthinking and come in already."

I sigh. Caught. When I enter the room, a middle-aged version of me sits up in her hospital bed.

"Hi, Mom."

"Whatever Carolina was saying about me, she's fibbing. I'm a star patient."

Marigold Frost is all stern nods and raised eyebrows to anyone who doesn't know her, but a smile slips through for me. Her graying-blonde hair rests in a plait over her shoulder, since Farewitches know ponytails stir up headaches after a long day in the kitchen. She was once a plump woman from sampling her concoctions as she went. But now, she's not so much warm loaf of bread as, well, breadstick.

When I came home, I thought she was just pale and thin from the stress of being the Holler's new mayor. But back then, our biggest heartbreak was still only Momaw's death, and we were both blessedly naïve.

After giving her a hug, I take my usual seat by her bed. "How is Mayor Frost this evening?"

"Fit as ever. I could debone a duck right now if you needed one."

My gaze narrows on her. We've got the same blue eyes and pale skin, which means the same purple eye bags when we're utterly spent. But my mom has always been a better liar than me.

Marigold Frost, current mayor, has overseen Foxe Holler with the thoroughness and care of a chef in her kitchen.

Marigold Frost, former Farewitch and my mom, is also dying.

The lead apron came for Momaw Frost but stayed for my mom.

She pats the bag I brought with me. "Did you—"

I pull out a bottle of Cheerwine, cold and sweating. A spark lights her eyes. She downs the sugary drink in crisp gulps. In a recipe for Marigold Frost's immediate happiness, Cheerwine is the first ingredient.

"They don't give me any of the good stuff," she says after draining half the bottle. "You're telling me Jell-O is better for my health than this?"

I don't argue, giving in to a shiver instead. The room is chilly enough that it would be a good place to work with buttery biscuit or pie dough, but other than that, this place reminds me of a meat fridge. The only steady constant is the tight staccato of beeping machines. What happened to the daffodils I brought? Not a speck of yellow anywhere. Momaw would be appalled.

There's a tray of food my mom has clearly been avoiding out of sheer stubbornness. A small bread roll (visibly stale), the aforementioned Jell-O, a mass of what has to be collard greens—no bacon, of course—and some clumpy dish whose defining characteristic is Already Digested.

Mom yanks on my focus. "The nurses have been extra chatty. The way the hospital's squawking about you, it's like you've gone and won the lottery, girl."

Oh no. I'm too late.

I hoped to talk face-to-face first, before the he-said, she-said network of town got busy. Momaw's voice rings strong in my head: *Don't be green, girl.* Foxe Holler loves its lore and loyalty. If I befriend the wrong legend, make the wrong decision, bitter and upset townsfolk might try to debone *me.*

My mom raises both eyebrows, her way of being more tactful than her own mother. Unlearning generational bad habits and all that. "Does the Warlock really write in script?"

"What?" The letter burns in my pocket. Maybe I should check if it's actually burning. "Oh, uh, yeah. His cursive is actually pretty good."

"Phew. I don't think that old man knows what century we're in. Glad to know I'm not the most outdated soul in the Holler."

"Least not while Beulah Buchanan and Gertha Fudge walk the earth."

"Those two old busybodies could subsist on Communion wafers and hard candy till Judgment Day." She eyes me real good. "You, on the other hand . . ."

Here we go. "Don't start, Mom."

"You eating?"

"You know how busy the shop gets. I'm surrounded by food if I want it. I'm fine."

"A hot brown would do you some good; your nail beds are blue—"

"What did we talk about?"

"Yes, yes, commenting on bodies, I know. I don't want to be another relic of a matriarch." She props herself up, flat biceps shaking, and I catch her wince of exhaustion. I'd do anything to take some of the pain away.

Anything? Like heal a dangerous Warlock just to get access to his magic or money?

"What did he offer you?"

I release a breath, ruffling my bangs. Like the undercooked center of a cake, there's no avoiding this. Eventually we'd eat our way here. "He said I'd be compensated *handsomely*."

"Ha! Lies. That Warlock's been hoarding money and magic in that decrepit old mansion for decades. Centuries, who knows. Doesn't spend a single wheat penny."

"If he really is as old and powerful as everyone says, what's the harm in a quick checkup?"

"Ignoring the fact he's been a blight on this Holler for as long as anyone can remember?"

"*Can* they remember?" The Holler has a growing population of old women whose memories are selective. "He might be familiar with cures, or magic we've never seen before. Combined with our recipes, it might make a difference . . ."

"And what's the isolation done to his mind? He could be eating cute young blondes for dinner. He certainly isn't going to the Piggly Wiggly for groceries."

This is getting ridiculous. We don't even *have* a Piggly Wiggly.

But logic doesn't matter here. Because for as long as Witches have been butting heads in this town with anti-magic zealots like Gertha Fudge, they've liked Warlocks even less.

Small towns might warm up to grassroots magic and neighborhood Witches, but powerful beings like Warlocks don't usually settle in one place, where their magic wouldn't have room to expand and consume. History shows us Warlocks often monetize what Witches are already good at, then demonize midwives and kitchen girls for those very same skills. That rivalry is why the Witches in this Holler will withstand the threat of the Widow Witch and the damage her reputation does for magic, but *heaven forbid* a Warlock sends a letter.

I square my shoulders and try to look as mature as possible in overalls. "I know Warlocks have disappointed us before. We paid them to help cure Momaw, and they gave us a whole bunch of nothing. *I know.* But I also know what bills got paid or didn't based on the groceries in the fridge." I gesture around the room we basically mortgage. "We live in a town smaller than the population of a liberal arts college, Mom. The Apothakery is busy, but if five people go vegan, we won't be able to afford ingredients, and we sure as hell can't pay the hospital."

"Vegan? Here? Girl, Beulah Buchanan thinks we still use lard in the pie dough, and I don't have the heart to correct her . . ."

"*Mom.*"

"Honey, I'm going to be too tired to argue with you soon." She downs the rest of her Cheerwine. "Focus on the Apothakery, on our neighbors. The good folks we know. Do not accept the Warlock's offer."

Is that an order? I want to snap, my frustration surfacing. Or my hunger.

When she crosses her arms, I know the conversation is over.

"Shouldn't you be out on a Saturday night?" she adds, like she's just asking me for a mint and not commanding me to avoid a mysterious and treacherous ancient Warlock in an isolated danger-palace far from everything and everyone I know.

I slump back in my chair. I'd call her out on the lousy diversion if I weren't so tired. "With who? Ms. Buchanan and her poodle?"

"I don't know, a *date.* Just because we Frosts don't take husbands—"

"Word choice."

"—or partners, doesn't mean we have to be celibate."

"Ew, Mom, really? *Word choice.*"

The Frost women before me have always gotten away with tolerating men just long enough to keep the Farewitch line going. Our family's tradition is the source of consternation for the conservative old church ladies, who love to gossip about *promiscuous* Witches. Because of the Widow Witch, we Frosts aren't the only folks in the Holler who dodge marriage, but the church ladies are too afraid of the Witch to make a true fuss over neighbors living in unmarried dens of sin. Feeling conflicted about this no-win scenario is one of their top-five hobbies.

"Just don't spend all night looking at all those old recipe books and family grimoires," my mom adds. "I've told you before, you won't find anything in there."

Same argument, same ending. I want to holler in frustration. Our kitchen grimoires are our bibles. *What if we missed something? What if* I *missed something?* These thoughts keep me from sleeping most nights.

Especially considering the Farewitch of Foxe Holler is a fraud.

Sure, I can cure concussions with apple dumplings, inflammation with butternut squash, a bloody nose with hush puppies, and the flu with burgoo. I can hold my own with remedies that keep the Holler running. But if I can't puzzle out the mysterious wasting disease eating away at the woman who raised me, and the woman who raised her, what kind of Farewitch am I?

I don't get the chance to mount a final protest because at that exact moment my nemesis walks in.

Silas Key, I can admit, is an objectively stylish force in his usual three-piece pinstripe suit, which today he's traded for a linen version for the warmer April weather. But that doesn't matter, because every time I see him, he looks increasingly like a formidable mayor while my mom looks less and less like one.

"Silas," I say. More of a grunt than a greeting.

Bless his heart, he tries to smile, but my scowl probably doesn't make it easy. "Ah, Honey. Delightful."

He's my mom's number two, the person who would take her place when she . . . if she, I mean . . . Well, in so many words, Silas is me. Marigold Frost goes around collecting people-pleasing young folks to fill her chef's clogs.

But my mom doesn't need a Silas, a number two. She's going to get better; I'll see to it. Even if it means I *don't* avoid a mysterious and treacherous ancient Warlock in an isolated danger-palace far from everything and everyone I know.

Silas brushes a perfect comma of blond hair off his forehead. "I'm sorry to interrupt the obviously jolly energy in the room, but I need our mayor to sign a few documents."

"Too tired," my mom sighs.

"Marigold."

"Silas."

"*Marigold*, do we have to argue like an old married couple every time I need you to do a single clerical task? You're still the mayor on a Saturday, you know."

"Frosts don't have husbands—"

"Or partners," I interject.

"—or partners, Silas, you know that. And I enjoy our bickering."

He rolls a pair of brown eyes. "So you're not too tired for that?"

"We'd never work, anyway. Marriage would take the fun out of this."

"To clarify, would that be because of our quarter-century age gap, or the fact that I'm looking for a *husband*?"

My mom throws out a hand. "Fine. Hand them here. You can entertain me with the story of your latest date, because my daughter isn't going on any."

Her assistant slash number two slash secretary grimaces as if he's recalling a particularly terrible memory. Interesting.

"I need to talk with Honey while you sign." He sets a manila folder on my mom's blanketed legs and turns to me. "Mind if we speak outside?"

Every private conversation I've had with Silas always ends with the terrible taste of bad news in my mouth. Suddenly, I crave nothing more than the butter haze of the Apothakery's warm yellow kitchen. My skin is freezing over in this place.

"Actually, I'm late for a date with my apartment."

"What, a whole jar of cornichons and a book with subpar smut you've read ten times already?" He looks at me like Mom does and it's not a stare I appreciate.

"Don't dismiss my refined palate."

"You see your apartment all day. You sleep where you work. I just need five minutes."

Resisting the urge to grumble, I give my mom a kiss goodbye. Visiting hours always taste a little of guilt. Just because I like being alone on a Saturday night doesn't mean *she* enjoys spending so much time alone. I get to go home to a robe and a container of reject cookie scraps in the freezer. She has to stay here.

I slip into the hallway with Silas.

When we're alone, he looks me up and down—is that dissatisfaction with my overalls? Not today, sir—and smooths the waistcoat of his suit. I know he's only a few years older than me, so I despise how consistently put together this guy is. We're supposed to be equally stressed and overworked. The code of thirtysomethings.

Where's his *messy*?

He clears his throat. "Can we be friends?"

"You're preparing yourself to replace my mom."

"Like I've told you a hundred times, I'm simply trying to create contingency plans here. I've been your mom's mentee for six, going on seven, years. You're both in denial, but you've got to trust I can handle this responsibility."

Now, as can be summarized so far, I don't usually stoop to gossip. But in a holler where the phone lines fold in storms, access to any network could blink out from one gravel road to the next, and many folks simply don't trust the devil's tool of Wi-Fi, sometimes gossip is the most efficient form of communication.

A cast-iron skillet is my weapon of choice, but I go for my backup—information. "Like how you handled that date of yours last Saturday night?"

He groans, pressing a gold-ringed thumb to his temple. "One bad public date and suddenly I'm the sole topic of the Bible study group."

"I'm not in the Bible study group, but you were. According to my sources."

"Jesus. Christ."

A few nurses at the station down the hall look up.

"Don't let the church ladies hear you say that," I say. "They'll send Pastor Webb after you. Heaven forbid they don't let you be the next mayor. A tragedy, really. *Were that to happen.*"

"First of all, something is off about that man."

Okay, that we can agree on. I don't attend myself, but I know Witches often make an appearance in his sermons, and not because they're holding a toy drive. "I always thought he was at high risk of becoming an actual spider."

"Secondly, Samson was never going to work out; he's a Libra for chrissakes. What I don't understand is why my love life is more interesting than how Noxie on Shirley Street shot off her husband's toe last week."

I shrug. "She does that once a year. And because your date threw a literal biscuit at you. Kitty's Kitchen doesn't even *serve* biscuits."

"Your guess is as good as mine. He pulled them right out of his Longchamp."

"If that's how you handle tricky situations, I don't know if you'll be the best mayor to follow my mom." Okay, low blow, but I passed desperate a long time ago. Does he understand I'm willing to take a whole slew of questionable risks to keep him from being Mayor Silas Key? Nothing personal.

He sighs. "Listen, you have no idea how hard it is to date in a town this size. I would be a ten in Manhattan and here the best I get is a tourist who's only visiting to rent a log cabin to *get away from it all*."

Well, crap. Now I feel a little bad. He's right: We're operating on totally different playing fields. Olive branch, then. "Your date—*Samson*—came by the shop the other day looking for something to cure a pinot grigio hangover. He looked like absolute hell."

"See? A pinot grigio guy. Never going to work." His *I'm serious now* forehead scrunch reappears. "I'm doing my best here, but your mom can't be my mentor *and* my opposition. You've got to make her work with me. She'll listen to you. I'm trying to be a young mayor in a town of four thousand—*maybe*—that barely has its own postal code. I want friends, not enemies. More folks ask me every week where their mayor is, and I can't deflect forever."

And Carolina's deflection spell and warding around my mom's hospital room can only keep folks from snooping for so long. If I could banish the image of my mom—ghostly, thin hair, hollow cheeks, looking way too much like Momaw in her last months—I could put up more of a fight now. But I can't. I just need her healthy. "You're right. I know my dating life wouldn't be front and center like yours."

"If you had one."

I *almost* laugh. It was a good one. "Ouch. I don't know about this friends thing."

"At least help me by dating someone, so we can keep her distracted."

"She does enjoy trying to set us up. My mom does know you're gay, right?"

A delicate half chuckle passes between us. Quiet, but it's there.

Okay, I suppose I *could* make more of an effort here. "Maybe we should get dinner. Just the two of us. Talk outside of this hospital room for once."

His eyebrows go up. "*You* know I'm gay, right?"

My hand goes to my invisible pearls. "*What?*"

"Ah, that was your sarcasm. I see."

"We both know we're way too busy for dinner, anyway. It was a trick question."

Silas clears his throat, looking away. "Listen, I don't want to add to your plate . . ."

"Oh, please do." Folks have been adding to my plate for years. It keeps piling up and I just keep . . . not eating it. One day, I'll inhale it. Catch up. *Somehow.*

"We're going to need more medical care than Foxe Holler can

provide. We should think about moving Marigold to a larger city, a proper hospital. Or if necessary, find excellent hospice care." He tugs at his waistcoat, a nervous tic of his. Never a good sign. "Your grandmother passed away after battling this same unknown thing for a year. And Marigold's been here nine months now . . ."

The acid in my empty stomach bubbles. The urge to vomit is stealing every tablespoon of weak focus I've got. *You've tried everything in those grimoires, girl,* Momaw would remind me. I've had time to exhaust my options, but with all the potential cures I've created, all I've done is exhaust our pantry and bank account.

Silas faces me, as if to make this fast, efficient. "Your mom is getting worse, quickly. Nurse Carolina and I think she has a few months left, at best. We need an answer. Now."

Chapter Three

MONDAY, APRIL 4

Honey's Helpful Hint, from
*Honey Frost's Southern Cookbook
for Recipes Gone Wrong*:

**Strength in coven, fire in the oven,
for curses most foul, seek cures of fowl.
For the precious wares and the gravest cares,
find thee fast a Farewitch lair.**
—a Farewitch fable

On Monday morning, I fasten a note to the Apothakery's narrow yellow door.

BACK SOON. PROMISE.

Our dangling wooden sign out front seems to scrutinize me from its high ground.

Fine—I know I'm not kidding anyone. I didn't close the shop today on a whim. Thinking ahead, I delivered this week's orders yesterday when most folks were sitting down to dinner. Even the banana cake for Nurse Carolina's niece, who has a *very* important eighth birthday party on Wednesday.

I didn't get to bed until the rooster living out back woke up, but what is sleep, anyway? I'm already used to getting less rest than my bread dough. The gluten can relax, but a Frost can't.

Word will get back soon enough that the Apothakery didn't open today, that for the first time in its history, it closed without warning or explanation. As long as the town has feared the Widow Witch, the Frost women haven't taken a break. When my mom gave birth, a retired Momaw Frost just stood in. When Momaw passed, my mom just put *grieve* on a to-do list.

But I'm ready to see this through, for my mom . . . even if she has no idea where her daughter is this morning.

Making what is perhaps one of my more foolish decisions, I drive the old Frost family pickup truck to the edge of the Holler. The *edge* edge.

With shut-eye eluding me since Saturday's hospital visit, I used what little time I wasn't baking to research and try to make sense of the Holler's history with Warlock Knight.

Storms and droughts and crop infestations and barren seasons for livestock, tornadoes and floods, an earthquake or two . . . There have been plenty of newspaper-worthy environmental oddities here. When the online records ran dry, I unearthed Momaw's newspaper clippings from the attic, ignoring the nostalgic pain. Having grown up poor, Momaw was a hoarder in her old age, and kept boxes of announcements, births and weddings and funerals. Boxes.

Then I cross-referenced town news with the rumors the neighbors love:

He ruins crops, particularly around the summer solstice.

Hens won't lay eggs if he's within fifty miles of town.

He burned the town's library in a spell gone wrong.

But I quickly hit a wall. If the general assumption is he's immortal, he could be the destructive magical force behind everything odd. Or nothing at all.

Everyone in the Holler knows why the library burned down twenty-five years ago—reckless magic caused a fire that took several lives—and that it was never rebuilt. Too expensive, when the town needs to pave roads and keep the hospital running. The exact cause—Witch magic or Warlock magic—was never determined.

Around the same time, the Warlock simply disappeared from Foxe Holler. No goodbye. Rumors or not, folks love to point fingers, and there's no counterfeiting the fear I saw in my customers' eyes. Maybe the blame that hitchhikes to a tragedy like that is enough to drive someone into isolation.

I'm going to say hello and find out.

Eventually, finally, I turn onto a narrow gravel road leading up into the hills, and soon gravel becomes dirt. By the time I pull up to the iron gate of an estate cocooned in black birch and pine trees, I'm not sure I'm even in the same holler anymore. The winding, unpaved dirt back roads add time, but this is ridiculous. No wonder the Warlock never comes to town. The gas money would bankrupt a person.

Dense foliage curtains everything beyond the gate like the stage of some forgotten performance. Any mansion remains completely hidden from view. The iron metalwork of the gate twists in elegant script above its large winged doors.

KNIGHT MANOR

No harm in an informational interview, right?

With the lush woods and flora, oddly thriving for this early in April, anyone monitoring the gate might not see me coming, and in the Holler, a trespasser flirts with getting shot. No thank you. After throwing the truck into park, I hop out. The 1968 Dodge D100 pickup is avocado green, freshly washed in preparation for Today's Ill-Advised Adventure. I want to make a good impression. For some reason. Maybe Warlocks are impressed by good vehicular upkeep. Old men like cars . . .

Approaching the gate with caution, I palm the iron, looking for any intercom system. Then, just like the small black letter, the iron burns a gentle, hot kiss into my hand.

The immense gates swing inward, shrieking. Like someone

hasn't opened them in a lifetime. When was the last time someone visited?

When was the last time someone *left*?

The coffee in my gut churns. That was too easy. Someone's expecting me.

He's expecting me.

No turning back now. *That would be rude, girl,* comes Momaw's voice.

Back in my truck, I creep through the gates, only a big toe to the gas pedal. Edging up the gravel drive, I think I spot an old tobacco barn, but the woods and landscaping aren't just thriving. They're *overgrown.* Finally, the meandering drive comes to an end. I park at the steps of Knight Manor's front entrance, and slide-fall out of the truck. All I can do is stare.

When my mom said the Warlock didn't spend a single penny on *that decrepit old mansion,* I thought she was exaggerating. But Marigold Frost is a baker, and a teaspoon is a teaspoon, not a smidge more. Precision is ingredient number one.

The town rumors got *decrepit* right. But everyone got everything else wrong.

Before me is an old behemoth of a house with a wide porch that disappears around either side of the place. Every surface and support beam seems made of wood, and it must all be original, because it's now more mushroom than bone colored. The only parts of the house that aren't wood are the one-two-three-four-*many* stone chimneys. I can't tell if the house is supporting them, or if the chimneys are the only thing keeping the whole place upright.

Knight Manor isn't a mansion. It's a farmhouse.

A memory takes me so quickly, my sharp laugh sizzles out.

This farmhouse reminds me of Momaw's. Same screen doors, same decaying carved window eaves, same rocking chairs on the front porch. With Momaw retired and able to babysit while my mom ran the shop, I spent endless time there as a girl. Even nights. Those sleepovers are my best memories of Momaw. I can almost hear the reruns of *The Golden Girls*. We'd play gin and rummy until Mom picked me up.

I barely catch the sob before it escapes my chest. *Breathe.* If I'm having this much trouble outside the house, I'll be doomed inside.

The rumors suggested some haunted hellscape. All I'm seeing is a *Southern Living* cover reject. How much do the folks of the Holler really know about the Warlock they fear? Or do they just listen to Gertha Fudge's rants?

But as I focus, I notice the abnormalities.

What started as a traditional two-story, probably nineteenth-century farmhouse now has a dozen additions tacked onto the original heart of the structure. Like the first godawful, confused layer cake I ever baked. A house this size is expensive. *Big like old money, not new money,* Momaw would've said. There are no fancy cars in the driveway, or any cars at all. Odd, since the Holler's public transit system consists of the church van or the bed of someone's pickup.

The cracked, wavy glass windows were once elegant, but now vines rip at the rotting window frames and shutters, and birds' nests barnacle for purchase. Ivy crawls between cracks in wood, threatening to pop loose a nail like floss hunting between teeth for a poppy seed.

I would know. Lemon poppy seed is a favorite flavor for the Frosts.

But the Manor banishes any hunger. My gut knots as a crisp April breeze edges under my clothes. It's cooler up here than it is in town. Wild vegetation infests the sprawling grounds (farmland?), but this grand house is the first infected molecule of the plague. Now, truly realizing how far out here and alone I am, I feel silly, way in over my head. If the house looks this sick on the outside, what is the Warlock like on the *inside*? If my mom's right about the suspiciously aggressive isolation, is she right telling me to refuse his offer altogether? By trying to save her life, am I just going to risk mine?

What am I *doing* here?

I could turn back. Tell the nurses to keep trudging along, trying the same solutions, give Mom the same Jell-O, in the hopes she might get better. Keep combing through cookbooks and recipe journals and grimoires for that fateful recipe I know has to exist. We could all simply return to the usual routine.

Screw that.

My mom has until July, if we're lucky. I know exactly what I'm doing here. If I help this Warlock, he might help my mom in return. Or his archive could. Shoot, at the least, he could pay well enough for me to shuffle more money toward her care.

Behind its screen, I knock on the main front door. When there's no answer, my nerves make me try the door, just in case.

It swings open without resistance.

Relief quells my panicky stomach. Interesting. But also unnerving. Am I being watched, or is the house always this hospitable? What if I *hadn't* come? Would the Warlock have stomped into my shop this morning to track me down?

"Hello?" I call into the foyer.

Black-and-white tile bounces the echo back to me. Empty.

Lord, the sudden aroma of the cedarwood takes me right back to Momaw's. All that's missing is sugar and cinnamon toast.

The memory comes with a homing beacon of an instinct and I head for the back of the floor plan, where I'm positive the kitchen will be. Logically, it's safe to assume he'll interview me there. This doesn't *feel* like trespassing. I think. I'm welcome, right?

As I go, the place is an absolute rabbit warren with halls and nooks and spiral staircases that climb nowhere. The scent of loamy earth follows me, but I can't tell if it's the soil-giving-life type or the decaying-into-the-ground kind. Everywhere I look, tiny intricate carvings of plants and herbs decorate the crown molding, the banisters, even the wood doors. Stained glass windows bloom from the walls, the glassy images of basil, rosemary, sage, and thyme tossing slants of green-tinted sunlight into the otherwise dim and dusty house.

If this man weren't a Warlock, I'd say a Greenwitch lives here.

So far, the inside doesn't promise to remedy any deficiencies in confidence the outside creates. It's in such a state of disrepair, my brain demands order, so I quickly make a mental list of all the ingredients for this disaster of a recipe:

½ of a dining room table, leaves missing
12 dining room chairs (for *what* people?)
7 random trunks, empty, possibly once for clothes?
A healthy number of rugs and quilts that all need cleaning
Countless potted ferns and palms, arranged evenly throughout the first floor
Banjos that seem to multiply every time I look away
A grand piano, under a painter's tarp
A child's bike?

But even with my curiosity, I don't meander. I'm here for a reason, and I have a feeling the less time I spend wandering around this place, the better.

Just as I thought, a narrow door tucked away at the end of a hall, close to the dining room, at last reveals what I'm looking for.

Despite the rest of the place, the house's kitchen is . . . *Wow.*

I spin in place as I take in literal walls of windows.

Several look out toward the front porch and the drive even though we're at the back of the house. The kitchen must be one of the later additions tacked on at an impossible angle. Warlock magic, or shoddy architectural design? The windows offer the perfect view of unwanted visitors; someone in the kitchen definitely could have seen me coming. Copper pots hang from the tall ceiling alongside dried bundles of herbs, directly over an island the size of a pontoon boat. There's even an elegant gas range, and there next to—

Lord above, it's an AGA stove. With five ovens. Five! The glorious beauty is a welcome shot of comforting espresso to my unease. Gorgeous. The Apothakery has two ovens, sometimes, and I'm constantly fighting the two devils over their cold and hot spots.

All right, I'll admit it. Knight Manor has one helluva kitchen.

As I move to get a better look at the AGA, I trip over a loose tile and nearly land on my face. A tile I'm pretty sure wasn't unseated before.

My cheeks warm. Can a house be annoyed at someone? If what I've heard is true, the Warlock's magic would be powerful enough to saturate this farmhouse with . . . personality.

Great. This should be fun.

Then there's a shuffling sound, and I whirl around.

When I listen, it's quiet again. I'm alone. A shiver runs through me so fast, my arm hair rises. *Get it together, Honey.* Probably a bat, by the state of this place. Could be the old house settling. I get the impression lots of things here squeak. I pray there are no mice.

Extra careful stepping over the tile now, I head for the massive fridge.

The heart of a house, a fridge is where Farewitches start, if we make the rare house call. I'm a professional, but also nosey, and scouring a fridge can be a great step in the right direction toward a diagnosis.

On cue, the fridge's double doors screech when I yank them open. A viciously sour smell smacks me in the face. We've got grape jelly, probably to go with the peanut butter on the counter. Soy sauce. Two cartons of eggs, somehow not the source of the smell. An obscenely large bunch of radishes that would love some butter and salt. Kids' Yoo-hoo drink boxes taking up extensive shelf real estate, and a single chilled bottle of what is either rice cooking wine or baijiu. Lastly, apple butter.

Mine, from the Apothakery. I'd recognize those jars anywhere.

The inside is as pitiful as the smell promised. But as I close the doors, a weird sort of smile inches onto my face. This looks like my fridge on particularly busy weeks.

Then someone giggles.

I whirl again and come face-to-face with a severe-looking older woman eyeing me across the island, arms folded and mouth cross.

"Ah!" I slap a hand over my racing heart. Wait—*I'm* the one who doesn't live here. "Sorry, ah—did you . . . did you giggle?"

The woman's narrow cold eyes are gray, like her hair. "Do I look like I giggle?"

I make the mistake of taking a second to answer. The hair, perfume, and cardigan-skirt set are giving off major grandma energy. Momaw gave me plenty of those stern looks. Suddenly, I feel underdressed in my overalls, even though they're my *good* ones, linen, instead of my usual torn denim.

"Ah, no. I mean—I'm sorry. The front door was open, I think, and I didn't want to be late just standing in the drive, so I thought I'd wait here, and since I was invited, I figured no one would mind if I let myself in—"

"Please, Ms. Faust, no need to pontificate."

"It's Frost. Like *frosting*."

"I'm sure."

Frost like *frigid*, I should've said. I throw out a hand. "Honey Frost. Farewitch of Foxe Holler." I sound like I'm asking a question, unsure. "Stellar to meet you."

The older woman looks down at my offered hand like I'm holding a cracked, goopy egg. She doesn't shake it. "We know who you are. Mr. Knight is unfortunately expecting you." Her voice lowers and I swear the sunlight vanishes for a second. "We didn't think you would show."

I remember the Warlock's letter. *Regretfully. Unfortunately.* What is it with these people?

"I'm the Holler's Farewitch. I can help anyone, or I can try." Nice. Real confident. "All someone has to do is ask."

"People-pleasing is a trauma response, dear."

Surprising that the fifth member of *The Golden Girls* is online enough to know that vocabulary, but I keep that retort to myself.

I'm getting tired of this woman's crusty top layer, but I'll find some way into her goodwill. I'm good at wiggling into places I'm not supposed to be. "Right, well, thank y'all for having me."

She cocks her head; the French roll of her hair doesn't roll a bit. A single hair doesn't even flutter. "How much do you know about the Warlock and Knight Manor?" It's almost like she's surprised I remember why I'm here.

"Admittedly, only whatever the rumor of the month is . . ." My words die under her withering stare. Now that I think about it, I've never seen her before at the shop or in town.

Who *are* these people tucked away at the edge of the Holler? If I had to guess the true identity of the Widow Witch, this lady would be in my top three.

"Where are the rest of the staff?"

"It's just me. And before you ask, I'm no Witch. The Warlock is the only one with magic in this house."

"Excellent," I say, mustering confidence I don't feel. That explains the state of the upkeep. "Independent working women, us two. Solitary work is good for the soul. *Don't bother a cake; you have to leave it alone to cool right.*"

She scrunches her nose. "Do you often talk to yourself in inspirational quotes?"

"Oh, it's something my Momaw used to say. I'm writing her advice into a cookbook. *Honey Frost's Southern Cookbook for Recipes Gone Wrong*—"

She heaves a sigh. "You have an hour to make something for Mr. Knight. Consider it your interview."

Hold on a mother-loving second. "Uh—I'm sorry, what—"

"Is there a problem?"

She has a few months left, at best. We need an answer. Now.

A pitiful Farewitch, I might be. But a slipshod daughter? Never. I can do this. "Not at all. May I meet the Warlock now? I need to speak with him about his illness before I begin."

"No, you may not."

What. She's kidding.

Farewitches draw from a common source of power with intention and the right ingredients, but each of us inherits our own unique twist to the magic that helps us find our focus in the kitchen. A magical thumbprint, of sorts. I might not be the best Farewitch, but I know my strengths, and my particular magical affinity requires the patient.

"I'm sorry, but that's not how this works. I have to see him to begin my process and make a preliminary diagnosis. Farewitch magic needs—"

"That won't be possible. He's busy reinforcing the wards around the Manor."

"Warding? Against *what*?"

She looks down her nose at me like I should already know.

What in the hell is going on—I'm invited! How's he going to try what I make if he doesn't show up? I came here to cure an ailing Warlock who, despite having some monstrously powerful magic according to the town, obviously doesn't possess the right kind or amount to heal himself. The mysteries keep building and I've had enough.

"He needs to make an exception. Otherwise, I can't do my work, Ms.—"

"If you can't find a way, then make one. *Otherwise*, leave." Glare. "And you may address me as Ms. Zeen. I'm the Governess." Her eyes wander over me again, mouth wrinkling up like the shriveled skin of roasted potatoes. Yup. Definitely the overalls. She's clearly offended by clothing on the onesie family tree. "I don't believe Warlock Knight is going to like you one bit," she says, and then turns on one kitten heel and is gone.

He'll get over it. That's what I *want* to say. But what comes out is a lackluster "That's unfortunate" the Governess doesn't even hear. I will most definitely be leaving *that* prickly pear of a cake alone to cool.

Once again, I'm by myself in a large empty kitchen, feeling more alone than when I arrived.

There's another giggle.

Maybe not so alone.

This time, I spy a fleeting glimpse of round cheeks and a small head of dark hair disappearing behind the kitchen door. So I'm *not* losing my mind. That explains the bike and the small sticky fingerprints on the fridge. Everywhere.

An idea forming, I side-eye the AGA stove. Now there's a friendly face.

We Frosts need to be moving, to be productive and creating. Takes the edge off. I've got to think clearly enough to brainstorm a recipe for a patient I'm not allowed to meet. So I do what I do best when I need to calm my nerves.

Baking is an optimistic term given the ingredients I have access to. This is going to be more creative compiling. But *The Frosts' Creatively Compiled Concoctions* wouldn't create a line out the door of the Apothakery, would it?

I wash my hands and pick the right temperature on the AGA. The steady heat chases away some of this cold, damp quiet. After some hunting, I find a loaf of simple country bread, cinnamon, sugar, and yellow butter that softens easily near the ambient warmth of the AGA, making for an easy smudge on thick slices of the bread. Next comes a good dusting of cinnamon and sugar. When the slices look like little sparkling faun-colored pillows, I toss them all onto a baking sheet I have to clean twice before I trust it.

Normally a Farewitch doesn't presumptuously take over a kitchen, especially when she hasn't seen her patient, but the Governess did say I only have an hour . . .

The moment the first notes of warm cinnamon fill the air, I feel better. This was a quick staple breakfast in the Frost household. The ingredients are always in the pantry, and it can be eaten in one hand while the other sets a mise en place. It also has the unfailing added benefit of luring almost anyone into the kitchen who's still sleeping. Or hiding.

Sure enough, a small figure pokes his mop of dark hair around the doorway. By the time I pull out the tray of perfectly GB&D toast, I'm staring at a little boy.

He stares back.

Eight? Nine? I'm not great with kids' ages. I'm an only child like my mom.

"Hello there," I say. "Have you eaten? Lunch?" Now that I can see him, he's wearing pajamas with all sorts of dogs on them. "Or breakfast?"

I transfer most of the hot toast to a platter and push it in the shy boy's direction across the island. Then I grab my own slice. The cinnamon hits my tongue and I grin for the first time in days. I knew it—I've surpassed my mom's own recipe for this. I'm now Queen of the Cinnamon and Sugar Toast. She'll have to accept humble defeat.

The boy looks from the toast to me. Back to the toast. His hair is black as my cast-iron skillet, and he's pale but not sickly, like someone slathers him with plenty of sunscreen. When he inches closer, he's only at eye level with the counter. He seems small for his head size. Or is that a weird thing to think? How tall are nine-year-olds?

"I like your overalls," he whispers, bright intelligence hovering in his hazel eyes.

Oh, I like this one. "Thank you, they were on sale—"

Before I can blink, he grabs three slices and bolts.

Huh. I'll take the clumsy robbery as a compliment. And if a little boy lives here, the farmhouse can't be that dangerous, can it?

Just then, a copper pot falls from its ceiling rack, landing right on top of my platter of toast. The ceramic platter cracks under the direct hit.

No harm in an informational interview, my ass.

If the house is already throwing tantrums . . . Well, ask any Witch: That doesn't bode well for the mental state of the house's owner. The half-chewed toast in my mouth goes dusty to my taste buds. I ignore the mess and take a step back from the island.

What in the world am I going to make? It for sure won't be the toast, especially now that it's got extra ceramic crunch. This is ridiculous. I can't work with an agitated kitchen, and I can't work with no patient. I'll just wait, run out my hour. He has to show up eventually. The kitchen is the heart of the home, after all.

Heart and eyes: The kitchen's entire back wall is all thick-paned windows and stained glass looking out onto the rear of the property. I creep closer to the back windows to peer out.

Even from here, I can tell the grounds behind the Manor aren't just trees and shrubbery—they're Gardens, capital letter and all. Devoted to what looks like everything from flowers to vegetables to fruit. All perfectly situated for morning sunlight instead of harsh afternoon heat. Meticulously kept. The smell of wet soil and deep earth is strongest here, too. Inside, potted vines and ferns and herbs surround me. I'm starting to feel like I've wandered into a farmhouse that really wants to be a greenhouse.

I brush my hand along shelves and countertops, expecting dust. Instead—soil.

That won't do. Clearly no one's used this kitchen to prepare anything more than a PB&J. Someone here cares very little about what strangers from town can see from the road, and an awful lot about what they can't.

But the bones of the place are good. I can work with this.

While I wait, I clean up my food prep and fetch a few basic grocery items from the truck I brought along. The Governess said don't wander, but I'm going to assume the front lawn is safe.

I end up staring at the frightful contents of a pantry so neglected, I didn't even see it tucked behind a large palm tree until a second inspection of the kitchen. If I'm not hallucinating, it looks like all the spice jars are filled with plant seeds—

"Are you auditing the pantry?"

A deep voice startles me into spilling a box of Goo Goo Clusters. The chocolates are so old, they hit the tile floor with echoes that are sure to wake any vengeful spirits slinking about this odd museum of a farmhouse. I turn and find a dark-haired man staring at me by the door.

My brain is still in list and recipe mode, so the first items I notice about him are:

1. He's pale except for twin patches of color on his cheeks, like the sun spots on my mom's hands from baking too often by the window.
2. His age. Or lack thereof. His thick hair is long enough to fit into a hair tie. And his hairline—eleven out of ten. But gray smudges his temples like lipstick on a wineglass. He could be a sun-beaten thirty or a wonderfully taken-care-of fifty.
3. He's covered in dirt.

"Oh, sorry, er—I haven't had one of these in a long time." I'm still holding the empty Goo Goo Cluster box. Shameful recovery. I gather up the fallen chocolates and leave them in an awkward pile on the island. Right next to the destroyed plate of toast. The man watches me the entire time, his expression a stern, unreadable mask. I can't tell if he's annoyed to find a random woman in his kitchen or if he's annoyed to learn said random woman is already breaking stuff.

On cue, he looks at the toast.

"To be fair, it was the pot's fault," I blurt without any context.

A bubble of silence follows. The moment I'm not trying to push my buttered food therapy out the door, my people skills dissolve. Wow. Minus ten first impression for me.

He speaks first. "You're younger than I was expecting." His voice is low and terse, brow furrowing. Definitely annoyed.

"Oh." Pause. "Thank you?" Oh. *Oh no.* "You're him. Warlock Knight." *You're not what I was expecting, either*, but I don't say that part out loud.

He frowns, maybe confused. "I'm the gardener."

My hands unclench with relief. "Ah, okay. *Lord.* Good to hear." That explains the dirt. Crisis dodged. Pilfering the pantry and tossing his sweets to the floor is not how I wanted to meet the Warlock, even if he is the one avoiding the very guest he invited. "Everyone in town's out of their wits afraid of the Warlock, and I didn't know what to expect . . ."

In the following silence, which there's a lot of, I absorb more details.

He wears gloves and practical boots, a white Henley that keeps the sun off his arms. Bandana around his neck. He's lean in an on-his-feet sort of way, not a gym-membership way. A smudge of soil everywhere I look. Bright hazel eyes, black hair—*hazel eyes.*

My brain fires up like the Apothakery's old microwave. "The boy I saw around here, is he yours?" He must be. Maybe the Warlock allows his employee to bring his son to work. That's nice. Although that doesn't explain why the boy was in pajamas . . .

"He's just my ward," the gardener says in a clipped tone as he steps farther into the room, leaving behind two muddy boot prints that have no place in a kitchen. No wonder the Governess is tense. "Distant family relation."

I'm probably imagining it, but I almost hear a hint of sadness flavoring his voice. The kid seems like he brings nothing but constant amusement and joy. I glance around at the plant life. "Your herbs are gorgeous. I've never seen basil so healthy."

A perplexed flicker jumps into his eyes, like he doesn't get compliments and so doesn't know what to do with one. But then the stern mask is back just as quickly.

I try again to keep this one-sided conversation going. "Although it doesn't look like you ever pick them."

He tugs at his gloves. "No one around here cooks to inspire the need."

Clearly. This is 100 percent an ingredient household. And barely. "A shame. April is a bit late to plant a garden, isn't it? Doesn't the soil warm up around here by March?"

Although we are up in the hills, far from town. How would I commute here and back to the shop every day to check on a patient who lives here? Farewitches need to be close, at least with new customers they're still diagnosing. If I'm at my apartment, I'll never be able to study the Warlock's habits, his eating, examine what I can help change from a nutritional perspective. I'd spend a precious day's worth of baking in the truck.

The man's gaze darkens, like he didn't expect a Farewitch to have gardening knowledge. But every Farewitch knows food and farming and the land are inseparable. "The soil around the Manor stays colder for longer."

That's . . . odd. I don't ask my hundred follow-up questions, but I don't get the impression the soil is finicky because of an errant mountain cold front. What kind of magic does the Warlock practice, again? Even if the details are fuzzy, maybe the rumors come from truth. Our library *did* burn, so perhaps elemental magic was at play? But that's usually lower magic, grounded and tangible, a Witch's favorite kind.

And elemental magic won't help cure an ailing Farewitch's wasting disease.

"I'm Honey Frost," I say. "The Farewitch Mr. Knight requested." Perhaps the Warlock's biggest mistake. But he doesn't need to know that if, just for my attention, he's willing to trade extensive magical knowledge that could help my mom. Bake it till you make it.

The man doesn't give me his name. "How did you get in here? Past the wards?"

The question is innocent enough but his voice is gruff, unwelcoming. Maybe I hit a gardening nerve asking about the soil. "The door was unlocked."

"It doesn't unlock for strangers."

"I've been invited, haven't I?" The Warlock asked for me by name. I know what I can bring to the table. Or try to. Literally. "Since it's possible I'll be working here alongside you and the garden, I'd like to make sure we're planting a large variety of herbs. And some of the less common herbs, too."

He doesn't answer me. I think his stern stare is about to be a glare.

I push on. "I'd also like to see what you already have planted. I'm not sure how long I'll be here, but I'd love to know what produce is coming down the line further in the season."

Still no answer. He stalks farther into the kitchen, shoulders rigid. A small whiff of fresh soil and the color green follows him. I wonder if that smell can be bottled—

None of that, girl, Momaw Frost would warn me. Farewitches do *not* have time for men.

"Another thing—I can write all this down—but it's going to get hot in here and I'm not sure the plants will thrive once I begin. They're probably used to the low heat of the AGA, and I don't want to shock them with new temperatures, what with the gas range going regularly now, too. Especially in May and June."

He stops a few paces away from me, like I'm some feral, trespassing

Farewitch, and in a tone that is most definitely not a question, asks, "Any other requests."

In a sharp split second it hits me like a copper pot on a plate of toast. "You're . . . not the gardener. Are you."

"Oh no, I very much am. I just also happen to be the Warlock of Foxe Holler."

Fu—of course he is.

Chapter Four

MONDAY, APRIL 4 (STILL)

Honey's Helpful Hint, from
Honey Frost's Southern Cookbook for Recipes Gone Wrong:

When frying, work in batches and let the oil return to a high temperature between batches. Do not crowd the frying skillet. Flavor needs space, and even the best-tasting snacks can get soggy and spooked.

"You can address me as Mr. Knight."

He lifts a stool in one hand and brings it to the island. It doesn't fit the height of the counter, but everything is a little out of place in this farmhouse. Including me.

I can't tell if he's pissed or just grumpy. *Both.* He's harder to read than Momaw's Woodford-fueled handwritten recipes. Clearly no one expected me to show up this morning, and I've for sure lost this job before getting hired.

He doesn't wait for any kind of apology for the social blunder. "To be frank with you, I don't have the luxury of interviews at this point, but Ms. Zeen keeps the Manor running, and she insists on formalities. So, here we are."

A test recipe. Right. The whole reason I'm here. I give him a subtle once-over, reviewing my usual mental checklist. Eyes, focused. Walk, even. Skin, pale but not deathly sallow. Speech, clear. Situational awareness, solid. Attitude? *Needs improvement.*

He looks relatively healthy on the outside, although I know that doesn't mean anything if he's suffering from a chronic illness of some kind. There's a world underneath our skin other people aren't always privy to, and food can't fix everything. But how am I going to even begin to try to heal him if no one will tell me what's wrong?

Doesn't matter. I'm here for my mom, and I'm a Frost to my core, made of grit and gristle (which also happens to be the name of the only late-night restaurant in town, the Grit & Gristle). There aren't many folks with magic in a town this size, but just because I've never healed another magical being as powerful as a Warlock doesn't mean this is going to be another situation like my mom all over again.

Besides, this is where my unique twist of magic comes in handy.

I move around the island, the last barrier between us, and stop directly in front of his stool. This is likely the only time I'll ever be taller than him. My hands go out, palms up. "May I hold your hands for a moment?"

That shakes his stern mask for a hot second. "Absolutely not."

Bothersome, but now we're getting somewhere. Could his illness originate on the skin? An allergic reaction of some kind, or an autoimmune response concentrated in his extremities? Perhaps direct skin contact with something in his garden is to blame. Maybe I'll get lucky and this whole situation is just a bad case of poison ivy.

"I know this is sensitive, Mr. Knight, but I need to touch your skin to even begin a recipe. I always start here. Anything about your health remains confidential with me, I promise."

He doesn't look convinced. "Is this what a typical house call from a Farewitch entails?"

"We don't really do house calls anymore." *So appreciate it*, I want to add, but I play nice.

"I didn't realize this process would be so . . ."

"Hands-on?" Ha.

His severe indifference slides right back on. Not one for jokes, then. He raises his gloved hands. "These stay on. No exceptions."

"But I have to touch you—"

"Then you'll have to touch something else."

Silence.

His eyes squeeze shut half a second. "That did not come out correctly."

"No, it didn't." I bite my tongue to keep from grinning. "Okay, gloves on. No hands. May I?" My palm hovers by his cheek.

His brow sinks over his eyes. I can see he's weighing whatever pain he's in against tolerating my presence. I'll try not to be offended.

"If we must." Discomfort hangs on his gruff whisper, and it sends a bolt of nerves right down my spine.

"We must." My palms go around his cheeks.

He stiffens, his mouth tight. In the way, *way* back of my mind, I wonder when someone last touched him. His skin is warm, from sun. Slightly scratchy, stubble coming in. I feel the oddest desire to run my thumbs over his sun patches— *Focus.*

Right. I can't forget I'm at the mercy of Foxe Holler's most powerful resident.

Witches practice lower magic, more grounded and practical, and so we craft stable, homegrown networks of community power. Warlocks, however, practice higher magic, amorphous and capricious spellwork that likes to react to their moods and impulses. So, more powerful in theory, if only because it's explosive.

Despite our differences, both Witches and Warlocks draw power from the land. Someone's magic is strongest when it's local and has time to grow roots. The land can only support so much magical energy, though, so being a small town means Foxe Holler has just a handful of other Witches. I don't even *know* another Farewitch, besides my mom. With that constraint, and their higher magic that guzzles energy, Warlocks often become solitary travelers, independent yet isolated and restlessly nomadic. Their power easily becomes volatile.

Higher magic, higher reward. Higher risk.

Which is why the folks of Foxe Holler trust neighborhood Witches but not Warlocks. Except—*this* Warlock is the exception. He's been here, in this spot, for ages. Ironically, that might make the town fear him even more. Unpredictable higher magic is one thing, but a Warlock who stays put and lets his power burrow and calcify?

As I hold his face, his breathing is impressively controlled, even if the tension in his body is screaming. Something haunted hangs in his eyes that I can't place. I close my own, my thumbs brushing over his jawbone. And then I let my magic do what it does best.

Fragments of old moments in time dance under my eyelids.

The memories begin.

They don't come through as a best-of highlights replay, or in clear images, but appear in notes of flavor, feelings that come with a taste. But darkness hits me with every cabinet in the kitchen of his mind that I try to pry open. Not empty, but the memories are shadowy. Hidden.

I concentrate, edge closer to him, my eyes pressed as tightly as my fingers on his face.

Finally, I tug a few glimpses into the light.

A summer picnic, out in the yard. A birthday? The Manor is fuzzy, and looks more like the farmhouse in its original glory before the quirky additions and neglect. Then a woman, her black hair in a bun, great cheekbones. A silk scarf around her neck gives her gobs of elegance points. Chinese jade rests at her throat, green pendant twinkling in the sunlight. She smiles at me—

The Warlock's gloved hands tug on my forearms, and the memory vanishes, but I let it go. Farewitches only take what we need. My eyelids flutter open.

His breathing comes fast now, no longer controlled. "That's enough."

My hands drop and I back up. "Thank you."

Wide hazel eyes look away, avoiding mine. "What could that possibly have told you that I couldn't?"

That's another trick of my memory magic—a patient never knows what I see. They usually just feel tired or hungry after I poke around. "It tells me you shave with a straight razor and need better sunscreen."

The glare returns. We're back in business. But I don't need him to like me. I just need him to like my food.

At last, an idea for a recipe blooms.

So with the Warlock watching my every move, I get to work on my real interview.

I wash the produce I brought and get hot oil going in a skillet. It's not *my* skillet, and there's rust on the bottom, but it'll do. I know this recipe by heart, but this edgy silence will drive me mad, and my mind needs something to distract me from my nerves.

"Your letter said *the situation is advanced and beyond my efforts*."

My back is to him at the stove, but I can see that fixed scowl of his perfectly in my head. "I don't look ill on the surface, but I wrote you the truth. I also said you would be compensated handsomely if I hire you, and part of that payment is for discretion. The less you or anyone else knows, the better. Do we have an understanding?"

I'm more than familiar with the mental and internal toll of an invisible illness. Momaw kept her decline secret as long as she could. My thoughts always trickle back to her in these anxious moments, when I wish I could hear her voice on the phone.

"I wouldn't worry," I say, trying to focus on slicing. "Everyone in the Holler thinks you're over three hundred."

"Everyone just *assumes* all Warlocks are ancient?"

"How far off am I?"

"I'm very well not three centuries old, thank you."

"Hmm. Disappointing."

He scoffs. "Like a Witch, I have a regular human lifespan. If

Warlocks were immortal, you wouldn't be here, would you?" Then, lower, an aggravated mutter: "We wouldn't even be in this mess."

Good point.

I set out a shallow dish of spiced flour, a bowl of whisked daffodil-yellow eggs, and lastly, cornmeal breadcrumbs I toasted myself out of old cornbread from the Apothakery. "Have you gotten any kind of diagnosis from a medical doctor? What did Dr. Virgil say? You must've seen him first."

"No doctors. It's not a regular illness. It's magic in origin."

At the severity in his voice, my heart stumbles. My first thought jumps to *curse*, but curses are Witch territory, our kind of practical magic. I'm not sure Warlocks can even *be* cursed. To them, it might just feel like the sniffles. Even if a Warlock somehow fell victim to a curse, they could likely just undo it. And there are better ways to lift curses, usually with a spell, not with a Farewitch and her food.

This is something different.

Even if it means he sends me away, I have to be honest when it involves someone's health. I look at him, my fingers coated in a hearty combination of gluten and egg. "While I appreciate your interest in my skills, I typically heal common physical ailments. The non-magical kind."

"I don't invite outsiders here lightly. Indulge me," he says, but his attention is on something beyond the back windows, the gardens. There's that haunted *something* again. Sadness? Or guilt?

"If it's magic in origin, have you consulted with other Warlocks?"

"Discretion, Ms. Frost." His tone doesn't leave any air for debate. "How does your magic work, exactly? I didn't know your predecessors, and I've never met another Farewitch."

He wouldn't have, not here in the Holler. Witches know Witches, and Warlocks know Warlocks. But the two groups don't mix. The last Warlock to actually live here in the Holler was . . . I have no idea.

"Farewitch magic is basically practical healing made stronger. It's not automatic by any means. I suppose it's a . . . triangle of sorts."

The oil is almost ready, so I turn back to my ingredients.

"We start with the same ingredients, tools, the pantry anyone might have access to. Then we add our magic that comes from intention, spells, rituals, incantations, the inherited family recipes. The lore of ingredients or sigils, folk knowledge passed down through generations . . ." He's got me so on edge, I'm rambling. "Lastly, Farewitches manifest a unique affinity. It's like a thumbprint . . . Or, it flavors *how* our magic helps people."

The oil is perfectly hot. I drop my scraggly clumps of flour into the skillet, one at a time so the oil can keep up its heat. The noise of the robust sizzle dances around the kitchen. Flour and cornmeal turn crispy. Garlic and onion and oregano and paprika tickle my nose. The place begins to smell like a real kitchen and not a floor model of one. What's magical is how frying oil instantly makes a place feel lived in. A house into a home.

"Do other kinds of Witches have affinities within their magic?"

"Sure, though they might refer to it in a different way. But a Farewitch is always born with an affinity. They usually repeat through bloodlines, though not always. My grandmother's was a skill with herbalism. And my mom's was—*is* elemental magic. Fire and heat. She can manipulate and control temperatures. A coveted affinity for a Farewitch, obviously."

"And yours?"

I hesitate. Farewitches don't consider our affinities secret or private by any means, but when I tell someone mine, they ever so gently pull back. Like I might steal something from them, when in reality I'm just listening to what their memory wants to tell me.

He shifts in his stool, restless at my lack of an answer. "I need to know if your magic will only help me live longer with the illness, or if it will actually fix the problem. Does your healing promise me time or health, Ms. Frost?"

I drop a plate of expertly golden-brown fried green tomatoes on the island in front of him. "I've found, Mr. Knight, that the key to health is usually time."

He leans back, staring at the tomatoes. And staring. If he wore glasses, the lenses would steam. The Warlock of Foxe Holler has apparently met his match in the form of fried *Solanum lycopersicum*.

I nudge the plate. I *know* I've chosen the perfect recipe. He might be a stoic wall, but his memories aren't, and he should feel some type of good after eating this, whether physically or even just emotionally. "Don't let them get cold."

In a gesture that's alarmingly endearing, he picks up a fork and knife to saw a tomato into neat pieces. I notice the utensils then—carved Chinese characters crawl up the intricate stems, but the fine silver is old and tarnished now, like the rest of the farmhouse. Folks usually eat my fried green tomatoes with their hands. He's gruff but he's got manners.

But he still hasn't removed his gardening gloves, even to eat. I take it back. Unsanitary. Although if it's because of his illness, it's not my place to question him, especially since he's had decades of isolation to hone his quirks.

It's been a while since my heart's gone wonky waiting for someone to try that first bite of my food, and I realize I'm holding my breath. This isn't just any customer. If he doesn't like it, will he obliterate me on the spot? Or worse—insult my cooking?

He places a chunk of tomato on his tongue and chews. As his jaw works, his shoulders release the smallest, tiniest edge of their tension.

His eyes close.

Victory. I slide a ramekin toward him. "I like to dip mine in apple butter. Sweet and salty."

A dollop goes on his next bite.

But then he sets down his utensils and stares at his barely touched plate. Two bites and he's finished? I bartered my coveted molasses fudge for Farmer Kelsey's tomatoes! Maybe I've miscalculated, overestimated the recipe and my own skill, flown too close to the culinary sun—

His eyes find mine. They're already brighter. Color fills his cheeks. "Don't avoid my question: How does your magic's *thumbprint* work, exactly?"

Swallowing a satisfied smile, I manage to breathe. "Any Farewitch knows fried green tomatoes are good for curing the blues, especially seasonal affective disorder. But my affinity is memory magic. When I touch someone with intention, they show me a memory of a meal, their body's way of telling me what it's craving, what it needs. That's where I should begin treatment. The strongest cures come from the strongest flavors: the ones we've had before."

"That's the magic."

"And the limit. For me to see a memory, it has to involve food. Luckily, we spend a lot of our lives eating, and the best memories usually happen over a shared table."

He pushes away his plate. "You took a memory from me?"

"You *shared* one. I never take—you still have it. With a new patient, I need skin-to-skin contact. I always get permission to touch someone." I'll blame his blunt questions on a Warlock's typical ignorance of anything Witch related.

He eyes his food with caution. Maybe the memory I saw that looked harmless to me has reminded him of something painful.

Clamoring for an explanation that might save me, I add, "Also, the old ladies in the Friday cards group claim your family used to hold parties here. A favorite menu item was supposedly the fried green tomato hors d'oeuvres, so I figured you must have eaten them ages ago, back in . . . well, *back*."

His gaze narrows further. Crap. Is he . . . mad? Upset that I just called him old, or that I clearly uncovered a very invasive weed he's spent decades trying to smother? I was elbow-deep in powdered sugar yesterday and now I'm tiptoeing around a Warlock in an isolated house with no one around to hear my screams. *How in the hell did I get here?*

His stool screeches across the tile as he stands. "My memories are private. This entire endeavor is a mistake."

What. I cross my arms. "You're ill. I don't think you have a choice."

The intimidating facade on his face slips like an egg on nonstick, but only for a second. "I'll find another Farewitch."

"Be my guest. Foxe Holler's only got me, and another Farewitch would never leave her own community. You and I both know local magic is the strongest."

"Leave. Now."

"Hell no." I didn't close the shop, lie to my mother, and drag my ass all the way into the boonies of the boonies for a *No thanks*. "That meal was perfect and you know it."

Just then, the lights in the kitchen flicker off. The air stills, dead. Out of the corner of my eye, I see plants begin to grow exponentially fast from their pots, vines racing across the tile for my feet.

The Warlock is in front of me before I can blink, his shadow looming over me. "I don't need a child Farewitch lecturing me about my own magic. I'm more than familiar with the consequences of its shortcomings. Get. *Out.*"

My cheeks burn. More than the thought of the Warlock's plant monstrosities dragging me to the depths of his garden to suffocate me, that *embarrassment* at being called out for my inexperience does it.

Fine. Maybe I am a crappy Farewitch. But at least I was willing to listen.

As I stomp back through the maze of a farmhouse, my thoughts reel. I didn't ask for this. Any of it. The job, the town, the shop, the legacy. I'm not even sure I want it. All I want is for my mom to celebrate her next birthday. If I can't tunnel my way into this Warlock's life long enough for his magic and knowledge to point me to an answer, then forget this mess.

I'm yanking open my truck's driver door when I hear the porch creak.

"Wait."

I don't know what it is, but something in the Warlock's voice makes me turn back around. Unbelievable. Farewitches are just people pleasers with aprons, it's true. But it's more than that. I can't abandon what might be my last chance at finding the cure for my mom. A Farewitch doesn't give up so easily.

On the front porch, his arms are crossed. "Unfortunately for the both of us, you are the last option I have. You're also the only person not afraid to come here."

"I'm not surprised," I reply, keeping a healthy distance. "Your house needs to learn to trust new people. Or at least not pelt them with pots."

"I've lived here for years and I don't trust anyone. Why should it?" His expression remains completely unreadable. Never have I heard such a cranky non-apology. "You have the job if you want it."

My heartbeat jumps like a mixer on high speed. *No freaking way.*

"You'll have to live here, of course. I presume that won't be a problem."

My mixer heart zooms faster and starts sparking. Wait, what—

He pulls out a folded square of paper as he stalks down the porch steps. "This is the fee I can offer you. Half now, half at the . . . end."

Numb, I meet him at the bottom step and take the paper. Fingerprints of soil cover the pages. Like he's been holding on to it for a while, waiting. I look at the amount.

My cinnamon toast does a choreographed dive routine in my gut. With this kind of money, I can do something *real* for my mom.

Or doctors can, with bills paid in full. I could send her to a big city with better healthcare and even rent an apartment to be close to her, *all at once.*

But I wouldn't be able to do that part. Because I'd need to be here. With the Warlock.

My mouth is open, but I don't care. He's still scowling when I look up at him. His face must freeze like that. "This is beyond . . ." I don't know how to finish. I got the job.

What if I can't cure him? And I can't abandon the Apothakery to work for one person, for who knows how long.

It's not a regular illness. It's magic in origin.

An oily tang sits on my tongue as I swallow down the terrible feeling that my mom's illness is also viciously beyond any regular physical disease. If I send my mom away to another hospital on the chance she might get better, I won't be with her during what time she has left. Would a different doctor even be able to figure out what's wrong with her? She'll fret knowing her daughter closed the treasured Frost Apothakery and *that,* of all things, might kill her first.

"This is generous, Mr. Knight." Deep breath. "But to be honest with you, I'm not sure you're worth it." I turn and move to leave.

"You're looking for something, aren't you?"

I halt.

"I have an extensive archive of books. Old texts, grimoires. That's why you came. I'll give you access to my archival library."

How the hell does he know this? Are there Holler rumors about *me*? Maybe the worry is just that clear on my face. I've never been able to master a stoic mask like he has. Farewitches feel *a lot,* and we need that emotion. We bake it right into our food.

I shove down the unease clawing at my chest, and turn back. Again. "I can't just close up my shop. I have no idea how long this is going to take."

"Let's be frank with each other, Ms. Frost. You're clearly a young

Farewitch who is desperate enough to close her shop once already." He grits his teeth, like conversing with me is painful. Likewise. "Unfortunately for the both of us, *I* might be *your* best option."

Crap. I can't refute him there. He's right about one thing, maybe the most important thing: The money is stellar, but the knowledge is invaluable.

"I'll sleep on it and call you."

"I don't have a phone. I'll give you three days to get your affairs in order."

Infuriating man. "I'll *think* about it."

Back in my truck, I want to scream into my steering wheel, but the Warlock is still watching me. He doesn't step off the porch's last step. Odd. Are the wards he mentioned here to keep people out, or something in?

Or someone.

The idea of a trapped Warlock would probably comfort folks in the Holler.

But if he's trapped somehow, he's not the only one. I swallow. What would Momaw or my mom do now?

My pride crumbles. They were stellar Farewitches. I'd sell my soul for a teaspoon of their fortitude.

We need an answer. Now.

I launch out of my truck and storm back toward the porch for a. Third. Ridiculous. Time. I must look wild, because the Warlock's head tilts in concern. Planting myself right in front of him, I try my best to hide my shaking fingers, hands, voice.

"I want any and all—*all*—archives of yours at my disposal."

His lips twitch. "The kitchen and library are yours. But the rest of the house is strictly off-limits at all times. No ex—"

"*No exceptions*, yes, I got that part. And if it becomes clear I can't help you?"

He grimaces. Picturing the worst-case scenario, or a stranger living on top of him in his precious seclusion? Definitely both. "I won't take it personally. Further questions?"

A million. *Why are there so many terrible rumors about you? Why did you disappear twenty-five years ago?*

But none of that matters right now. I'll find out myself, one way or another, only after I cure the person I love most.

"I want my own room," I blurt. "And bathroom." I need a win today.

"I certainly wouldn't ask you to share with Ms. Zeen. Any *other* requests?" He taunts me with the same sarcastic tone from earlier. "If not, Friday is your first day."

That's that.

When I'm halfway back to the truck, he calls out one last time. "Your tomatoes—they were . . . adequate. How did you know I would even like your recipe?"

Adequate. Pah. They were phenomenal.

"You already had my apple butter in your fridge. You liked my food before I walked in."

Then I give what I pray is such a casually blasé bow at the waist, no one can tell I'm cracking on the inside.

And I hope, so fiercely, that it irks him to no end.

My truck tires screech on the gravel as I peel out and leave him on the porch, his heavy dark gaze hovering in my rearview mirror.

Chapter Five

FRIDAY, APRIL 8

Honey's Helpful Hint, from
Honey Frost's Southern Cookbook for Recipes Gone Wrong:

Do not rush your process, ingredients, or oven. You cannot bake quickly. You can only bake incorrectly.

It's only fitting the first time I move in with a man, it's for work.

I park my purring Dodge off to the side of Knight Manor, although there's no one else to make room for. An older pickup I just now notice is napping under half a tarp, hidden in the greenery. Like everything else, it looks forgotten. For errands? They can't get everything delivered, can they? Have I even seen a postman—a mailbox?

I can easily imagine the Warlock's answer and scowl. *Mailboxes imply we're open to correspondence.*

Heaven forbid.

After my interview turned tribunal, I slapped a new sign to the shop's yellow front door.

ON VACATION. BACK IN THREE WEEKS.

Even my rest is a lie. Can a Farewitch cure a powerful magical being in the time it takes to get a sourdough starter going? No idea. Sounds like a feat on par with mastering a Julia Child recipe.

How to Cure Your Warlock in a Weekend. The title of my next cookbook.

Then I spent the rest of the week at the hospital with my mom, or in the Apothakery furiously baking and replenishing stock for the more common ailments and standing orders. I stopped counting my all-nighters. Somehow, I still managed to deliver everything for my regulars across the Holler. Can't leave my neighbors up a creek. I'm a Farewitch to *everyone.* Even if everyone doesn't believe it.

But deprived of their usual steaming skillet cinnamon buns and biscuits for a week, my neighbors eventually connected the dots. A dash of panic ensued.

The last couple of days, whispers followed me on errands in town. Harsh looks at the post office, upturned noses at the market, even major side-eye at the consignment shop, where my overalls addiction keeps them in business, thank you. A gaggle of aggrieved church ladies even shadowed me, close as hungry barn cats. For ladies who distrust magic as much as their spitfire leader Gertha Fudge, they sure do believe awful hard in it.

"One does not simply close Frost Apothakery, child!" they shouted at me across the town square. "And most certainly not for a dastardly Warlock!"

Friday came blessedly soon.

Now, as I stare up at the neglected farmhouse laid bare in the morning sunlight, the fear in town taps like Ms. Buchanan's poodle's claws across my mind. Inhale. Exhale. Hay, grass, horse somewhere in there. The familiar fragrance of the Holler anchors me as I enter the Manor and seal my fate.

Inside, I dump my skillets in the kitchen, away from overhanging pots. I half expect an ambitious vine to steal something. Farther into the room, a massive picnic-style kitchen table looks like it can seat twelve, fourteen, sixteen . . . You could bowl on this thing. When it's not throwing a tantrum, it really is a kitchen for entertaining, for family gatherings and celebrations of hearth and home.

For *what* people?

My favorite cast-iron skillet looks pitiful on the floor, and glares at me, rather rudely. It can sense this is not its kitchen. I glare back. We don't have a choice, do we?

But: Who *will* run the Apothakery if I need to stay longer? I can handle living with a dangerous Warlock. But I cannot, under any circumstances, stop working. The residents of Foxe Holler make for some cantankerous customers, but they're mine.

Ten minutes and a slow, clumsy ascent up two flights of stairs later—governesses apparently do *not* help with luggage—I stop in a narrow hall on the third floor, in an entirely new wing I don't think exists on the outside. The farmhouse's guts do not at all match the blueprint of its exterior.

Warlock magic has to be at play here, yet he couldn't have magicked in some elevators?

Rows of closed doors line the narrow hall, probably bedrooms for a fuller home, with life and laughter and generations. Again, for *what* people? How did such a spacious farmhouse end up so vacant? What went wrong? Then I think of how quickly my own family shrank to two. Death moves fast. Grief doesn't. Empty space grows like a weed.

It's easy to find the single open door on the floor, the room the Warlock has assigned me *against his better judgment*, says Governess Zeen. I drop my suitcase on the floor of my new home for the next three weeks.

Like the stairwells and halls, this room is dark, nearing frigid. The bedroom is small but no smaller than mine above the Apothakery. There's a creaky writing desk and chair, and a trunk that appears to be full of vintage paper sewing patterns. The old hardwood floors are on full display with the sparse furniture. There's a single twin bed.

The Warlock obviously doesn't think I'll be having any guests.

I half wheeze-chuckle to myself. Silas would find that funny. If we were friends and told each other those sorts of things.

"Ms. Frost, if you're winded after a staircase, this house is going to be terribly difficult to navigate. You should eat more protein."

Governess Zeen stands like a gargoyle in the doorway, arms crossed over a brand-new cardigan set. Almost-black navy, this time. I guess the beige was too colorful.

Two *staircases*, I want to say. "I'll remember that, Ms. Zeen."

Rigid as ever, she watches me drag my suitcase into a corner. "Your washroom is down the hall. It hasn't been used in ages. I hope that's not too rustic for you."

I wave a hand nonchalantly. Now that I've entered a new decade, I need the daily steps, and I'm no stranger to an outhouse (thank you, Momaw). I don't mind a few dust bunnies.

Momaw's farmhouse got its fair share of dust, but whenever she said *dust bunny*, I only heard my name. From then on, my mom and Momaw and I would spend hours hunting imaginary *dust hunnies*, giggling until our sides hurt and we downed warm honeyed milk to calm down before bed. A phantom warmth floods my veins as the memory hugs me tight. Too tight.

"I hope you don't daydream when handling knives."

I snap back to the present. The Frost women at their best, vibrant and laughing, is only a memory now. "Sorry. I haven't slept much the last couple of nights." *At all. Never.*

"If you need anything, feminine products and the like, you can find them in the cabinets underneath your washroom sink."

I hide a smile since it might scare her off and ruin this atom-small moment of bonding. No need to mention I haven't had a regular period in years. Stress, the gynecologist says. *Or a gift from above.* I don't have time to leak when my job demands I'm on my feet all day.

She purses her lips. "The rules, Ms. Frost: Stay in the kitchen. Do not wander the house, especially at night. And whatever you do, refrain from bothering the plants."

So far, the only areas I've been allowed to see except the kitchen are the stairwells and halls. As per The Rules.

"Lastly, the Warlock's gardens are strictly prohibited."

"Of course, why wouldn't they be?" I mutter. Not quietly enough, based on her glower. She'd fit right in with the church ladies. Although none of them would dare work for a Warlock.

When she leaves, I unpack one thing first: a framed photo of Dolly Parton. It's no coincidence Dolly's hair reminds me of Momaw's. Sometimes, it's easier to look at than actual pictures of my Momaw.

I prop my good luck charm on the nightstand, then take a gander at the view outside the single wavy-glassed window above the desk. It looks out over the gardens behind the house.

Strictly prohibited.

A Farewitch can appreciate a tight SOP. I get it. Every kitchen has rules.

But I don't care for his.

I immediately head for the gardens behind the house. He's paying me to cook, and I need ingredients. Does trespassing count if you live upstairs?

Quietly as possible, I creep out the side screen door near the back of the kitchen and onto the section of the wraparound porch that looks out over the back of the grounds.

The Warlock's gardens.

Just from the porch, I can tell these gardens didn't grow overnight. He's been toiling out here for decades, yet not one rumor about him mentions gardening or herbalism. Someone who spends this much time on a craft but doesn't want to show it off . . . Odd. Gertha Fudge will tell you how the cow ate the cabbage over her pineapple canning. Even Ms. Buchanan gushes about her poodle, in a charming, gab-you-to-death way.

Something tells me this man's not simply a grumpy recluse.

Between my interview and today, I scrambled to learn anything more I could about the Warlock. Seemed the wise thing to do before making an immensely powerful magical being my roommate. My thoughts wander back to the timing of the library fire and the Warlock's disappearance from the public eye. Connection or coincidence, I'm not sure yet.

A buzzing noise sounds then, too loud even for the dragonflies around here.

My phone! Given the poor state of cell service up in these hills, it must've finally wrestled up a signal being outside. Sure enough, one tiny bar struggles for life.

Mom.

I silence it.

There is the slight possibility I might have neglected to tell her my plan. Or that I came here at all and specifically ignored her warning. As I brainstorm how to avoid my mother, my phone rings again, like maternal clockwork. This single bar of service is really earning its rent.

This time, I mentally prepare myself for a real dressing-down, worse even than the first and only time younger me used soap to clean the cast iron.

". . . Hey there, mother dearest."

"Little miss, you best not be avoiding your pitiful mother."

I feel lighter than angel food cake hearing her voice, the fire I know so well flavoring her tone again. But if Mom is having one of her good days, she'll be fixing to scold the legs right off my chair.

"I hear you've accepted the Warlock's offer."

Lord, here we go. "You and every other soul in town, apparently."

But she's confined to her hospital room, which means . . . Silas. *Rude.*

"This *is* Foxe Holler, daughter dearest. When folks think of magic, the Widow Witch always comes to mind. The whisperings lately are even more damning than usual."

"Whisperings from who?" I'm getting fed up with all this speculation. Just because someone is odd and lives alone doesn't mean they deserve to be shunned. "The church ladies? Please. Gertha Fudge never met a rumor she didn't like. She's *always* wanted to leash magic."

"Even if the Fudges of the town dislike magic, *we* know magic isn't inherently bad. Whatever higher magic the Warlock practices doesn't bother me," she continues. "It's *men* with magic you want to be wary of. Are there any women in that house with you?"

"The men include an eccentric gardener who doesn't believe in phones and a little boy. I'm fine."

"Even so, I had Carolina place a protection spell on you while you're up there. Warlock-proof. She's a good Hearthwitch, but it won't last forever."

Proof against what, exactly? He's grumpy as all get-out, but the Warlock has not raised a single menacing finger toward me, to the point I don't even know what kind of magic he possesses. What good is this higher magic the Witches bemoan if a Warlock doesn't ever use it? The most dangerous thing at this Manor thus far is the kitchen.

"Does she have any spells to protect me from the house itself?" I ask dryly.

My eyes roam the skeletal facade of the farmhouse, which must be hiding other forbidden pockets and rooms. I can't tell how a Warlock's supposed extensive library of invaluable magical texts would even fit inside this place. So many shadows for secrets . . .

I pace down the side steps and to the gardens as we talk, letting the bar on my phone decide my direction. Green surrounds me. Bushes and trees and flowers and vegetable beds. Blooming plants and thorny ones, edible and, I'm sure, poisonous. Even a cactus, though this is not the right climate. Magicked to thrive, no doubt. Bees and hummingbirds and dragonflies buzz by. Roses and sunflowers and squash blossoms and strawberries.

Care and attention. Life, not destruction. I've never been in a place so active with growth yet so grounded in delicate silence at the same time. Where the inside of Knight Manor is decaying, the gardens are blossoming with life.

"I've been thinking—if the Warlock's health is off, unbalanced, his magic would be, too, right? Magic is strongest when it's local, so an ill Warlock's power could—"

"Cause weird occurrences . . ." my mom says, catching on. Moms are great for brainstorming. "Still, whether his reputation is based on intention or accident, the Widow Witch has more than earned hers. If that man's caused an imbalance of magic, she'll hunt it down and you'll be caught in the cross-spell. She's a Hedgewitch, after all."

A seven-course meal of flavorful language runs through my head. I've never met one, but Hedgewitches work magic between dimensions of being. Life and death. Present and past. Reality and illusion. If anyone comes close to having the grand—and uncontrollable—higher magic a Warlock does, it's a Hedgewitch.

Witches live by the creed that all magic is neutral, and that *rotten* magic simply comes from poisonous intention and misuse. But there are some forms of power more unstable than others, more prone to mirror emotion and the darkest parts of ourselves. More prone to terrible debt. No matter what, all magic has a cost, and the universe always hunts for balance.

I wonder if other towns have a Hedgewitch problem like us. Maybe they have their own threats. Maybe the big cities have more than one. Shoot, Foxe Holler could be the safest place of the bunch.

"All the more reason everyone needs to be at full strength," I counter. "That means you. I'm going to have you healed in no time. I think I'm close to finding the right recipe, and his archive of spell books—"

"Don't heal the Warlock, Honey." Her voice dips but it might be the static of the shoddy connection. "You're my only child. Whatever debt you gather there isn't worth it."

That's like saying you're *not worth it.*

"Honey, if there were ever a moment to mind your poor mother, this is it. What in heaven compelled you to accept his offer?"

That's the moment I've had enough. "After how Momaw passed, did you really think I *wouldn't*?"

That shuts her up. But she needed the reminder. There is no sugarcoating this wasting illness into submission.

Farewitches are supposed to have decades of formal training; apprenticeships with other Witches as their mentors. Momaw wallpapered her old farmhouse with maps, and whenever I stayed over as a girl, she would point to places I'd never heard of, a wild story for each one. Through my twenties, I should've had time to keep learning. I'd start my training only *after* I'd seen those storybook places, perhaps gone to culinary school in France, tried a barraquito in Tenerife, baked a lover a birthday cake . . .

All of the Frost women should have gotten more time. If I have to sacrifice some of mine so my mom can have more, then prepare the pyre.

Then I realize why my mom's call settles so oddly in my chest. "I thought you'd be more distraught over the part where I *closed the Apothakery*."

"Folks won't wither and die if you don't fill their orders for a couple weeks."

"The church ladies might."

"I'm more distraught over the company you're keeping."

"I can't figure out why everyone is so afraid of him. Including *you*."

She won't like being lumped in with Gertha Fudge and the quick-to-judge church ladies. She sighs. The phone line crackles. I've caught her. "You leave the minute there's a sign of something unsafe. You hear me?"

Everyone in Glasgow can. "Loud and clear." I think about the rotting floorboards, the crumbling roof, the suspicious substance growing in the grout in the bathrooms, the black dust that makes me want to Google *Can you get black lung from a butler's pantry?*

"You know, your father didn't have magic and it made things so much less complicated. Simple."

I stop strolling. She never brings up my father. She's being . . . frighteningly nostalgic.

"And this is the first time Frosts have closed the shop. You could actually find yourself with extra time on your hands."

Moment gone. What was reminiscing was actually an A+ subtle guilt trip in disguise. "Any extra time I have, I'm going to prepare my regular orders so I can drop them off whenever I head back into town." *And I'll be scouring a library.*

Her sharp huff cuts through the poor cell service. "Rest can be rest without being productive rest, you know."

"Says the woman still managing the town's sanitation schedule from a hospital bed."

"You and Silas have been talking too much."

I agree.

"If you don't show up to visit on Saturdays, I'll know something is wrong. Unless you've got a date or some such, then don't worry about little ole me."

So much for her pitching a fit.

"I'll give you a few weeks to make this work. Eyes open, girl. Be smart, be careful."

Exhaustion creeps into her voice now. We've only been on the phone a few minutes, but she's already spent.

Like a good mom, her concern just makes my own uncertainty flare. "What if I can't cure him?"

"Just remember to stick to the basics. In our line of work and magic, the right cure is usually the simplest." Pause. "Just in case, hang up a horseshoe for luck." Pause. "And eat your breakfast. Black coffee does not count, young lady. Dehydrates your skin."

Here we go. Even in my thirties, I can't escape parental lecturing. "Not much cell service up here in the boonies. I'm losing bars—"

"Remember, don't leave dishes in the sink! You'll invite nightmares—"

"Love you, too, see you tomorrow—oops. Connection's dropping. We might cut—"

"Don't you dare hang up on me!"

"I can barely hear you. Truly, terrible service out here . . ."

Then I definitely dare, and hang up before I have to do my impression of going through a tunnel. No one wants that.

In the calm of the garden, I breathe in. Honeysuckle. Basil. And sweet, sweet silence. No wonder the Warlock spends all his time out here. Or doesn't have a cell phone, for that matter. He's starting to make a little sense, crumb by crumb.

The basics.

As I think, I twist off a sprig of fresh basil, half expecting something to pop out of the ground to bite off a pinky. The Warlock's magic somehow involves his plants. I rub the delicate basil leaves between my fingers, inhaling the distinctive fresh smell. Perfect.

And just like that, I know the first recipe I'm going to make for him.

Chapter Six

FRIDAY, APRIL 8 (STILL)

Honey's Helpful Hint, from
Honey Frost's Southern Cookbook for Recipes Gone Wrong:

Start with the basics. The best recipes—and epicures for the soul—are often the simplest.

I am being *bullied*. By a kitchen.

I can't get the gas range to give me boiling water. Then the fridge refuses to open. Suspicious. When I turn back to the island, my plucked basil is gone. As another stupid tile trips me, at that very moment, the farmhouse sink goes rogue and unleashes watery hell on me. I try to shut it off with furious fingers, with no luck.

Dripping, I look up at the ceiling. "If you didn't want me to be here, you wouldn't have unlocked the front door," I shout skyward. This house has a level of sentience somewhere between goldfish and poodle, but where is its soul, its heart? Definitely the kitchen, if you ask me. "He asked me to come here. He needs my help. Be nice."

After a moment of silence, the sink sprayer shuts off.

The gas range under my pot lights.

The fridge doors swing open.

And a greedy ivy plant releases the pantry's doorknob.

Now we're in business. "Thank you," I say, tossing my soaked kitchen towel onto the island.

After the water boils, I pour it over some tea bags and, after a bit, pour everything into a pitcher with sugar I muddle with crushed basil.

Usually folks use mint, but I find that the basil, which has reappeared, cuts through the gargantuan sweetness. Lastly, slices of lemon.

Hallelujah! Momaw Frost's famous Southern sweet tea.

Typically good for headaches, but also known to cure a whole mess of little annoyances. *The basics.* After all, it's sugar, and what malady doesn't often involve a headache? Usually, the benefits of my recipes begin physically, relieving symptoms. Then the longer-term advantages appear. A healthy mind so often follows and depends on physical health.

Another thought occurs to me: If the Warlock's magic enlivens his houseplants, then it's likely in the herbs and produce he grows. Since magic is rooted in the land, sourcing ingredients right from the Manor's backyard might make my recipes especially strong. That could be the key. Using the same old ovens and supplies isn't helping, so maybe all I need is a new kitchen to jump-start my recipe testing for my mom. In the morning, I'll try a recipe I've already crossed off, see if the new environment changes anything. Then when I visit on Saturdays, I'll bring what I can for her to try.

My spirits lift. It's theoretical hope. But hope nonetheless.

Then I wait.

And wait. At the kitchen island, untouched glasses of ice sweat in the warmth as the sun slants across the kitchen. But no one comes.

Screw off-limits. The gardens didn't get me, and I won't let the house, forbidden rooms or not. If no one is going to indulge in what I was hired to do, then I'll find them first.

As it turns out, it's much harder than I expected to hunt down a Warlock in his own home.

Every time I pass a room that gives me a peek into his life, the door slams shut. As if the house senses my curiosity. I almost lose my nose a couple times. Every carved molding is a sculpture of ferns and vines of ivy, and stained glass windows cast colorful silhouettes of more flora across the patchwork rugs. The wallpaper changes from room to room, sometimes mid-wall, but it always involves plants.

The more time I spend in these neglected halls, the less I'm sure one lone Farewitch can cure anything or anyone in this place. I can feel it, a fuzz on the tongue: Unease and rot have been growing in this skeleton of a home for decades.

Sticking to the safe hallways, I wander through the house until I hear noises. Second floor. End of the hall. A door is ajar, hiding a conversation. There's another voice, much softer, with bright edges. If the Governess gets angry with me for trespassing, so be it.

I take my chances and step through the cracked door.

Chalkboard. An easel with paints and brushes. Low bookshelves, for a shorter person. Smells of eraser shavings and Governess Zeen's perfume cling to the small room. A classroom. Or a farmhouse version of one.

There, sitting at the only desk, is the boy from the kitchen.

The moment he sees me, he launches out of his seat and runs over. His hazel eyes wink up at me. "Did you make more toast?"

I chose a good door. Smiling, I say, "Is that a formal request?"

There appear to be no computers or projectors in here. Maybe I can find an extra old laptop lying around the Apothakery to donate—oh God. Does this place even have Wi-Fi?

The boy distracts me from the major red flag with a pair of doe eyes. "I love the sugar bread. We only ever have *oatmeal*." He utters it like a curse.

Despite the toast heist, the boy hasn't absorbed any of the Warlock's withdrawn prickliness. I wonder how long he's been a ward here.

Standing by the chalkboard is Governess Zeen. She looks down her nose at me. "You're interrupting Spanish lessons."

The boy leans in to me to whisper as all children whisper, which is not at all. "That's Ms. Letha Zeen. You know she's serious because her name is only one letter away from *lethal*."

"There are many lethal things in this house," a rough voice says.

I jump ten miles to heaven and whirl to find the Warlock directly behind me. How did he move so quietly? Was he watching me this whole time? I think I see a brief glimpse of delight before it fades into a pointed scowl. He's enjoying this.

"Hence why areas are off-limits and why we don't wander," he says.

Ms. Zeen tosses a textbook onto her instructor's table in defeat. "Good afternoon, Mr. Knight. Now you're *both* interrupting Spanish."

He takes the slightest step back.

So, the Warlock of Foxe Holler is intimidated by his Governess. Understandable. The woman's cardigan set is as pristine as a wartime general's uniform.

"I thought French was Friday and Spanish was Monday."

"German is Monday. French is Tuesday, and Mandarin and Cantonese on Wednesday and Thursday. Really, it's all on the schedule I made you."

The boy, ignoring them, offers me his hand. "I'm Lazlo. I'm almost a teenager."

"You're nine," the Warlock rebuffs.

Then he does the wildest thing. He *ruffles* the boy's head of hair. *Affectionately.* Lazlo rolls his eyes. "I'm *almost* ten." He's still beaming up at the Warlock. Beaming. Up at Warlock Knight. What kind of screwy parallel universe have I stumbled into?

So quickly I almost miss it, that dark shadow flashes across the Warlock's face as he looks at his ward. It's almost . . . melancholic. Then it's gone, suffocated under a frown.

I recover from my shock enough to shake the boy's little palm. "Pleasure to meet you."

Ms. Zeen sighs from across the room. "Lazlo, please resume your verb conjugations."

Lazlo scrunches his face in disgust. The Warlock holds a long finger to his tight lips and mimes a playful *shush* at the boy.

Definitely slipped into another dimension. I knew the house let me off too easy.

"You'll be sure to get along," Governess Zeen says to me when she reaches us and Lazlo's back at his desk, head bent over messy papers. "Given your nearness in age."

I feign a smile. War, is it, then? "I have a young face. Not as many wrinkles as others."

Next to me, the Warlock snorts.

Ms. Zeen's eyes narrow. "How old *are* you, dear?"

"Old enough. *Ma'am.*"

"Why isn't your mother still the town Farewitch?"

"She needed to be the mayor."

"Have you ever heard the saying *Don't trust a skinny chef*?"

The Warlock steps between us. "That's enough, Ms. Zeen."

So not too intimidated to stand up to the woman once in a while. *Standing up for me?* Odd. But I'm not one to let grouchy old women scare me. If I did, I'd be out of business.

I give her a sugary grin. "Ms. Zeen, you should have eaten some of my fried green tomatoes. The oil might help grease your insides so you can pass that stick through your colon."

Except I don't say that. I'm a polite Southern lady. Manners.

What I really say is "There's a batch of my Momaw's basil and honey sweet tea in the kitchen. Please help yourself."

"Not my preferred cup of tea." Ms. Zeen returns to the chalkboard, leaving me alone with the Warlock, which isn't much of an improvement.

He turns to me. "Follow me. I have something to show you." Then he leaves the room without warning.

Oh joy.

We traverse the second floor in the opposite direction, across the entire Manor, which physically *cannot* be this wide on the outside. A Barbie-Escher Dreamhouse, for sure. We pass endless closed doors.

Locked, probably. What's he possibly hiding behind all of these? I try to match his pace, but this fellow has some grasshopper legs. Long and lean and—whatever. He never lets me out of his peripheral vision, anyway. He really *doesn't* want me to wander.

When we reach the top of one of the four staircases I've seen on this floor alone, he finally speaks. "I told you the rest of the house is strictly off-limits."

This hallway looks familiar. We're on the third floor now, where my room is. I think? "Everyone disappeared on me. Lazlo's delightful, by the way." I remember the way he spoke to the boy, without the rough edges of his usual demeanor. "You said you don't like anyone, but you're awfully nice to him." Tread lightly, tread lightly.

He almost looks surprised but quickly throws a mask back in place. But not before I see that bruise of sadness in his gaze. Maybe I'm *not* imagining the haunted look. "He's a child. Despite any rumors you might have heard, I'm not unkind to children."

"I thought I was also a *child* Farewitch."

He opens his mouth, then closes it. No retort, then? Though I've played myself, because now I'm extra curious what our age gap actually is . . . for research.

"Everyone under forty looks the same to me," he finally says.

We're going to have to get along for me to have the best chance of healing him, so I try a different tactic. "Can I at least have a tour? A small one." No one has seen the Manor for a long time. Now that it's clear he didn't lure me here to use me as fertilizer for his garden, I'm nosey.

He frowns. "You've seen the kitchen. The foyer—a large empty waste of a room. The other rooms on the ground floor are empty common rooms, washrooms. We have a parlor, but it hasn't been touched in ten years. Ladybug infestation. There's a reading room—"

"Let me guess: It's empty and hasn't been used since dial-up."

"No, Ms. Zeen does her sewing in there. Keep up. We have a

dining room, when there used to be gatherings and holidays. Now another waste of space."

"Where does everyone eat? The kitchen table?"

I kid you not, the man has to process my question to answer. "Our bedrooms."

For the love of— "*Together,* I mean. With each other. Communal meals."

"I don't understand. I usually eat standing in the garden. When I remember."

I halt in a random hallway.

He stops when I don't follow. "You look like you've swallowed a cicada, Ms. Frost."

Breathe, Honey, breathe. Like Momaw Frost said when little me was just learning, and the centers of my cornbread were raw but the tops were burning. *Breathe,* like my mom repeated to me over and over again at Momaw's funeral.

When he remembers. Good. Lord. When he starts walking again, I stomp after him. "You can call me Honey."

"Is that a family name?"

I try to hide my surprise. An actual question about me that isn't about being a Farewitch. I nod. "Lots of Frost Farewitches have been Honey. It was that or Hazeleen."

He flashes me one of his blander scowls, which I know now is his default. "I won't be calling you an endearment. I've never called anyone *honey.*"

Without meaning to, my head jerks in his direction at my name. I'm not sure how that information makes me feel. It settles in my stomach like a bubbly drink. Fizzy, jittery. Has he always lived alone? "Everyone uses it. It doesn't mean anything to me but my name anymore."

He scoffs like that statement bothers him. But I have no idea why it would. He clears his throat. "And your husband calls you . . . ?"

Another personal question, albeit a clumsy attempt to pry. We're making leaps and bounds today. "If I had one? Often. Because he'd have a phone. And answer my questions."

Indignance sparks in his face. It's worth it. I don't know what makes me so bold. Maybe I'm hangry. I've been running since I got here.

"Not that the verbal-only tour of the Manor isn't stellar, but you seem like you've never invited a guest into your home before. Ever."

"We're not a bed-and-breakfast, in case you were under a different impression."

Bless him, he has the confidence. "Your spooky gated entryway might be responsible for that. It's a tad deceiving."

"It serves its purpose. I don't like new people."

But I don't think that's it. I think he's worried new people won't like him. "You at least need a mailbox. We can't all communicate via the United States Postal Smog."

His lips switch to the side. We're miles from a smile, but I still let out a mental *Hurrah!*

Which ignites the other question in my brain-stove from earlier, now that I *might* have his guard down. "Can you tell me about your magic? It's not as effective as memories, but that could help me understand your illness."

His shoulders go stiff like I've asked him if he prefers boxers or briefs. "No."

"We still need to go through your symptoms, your family history—"

He makes a turn down another hall, ignoring me yet expecting me to follow. Another nonanswer. It's totally pointless trying to talk to this man.

Finally, he stops outside a set of carved oak double doors. As I approach, I make out the details of the artistry that has to be hand carved: lighter wood inlays of bamboo stalks, vines of ivy running around them like a woven tapestry. The size of the doors hints at yet another room that can't possibly exist based on the Manor's silhouette from the outside.

Without preamble, he pushes the doors wide and says, "Beyond the kitchen, you're allowed in this room and this room only."

"Does this place at least have Wi-Fi?" I ask after him.

But he's already disappeared through the doors. Jackass. *Definitely* no Wi-Fi, then.

I follow him in—and stop short.

Eclectic chaise longues and tiny cocktail tables greet me, and windows promise wonderful natural light if ivy weren't overtaking the exterior of the farmhouse, covering the glass. An impressive grand piano anchors a corner of the room, and beyond that is a huge stone fireplace for robust family gatherings.

It's a lovely sitting room . . . but also not lived in, another ode to a time before.

As my eyes adjust to the dimness, I can see this room is just a foyer. I step down into a sunken level off the first, into another, even larger room that has me salivating (no small feat).

Floor-to-ceiling bookshelves, ladders poised to reach high shelves. Rows of mahogany worktables and cushy chairs comfy enough someone prone to naps might succumb. Dozens of lamps chase away gloomy shadows. A narrow balcony winds the perimeter of the room, with a spiral staircase that twists down, down, down to other levels. There must be a door into the library on every floor of the house. A thousand tomes stare back at me, new ones with shiny leather to wrinkled fellows to treasures so loved they don't have covers anymore.

I'm here to cook, but *this* is what I really came for. Warlock Knight's library.

While the rest of the Manor smells of soil and bad dreams, here I get a robust whiff of paper, leather, burnt wood in a real fireplace. Some of my stress falls away. I could curl up in here for hours, days, lost in a book while a pot of something is on the stove.

Oh yes.

Oh no.

It's *perfect.* Too perfect.

Another odd feeling creeps in. The Warlock put my room on the same floor as the library, the one place he knows I'm interested in. I'm . . . touched? Then I remember it's probably just to keep me from wandering around too much, not to make my life easier.

As I move through the room, perusing shelves and cabinets, my mood keeps lifting despite my best efforts to be surly about this whole living-with-the-Warlock situation. Novels, records, historical texts, grimoires, flora and fauna guides, spell books—I see it all.

This endless collection of books *must* have something new to help my mom.

I can feel it. I can believe in the possibilities here.

Fingers impatient, I start lifting books from shelves. I wonder if there's anything about the Warlock himself, his past in the Holler. If he would tell me what kind of magic he has, I could narrow down the rumors worth examining, or disproving. This looks like a collection he's been building for centuries—why would he care about burning a small-town library? Ms. Zeen also doesn't seem like the type of woman to tolerate sharing a home with a murderer. She'd probably do the murdering herself.

Depthless rabbit holes, all of this. I bite my lip as I think, making to-read piles. As I survey one of the stacks, a framed picture suddenly falls from a shelf to the wood floor, clattering like all get-out. At least it wasn't aiming for me this time. Almost like the Manor is listening to my inner curiosity, trying to be helpful.

I cradle the small framed photo. A young woman smiles back at me from a black-and-white portrait. Midnight hair, sharp cheekbones—it's the woman from the Warlock's memory. There's that jade pendant around her neck. Her resemblance to Warlock Knight is even clearer in this picture—

"Already snooping?"

I nearly skyrocket through the roof, a repeat of the classroom. "Jesus!" I jump away from the man who has now managed to sneak up on me twice. A third time and my soul will vacate my body. "Wear a bell or something. And I don't think it's snooping if I live here. *Sir.*"

He watches me with stern hazel eyes. "In spite of any reservations you might have, if I can't convince you to stay, I hope my library and archives will."

The words almost sound like a threat. He spies the picture I'm clutching to my heaving chest. His expression goes from stern to downright displeased. With a swift, gloved hand, he pulls the frame from my grasp. "Where did you get this?"

"The house threw it at me." Not a lie.

One black eyebrow goes up.

Still jumpy, I scramble to fill the pause. "Who is it?" *Open up. Give me something!*

"Someone no longer here." He places the picture face down on a table. "How is your room?"

"Too close to Governess Zeen's, but I'll take it."

A knowing *Ah* comes from his direction.

"She said you wouldn't like me," I offer, trying to break this weird tension.

He doesn't deny it. Or reply at all. Instead, he runs a gloved finger over the piano. Dusty. No one's played in ages. The whole house is like that, either dust or soil.

Cautiously, I break the silence. "Do you have any other family around?"

"Please don't feel obligated to get to know me, Ms. Frost. As you proved in your interview, you don't need to in order to be a sufficient Farewitch."

Bristling, I square my shoulders and look him in the eye. "It helps to know a patient when I begin baking. Consider all inquiries of the most casual kind, *Mr. Knight*." I can dance this jig of formality, too. It takes two slices of bread to make a stubborn sandwich.

His frown twists into a scowl. "Just Ms. Zeen. She's not related by blood, but she's like family. I maintain the defensive warding outside the Manor, and she keeps the inside from falling apart. When she's not tutoring Lazlo, that is."

"Heaven forbid you should try to teach anyone fractions."

No grin. Shoot. I'll keep trying.

Obviously Ms. Zeen is more than *like family*. A farmhouse as large as this takes managing, but is there some other handshake deal that connects her to the Warlock? Or are they really just the closest thing to family each of them has? For that matter, I haven't a clue what the Warlock does all day in this house when he's not with Lazlo. Or gardening. Maybe there's a network of Warlocks keeping him busy with tasks, some department of correspondence via ominous weather patterns.

Again, I'm struck by how much we Witches don't know about Warlocks. It makes me wonder what we don't even know about other Witches, like the Widow Witch. The best source of trustworthy information will be my own research.

"Lazlo doesn't go to school in town?" I ask.

"No, he's . . . a strange child," he relinquishes.

That's comforting. "You're sure he's not your son?" I ask, mostly joking. *Not really.*

He expels a breath, deep lines of tension crisscrossing between his brows, almost like talking causes him physical pain. A symptom, pushing to the surface? Then the tension is gone, and he's his usual glowering self. "He's a distant relation. His parents suddenly passed and I was next of kin."

"Oh. I'm sorry to hear that." Crap. Stupid of me. This is clearly a sore topic for the now-very-small Knight family. Like my Frost family of two.

"He's only lived with us here for a year," he adds. "It's an adjustment. Change is hard. Especially when sickness is involved."

"I understand." I certainly do.

We don't say anything further and I can feel him pulling away again, the stony planes of his face hardening into a walled fortress.

Before I lose him, I ask, "How did you know I'd be interested in your library?"

He crosses his arms. Dirt smudges his shirt. He's been in the garden. "A rumor told me you're often found scouring old recipe books and kitchen grimoires in your free time."

The gossip highway of Foxe Holler strikes again. "I dabble."

"Must be difficult to find what you're looking for without a library in town."

A rumor told me you flambéed it. "Research is complicated, I'll admit. It's tricky to find PDFs online of community cookbooks with print runs no bigger than the size of a congregation. That is, if folks even have the tech to do that."

The stare he gives me then is so intense, my spine goes rigid. "What are you looking for in all those books?"

I think about the secrets around me, the archived and forgotten information that might be able to save my mom. Say the answer is hiding here: How would I even go about finding it in a library with more square footage than the state fair? I might cure the Warlock before I ever scratch the surface of my other research. And then why would he let me stay?

I can't say the wrong thing and lose it all. Not now.

What *am* I looking for? More sunrises. More laughs. A happy ending. A second chance. They all have one thing in common.

"Time," I whisper.

His eyes narrow with pointed curiosity and his voice dips deep, raspy. "Aren't we all."

Impossibly, my shoulders shiver and my cheeks heat at the same time. Is this how he felt after I fed him food from his memories? Brutally sliced open and bare for the world to see? I've known him for less than a week and he can see right through me. Is *that* his magic?

A terrible thought occurs to me then. "Is there anyone else who takes care of Lazlo with you besides Ms. Zeen? Another guardian? Extended kin?"

"No. Just me." He heads for the doors, as if he can walk right out of our conversation.

So if I fail and can't cure his illness—what happens to Lazlo?

My gut turns over. I can't face another dead end. Not with an adorable little boy thrown into the recipe. "Mr. Knight, I appreciate your *reluctant* faith in my abilities, but I don't think I'm the right person for this job. If this illness is as serious as you suggest—"

"It is." He stops, turning back to me. "Ms. Frost, I'm dying, and based on the progression of my illness, I have strong reason to believe I shall expire on my upcoming birthday on the summer solstice."

I choke. "*Excuse me?*"

"The summer solstice. The solstice during the summer months. Not the December one. The twenty-first of June. Am I being clear?"

My brain misfires. I've poisoned myself delirious with bad basil, that's the only explanation. "That's in ten weeks!"

"Yes, dreadful," he sighs. Like he's simply waiting for me to hike up some skirts and flee. "Best bake quickly."

Chapter Seven

MONDAY, APRIL 11

71 DAYS UNTIL THE SUMMER SOLSTICE

Honey's Helpful Hint, from
Honey Frost's Southern Cookbook for Recipes Gone Wrong:

Don't leave dishes in the sink or else you'll invite nightmares, and always hang up a horseshoe in your home for good luck.

The Frost Family Apothakery has officially been closed one week.

Chaos reigns. The dash of panic is now a full-blown, heaping tablespoon.

During hospital visiting hours over the past week, Nurse Carolina saved me from a waiting room of demanding townsfolk. No one has anything better to do than bother a girl dropping off a pan of sorghum-syrup sweet potato casserole. Half the town is furious I've closed the shop ("and for a Warlock, no less!"), and the other half is now requesting house calls, like my workload isn't gastronomically astronomical as is. Because I can't help myself, I agree to make consistent special deliveries for some of my sweeter regulars.

I'm starting to admire the Warlock's skill with the word *no*.

If only my neighbors knew the unparalleled and beloved Mayor Frost is suffering from whatever illness took Momaw, their previous Farewitch. I've never itched to scream out the truth before now. But Mom would never allow it.

Not unlike how the Warlock failed to mention he's literally *dying.* Not just gravely ill. No, that would be too easy.

After he yanked that particular dusty rug out from under me with his admission a couple days ago, I saw no sign of him all weekend. All this fuss to get me here and then he doesn't even bother to show up to try my food, *his potential cures.*

Governess Zeen also wants nothing to do with me and only appears to make copious amounts of hot tea. No idea how she prefers that dishwater stuff over my sweet tea. The old bat must subsist on terror and dust alone. Occasionally, Lazlo snatches a snack and flees. He's friendly but also might think me a spook, or a storybook crone fattening him up to eat him.

So when I do find a spare minute to scarf something down, I eat alone.

On top of everything, my mom called me bright and early this Monday morning: *No luck with the sorghum sweet potatoes. Still feeling wretched, my joints are screaming with the rain this month . . . Keep trying, probably just a bad batch of potatoes . . .*

By noon, I'm in a mood so sour, I'm turning milk to buttermilk with a glance. Literally. The house itself must sense my mood, because it doesn't bother me.

So I decide to bother it.

My quarrel begins with what I've ignored so far: the inexcusable seven-layer cake of anonymous grime on every surface. The entire Manor looks like it's under a musty camera filter. The only place cobwebs don't hang is between the plants. I can't cure the Warlock's bad mood, but the state of this place could very well be partly responsible for his plague-like stuffiness.

A Frost woman is a helligan of a resilient creature. But can I cook, bake, decorate, knead, sprinkle, poach, and sear on countertops and in pans where dust is always the first ingredient? No way in hell.

Hoarder that she was, Momaw Frost would somersault in her grave if she saw this place. *Cluttered kitchen, cluttered mind, girl.*

I leave the knife I was furiously sharpening in the kitchen (for the best, can't let my kitchen safety escape with my patience), and when I get to the third floor, I'm huffing. I think the house added extra stairs just to delay me. At the opposite end of the hall, far from my own bedroom, the very last closed door is secluded in an alcove, by itself.

I pound on it.

I guessed right. For the first time in three days, the Warlock deigns to honor me with his existence and opens his bedroom door. His mistake.

"*You*," I say. Strong start.

His eyebrows go up. "Have I missed an argument we had I wasn't there for?"

He's in his usual gardening uniform: Henley, boots, bandana. He never wears a hat, hence the sun spots on his cheeks. And he's covered in soil, again. I bet he left footprints on as many staircases as possible, just to irk me. His dark hair curls at his temples with sweat from the sun. So he *was* in the garden, on the other side of those windows, while I was in the kitchen. Alone.

"How am I supposed to cure you if I never see you? You wanted me here as soon as possible, neglect to mention *you're dying*, and then you never show up to meals."

His annoyance morphs into indignation. "Me? *You.* You took basil from my garden."

Damn. So he did notice. "Yes, for the sweet tea I made that you never drank. Are you saying I can't use the herbs growing out here? They're herbs! That's what they're there for."

He wrings his gloved hands. Agitated? Crafting a spell to wish me out of existence? "You may use them, but only if you ask me first. The garden doesn't like to be touched by strangers."

If all the plants around here are as sentient as the house . . . Fine, I probably should've asked. "Only if you promise to eat what I make you."

He runs a tongue over his front teeth. That one tiny movement steals my focus. "As long as you promise to improve your mood. The plants can feel you're upset and they're withering."

"Withering?"

"Withering, Ms. Frost. *Withering.*"

"If they're withering, it's because of the state of this place," I retort, remembering why I climbed the stairs in the first place. "The house is a mess. It needs to be cleaned, and not by me. I'm a Farewitch, Mr. Knight. Not a maid."

"The house is fine."

"*Fine?*" I edge closer to him but he doesn't back up. "This is a gorgeous farmhouse and your ancestors would be ashamed—*ashamed*—to see the state it's in. What are all the wards for, anyway? To protect the dust? We're cleaning. Now."

He looms over me, a monolith hovering at the edge of his shadowy bedroom. "As much as I would adore watching a smart-mouth take her chances with the forces I'm warding against, the wards protect us, *Witch*. All of us. Besides, this house does not like to be jostled."

"The house can get over it. I can't work in filth. Your plants sense moods, my ingredients sense bedlam."

"*Bedlam* is a strong word."

"The hardwood under the furniture is a different color. *Sir.*"

His eyes roam my face, probably looking for weakness. He won't find any. "I said no." Then he shuts the door in my face. Or he tries.

Before he can, I jam my heavy clog in between the door and the frame.

The *look* this man gives me. My insides curdle. I should . . . not have done that.

But I'm committed now, come hell or high water. I cross my

arms, trying to fake enough confidence he doesn't notice the sweat on my upper lip.

Shadows dance across his face; his eyebrows pull in, frown deeper than I've ever seen it. I suddenly feel very small, very young, and very much out of my depth. I swallow the dryness in my throat. *This* is the Warlock my mom warned me about. This is the Warlock the town fears more than the Widow Witch.

Before I can run, strong hands go around my waist on both sides. Then he *lifts* me right out of his doorframe and sets me back into the hall like I'm no bigger than a misbehaving poodle but twice as troublesome.

The door slams and I'm alone.

My gut nose-dives. If I'd eaten breakfast, I would vomit it up with relief. I take deep breaths, letting my nerves recover. When it's clear I'm out of immediate danger, I get angry all over again. This man doesn't get to close doors mid-conversation with me.

The house must be siphoning off my sanity tablespoons at a time, because somehow, I'm brave or delusional enough to knock again.

I know he won't answer, so I call through the door. "If you don't work with me here, I'm going to help myself to your garden. I'm armed with nothing but a pair of dull sewing scissors from 1979." *Probably not as old as you.*

Silence on the other side.

"They're *very* rusty."

The door flies open and the Warlock steps around me into the hall. "Lazlo!" he shouts to a room a few doors down.

Another door cracks open and the boy appears, textbooks in his arms, most upside down. "I wasn't skipping class, promise!"

The Warlock dismisses the excuse with a wave of his hand. "We're cleaning. Now."

Confused, the boy drops his books and follows his guardian down the stairs.

"Don't forget the fireplaces," I call after them, flush with a pride that won't quit tingling under my skin. I did it. I made the Warlock of Foxe Holler follow *instructions*.

The Warlock gives me a murderous glance over his shoulder. "Yes, ma'am," he drawls in reply, voice low.

My cheeks go so red. Something in this house is burning and it isn't the oven.

The farmhouse gets its first bath in decades. Nowhere is safe.

I play the Dolly Parton I've got downloaded on my phone obnoxiously loud so I can't hear any complaining.

Ms. Zeen, Lazlo, and I tackle our bedrooms and the library and classroom, while the Warlock takes everywhere I'm not allowed to explore. Windows are open, rooms aired, floors shined. Rugs beat, limescale scrubbed, bookshelves dusted. Snaggletooth vines come down from windows outside, and sunlight returns to Knight Manor. We even have skylights!

The house tries to fight, doors locking me out and in, floorboards lifting and sinking. A few bats fly out of dark crevices, but that delights Lazlo to no end.

Eventually, the house gives up. About the same time, I notice the Warlock's permanent glower loosens and a bit of guilt simmers off as he watches Lazlo chase bats through the house to the rhythm of Dolly.

Even Ms. Zeen looks like she might hate me just a little bit less. Or more? Pleased with the cleanliness, or seeing me cough on bleach fumes? Hard to tell.

What I do know is, the mysteries plaguing this house start with the Warlock and Ms. Zeen. They're tied together with some secret as knotted as the Warlock's vines slithering around. The Warlock is Lazlo's only kin, but there's more to that story. I can see it in the melancholy that overtakes his gruff facade whenever he looks at the kid and doesn't think anyone else is watching. These three came together in a strange emulsion and are gatekeeping the recipe.

But until I can crack open the Warlock's hard-boiled, bad-egg mood, I can at least make this house feel like a home for Lazlo.

By late afternoon, I conquer the last battlefield: the kitchen.

Elbow deep in a farmhouse sink full of sudsy water, I wonder if the Warlock's magic could've done all this for us . . . Knowing him, he'd say no just to make me work for it.

But I don't mind the hard work. It reminds me of the Apothakery, and a twinge of homesickness for that butter-yellow door pinches me.

Unsurprisingly, no matter how hard we clean, I can still smell soil.

Though I don't mind it, now that dirt isn't on my countertops. It smells like summer, like the produce harvests that come with my favorite holidays on a Farewitch's calendar: rosemary and lavender for Beltane on the first of May, lemons and tomatoes for Litha and the summer solstice, corn for Lughnasadh in August—

The summer solstice. When the Warlock thinks he'll die. My mood trips.

He still hasn't told me about his illness.

Dishes done, I get started doing what chefs do best: making new dirty dishes.

I blend butter, sugar, eggs, flour, and coconut, a peaceful smile on my face in the newly pristine kitchen. Shortly after I start toasting shredded coconut, the Warlock enters the kitchen. Unrequested. I must be seeing things.

As I bake, he fills a tin and begins watering various potted plants around the kitchen. There's a pail in every room of the house I've been allowed to see, no doubt his sole decorative contribution to the Manor's aesthetic.

He's even more silent than usual, like he isn't here at all. A ghost. But my shop is always such a storm of activity and stress, this shared quiet is peaceful.

It occurs to me then. He's *stalling*.

He reaches the plants closest to me but stays on the other side of the island—far from the knife I was sharpening earlier. Smart.

Then he clears his throat. "I had several time-sensitive tasks to wrap up in the Manor this past weekend. And research. That's why I wasn't around."

That's probably the closest I'll get to an apology. Not wanting to push my luck, I act unbothered as I toss in baking powder and salt and vanilla. "Is that what you and Ms. Zeen are up to all day? Did I interrupt all manner of nefarious Warlock projects when I arrived?"

No need to clarify if I mean the Warlock or the projects are nefarious. He can handle some mystery.

"If you must know, Warlocks choose a specialty of study, separate from their own personal magic. I chose curse magic."

"But don't Warlocks think curses are lower magic?"

"They do. But I've learned Witch magic can be . . . creative." He pauses. When I glance up, he's already looking at me. "As you can imagine, not many Warlocks research curse magic, so I'm often the person other Warlocks write to with questions. I try to answer where I can."

So I *was* right. Kind of. He's a consultant on the Warlock information highway, with crappy work-life balance. Typical of them, doing everything formally by letter. If he only learned how to use email, he'd have twice as much free time to get healthy.

"This house requires significant upkeep. The wards alone are an undertaking," he adds. "I haven't managed all of it well, since . . . the illness." He forces out the admission like it almost finishes the job and kills him.

Now I feel bad. I'd lit into my employer *and* patient. Swell job, Honey. But I can't help wondering, what are we warding *against*, and should I be carrying pepper spray? My gut tells me this isn't the time to ask. He's actually talking, giving me more info than I've gathered alone.

"I didn't mean to ambush you earlier," I say. "Bad mood—family stuff. I'm sorry."

"But you did mean to threaten my plants." His annoyingly stoic expression doesn't falter, so I can't tell if that's a joke.

To be safe, I keep my eyes on my batter. Next, I pour in the PET milk, a.k.a. evaporated milk. As I fold in the toasted coconut, the Warlock clears his throat. "You're right. The cleaning isn't your job."

Outside, I shrug as I pour batter into two waiting round cake pans. Inside, I'm ecstatic. Was that a delicate little *thank-you*?

"I noticed you stock my apple butter, but I've never seen you in the shop. Should I be complimented or insulted?"

He lowers his watering pail. "Despite his eccentricities, our postman will begrudgingly pick up and make small deliveries for me, if I leave him a note and payment. I sent him in for a few jars when I was thinking of hiring you."

"So we *do* get mail and deliveries. Good to know." The Cumberlands' general store made it clear I'm not welcome until I reopen the Apothakery. "I need to send out some orders while I'm here. My older customers can't just pop over to a Farewitch in the next town over. And my younger ones with children don't have time to make a casual half-day round trip."

"Good luck. He doesn't come close to the Manor. He parks at the bottom of the drive, hauls everything up and tosses it near the porch, then dashes. I've never seen his face."

"Ah. Eccentricities."

"Eccentricities."

As I slide the cakes into the AGA, I think back. Have I seen a courier buying apple butter? I only know the Holler's postman sticks to his routes and is kind to the church ladies—they praise his calves constantly—but he, like the Warlock, is one of the few folks I've never formally met. Am I so wrapped up in my day-to-day tasks at the Apothakery that I never noticed him? I need to look up once in a while at the people I'm feeding.

At last, the Warlock joins me at the island, watching the dance of my hands as I gather the ingredients for frosting. "The Manor has yet to scare you, however." His words are low, cautious. Hanging on the *you*. A question.

"Not true. I'm just scared of other monsters more." Like incurable illnesses. As I whip leftover coconut pieces into the frosting, my muscles take over, like I'm right back in the kitchen with my mom, and I unconsciously hold up a spoon of frosting to the Warlock—then catch myself and hand him the utensil instead.

I almost, disastrously, spoon-fed the Warlock of Foxe Holler. *Scream.*

He either doesn't notice or ignores me, but takes the spoon. His eyes widen, but all he gives me is a hum of acknowledgment, the sound deep in his chest. Watching him lick the spoon is way more enjoyable than it should be.

I need a change of subject. Now. "Tell me about your symptoms while we wait for the cake."

"If we must."

"We must. How will I know if my recipes help relieve any pain if I don't know what the pain is?"

He avoids my gaze. "Lethargy. Irritability. Constant bodily aches."

"You might be on your period, Mr. Knight."

That gets me eye contact. I wish I could tell if he's laughing on the inside or about to blow a fuse.

"Does dying count as a symptom, Farewitch?"

"Ha. Funny. We'll have to go to the farmers' market together soon, to look over ingredients. I need to see what you're drawn to, what you might like to eat—"

"No."

"No?"

"I don't leave the Manor."

"Excuse me?"

"The Manor, Ms. Frost. The grounds. Property. Call it what you like."

I think I assumed no one in the Holler ever sees him because he just . . . comes out at night. Or something equally as vampiric. "You never leave. Never never."

"Correct."

My attention homes in on him. "Have you *ever* left?"

"When I was young."

"And when was *that*?"

His lips purse. Just when I thought I had a grasp on his oddities, here we are again. I have a hard time believing this Warlock is afraid of anything, but something has him cautious.

"Don't leave? Or *can't* leave?" I press.

"The difference in semantics is irrelevant in my case."

"Okay, so *why* don't you leave?"

"A number of reasons."

"Great, plenty to choose from."

His eyes narrow. "The less the Holler sees of me, the better. That's the only answer you need."

As if the universe is a dramatic, mischievous thing, at that very moment the afternoon glow outside vanishes, like someone dropped a giant lid over our soup pot of a farmhouse.

An earsplitting *BOOM* of thunder shakes the Manor to its foundation.

Unabashed fury cracks the cold stone of the Warlock's pale face. His teeth clamp together, jaw working, as he looks heavenward to the ceiling.

"Not now," he growls to the sky.

Chapter Eight

MONDAY, APRIL 11 (STILL)

71 DAYS UNTIL THE SUMMER SOLSTICE

Honey's Helpful Hint, from
Honey Frost's Southern Cookbook
for Recipes Gone Wrong:

Salt. Vanilla. Spice. The smallest ingredients have the biggest flavor.

Warlock Knight moves to the window with efficient speed, neck craning as he peers out into the sudden gloom.

The wrath in his expression makes him look older. Weary. Primeval.

I check the oven—still on. Cake baking, oblivious. Phew.

Governess Zeen races into the kitchen, kitten heels clicking. "No warning?" she asks, checking locks on doors and windows. Her posture is battle ready.

"None." The Warlock's face drops. "Where's Lazlo?"

"He was right behind me—"

"Here!" The boy in question skids into the kitchen, socks slipping on the freshly shined floor. He flies right into the Warlock's open arms.

"Remember, this is no different from any other time," the Warlock says to him. "Do not leave the kitchen—stay close. The wards are strongest closer to me."

"Excuse me," I say, watching the entire exchange, motionless with nerves. "Not to be a bother, but are we under *attack*?"

I'm not sure it's possible for this Warlock to be afraid of anything, *but.* The opposite of confidence dances on his face as he looks at his ward. Goose bumps dart across my neck. I'm missing something here, but my gut agrees: If there's any kind of distress, the most important thing is to keep Lazlo safe.

"I'm a bit frightened," I announce. Play along, I can do. "Would you mind standing with me, Lazlo? I could use a friend."

Lazlo speeds over, determination on his soft features. He runs right into me, hands clutching at my apron. "I've got you, Ms. Honey."

The Warlock sends me an odd look I can't for the life of me place. Appreciation, but with . . . regret? Can gratitude be regretful? To be fair, if it could, he would nail it.

Another tremendous *BOOM* shakes the Manor. Windows vibrate and planters topple over, soil spilling across our clean floor. Ms. Zeen grabs the island for balance. The room keeps darkening with the outside world.

The Warlock throws himself at the back door to the gardens, the closest entry point into the kitchen.

"Are we at the center of a tornado?" I ask, glancing at my cake. Still level, miraculously. Perks of being a Farewitch.

"If only," the Warlock says with a lot less urgency than he should, eyes on the gathering storm outside.

Not storm. A *cyclone.* What in the—

Something tugs at my apron. Lazlo stares up at me with wide eyes. "Do you . . . do you ever bake any sweets to cure being afraid?"

My heart seizes up like a drying slice of citrus. "Of course. But try this for the time being." I take one of his hands, giving it a hearty, reassuring squeeze.

We don't let go.

Lightning strikes the sky. Lamps flicker but the electricity holds. Wind tears at the windows, as if we're in some nightmarish snow globe. Shadows seep under the garden door, like dark and twitching tentacles.

Squalls *and* shadows. Perfect.

"She's stronger than last time." Ms. Zeen's voice carries none of its usual control. "The last few solutions we tried won't work twice."

Seeing the Governess actually concerned makes my stomach flip. If someone doesn't tell me what's going on, I might retch soon, which won't be pretty because I haven't eaten much today so it'll be more dry heaving than anything.

The Warlock looks wildly about the kitchen, then does a double take. At me. "Then we'll try something different."

He reaches me in three long strides, avoiding fallen pots and broken plates. He rests a gloved hand on Lazlo's head as he looks down at me.

"Can you trust me long enough for a favor?"

BOOM.

As some harbinger of death descends on the farmhouse, all I can think is *Mom was right.* Right about living in a forlorn and antiquated, pitiful haunted house on the outskirts of town with a Warlock supposedly responsible for a history of vicious magic, fire, and death.

But heaven help me, I nod back.

The Warlock steps closer, Lazlo secure between us. This is the nearest we've ever been.

"Wish for something small, Ms. Frost."

"Um. What?"

"Something inconsequential that might solve your—our—problem."

"I don't understand."

He bites the inside of his cheek, clearly frustrated. "Isn't this disturbance getting in the way of your baking? Isn't there *something* you'd like to do today you *can't* when the weather is bad?"

The man is off his rocker.

Lazlo tugs on my hand. "Wish for something small to make your day better." He stares at me expectantly, so hopeful.

"Sure . . . I . . ." Play along, Honey. And then it clicks. *Of course.*

I finally know what Warlock Knight's magic is.

"I wish I could have a picnic in the gardens today. Where I can nap in the sun."

The Warlock smirks, and I can't tell if that one gesture is comforting or terrifying. He turns toward the ceiling, holds up a gloved hand, and *snaps*.

Light bursts into the kitchen.

The shadows disperse. The shaking quiets. The storm outside shivers to nothing.

In minutes, the early-evening sky looks exactly like it did moments ago. Whatever was wreaking havoc on the farmhouse is gone. Not just gone. *Expelled.*

The only lingering sign of the Warlock's magic as it vanishes from the air is the faintest taste of . . . thyme, dissolving on my tongue.

Powerful magic, indeed. I'm beginning to understand these fear-soaked rumors about the Warlock and his history.

In the following stillness, Ms. Zeen rights overturned pots while the Warlock sweeps scattered soil. He moves slowly, like he's waking from a nap. His cheekbones stand out and I think he's paler, the color of an onion. A tired onion.

With the danger gone, Lazlo releases my hand. He steals some shredded coconut scraps on the counter and escapes back to his room. Like everything is just fine.

I finally break free of my paralysis to sputter, "What the hell was *that*?"

The Warlock and Ms. Zeen answer at the same time.

"The Widow Witch."

Now I know they're off their rockers. "*The* Widow Witch?" Giving my voice wrinkles, I recite the church ladies' favorite bit of story:

"The Hedgewitch notorious for leaving a single widow in her licentious wake each spring."

Ms. Zeen harrumphs at me. "Is that your best impression of an old woman?"

The Warlock looks her way. "You do use words like *licentious*."

"Hush."

My hands land on my hips. A real Witch, sure, she is. Missing husbands, sure, there are. But . . . "No one here is even married. What could she possibly want with us? Why would she risk hurting Lazlo?" He's a literal child!

I don't get an answer because just then the Governess suddenly points to a corner of the kitchen where dirt cakes the tile. "Mr. Knight, look."

No, not dirt. Scorches. But not just any normal fire damage.

Seared into the tile floor is a streak of still-burning letters. A message.

YOUR TIME IS MINE.

"What does *that* mean?" I ask, glad the Warlock chose to send me an old-fashioned letter earlier this month. The Apothakery's old floors would not hold up against fire and brimstone.

Ms. Zeen and the Warlock exchange a knowing glance.

"It just means I need another rug for the kitchen," he grinds out. "It's nothing, drivel. The Widow Witch delights in wreaking havoc. Likely just so there's a need for her chaotic sense of balance and order."

My fingers go cold, the tips white and numb. Staring at my humble Farewitch hands, I see burns from fights with the oven, but never a real brawl. If the Widow Witch's body count is accurate . . . I am woefully out of my league here.

"But why you?" I ask. He doesn't answer, and that tells me

everything I need to know. "What did *you* do to piss off the Widow Witch?"

"I might have upset her a time or two over the years," he sighs. "Warlock magic can sometimes leave things . . . messy. Unbalanced. And the old bat is petty."

Fine, keep the sordid details. "Does she ever manage to get inside?"

"She very well might have today." Ms. Zeen pins the Warlock with a stare.

He coughs, focusing hard on rehanging a vine over the kitchen table. "I wasn't paying as much attention as I should. My wards flickered."

Because I was peppering him with questions. Crap. Warding for a Farewitch isn't really a conscious thought; it's more just an intrinsic guarantee since our shops absorb magic across generations. I assumed warding worked the same for Warlocks, but they don't have those deep generational roots of inherited power and protection, do they? If Warlock Knight has to spend all his focus and energy on warding, watching for peril, no wonder he's so withdrawn.

Ms. Zeen's expression grows puzzled as she surveys the damage. "That's the strongest storm from her yet. It should have floored the house. Something besides the usual wards stopped her today."

"Odd," the Warlock mutters. "She's only interested in correcting imbalances of magic. And if there's unbalanced magic, her power is usually weaker. It's *why* she always collects on her deals in the first place."

I squirrel away that clue, and another rumor begins to unravel: Maybe the Warlock isn't responsible for destroying crops. Maybe the Widow Witch just follows him, her magic affecting the environment as she tries to balance some debt of his. But what debt has the Warlock accrued?

The Warlock turns to me with a hard stare. "We should be licking our wounds." Then he's stalking toward me, broom in hand, like I'm a mess he's going to tackle. "*You* have a protection spell stuck to you. I could smell it on you the moment you moved in."

My neck tingles. He smelled me? Oh! *Carolina's spell.* I owe her a massive thank-you. "My friend is a Hearthwitch, and she crafted it for me. But I didn't ask her to." For some reason, it's important he knows I didn't come here expecting the worst of him.

"The spell has impressive range. I suppose not every resident of Foxe Holler is extraneous."

"Like how every Warlock isn't his worst rumor?" I shoot back.

One of his thick black eyebrows goes up. I've noticed they stay untouched by time even though his hair is peppery gray at the temples. His eyes flick over me. "It's not just that spell."

I *know* he's studying me like a magical puzzle, not checking me out. But I still feel naked under his scrutiny. "Uh—well, Farewitch magic bakes into a space over generations. The protective and healing qualities of our spellwork can flavor a house, like a cast-iron skillet. Maybe my magic has settled into this kitchen a little and helped."

If that's the case, I've never seen it work on someone else's kitchen so quickly. I don't even sound convincing to myself. This man's sharp attention makes me ramble. The Warlock reaches around me, close, to lean the broom against the island. That thyme smell overwhelms my nostrils. My breath hitches, like my lungs are greedy for it.

"Whatever magic you have, Ms. Frost, it isn't little," he says, the words soft. I don't see his expression before he moves away. "The sooner we clean this up, the sooner you and I can both get back to work."

I respect the skill at compartmentalizing, but *still.* This is the Widow Witch, not a carpenter ant infestation. The Holler expects her once a year—how often does she terrorize the Manor? But they're already cleaning, and after my earlier blustering, I refuse to be caught as the only person sitting on my hands.

Ms. Zeen continues tidying up the aftermath while the Warlock brings traumatized plants to the farmhouse sink. He refills them with loose soil, and I join him to wash the dishes I'd used for the coconut cake.

If we're all going to just carry on as normal, I've got questions.

"Tell me about your magic," I say, ignoring his immediate apprehensive frown. "I need to know more to find the right recipe, or craft one from the skillet up. You have to give me something to work with."

Could be it's because we're shoulder to shoulder, not eye to eye, at the sink—he allows the interrogation. "It's a higher magic called the Language of Small Wishes."

"*Wish* magic?"

The lore around the more mysterious higher magics, those older powers rare even for Warlocks, has always intrigued me. For all their lessons on magic as I was growing up, Momaw and my mom never bothered much with the topic of Warlocks (*Waste of your time, girl, you won't ever meet one*). No wonder the rumors about him never got specific enough to mention the actual classification of his magic.

He nods. "Narrow, limited wish magic. I can't conjure wealth or send someone to the moon. Small Wishes, asked for in small ways. It's a word puzzle of sorts, language you have to play with more than a firm set of rules. I can grant my own wishes, but only simple, mundane tasks. And I can't grant the wishes of the people whom I, well, live with. Or have, for a long time. Family, whether by blood or bond. Like Lazlo and Ms. Zeen."

Immediately I think of my mom. I can't help it. Could there be some tiny, perfect way of phrasing a wish that could save—?

"Before you ask, no, I can't cure someone of anything. Disease is complicated. Otherwise, I would have figured out my own malaise a long time ago."

Makes sense. Power needs checks and balances. Witch or Warlock, magic can't create life from nothing. I try not to show my disappointment. What's one more closed door? I've knocked on so many since my mom became sick. And the Warlock doesn't need to know about my mom. I don't want him to feel I'm just here for her . . . even if that's why I came here originally. Like any good Farewitch, I *do* want to find him a cure.

"And the gardening? Do you make the plants grow?"

"That's a balance of both the manual and magic. Like a Farewitch, I have to begin with something concrete—seeds, planting, watering—do the work myself. But along the way, I can give my plants a bit of help. Make them stronger, immune to pests, withstand a frost. I can grow herbs and flora you won't find native to the area. Or have tomatoes all year long. Make colossal strawberries." A twitch of his lips. "I like to be outside, to use my hands. I'd work in the dirt even if my magic were limitless."

As he talks, he moves his traumatized yet freshly watered plants and their pots from the sink to the counter.

"You know, if I had Wi-Fi here, I could look up some of this stuff about Warlocks." I'm just thrilled he's talking, even if his *opening up* involves rusted hinges that scream and resist.

"That cell phone of yours isn't all-powerful?"

"Not this far out. Think about it. So many questions you wouldn't have to answer."

His voice drops so low, I almost don't catch his next words. "But then who would I have to aggravate and pester me?"

I have no idea what to say to that. I'm not sure he even meant me to hear it.

He seems to register his own words half a second too late and quickly adds, "Would you like to try another wish?"

"*Please*," I say with an embarrassing amount of eagerness. I've never met anyone who belongs to the school of wish magic before.

Ms. Zeen looks up from her cleaning. "Sir, you shouldn't—"

"It's all right," he calls to her, turning to fully face me. "Go ahead, Ms. Frost."

"I wish . . . I had enough room in this sink to . . . bathe."

Wow. Pathetic. But he doesn't react to the silly phrasing. I can learn.

He snaps, the sound dull through his gloves. In a blink, all the dirty dishes and utensils are clear and dry, resting on the counter. The sink is completely empty.

Herby thyme hits my tongue again, and I beam. "*That* is stellar."

His shoulders relax. Or slump. "I won't always be around to wash your dishes for you. Don't get used to it."

"Too late."

"Your health can't take that, sir," Ms. Zeen scolds.

My Joy sputters. "What do you mean?" Then I notice his eyes, sunken in the purple shadows of his sockets. Of course. He's not just tired—he's exhausted. Are his symptoms finally showing?

He waves a hand at his Governess. "Small tasks like that don't bother me. Ms. Zeen is just overly concerned for me."

"Someone has to be, sir."

His chest swells, as if he's trying to catch his breath. "I don't use my magic very often as of late. Being ill . . . I try to conserve my effort. My power. Before, I could have banished a dozen storms from the Widow Witch if someone had wished it."

As a Farewitch, my hands are my best kitchen tool, and they always ache to touch. But I resist the urge now. Lord knows what kind of trouble a reassuring shoulder pat would get me in. "Your magic—it's weakening as you do."

The grim set of his mouth confirms it. "I prefer to keep the information private."

And here I asked him to demonstrate for me, like a card trick. I deserve Ms. Zeen's scornful stare. "Do you keep your wish magic itself secret?"

"Not secret, I just don't advertise it. Magic like that encourages people to . . . lean in."

Funny. I hide my memory affinity because it makes people lean away.

"Enemies?"

"Enemies, neighbors, humans. People only ever see the wish I can give them."

A spark of empathy lights through me. I wonder how many people in his life have seen only a Warlock and his magic, only what he could offer them. He wouldn't know who liked him for his company or for his magic. Not unlike being a Farewitch. Would my neighbors give me the time of day if I were just Honey?

But I wasn't even going to take the job until he promised access to his books, so am I any better than any of those folks? I suppose I shouldn't care. I'm not here to be his friend. I know this, he knows this.

Still, I make a mental promise to myself. No more wishes, even the smallest of the small. Magic always takes a physical toll on any Witch or Warlock, but his seems to drain him at an unusually fast pace. "Any other enemies I should be briefed on?"

The Warlock's expression hardens again. "That's enough for one day."

Lazlo rockets back into the kitchen, disappears into the pantry for a hot minute, then bolts away with an armful of packaged snacks. I smile. At least there's *one* thing in this world this prickly Warlock is soft for.

Then something explodes.

Okay, not an explosion, but it *feels* like one. After the Widow Witch, my nerves are fried like fritters, and the Warlock's hazel eyes are staring at me, and it's all just A Lot, so of course the oven buzzer sounds exactly like an explosion. Honest mistake.

I startle so hard, my shoulders hit my earlobes. "The cake!"

Thank Dolly for timers. Against all odds, the cakes are fine. Two perfectly golden rounds of coconut cake come out of the AGA.

By the time we finish re-cleaning the kitchen, the cake is cool enough for me to frost and slice. As I inhale, I'm on a beach somewhere, demolishing a piña colada. The Warlock's probably never been to a beach.

I quickly push away the mental image of him wearing swim trunks and slide a slice toward him. "Coconut cream pie cures pet allergies, but coconut cake is for plant allergies."

His brow furrows. "I'm a gardener. I'm around plants as long as the sun is up."

"Exactly. Since we're not sure what your illness is, and I didn't even know your symptoms ten minutes ago"—pointed look—"I was thinking, you spend so much time in your gardens, what if there's something causing you harm, in tiny doses? Repeated exposure? We'll rule out the basics first."

"Phytotoxins?"

"Crafting an antidote or a poison just depends on the dosage."

He seems ready to protest the idea again, but something shifts in his expression. Like he knows something I don't. "That's . . . not a terrible idea."

"Thank you?" I hand him a dessert fork. "Guests and patients eat first."

He accepts the offering. "I'll take this to my room."

"You're leaving? How will I know if you show improvement?"

He's already slipping toward the door. "I'll tell you."

"At least send Lazlo back down. He only grabbed Goldfish and a packet of taco seasoning. He has to be hungry."

When he doesn't acknowledge he's heard me, I vault around the island, placing myself right in front of the Warlock before he can leave.

He halts. "Do you *ever* tire, Ms. Frost?"

"This"—I gesture between us with my own tiny fork—"needs to work. I can't guarantee a recipe will succeed, and you don't have to like my food, but you *have* to show up to try it."

His heavy look lingers on me. "I promise." Gruff, clipped words. He sidesteps me. "For Lazlo." Then he's out the door.

Show up for yourself, I want to shout.

Ms. Zeen takes a coddling sip of tea as she eyeballs me with the judgmental stare of the century. "Bold of you." Another sip, even more delicate. The tea can't be so hot it needs *that* level of care.

I don't need this right now. "Have I done something wrong? Offended you somehow?"

She sighs, primly, if that can be done. "Mr. Knight used to think everything could be solved with magic, but that's only haunted him. So now he treads carefully. If you take the aloofness personally, you'll only get any sensitive feelings of yours hurt trying to understand mistakes much older than you."

"Is it because of what happened a year ago? How did Lazlo end up here, exactly?"

"You don't need to know everything, girl."

So we're back to our usual skirmish, are we? I thought she might trust me now, just a little. "I need to understand—"

"You *need* to do as you're told. Which is to cure the sickness in this house. Mr. Knight's magic lives here. He is the Manor and the Manor is him. Why do you think he has not been able to leave in twenty-five years?"

"He only said he doesn't *like* to leave." Not that he *can't*.

Her question sparks another already lingering in my head: Why would a Warlock with wish magic specialize his studies in curses? My apron suddenly feels way too tight around my growling stomach. Hunger, unease. They're indistinguishable.

The old woman doesn't reply as she heads for the door, sending a look of derision at the coconut concoction as she passes the island.

"Your cake looks dry."

Chapter Nine

THURSDAY, APRIL 14

68 DAYS UNTIL THE SUMMER SOLSTICE

Honey's Helpful Hint, from
Honey Frost's Southern Cookbook for Recipes Gone Wrong:

Garden-fresh cucumber Benedictine will keep tongues—and tempers—cool.

Just as I open the fridge on a morning a few days later, I hear the sound of utter disaster pulling up in the driveway.

I know that old, curious humming, like the beginning of a menacing, minor key hymn.

Buick motors.

Oh no. I bolt for the foyer. If I can intercept—I fling open the front door to find an entirely new kind of cyclone of chaos.

Too late.

Sure enough, the church ladies of Foxe Holler are wearing holes in the front porch. May the gods of neighborly duty spare me.

I tighten my apron, battle ready, and step out onto the porch, blocking the door. "Good afternoon, ladies," I say, extra sweet while I scream internally. Maybe I can fake a plague.

What are they *doing* here? No one has bothered with the Warlock for twenty-five years, and now they pick the minute I arrive to work up the nerve. Their fear seems only as strong as it is convenient.

"I see you're still wearing those clogs, Miss Frost."

Seems I'm not the only one ready for a fight.

The older woman in front steps forward, her chin high in the air, red lipstick popping against her dark skin. Her cane echoes each time it strikes the porch. She's known to wield the thing like a scepter, as much for style and show as support. Forever in charge of church luncheons, she's the unofficial monarch of the church ladies. Even though she has no magic herself, her power over the Holler works like the most brutal spell. Or curse.

"Hello to you as well, Ms. Fudge. And I need the clogs for my job, since I stand and bake all day."

Gertha Fudge and the ladies behind her drop their gazes in unison. It's not Sunday, so their dress code is humble, but there are still straw hats and pantyhose for days.

"No good for the hips," mutters one.

Another clicks her tongue. "Or the posture. Look at the poor girl." Murmured agreement goes up from the cloud of perfume.

Just as I'm plotting how to warn the Warlock, Lazlo, Ms. Zeen—*Run for your lives!*—a bark comes from the back.

Beulah Buchanan pushes to the front, her poodle in tow. Beauregard sniffs around our feet, caring only for smells and not this sideshow. "You move like the dead, Gertha. Quit taking up the whole porch with your clucking and make room."

Ms. Fudge leans away from the poodle. "Why you insist on bringing that hound everywhere, Beulah, Lord only knows."

"At least he's got bark to his bite."

Most of these women have come to me for help with an ailment at some point, when Gertha Fudge wasn't looking. Nothing like pain to make a believer in magic. What experience I do have with their memories tells me something nostalgic will encourage some needed calm before this gets out of hand and I'm refereeing a church-lady brawl. Some of their strongest memories are Gertha's church luncheons . . . An idea comes to me.

"If y'all stay *right here*, I can whip us up some Louisville

Benedictine sandwiches." I usually add bacon, but with this group, the pork fat might close one too many arteries and off someone.

Ms. Fudge strikes her cane against the porch once more. "This is no social call, girl."

Now that's almost more worrisome than anything. Guests refusing refreshments? But I can barely corral these women in my own shop. What makes me think I can thwart the Golden Girl intervention here, now? Not that Gertha Fudge visits my shop.

Fudge has despised magic for as long as anyone can remember, since the Widow Witch took her husband, but frankly, there's not much she does like. If she didn't hate magic so much, I'd think *she's* a Hedgewitch. The woman practically lives off terror, and she doesn't need anything more powerful than her own streak of meanness—*that's* authentic.

"Why are we here again? Oh yes. We're storming the castle." Ms. Buchanan rolls her eyes at the other ladies, who are still stiff with apprehension.

"We're here to see to your well-being, Miss Frost." Gertha Fudge uses her cane to smack down the ragged doormat buckling around her feet. "Don't touch anything, ladies. This place reeks of rotten magic. Y'all are afraid the Widow Witch will disappear your men, but this Warlock will corrupt you so fast, not even the Lord can help you outrun the sin."

The women mumble their agreement, their chatter growing.

"And don't stare into any windows. That's how the Warlock steals your soul."

"That's *mirrors*, Kitty."

"I will say, I bet you the acoustics in there would be something else."

"Oh hush, Blanche, you got plenty of space in the church."

"Well, my mama's great-aunt says the library isn't the only thing in the Holler he's burned down over the years. He'll come for the church one of these days . . ."

Despite an oncoming headache from the perfume, I try to listen. A homegrown network of chitchat can reveal gems. These ladies have been *around*, and I need all the information I can get about the Warlock before his isolation. But I'm realizing their gossip is unhelpfully biased, like they're only familiar with the lore of a different, monster of a Warlock in their minds.

They're vexed, though it sure as hell isn't about my well-being.

"Ladies, let Pastor Webb say his piece."

A man stands behind the church ladies and only now steps forward. He's wearing a polo shirt and slacks that must be the Pantone color *Internal Revenue Service*, and his round beige cheeks make him look ageless, a computer-generated profile. His short hair is a dusty oatmeal, from gray or balding genes, I'm not sure. His genes didn't give him any magic, that I do know.

Pastor Oris Webb.

That headache finally surfaces.

His eyes, cold and artificially bright as lab-made blue raspberry, land right on me. "Peace be with you, Miss Frost."

Now I see why the church ladies are so brave today.

"The town is disheartened you have placed yourself in the employ of the Warlock, Miss Frost, especially given that your actions reflect on our mayor." As Webb speaks, he tosses a small golden apple from hand to hand. "Not to mention your own grandmother succumbed to an illness even hazardous magic from greedy Warlocks could not cure."

I squint against the morning sun but can't feel any warmth. The Warlock's magic leaves something behind, thyme on my tongue. The preacher man's presence does the opposite: The air between us goes thin, and he sucks any warmth right into his bubble of cold, dead air. I notice his slacks have no pockets and it's more disconcerting than everything else. Do servants of the Lord not need to carry a wallet?

"I'm the Farewitch. Everyone in the Holler has a right to my help." But I'm glad that, like Gertha, Webb never visits my shop.

Ms. Fudge points a wrinkled finger at me. "Your *real* job is as Foxe Holler's Farewitch. This whole charade is unacceptable. Deplorable. Improper. Reprehensible—"

I lean against the doorframe. There are plenty of synonyms for *unacceptable*. We could be here a while.

"Get to the point, Gertha," Ms. Buchanan drawls, winking at me.

"Mind yourself, Beulah!" Ms. Fudge slams her cane on the porch once more, like a gavel. The other ladies hush, eyes darting everywhere. "Being on the books of a Warlock is one thing. But abandoning the Apothakery to do so is quite another."

"I'm not abandoning anything. I closed the shop for three weeks. *Three.*"

And I'm already down one. While the rest of the Holler is praying for the wedding season and the Widow Witch to hurry up, I wish time would just *stop* so I can catch up. With the Warlock's casual mention of dying, that window of time I gave myself seems silly.

In his library, I've already dug up handwritten recipe books, diaries, betting logs, financial records, grimoires, farmers' almanacs. Any kind of written text, his archives have it squirreled away. It's exactly what I hoped for. All that possibility. Wonderful . . . and overwhelming. Now, the ten—*nine!*—weeks until the solstice seem much too short.

"Three weeks, three years. It matters not to us. You are the Farewitch of this Holler, if a young and green one. After six years on the job, you should know better." Fudge shakes her head. "Especially after what poor Ambrosia went through. She would be the first to remind you of your responsibility to serve your *real* community."

My ears run hotter than spellfire. I push down the rage simmering in my core. How dare she use Momaw to guilt me? Vultures, all of them. Thriving off heresy and wrinkle cream.

"My grandmother would tell me to treat everyone seeking help fairly."

No fewer than four church ladies harrumph.

"An altruistic effort," Webb adds. "But your neighbors are worried for your safety."

I wonder if that includes him. Is that why Webb is letting Gertha Fudge take the lead here? Does he think I'll be more likely to listen to grandmotherly church ladies? "Don't worry, our neighbors have made their concern clear."

"Then you'll understand why we ask you to reconsider your choice. Warlocks invite powerful enemies. Don't become another victim of a fairy tale."

They've been here ten minutes and already assume they know everything. How can Ms. Fudge strike someone off her prayer list, a man she *doesn't* know, with such vigor? Now that I think about it, she's old enough to have known him *before* he became a recluse . . .

But my gut says there's simply too much guilt in the Warlock's eyes to leave room for the bloodlust folks believe is festering under his roughness. Whatever secrets he's hiding . . . they're locked away not because they're dangerous, but because they're painful.

Regardless, it's clear Foxe Holler doesn't know much about the Warlock at all. Maybe it's best to keep it that way. The fewer questions they ask, the better.

"Sorry to disappoint, but I'm not a prisoner," I say. If anything, my world has always been my kitchen, and now it's bigger than ever. "As every Witch will tell you, magic is neutral. And the sole purpose of mine is helping people."

"Allow me to get to the point," Webb says. "The Widow Witch hasn't yet tithed a husband this year, and the longer she waits, the more the town grows concerned she could be planning an even greater reckoning. There's a strong chance she could use the Witches' upcoming holiday—Beltane, isn't it?—as the moment for her confrontation. For safety purposes, it could behoove us to cancel the festivities your kind was planning."

This. This is why Webb came all the way up here only to use his church ladies as his megaphone. If it's their initiative as concerned neighbors, it doesn't look like Webb and his dogma have too much influence.

"Take heed, Miss Frost," Ms. Fudge says. "Wise Pastor Webb speaks truth in his sermons, which you would know if you attended service. The Warlock *is* a threat. Destruction always follows that kind of unchecked power. Witches are trouble, but a devious Warlock is worse. Now is not the time to be in bed with one."

My cheeks flush. "I'm not in bed with—*I'm* a Witch!"

"Hmph. A *Farewitch.* Magic might be a plight against God's natural order, but your magic is less threatening than a mediocre Hearthwitch's. Should we worry ourselves over violent scones, ladies? Or donauwelle for demons?" she asks her followers.

Nervous chuckles float on the April breeze. "I don't even make scones," I mutter. Though, if I ever finish writing my cookbook, I'm drafting *Donauwelle for Demons* next.

"And how you can work in this dungeon . . ." Ms. Fudge trails off, eyes peeling back the Manor imperfection by imperfection.

"Hey!" We cleaned this dungeon. The dungeon looks *nice* now. There are candles and the smell of cinnamon and the Warlock even let me clip three whole fresh flowers from his garden for the island. This is *my* creepy Manor and no one insults it but me.

On cue, the glass in the front windows shivers. Threatened and threatening. The last thing I need is an old lady in the ER with concussion-by-fallen-shingle.

"So all magic is bad magic, then?" I try to find a sympathetic weak link, but no one will turn against their luncheon leader. Especially not now that I've drawn a line in the battlefield flour by closing my shop and allying myself with a Warlock. An outsider. Imagine, holding a grudge so tight, they stay angry at the only Farewitch they have to keep their maladies at bay.

For all their gossiping, these women haven't even figured out their own mayor is dying as we speak. For a hot second, I want them to. I want their white eyebrows to climb high with shock. That would teach them to speculate about other people with blind prejudice.

"What in high heaven is all this commotion?" says a voice from the doorway.

Governess Zeen stops behind me, one foot still in the foyer. She collects herself quickly, donning a mask of stone when she sees Gertha Fudge.

"Why, Letha Zeen," Ms. Fudge croons. "I wasn't sure you were still alive up here, taking care of a Warlock. Wayward souls don't do this Holler much good, but I'll still pray for you."

The record should be clear: Governess Zeen has all the frightening parts of Momaw Frost without the grandma hugs, and scares me a helluva lot more than the Warlock. Most days. But such a foul taste lands on my tongue listening to Fudge condescend Ms. Zeen on the steps of her own home. My good mood extinguishes, and I snap like a dried angel-hair noodle.

"Maybe Ms. Zeen's kindness doesn't depend on having an audience, Ms. Fudge." Arms crossed, I stalk forward, making sure my clogs are *obnoxiously loud*. I let the sugar leak out of my voice. "I could make y'all all the sweets in the world and you'd still turn out *sour*."

Jaws go slack. Ms. Zeen glances at me, her stern facade slipping like an egg over nonstick. Ms. Fudge recovers first and throws back her bony shoulders. "Careful, girl, or you won't ever be welcome at church. Should you ever choose to attend, that is."

"Now, Gertha," Webb says, placing a gentle hand on Ms. Fudge's shoulder, his other still holding his apple. But his *gentle* is just slow and creepy, like a mannequin part come to life.

Ms. Zeen sniffs. "You toss people out all the time anyway, Gertha. It's your specialty. You're too hard on good people."

"Why—how *dare* you, Letha, after all I've done for you? *Life* is too hard on good people. Everyone needs to learn that." Ms. Fudge shakes her cane at the Manor behind us. "You tell this—this *ungrateful* boy that I will protect my town when he inevitably crosses the line."

I wave toward the house. "Tell him yourself. I'd be happy to go get him." *I would not. Please don't call my bluff.*

"No thank you. We don't consort with his type."

"His type is my type. So leave."

Ms. Buchanan is the only church lady who doesn't gasp, bless her. The other ladies throw breathy huffs in my direction.

Ms. Fudge points a knobby finger at me. "Back in my day, a Witch knew her place. Snubbing the warning of your elders will be your undoing, girl." Her watery eyes narrow. "Where the Warlock goes, the Widow Witch goes. Get out of that Manor while you can, before the Warlock steals something you can't get back. You might just save your soul. What's left of it." She drives her cane into the old wood boards of the porch, punctuating each word.

I must be delirious with adrenaline, because a hazy bubble shivers and swells around the church ladies and Pastor Webb, a glow that vanishes before I'm sure it's real. The *wards*. The Warlock's protective barriers have been poked enough, it seems. He was surprised the Manor let me in for my interview. But then why even allow these folks onto the porch?

Then I realize—that haze was the house *trying* to force out this intrusion, like it's detected harmful pathogens. But the wards aren't strong enough. They're weakening as the Warlock's magic wanes. The Widow Witch's impromptu visit likely didn't help, either.

Before I can ponder how long the wards might last, Pastor Webb steps *much* too close to me. His voice drops, mouth turning down. "I don't think a simple young Farewitch is the enemy here, Miss Frost. Magic is. Do not step in the Lord's way. Or mine."

My nervous system does a one-eighty at his change in tone.

Finally, he departs, still tossing that apple. With a last vicious glare at Ms. Zeen, Gertha Fudge and the church ladies follow, hobbling away with more speed than I thought possible.

Old Blanche has the balls to turn around. "You're lucky we're busy with Easter preparations. And we've never liked your Benedictine. It's not even green!"

A rotting shutter on the side of the house chooses that moment to detach and hit the ground suspiciously close to the old woman. She screeches and teeters away. I hope she's got a strong pacemaker.

"It's not *supposed* to be green!" I shout at her retreating back. That woman was plenty happy buying my food a couple weeks ago.

Shaking with rage that might be hunger and low blood sugar, I'm so furious I don't even notice Ms. Buchanan is still on the front porch, Beauregard eating what I hope is only a bug at her feet.

After a moment, Ms. Zeen coughs. "Well. Thank you."

I flash her a smile. Are we friends now?

The Governess grimaces. "I'm not that grateful."

Right.

Beauregard barks, and like some kind of pooch radar has gone off, a small shape skids to a halt at the open front door. Lazlo.

I don't have time to stop him before he flies across the porch to Beauregard.

"Well now, I thought I knew everyone in the Holler," Ms. Buchanan says, not batting a single cataract.

She does, but she also doesn't always recognize folks, what with her spotty memory. I'm just grateful Lazlo didn't appear before now. What would the church ladies have to say about a child living in this so-called dungeon?

"I've never seen a poodle!" Lazlo says.

The dog thumps a happy tail at the sudden activity, definitely falling in love.

Ms. Buchanan bends to Lazlo's eye level, which isn't far since she's already hunched. "This is Beauregard. Beauregard, say hello to this handsome young fellow."

The poodle licks Lazlo's cheek. The boy's smile breaks language barriers. Has the kid never seen a dog before? He grasps Beauregard's curly fur, and the dog presses into the scratches.

"His fur is the same color as my hair," Lazlo says.

"Would you like to play with him, sugar?" Ms. Buchanan says, sweeter than I've ever heard her.

Lazlo's so excited, he can only nod. She hands him the leash and then boy and dog run off into the Manor, before I can worry over how the house feels about pets.

"That pup needs a young one. Too much energy for these old bones," Ms. Buchanan says to me. "Would it trouble you if I came here to buy what I need? I don't care where you are, no matter what those old biddies said. As long as I can get my jam cake."

"If you're not afraid of the Warlock," I say.

She lets out a laugh that's both warm and a little bit terrifying. "I'm not afraid of anything. Especially a man."

Chapter Ten

SATURDAY, APRIL 16

66 DAYS UNTIL THE SUMMER SOLSTICE

Honey's Helpful Hint, from
Honey Frost's Southern Cookbook
for Recipes Gone Wrong:

When sourcing an ingredient you want, be willing to substitute. When sourcing an ingredient you need, be willing to trade.

Let it be known that the Farewitch of Foxe Holler is not a runner.

The baking life doesn't leave many opportunities for sprinting, and it's especially hard to run in chef's clogs.

And yet, this morning, I'm chasing a ghost.

When the blue blur flashes by out the window, sweeping past the edge of my vision, I vault into action, nearly breaking an ankle on the porch steps.

The fellow isn't getting away this time.

Truly, innocently, I *mean* to cut him off at the big willow tree to the north of the house, but the surprise attack proves too effective and I accidentally plow right into our postman.

We both go down, hard, into the dewy April grass.

I gather myself quickly, before he can flee again. "Why"—pant—"are"—pant—"you"—sneeze—"*running*?"

Foxe Holler's postman is lanky, about my age, and as he pushes himself off the ground, his dark skin shines with sweat. With much aggressive flustering, he shoves a pair of chunky black-framed glasses back onto his face. "Why are you *chasing* me, lady?"

"Because you're running!"

When I told the Warlock I'd catch our postman in action, swear on my mother's grimoire, he only said, *I think you've inhaled too much gas from the stove.*

I straighten my apron. First impressions, after all. "I need to order a microwave."

"Try that again?" The postman runs an exasperated hand over his closely cropped head.

Right. I am not losing my mind, heaven mark this fact. Even if I'm just staying a few short weeks, I *need* that harmless radiation power. The house will thank me when I'm gone.

"Hello, my name is Honey Frost and I'm the Farewitch. Pleasure to meet you. I need to order a microwave here to Knight Manor. Will you be able to deliver it? The bottom of the drive is fine. I can come down with my truck."

He gapes at me, adjusting his glasses. "You live here?"

"For now. Just moved in."

"Willingly?"

Okay . . . "I'm working for the Warlock."

He inches back. "*Willingly?*"

I don't have time for this. It doesn't make sense for the Holler to be so afraid of Warlock Knight when there are actually dangerous forces like the Widow Witch lurking about. We got lucky a few days ago, but if the house's wards are weakening, what damage could she do now?

Pastor Webb was right about one thing: The longer the Widow Witch waits to take someone, the more frenzied the town will become. Her victims are never *just* husbands, but brothers and nephews, fathers and sons, neighbors.

Maybe I need to expand my Farewitch repertoire from snickerdoodles to shields.

"Listen—what's your name?" He looks familiar, but everyone in a small town is familiar.

He throws back his shoulders, showing off his blue postal uniform. His shorts are a little too short on his long legs but he still gives the outfit dignity. He clutches a package in his arms like a newborn baby. "Rett Claywell. Postman of Foxe Holler."

"*Claywell* Claywell?"

"No, *Rett* Claywell—"

"You're Arna Jean's older brother!" I didn't recognize him in the heat of pursuit, but now I see the family resemblance: great cheekbones, lanky limbs, and terrible eyesight.

"*You're* the baker RJ talks about?" His incredulous voice makes me feel much, *much* worse about tackling the poor guy. "The overalls give you away," he clarifies.

Arna Jean Claywell and I met when she appeared at the Apothakery insisting on a summer internship (that didn't exist) while she was home from Howard University. She came back every summer after that. No idea why this genius of a Bookwitch picked my shop to learn about managing a small business, but whenever running the Apothakery felt like trial by fire, she made the oven heat tolerable. We'd daydream travel plans together, but the shop kept me too busy to go with her. Eventually, she graduated, we said our goodbyes, and I lost my intern.

My corn muffins were bland with despair for a week.

But I had no idea her older brother was the postman I was looking for. Things are looking up after face-planting in the dirt.

"Rett, first of all, sorry I tackled you." Get that out of the way. "And I appreciate your effort to deliver here even though it's clear you're not comfortable with Knight Manor."

His chest puffs out a smidge. "I always deliver my packages. *Always.* Folks deserve mail that isn't just bills all the time."

"But you know you don't have to drop things and run, right?"

"It's self-preservation. When you look like me, you don't approach an eccentric old loner's house. Even in the daylight. And in a uniform. Especially a uniform."

Okay, point taken. "He's not that old . . . Never mind. You don't have to worry about any nefarious magic, or—or . . . Why *are* you afraid of the farmhouse, exactly?"

He swipes a layer of sweat off his scrunched forehead. "Why *aren't* you?"

The Warlock asked me the same thing. Why do men always think it's strange when a woman isn't afraid of what *they're* afraid of? "Because the Warlock employs me to be here. It's my job. You get that. You deliver the Holler's mail, I . . . bake."

Not as strong a finish. But I don't have the bandwidth or time to be afraid of more than one thing at a time, and right now, the honor goes to *mysterious illness draining the life of my mom*, then *Widow Witch*, then *Governess Zeen*.

Then, maybe, Knight Manor and its grumpy Warlock.

Rett eyes me with lens-magnified distress. "I don't mean to alarm you, but I think you might be under a spell."

"I assure you, I am not."

"You're not being held against your will?"

"No."

"You're not the victim of a magical curse?"

"*No.*"

"You're not being forced to bargain for your ransomed soul?"

"What—no—Mr. Knight is a man who just also happens to be a Warlock. He's our neighbor, not a serial killer."

"Did he tell you that?" His eyes narrow. "Convenient."

Oh, for the love of— "Would I be asking you about kitchen appliances if my life were in danger?"

This stumps him. He extends the package to me. Despite the impromptu rugby, it's intact. "Heard. Even a haunted house deserves mail. But just so it's clear, I'll know if the Warlock ever delivers something . . . evil."

"Via the postal service?"

"You never know." He's absolutely deadpan.

I tuck the goods under my armpit. "Come on in for a bit. For iced tea? It's humid, and I tackled you. It's the least I can do."

His eyes widen as he stares up at the looming farmhouse. "*Inside* the Manor?"

I play my last ace, giving a casual shrug. "Arna Jean never believed any of that Holler gossip. Especially if Gertha Fudge was spreading it."

Rett's concern falters, gaze sharpening. *There's* that competitive streak I know so well in his sister. A Claywell right down to his willowy bones. Got him.

He adjusts his tie and knee-high socks. "*One* glass."

Ten minutes later, I'm serving the postman sweet iced tea in Knight Manor.

At first, the cabinet doors open on their own, like an oversized Advent calendar having a fret. Agitated little things. I'm guessing Rett only slipped through the Warlock's wards because I officially invited him in? Vampires would thrive in the polite South.

What in the Julia Child is going on with this house?

"Play nice!" I shout to the kitchen, confusing the hell out of Rett. But the kitchen calms down. It's been somewhat civil ever since I helped fend off the Widow Witch.

Bright side is, I think I'm beginning to understand this place. Rett is a brand-new person, untested. I, too, would be cautious of a stranger crawling around my insides. Ew.

As Rett takes a tentative seat on a stool, I open the delivery. My Weisenberger grits—excellent. I'm trying a Frost classic for the Warlock next. Truffle and goat cheese grits. Grits bolster a meager immune system.

As Rett sips tea, his wary eyes wander, cautious but curious, around the room. The kitchen behaves. "I feel oddly better than I expected to."

"Sweet tea. Good for the head."

"And bruised kneecaps?"

"Sorry."

"I'll forgive you if you give me the Wi-Fi password." He pulls out his phone. "And yes, I can deliver a microwave. This isn't amateur hour."

"We don't have Wi-Fi here. Yet. It's a whole thing."

"Doesn't Wi-Fi come with, like, the heat and hot water these days?" Zero sarcasm.

"You're very serious, you know. For someone our age."

"I'm a United States Postal Serviceman. I have to be."

Again, total deadpan. I like him. "I'd like to send orders to a few customers while I'm here." Two weeks left. Don't panic. "Some of my older folks need repeated remedies but aren't very mobile."

"My routes are structured. I can't just make extra stops for informal nonessentials. It's unprofessional."

"So you'll bring mail to the haunted house you're avoiding at all costs, to the point you'd rather toss packages at the flower beds and make a run for it than ring the doorbell. But you *won't* deliver cookies to the old folks' home. Have I got that right?"

"Yes, that sounds right."

"I see." I might let the cabinets have him next time. "I see that you're *ridiculous*."

He pokes the counter. "I'm trying to be the best postman I can be, which means ensuring everyone gets access to the postal service. But Pastor Webb's stopped Communion service for houses too far out, and he's got his followers thinking the post office should follow. The Marrow family is the latest to be too independent for his taste. *Conserve resources for the heart of the community*, he says. His church doesn't even pay taxes!"

I pause. Since when did Webb's interest in keeping an eye on folks expand beyond his churchgoing crowd? The Marrow name rings a bell. They're Witches—Greenwitches, I think. The Marrows have always kept to themselves, not unlike a certain Warlock. After witnessing Webb's fervor firsthand, I'm not convinced he'll stop with just families on the outskirts of town. Hell, everything and everyone in a holler like this could be *outskirts*.

"And *I'm* trying to be a somewhat competent Farewitch," I say. "Everyone deserves their packages. Everyone deserves their medications. Right? Or does Pastor Webb run the USPS?"

"He does *not*." His posture slips. "Touché." His glance goes sideways, a little too casual to be casual. "Mayor Frost is your mom, so you must know Silas Key."

". . . Vaguely." I'm not sure where this is going.

"I've been trying to get a meeting with him for a while. To talk about my route concerns and Pastor Webb."

"You want a meeting with him in exchange for helping me send out food." Which means I'll owe Silas a favor. My brains screams *No way*. "Deal."

The postman gives me what I think is his closest thing to a smile. "I have to get back, but thanks for the tea. Please refrain from tackling me again."

"I will if you leave packages like a normal person."

"No promises."

"Great."

"You know, Webb might be forced to cool off if Mayor Frost says something. It wouldn't hurt for your mom to make a public appearance once in a while." When Rett finishes the last of his tea, he stands. "Why'd the Warlock hire you anyway? I thought Witches and Warlocks don't get along."

I dodge the question. "He's ill. That's all I can say."

"Figured he'd invite you here at some point. He loves your apple butter."

"He said you picked some up for him recently. That might have gotten me the job, so thank you."

"Recently? No. He's left me letters with instructions to pick up and deliver from your shop for years."

My breath disappears, my brain a few steps behind. "Years?"

He doesn't hear me as he heads for the front of the house. "Oh, give RJ a shout. She just got back in town."

As soon as he's gone, my phone dings with a text from my mom. I've been graced with some rare inside service. Just a question about when I'm visiting next, but it reminds me of something. I hunt through my texts and find my old group chat with the other Witches in Foxe Holler: Carolina, Arna Jean, Ms. Marrow, her daughter (never answers). After graduation, Arna Jean left to travel before job hunting, but it's been years since I've seen her. She must be about twenty-five, the same age I was when I came back to the Holler.

Oddly nervous, I start typing.

kentucky fried coven

Welcome back, RJ
proof of life?

Arna Jean Claywell
Honeydewwww
what's this about closing the shop

Ms. Marrow
Hi y'all! Are we organizing something for Beltane this year?

Carolina Vázquez
I can host, but not if pastor webb is breathing down my neck
Why is he leaving me voicemails about you, Honey?

Arna Jean Claywell
Up to no good, honeydew?

Mom
Don't get me started.

Has webb ever been this fussy
about witches?

Ms. Marrow
Marigold! I haven't seen you in ages.
And not that I can remember, Honey.

Carolina Vázquez
But the WW hasn't been this quiet before either

Arna Jean Claywell
oooh shall we revive the betting pool?
put me down for 10 on noxie's husband

Carolina Vázquez
You'll never win that bet, he's immortal
Not literally, but you know

Mom
Shame on y'all

mom

Mom
Fine, I'll put 20 on him

Chapter Eleven

SUNDAY, APRIL 24

58 DAYS UNTIL THE SUMMER SOLSTICE

Honey's Helpful Hint, from
Honey Frost's Southern Cookbook
for Recipes Gone Wrong:

Opposites can be great complements, especially when it comes to texture. Animal crackers hold their crunch in banana pudding better than vanilla wafers, and their drier texture supports the intense sweetness of the pudding. They are one of the rare, perfect secret ingredients that Do The Most. Except when they're a mortifying means of unintentional seduction.

After another week of Farewitch best hits from the Frost family's kitchen grimoires—delicious, but no success with a cure—I decide it's time for an intervention.

"Did you know that poodles don't have fur, they have hair? Like us?"

"I admit, my knowledge of poodles is lacking," I say, listening to Lazlo as I shuck corn. Evening sun slouches through the windows, and bowls of fresh corn and leeks and okra cover the counter. My eyes dart to a clock on the wall by the pantry.

They better not be late. Food or time, a Farewitch doesn't like to waste anything.

Lazlo looks up from his notebook and a doodle that looks half dog and half flamingo. "It's why they don't shed. And did you know *poodle* is from *pudeln*—that's German for 'to splash.' Like a puddle. 'Cause they're water dogs. *Pudelhund.* They used to hunt ducks."

I move on to mincing serrano pepper. "I see German with Governess Zeen is going well."

Her homeschooling clearly doesn't include art.

"So they're excellent swimmers. Oh, and did you know—"

"Hey, kid."

"Yeah?"

"Ms. Zeen only let you come cook with me because I told her we'd work on fractions." I push a battalion of measuring cups toward him. "Help a lady out."

He heaves a sigh. "Math?" He shrinks down, chin on the counter. "But it's the *weekend*. And I'm not that bad at fractions."

According to Ms. Zeen, the kid is, tragically, that bad at fractions. Which is where I come in. Measuring cups are a three-dimensional lesson in portions. And I'm happier than I thought I would be with a little sous-chef in the kitchen. Relinquishing *some* control can be fun.

Even if said sous-chef keeps drinking the milk he measures and is easily distracted by canine facts.

"Mr. Knight would want you to try." The boy idolizes the man.

"I'll just be a gardener, like him."

"While a noble pursuit, there's still math in gardening." With a grunt, I drop a sack of yellow cornmeal in front him. "We're making corn pudding and cornbread. Both Southern staples, but baking is more precise than cooking. Measuring accurately will be crucial."

"*Cru-shul?*"

"Really important. You can't mess around with the measurements for cakes and cookies and breads. Baking is chemistry, but in the oven."

A groan. "I thought this was math."

"Here's our recipe. See these numbers? We've got to double everything since we're making two batches of everything."

We collect the ingredients together, and as I show Lazlo how to spoon the cornmeal into a measuring cup instead of scooping, he says, "Did you know a man tried to run the Iditarod race with poodles as sled dogs?"

The kid knows *Iditarod* but not *crucial*? "That sounds . . . bold."

He nods solemnly. "It did not go well." Shrugs. "It was the eighties."

"How do you know all this?" I pass him a small cheese grater and a block of cheddar for the cornbread.

"Books." To his credit, he attacks the cheddar with gusto . . . and then stuffs a hunk into his cheek when he thinks I'm not looking. "I would know a lot more if I could Google."

Shuffling sounds come from the door. "Mr. Knight, it would behoove you not to stand in the doorway. This is tornado country, not earthquake."

Glancing up, I see the Warlock stepping aside so Governess Zeen can march into the kitchen. "I didn't want to interrupt such a pertinent conversation, Ms. Zeen."

I ignore the sarcastic jab and choose peace today, waving him over. At least he's showing up now instead of brooding. "Perfect timing. I need help chopping squash." Lazlo isn't *knife-handling* certified yet. "Oh, and welcome to Sunday supper."

Stoic as ever, he stalks toward me. Now that I've seen his magic, I'm less afraid of him. Knowing how exactly someone could possibly kill me in my sleep, well, it's kind of freeing.

Pastor Webb's warning simmers on a back burner in my mind. Is that why the Warlock doesn't—can't?—leave his Manor? He's worried people like Oris Webb and Gertha Fudge will start asking too many questions? That can't be it entirely. The Warlock's stayed isolated for decades, yet Lazlo has only lived here a year. Although, the kid doesn't attend school in town and—that's not my job. I'm the Farewitch, not the boy's guardian, and I'm definitely no Governess Zeen.

I need to focus on the rhythm of the kitchen. Keeping the hands busy does wonders to chase away anxious thoughts.

When the Warlock reaches the island, I hold up a hand. "Wait—you can't wear those gloves while you cook." Honestly, this man. "You've got dirt . . . everywhere."

"I pulled this squash out of my garden with these gloves yesterday. I don't think my *dirt* is going to harm you."

I stick out a hip, which is less commanding when you're wearing an apron and said apron hides your lack of hips. But I can't come up with a good counter.

"Fine. We're making butternut squash corn pudding." The sweetness of the squash and corn work well together, and we've got leeks for subtlety and serrano peppers instead of jalapeño. "Farewitches make corn pudding to help with inflammation, which is the cause of many a problem. Though the squash is good for your spleen, magic or no magic."

He stares at my piles of ingredients. Judging? Displeased?

I scramble. "I'm making extra for a few folks." *Named Mom.* "Don't worry, I have separate funds I use for my customers. You're not subsidizing groceries for the entire Holler."

He stiffens, like I've insulted him, but then quickly absorbs a couldn't-care-less aura.

That's how Governess Zeen, Lazlo, and the Warlock are making Sunday supper in the kitchen. With me. Together.

And nothing's caught fire.

"What's burning?" Lazlo asks, mid-whisk.

Nothing's caught fire *yet.*

"My patience," Ms. Zeen says, slicing okra at the kitchen island. She wasn't happy about the post I assigned her, and keeps muttering *audacity* under her breath, although that could be *a dash of tea*. I can't tell—the kitchen is busy and loud for once.

I try a new recipe for the Warlock each day, which is as fast as Farewitch magic can work. The body needs time to digest the food and process the ingredients, to see if the recipe has an effect. Or not. The town expects me to reopen the Apothakery in a week. That's seven or so chances to cure the Warlock. But I don't feel any closer than when I started.

We've covered the basics: sweet tea for headaches; sorghum-syrup sweet potato casserole for joint pain; cornbread for general under-the-weather malaise. Coconut cake . . .

Nothing. Zero results.

My anxiety can't ignore the parallels. Momaw, my mom, the Warlock. Why are these three cures so stubbornly evasive? I've been trying different foods for months and months with my mom, and I'm running out of answers. The right recipes for both of them have to be here in the Warlock's archives. Like the sharp taste of bourbon in the first sip of a Kentucky Coffee, I can feel it in my belly. They *need* to be.

"Nothing's burning, thank you," I say, hopping over to the ovens. "The leftover bits on my cast iron are burning off. Life cycle of a skillet."

The Warlock looks up from chopping the squash. He's got superb knife skills even with the bulky gloves. 'Course he does. Unfair. "Again, I have to protest. It seems appallingly unsanitary to not clean them."

"We clean them." Lazlo's down to a tiny chunk of ungrated cheddar, so I free him of his task before he starts skinning fingers. "With water."

"No soap? Honestly?"

I point to a damning pile of other skillets off to the side. I've been working to free the house's cast iron from a glaze of rust since I got here. "*Honestly*, Mr. Knight, if you bring so much as a single sud near my skillets, I will mulch your mums. Respectfully."

His gaze narrows. "I dare you."

"*Respectfully.*"

"Twice," he says, teeth tight. "That's *twice* now you've threatened my plants."

I try not to focus on how his biceps flex through his shirt as he chops with increasing agitation. My head must still be recovering from all that church-lady perfume.

To distract myself, I check the consistency of Lazlo's dessert. The kid's a furious whisker, and stiff peaks become granite boulders real quick. I've graduated him from the corn genre of pudding to banana. The South loves its hash, mash, or mush.

Once the Warlock is finished with the squash for the corn pudding, I promote him to the fried catfish. Gloved hands hovering over the flour, egg, and cornmeal bowls, he insists on using a fork rather than perfectly good fingers to dunk the fillets.

"Sunday supper is a Frost tradition, and it requires happy skillets," I explain as I mix our prepped ingredients for the corn pudding: cheese, creamy milk, leeks, serrano, kiss of sugar, cornmeal, salt. And of course, gobs of corn. "No matter how busy the shop and life were any given week, my mom and Momaw and I protected suppertime together on Sundays."

Even now, I can hear Momaw Frost snapping instructions across the kitchen, wild gray hair held in place with illegal amounts of hair spray. When was the last time I cooked a full meal on a Sunday? Not for the shop, not to deliver to neighbors. Just for myself?

Probably the last time the inhabitants of Knight Manor had a real meal. These people have a kitchen table made for a mess hall, yet no one ever eats together.

Cue my intervention. A shared meal will be good for the Warlock, for this cranky house, for *everyone*. If I can get everyone spending enough quality time together, I might be able to tease out more information about the Warlock, some helpful nugget of history that could point me toward a cure for him.

Tonight's menu, a.k.a. my battle plan: okra, sliced and sizzling in a shallow skillet (Ms. Zeen); pan-fried catfish (the Warlock, begrudgingly); cornbread (mine, of course); and banana pudding courtesy of Lazlo.

"What about you, Ms. Zeen?" I ask. "What did your family like to cook together?"

The Governess tosses me a grimace. With her cardigan sleeves rolled up and wrinkled, she looks like a disgruntled wet cat. I can see where the Warlock gets his favorite expression. "Whatever was canned."

"Don't expend your energy, Ms. Frost," the Warlock says. "Ms. Zeen doesn't discuss her life before the Manor. Even I'm not privy to her rubric of friends and foes." His words verge on teasing, but I'm realizing it's unlikely even moonshine would get the woman to spill her past.

"Shall we speak of foes now, sir?" Ms. Zeen retorts. There's an undercurrent of a bite, evidence of a long-standing conversation between the two of them. Or argument.

He turns back to his catfish, silent.

A smidge of the kitchen's warmth dissipates. Warlock Knight is a man with history. Real enemies. What if the Widow Witch gets to him before I can cure him, before he can build his full strength back up? The bananas I'm slicing take on a sickly sweet overripe smell as I fret.

Jesus, I'm being silly. He's survived this long, right? This is probably how Ms. Zeen got caught working here. Somehow, the Warlock encourages strange fits of sympathy.

Brain buzzing with questions and nervous energy, I focus on beheading a row of peeled bananas. One thing at a time. Banana pudding, I can handle.

With the sunset turning the kitchen gold, the chorus of ovens, the smell of real vanilla—this is my orchestra, my science lab, my artist's studio. My good mood is impervious. Sundays are for warm cornbread and warmer conversation to fend off the Monday blues. I'm determined to give Lazlo, and the Warlock and Governess, this tradition of time together. Maybe they'll even keep it up when I'm gone.

As our supper at last cooks in the oven, I unveil my newest treasure from the pantry for those of us who are still single digits.

"Animal crackers!" Lazlo cries with delight.

"My secret ingredient," I mock-whisper. "Vanilla wafers get too soggy. Animal crackers hold their shape and crunch. They work much better with the soft pudding."

The Warlock sneaks a glance at us as I pour the cookies onto a cutting board and hand Lazlo a rolling pin.

"No dogs, right?"

"Nope. Just"—glance—"circus animals. Think you can smash these for me?"

"I'm no amateur at smashing, Ms. Honey." *CRUNCH.*

"Only *some,* we need half in pieces to mix in, and half kept whole—"

CRUSH. "Like this?"

I step back for safety.

He doubles down with the rolling pin and proceeds to beat the living crap out of the poor animal crackers. But only half. He *is* listening. I make a note to take this kid into town soon for some regular, normal human interaction.

I've overheard him talking to himself as he wanders outside, and he navigates the halls without looking up, having already explored the farmhouse down to its tiniest nook. He seems young for nine but at the same time like an impossibly old soul. Despite the care from Ms. Zeen and the Warlock, the truth appears in the quiet moments: Lazlo is lonely.

Now I understand why the Warlock always looks distressed around the kid. A melancholy Lazlo is like a hot brown on a day warmer than sixty. I can't stomach it.

Pleased with his pulverizing efforts, Lazlo gives a cookie to Ms. Zeen. She eats it with as much poise as one can eat a miniature mammal. He drops another in the bowl he's taken to leaving out for Beauregard.

Much to the Warlock's displeasure, Ms. Buchanan now visits the Manor whenever she wants to pick up jam cake, her pooch always riding shotgun. I should probably check if dogs can eat these clumps of corn syrup and soy lecithin.

Lazlo hands two cookies to the Warlock. For once, the Warlock isn't looking at his ward with guilt, and it feels . . . nicer than I thought to see that regret missing, even if it's temporary. The man swallows the cookie in one bite, like it's the best thing he's ever tasted. Lazlo beams. Then the Warlock offers me the extra cookie.

Distracted by the pure joy on Lazlo's face, I lean right over and inhale the cookie, no hands. My lips brush the Warlock's gloved fingers.

I chew exactly once before I realize my catastrophic mistake.

The Warlock's outstretched hand hovers, frozen, his eyes stuck on where my lips would have met his skin. For the first time, I'm grateful he insists on wearing those gloves.

The oven timer ticks in the background.

My voice fails, making the odd silence worse and my blush worse and just the entire situation *much, much worse*. The sharp cookie is lodged in my cheek, but chomping down will confirm the actions of my double-crossing mouth. They really do stay crunchy, stupid things.

Lazlo, bless him, doesn't notice the sudden awkwardness. Ms. Zeen sure does, though. No wonder Silas hates public dinner dates in this town.

Just then, my phone rings.

Thank. *God.*

"Back in a minute—!" I shout around a mouthful of cookie.

Refusing to dwell on this newest mortification, I dash from the kitchen. Only when I'm safely in the foyer and free of the Warlock's heavy stare do I swallow the godforsaken cookie and check my phone.

Erg. Speak of the Hugo Boss devil. After Oris Webb's visit, I don't have the patience for another man wasting my time right now, especially my mom's (not gonna happen) replacement. But I can't look the Warlock in the eye just yet. Or ever again.

"Hey," I answer, hoping it sounds like *Thanks, goodbye.*

"Hi—wait. Do you actually have my number saved as a real contact now?" Silas's voice comes through, recognizable but staticky.

". . . Maybe." I already regret answering. F minus in avoidant millennial, Frost.

"Does this mean we're friends?"

"Are you even allowed to make new friends in your thirties? It's probably breaking a rule of some kind."

"You are in your thirties, remember?" he drawls.

"And *that* kind of language is why we aren't friends."

"Listen, I'm outside Knight Manor but can't get close enough to the doorbell to ring it. The house seems to have warding, like Carolina has around your mom's room—"

"We have a doorbell?"

"Honey."

"Right, sorry, one sec."

Once again, I find myself the unintentional sentry of the farmhouse's increasingly busy entryway. Silas Key stands at the base of the front porch steps, a few paces from his parked hybrid. He's in yet another three-piece number, even on a Sunday evening. Pinstripes.

I cross my arms. "Estate planning couldn't wait until Monday?"

"Please, I don't spend my waking hours nudging your mother toward death's door. You do a fine enough job at that yourself." His eyes stick to the gloomy exterior of the farmhouse. It does look pretty menacing at dusk.

"I'm perfectly safe here."

"Right. Listen, if this Warlock has answers that might help Marigold recover, you've got my full support. But do not ask me to lie to your mother. She even knows when I haven't paid for parking. She can smell deceit."

His vote of confidence is unexpected. Appreciated? But it also means there's no denying how desperate we are, how *last chance* this last chance really is.

"I'm *fine*. And she knows this is just a temporary position. That *pays*."

"Ah. I'm guessing you're thinking of the latest hospital bills."

"Did you know health insurance is a scam?" Then it occurs to me Silas is here, in person, *on a Sunday*. Panic slaps a shiver right across my neck. "Silas, my mom—"

"She's *fine*. Relatively. You know, I don't *only* show up for bad news."

The nervous adrenaline thins in my veins. *She's okay, she's okay.* The relief tastes better than any animal cracker.

"I came to give you a heads-up, off the record. Pastor Webb is using the Widow Witch's absence to get folks riled up, and everyone's more nervous than ever. I've heard his sermons are leaning hard against magic. *All* magic. He's taken to preaching out in the town square."

"That is *exactly* bad news, Silas. Why didn't you just tell me this over the phone? Afraid my mom is tapping our cells?"

"Do you think your mom knows how to tap a phone line?"

Good point. "Next time, text me."

"Would you have answered?"

Another good point.

"Like I said, I'm here *unofficially*. No paper trail. Believe it or not, you and I are on the same side. But the mayor's team can't be seen playing favorites when it comes to the church and the

Witches in the Holler." He sighs and, for a moment, even looks stressed. "Oh, I've also been instructed to tell you to call your mother more often."

Ha, there it is. His ulterior motive for visiting. "Sneaky. At least she feels well enough to pester."

"When she calls, just expect your typical fear of Warlocks and higher magic. But stand firm, don't internalize that nonsense. We both know you can't afford therapy."

I'm about to stumble over a very unwitty comeback when I notice what's stuffed into his tote bag. "Flowers?" He's brought bright yellow marigolds. To visit me. At my mom's request. "Are you *sure* my mother knows you're gay?"

He rolls his eyes. "She told me to convince you it's an early gift to mark Beltane."

I snort. Sending flowers is her way of showing me she's watching, snooping from afar.

My mom's scheming reminds me I promised our postman I'd introduce him to Silas. I *could* invite Silas in for dinner. Feed him well before I drop the need-a-favor bomb. Any respectable Southerner would.

Before I decide, Silas takes a gruff call on his phone, which ends too quickly to be anything good.

"Connection dropped," he says, wincing. "Apparently, Webb is trying to call a town council meeting about canceling the Witches' Beltane celebration. Something about *pagan Hearthwitch rituals* attracting the Widow Witch. If the council meets, I'll have to be there as your mom's stand-in, but I won't be able to interfere or anything. Only the elected members can—Jesus, listen, I've got to go. I'll update you later. Take the flowers."

He shoves them at me. "Remember, call your mother, or I'll have to hear about it. Her rants, I swear. *She* needs a therapist."

"I know." Just add it to my growing to-do list.

"I mean it: Do not avoid her. Neither of us wants her jailbreaking from the hospital to—"

"I'm hanging up now, Silas."

"We're not even on the phone—"

I close the door but stall in the foyer, thinking. Worrying. If this conversation between the church and the town council escalates, folks are going to start asking more questions about their missing mayor. Even if the position is more ceremonial than democratically elected, Silas can't help Mom dodge her constituents forever. He might be on my side, but time isn't.

Cradling the marigolds, I return to the kitchen just as Lazlo says, "What does that mean, Ms. Zeen?"

"What does what mean?" I ask Lazlo, moving to the large farmhouse sink to put the flowers in water.

"*In-fa-chew-aysh—*"

"No schoolwork during dinner, Lazlo," Warlock Knight says before the kid can finish. Then his gaze moves from me to the flowers. And stays. The air shifts, like the Widow Witch has blown in a brand-new kind of storm. "Flowers?" he says, exactly the way I said it on the porch.

Ms. Zeen coughs.

"Early Beltane gift, from a friend." I don't mention my mom. Tonight, the thought of lying to the Warlock makes me feel like rancid oil for some reason I won't be examining, so I go with good ole omission.

The Warlock pulls at his gloves. Like they aren't already tight enough. "My garden has plenty of flowers already."

"That no one gets to see." I drop the marigolds into a vase with more force than necessary.

Okay, maybe my mood is pervious when it comes to hearing about Oris Webb and Gertha Fudge and their disdain for magic.

The oven timer dings.

We plate the food and set the table.

As we sit, Lazlo picks the spot next to me. On the other side of the table, Ms. Zeen is across from Lazlo and the Warlock is across from me. I notice the Warlock distinctly avoids sitting at the head of the table.

We eat.

The Warlock surprises me again by being the first to interrupt the clanging of utensils. "I'll regret asking, but *why* do we need Wi-Fi?"

Lazlo shouts "Dog facts!" at the same time I say "Recipes!"

Ms. Zeen's eye roll is nearly audible.

The Warlock looks between Lazlo and me. "One, *you* don't have a dog. And two, *you* have recipes. Surely you've found the collection of kitchen grimoires in the library by now."

Have I. My mood lifts at the mere mention of the sacred place. "Yes, but sometimes the church choir class of 1964 doesn't have the most current baking tips."

"You didn't find the recipe book exclusively devoted to scuppernong pies helpful?"

"You know what a scuppernong is? I'm impressed."

"And I didn't even have to Google it."

I hear it even though I don't believe it. "Did you just make a *joke*?"

His lips twitch. "Perhaps."

Ms. Zeen blows on her dinnertime cup of tea. "It was quite alarming, sir."

"I'll avoid it in the future, Ms. Zeen."

"Internet," I try again, "brings you into the modern age. That's reason enough."

"You and I didn't have Wi-Fi as children, so why does Lazlo need it?"

I pause, my fingers gripping my sharp, *throwable* fork. "How old do you think I am?"

"Don't answer that, sir," comes Ms. Zeen's sigh.

"Wi-Fi will make you more a part of the community," I press. Then pause. "All right, *fine*. The church ladies don't use the internet. But the online world can keep a person young even better than my food can." I also want Lazlo to have something to keep him busy after I leave.

"Ms. Frost, I gave up trying to be a young man for good reasons," he says.

"That's a shame. You'd be good at it."

Silence. The Warlock opens his mouth to respond, then changes his mind. Even Ms. Zeen actually looks up from her tea.

"Why is it so quiet?" Lazlo whispers.

The Warlock clears his throat. "I'll consider the Wi-Fi."

"Thanks, I already bought it," I blurt, gathering myself.

"You what—"

"And you have a microwave coming."

"*And*—are we now the Ritz-Carlton?"

"You know what a Ritz is?"

"The cracker?" Lazlo asks.

"I'm not Jurassic, Ms. Frost. I just don't have *the internet*."

"Y'all need to stop saying *the internet* like *the moon*." I aggressively stab an innocent piece of okra. "Microwave. Coming. Eventually. It's tricky enough getting things delivered in town, much less here."

The Warlock scoffs. "You're talking to the postman now?"

"And *don't you dare* ruin my hard work and frighten him off. Come say hello next time."

"*I'll consider it.* Any other requests?"

Lazlo looks up. "Can we—"

"Procure a pet of the canine variety? I told you, no."

"But Ms. Zeen likes the idea. She says being good with dogs will make me an *el-luh-jib-ble* catch for someone one of these days. Did you know that Elvis Presley liked to give poodles to his girlfriends?"

Eh, she's not wrong. "Dating standards have truly fallen," I say. "Do you have a boyfriend or girlfriend, Ms. Honey?"

Lazlo stares at me with two uncomfortably bright orbs. Why is the kitchen so hot? The ovens aren't even going any longer.

"Yes," I say.

"Ew," Lazlo mutters.

Another, more discreet pair of hazel eyes tiptoe in my direction. Or am I hallucinating?

"The AGA stove and I are in a committed relationship," I add, earning a giggle out of the kid. I'm wrong—the Warlock isn't looking at me at all, just Lazlo laughing. He's disinterested as ever. But I do catch the Governess giving the man some kind of warning stare. If folks would just say what's on their mind in this house, I *swear*.

"What about you, Mr. Knight?" I ask. "Never wanted to marry?"

Ms. Zeen lets out a cough that might've been a brave chortle.

Aha. A clue. I arranged this dinner to get information, and I've found that the right recipe for a person's best health often comes from a meal they shared with their partner.

The Warlock raises an eyebrow but refuses to look in my direction. "Have you?"

Lord, *I'm* supposed to be interrogating *them*. "I'm the town's only Farewitch—I'm busy. I have other priorities." Though, I've been busy for six years now. Longer. And counting.

Then a darker thought feasts on my attention: What if powerful magic *always* leads to loneliness?

Folks might blame bad luck on forces out of their control, and then their judgment twists spellwork into the enemy. Magic isn't bad by nature, but there are always people looking to exploit fear of the unknown and the different.

"Ms. Frost, are you with us?" The soft clatter of the Warlock's knife startles me.

"Sorry. Present." *Present?* Woof. Who is he, my professor?

"As I was saying," the Governess drawls, "Gertha and her biddies are just old gossips—"

"Except Beauregard," says Lazlo.

"—yes, dear, except Beauregard—and for all their complaining, they'd trade their souls for an ounce of magic to lord over the rest of us."

The Warlock's shoulders tense. "That could be why the pastor was concerned enough to visit my Manor. Someone who wants magic badly enough will try to control it. Fear and envy make people blind to consequence and cost. For all her violence, at least the Widow Witch understands balance."

His eyes flick to me.

"But you, Ms. Frost—you nearly invited these very same neighbors into my house," he says, dry as a second-day baguette.

"In my defense, the Church Cavalcade never made it past the porch." Rett, on the other hand . . . The house *did* let him in.

If the Warlock doesn't want strangers snooping around, he should be less enigmatic and—well, I can't control the will of an entire holler. I'm only one woman. Or I used to be. Just a daughter, when the recipe of my life was simple. But now I'm a Farewitch, a caretaker, a personal chef and quasi nutritionist, a Warlock whisperer, and a part-time fraction teacher. I'm the chance at survival standing between my mom, the Warlock, and a great big nothing.

"Besides, it's not a bad thing if the Holler becomes a little less terrified of you and your magic. *Sir.*" He can't fester in this farmhouse forever. "Folks would like you, if you let them."

"You don't even like me, and you're five and a half feet of bottled epinephrine."

"It's just caffeine. And vitamin D." I shrug. "Who knows, one day, you might even be able to go into town and buy apple butter yourself."

He gives me a look so furious I almost don't catch the slight shade of pink under the sun spots on his cheeks.

After supper, I stay at the sink to wash dishes.

A shadow drapes across the sink right beside me.

The Warlock grabs a dishcloth and starts drying the clean dishes. Low bar for men, but something behind my rib cage squeals at the sight of a man doing a household chore. Witches expect Warlocks to make messes, not tidy them.

We wash and dry, dare I say it, in comfortable silence.

Eventually, he speaks first. "Ms. Zeen also believes having more . . . visitors to the house would be good for me." His voice stays low, too low to reach the Governess and Lazlo at the table. "Perhaps you're right. I could be more amicable with those who make the trek."

Understatement of his ambiguously not-immortal life. Seems Silas *and* the Governess might be on my side. "You can unclench your jaw when you say that. Our postman didn't even flee in terror the last time."

When he doesn't reply, something else he said resurfaces, and I can't contain the troublesome Frost curiosity any longer. "Why does it matter?" I blurt.

"Why does what matter?"

"That I got flowers. That they could be from someone."

One eyebrow goes up. "Are they?"

"That's not the point."

"Then there's no point in discussing it," he says. "Ask me the question again when it becomes relevant."

The *nerve*. "But why would it matter?"

"Why would *what* matter, Ms. Frost? You are frustratingly vague."

"If I were seeing someone. Can I not date in my free time, while I stay here?"

To his credit, he doesn't immediately laugh at the idea I could have this thing called *free time*. He wrings the dish towel into a twist.

A tight twist. "That's not my decision to make. As long as you don't allow distractions to pull you away from your work."

"I don't think we're at risk of that." At this point, I should probably check the expiration date on my sex life.

He accepts a dripping mixing bowl from me. "Good."

"Right. Good." I look back to the dishes, trying to ignore the Warlock's elbow, which has somehow gotten *really* close to mine.

Then, without warning, he deposits the last clean dish on the counter next to me and evacuates the room like management's sprung a fire drill.

Every Warlock for himself, apparently.

Chapter Twelve

FRIDAY, APRIL 29

53 DAYS UNTIL THE SUMMER SOLSTICE

Honey's Helpful Hint, from
Honey Frost's Southern Cookbook
for Recipes Gone Wrong:

Remember to remove the skins and seeds of your scuppernongs; the inherent bitterness will make everything else sour.

The Warlock disappears for five days, but who's counting?

Me. I'm counting. Crossing them off on a tiny calendar in my room as we've approached the day I said I would reopen the Apothakery. Tomorrow.

Governess Zeen says he's deep in research for a client, another Warlock up in Louisville, and that he rarely surfaces during these projects.

Or he's avoiding me the way I dodge imitation butter. I'm not sure what's worse, vanishing or hiding. Both are synonymous with fleeing in my grimoire.

Still, I keep leaving him potential remedies in the kitchen. Bourbon butter cake, scuppernong pie (good for *tempers*) . . . I just hope he tells me if—*when*—something works. Lazlo cooks with me whenever he doesn't owe Ms. Zeen homework. While he sneaks more bites of food than he makes, his energetic chatter works like caffeine, and I'm able to whisk away my evenings in the Manor's library, digging through the archives for clues. Though with more folks in town requesting special orders and deliveries, I barely have time to hunt for that recipe that tastes *right* in my mouth before I even make it.

If I just had time to work harder, mine deeper . . .

But my woefully hopeful (wopeful?) estimate of the three weeks I would need is up and I'm no closer to cures for any ailment. I'm supposed to leave in the morning, and for the first time, the idea of returning to the Apothakery doesn't warm my belly like hearty soup.

So rather than packing like a sensible person, I'm nestled in a leather wingback, an old cookbook from a now-nonexistent gardening club in my lap.

Hours pass. I fall into a cozy rhythm of flipping pages, listening to the sigh of leather as I burrow deeper into my chair. I put a fire in the person-sized stone hearth, and the warm *pop*s keep me company on an otherwise quiet and chilly spring evening.

My entire life, I've been too busy to be bored. But when one of three other people in a labyrinthine farmhouse disappears, the extra silence echoes.

A rebellious frustration blooms inside me, like hungry yeast. Honestly, it's been fermenting for a while. Why is the Warlock so protective of his isolation? He could stand to lose his dismal reputation, not fortify the mystery.

The folks of Foxe Holler fear the Warlock—but what is *he* so afraid of?

My annoyed mood and that question have me pacing the stacks, trekking deeper until I reach a darker, forgotten corner where the warmth from the hearth doesn't venture. It's here I find a curious thing.

A single bookcase looms in its own locked enclave behind wrought iron bars.

I jiggle the bars, searching for a door. Who locks up books? Maybe the volumes I can see through the shadows are dastardly family photo albums with pictures of Warlock Knight dressed up for Halloween. The mental image makes me smile for the first time in a week.

But I don't have the magic necessary to break into this. If I were a Bookwitch, I could coax out a few shy volumes. My eyes catch on one with glimmering, gold lettering on the spine.

The *Foxe Holler Yonder*.

The town's local newspaper. Whole issues or clippings? Then I spot the detail that makes my chest tight: The year beneath the name—it's twenty-five years ago.

I need to see inside that book.

Pushing my entire body against the cage for leverage, I thrust as much of an arm as I can through the bars and reach, fingers wiggling. My middle finger grazes the spine. I'm so close—

The metal of the cage begins to burn.

Literally, *burn*, suddenly as hot as a cast-iron skillet right out of the oven, and my skin sears wherever it makes contact.

I yank out my arm so fast, I smell singed hair as my forearm grazes the bars. A scream builds in my throat but I clamp my mouth shut, biting my cheek so hard I taste blood and flesh. I drop to my knees, breathing through the pain. I've had my fair share of kitchen burns, but I can already feel the blisters bubbling, eager to burst—

Then the pain vanishes.

It's just . . . gone.

I look down at my hands. Nothing. No angry blisters, no charred hairless patches of pink and raw flesh. The only evidence of the last ten seconds is the adrenaline powering my heart.

Okay. The house's message is painfully clear. Don't touch the restricted books.

But . . . there's not a single burn on me. That thought almost unsettles me more. I'm a Farewitch. A burn, I can handle. Even a nasty one. But an illusion that can make me *think* I'm burning, with no relief from the pain? Terrifying.

This magic can't just be the house. After so many years, the Warlock's power and personality have probably soaked through this place like marsala in tiramisu. Unfortunately for him, this only makes me more determined to puzzle out his history. The one memory I barely managed to grab from him my first day was clouded, murky like bad creek water. Somehow, I feel as if the more he holds on to memories like that, the more they'll poison him.

His past has to be the key to his illness.

What the hell is in that book?

That question is how I end up right outside the Warlock's bedroom door at midnight.

I raise a fist. Lower it. Raise it a second time. *Woman up, Frost.* I switch hands, which helps, and knock.

No answer. I give him a minute in case he's sleeping. Do Warlocks sleep? They must, that's why he's not answering. He has lots of . . . subconscious spellcasting and omens to decipher.

Another knock.

This is getting ridiculous. He can't avoid me forever.

My third knock echoes with disappointment. I thought he must be up at all hours, like me. Kindred night owls. He *seems* like a personification of a brooding nocturnal strigiform.

Fine. So be it. I've haunted his house this long without any success; he probably thinks I'm a lousy Farewitch. But no one can tell me I don't give my all learning to be better. The bitterness in my throat tastes like the sour seeds of a scuppernong. Why do I even care if I don't see him on my last night? I don't need to say goodbye.

I know what I *do* need, though.

Ten minutes later in my bathroom down the hall, I sink into the perfect warm bath.

My sigh reverberates off the green tile. Bubbles tickle my arm hair that I swore burned off in the library. The warmth loosens a knot behind my navel. This must be what pasta feels like, steeping in its own juices, limp with leisure. No wonder it tastes so wholesome.

But my mind soon slips back to worrying. The Warlock will

become just another person I can't cure. Even if I were riding high on a full night's sleep and spent half my time between here and the Apothakery, could I really make this double life here at the Manor work for much longer? On top of helping my mom? I'm used to life yanking me in different directions, but this time, I don't feel the satisfaction of overachievement. Only overwhelmed, like I've got two cakes baking at the same time, except the catch is the ovens are on opposite sides of town.

The spiraling thoughts churn with heat under my skin, and sweat pools in my pores.

The Frosts aren't ones for *Small Wishes*. Only big moves, big confidence, big intention. Since I'm the only heir to the Frost legacy, expectations have always been high. I know that. *So well.* But it means that over the years, a single step forward feels akin to failure. What Farewitch can't handle her own Apothakery?

My cheeks flush, the bathwater almost too warm now. Anxious heat pumps through my veins. *Jesus*, it's warm. Typical Frost, turning a relaxing soak into a stressful self-interrogation. How long have I been in the tub? Shouldn't the water be cooling, not getting hotter?

In half a second, the uncomfortable warmth turns from stinging to a white-hot pain. My skin is on fire. Half faint, ears buzzing, I realize the water isn't just hot. It's nearly *boiling*.

I'm five seconds from passing out, but with my last ounce of energy, I flop over the side of the tub and onto the bath mat with a wet and undignified *SLAP*.

The relief is glorious and instant, like I've been dunked in an ice bath.

My skin cools, lungs open. The searing adrenaline dissipates, my pulse slows. Splayed on the bath mat, I'm a brand-new piglet, skin rosy like I got run over by a pink highlighter.

When I dare to peer back into the tub, there's no steam, no bubbles. No waves of heat. I dip a finger in the sudsy water. Tepid.

What. The. Hell.

Just like the metal bars in the library. It's like I've conjured the danger out of nothing, my imagination my worst enemy. The house is still playing tricks on me.

Antagonizing a maybe-sentient house is not a smart move in the middle of the night, so I throw a towel around myself and make a beeline for my bedroom. Not today, house. In the drafty corridor, my misty skin goes taut in the chill. I barely register my steps, brain on auto. Maybe the Warlock's illness appears as a loss of control? What does it look like when wish-granting magic goes haywire—

SMACK.

I swerve around a corner and run right into a wall that did not exist before.

Not a wall. A man. The hard chest of a man.

"You're *here,*" Warlock Knight mutters at the exact same time I blurt, "Good Lord, I thought you were a murderer."

As my pulse slows with relief, I notice he's looking at me with an expression verging on surprise. Or disappointment. "Careful, sir, someone might think you're relieved." Evidently, he was hoping I'd quit.

"Our three weeks are up, are they not? I assumed you left for good."

"You clearly don't know Witches very well, sir. Or me. We keep our promises to help."

Frustration overtakes his voice. "That's not . . ."

Then he does a double take, from my toes to my wet blonde hair.

My cheeks warm, my left hand keeping my towel in place. I probably look like a drowned dog, and feel just as ridiculous. Until I see he's still wearing his gardening clothes. Even the gloves. What, was he gardening at midnight?

Then I remember I've got my bangs rolled around one of Momaw's old mesh hair curlers, my secret to keeping them bouncy enough to stay out of my eyes while I cook. So I probably look like a drowned grandma-dog. Grandmutt energy for sure.

But he's not looking at my hair, bless him. His gaze sticks on my bare shoulders, then his mouth tightens and now he's looking anywhere *but* at me. Which mostly leaves fussy wallpaper to stare at. He moves to push past me, so I brace my free hand against his chest, pushing back.

"Are you avoiding me?" All my patience evaporated in the bathroom.

"We live under the same roof, Ms. Frost. That would be difficult." His gloved hand absently rubs his chest where my palm was a second ago, right over my damp fingerprints. "Where did you go on Saturday evening?" he asks, out of nowhere.

Whiplash. "Excuse me?"

"Before Sunday's meal."

I rub my temple. And the night started out so peaceful. Before Sunday . . . *Before the flowers.* Is that what this is about? Surely not. "I spend Saturday evenings with my mom."

"Why the same day?"

I keep my answer vague. "She, uh, likes the routine."

"And she will not visit you here? The rest of the Holler has no problem doing so."

Touché. "It's easier for me to visit her. She's busy . . . being mayor." I want to be intimidating and cross my arms, but can't risk letting my towel fall.

"Why do I feel like you're not telling me the whole truth, Ms. Frost?"

"Why do you have books locked up in the library, Mr. Knight?"

He finally looks at me, intense hazel irises peeking out from dark lashes. "That is beyond the realm of your concern."

He steps back, so I take a step forward. He doesn't just get to flee like some spooked armadillo. A spooked, grumpy armadillo. "*All of this* concerns me. You, the Manor, the locked doors—for chrissakes, the house just tried to make me into gumbo!"

Not the clearest explanation of what happened, but I don't miss how his gaze roams over me, searching. For proof of injury? "Don't worry. The house doesn't eat *stubborn*."

Good Lord. What *does* it eat? "My point is, the house is upset when *you're* upset. The kitchen hides my thermometers, the clocks never keep the same time, and I can't keep a candle lit to save my life. The more you brood—"

"I don't brood."

"—the more negative energy builds. I can't do my job if I can't trust where I sleep."

"Then leave," he says, a vicious edge to his voice. "You've given me enough of your time already."

We're still uncomfortably close, but after the illusions, I'm glad he's here, solid and real and smelling of summer rain. Yet the house's illusions are made of heat and burning and death. Strange. Doubly strange is how the fear of something else mutes whatever fear's still stirring in my chest for him. It's not gone, but it's diluted.

"My timeline of three weeks was based on finding a cure. I haven't found one yet, so I stay." For him *and* my mom. I don't realize I've made the decision until I say it. Already, an idea for reopening the shop while I'm here is forming in my head.

"How long?"

"As long as it takes." At that, an odd look passes across his face, one I don't know what to do with. "You asked me to be here, Mr. Knight. A Farewitch. To help you. Remember?"

"Perhaps I'm delaying the inevitable and don't deserve the help."

I can't be any more exposed than I am now, so I take a steadying breath and a leap of faith, and hope I come out unburned. Again. "Why? Are all the rumors about you in town true?"

He clasps his gloved hands behind his back. "That depends. What are they this year?"

"Pretty bad."

"I would be worried if they weren't."

"Murder."

"Uninspired, but expected."

"That you're a harbinger of droughts and famine."

"An old favorite."

"You make everyone's eggs rot and spoil."

"Interesting, that's a new one."

"Pyromania—"

He blows out a puff of air. "*Always* the library with these people."

"They say you burned it down."

The warm hazel shifts to a dark moss in the dim hallway. But even his glare is bizarrely comforting. It's still familiar, tangible. "Do you believe them, Ms. Frost?"

"Do *you*?" Should I be worried he isn't denying the accusations, or that he's accepting blame for crimes he knows he didn't commit? "If they're hung up on the library, why not open yours to the public? Or donate some of the money you definitely have to building a new one."

"You place entirely too much faith in people, Ms. Frost." He moves to pass me on the other side but I cut him off again.

"And you place too little faith in them, *sir*." I square my shoulders as best I can. This speech would be a lot more effective if I were clothed. "There's a chance I might not find your cure. Not when half the house is off-limits. The books—"

"For good reason, which is why I've warned you not to wander—"

"You promised me resources!"

"So work with the resources I've given you, and do not ask about the books again," he snaps, his harsh tone echoing. "Now move out of my way, Ms. Frost, and return to your room."

The third time he moves around me, I jump directly into his path.

At his incensed look, a deliciously feral delight curls in my gut. "Do not," he says through gritted teeth, "make me pick you up again."

I ignore the threat as a new thought occurs to me. "Were you awake when I knocked on your door earlier?" He doesn't reply, which is all the reply I need. This ridiculous man. "Why didn't you answer?"

His dark brows pull together. "Because you came to my bedroom. At midnight. It would not have been appropriate for me to answer."

I try not to blush but probably fail. "What in the world did you think I came for?"

"I—why *did* you come to my bedroom?"

"To ask about the books in the library!" Ridiculous, *ridiculous* man.

I force myself to take a breath, to really taste the anger on my tongue like I'm giving a sharp wine a second chance. His instinct is to ice me out, not burn down his obstacles. There's no way he's causing these illusions of heat by himself, not intentionally. This man's a lot of things, but he's not emotional.

The Manor, on the other hand . . . It feels like the house is losing control, more and more each day, as long as its Warlock remains sick. As his illness grows worse, so does the instability of his magic and anything connected to it.

The Warlock's jaw unclenches. "We'll finish this discussion at a more civilized hour. You're naked."

Good Lord. "Please, you're too old to be bashful and too young to be this serious."

A draft whips through the hall and I shiver. He leans forward and his immediate closeness, the ice in his eyes, is kindling for my gooseflesh.

"You should not roam the halls, especially at night, lest you find yourself an irresistible meal for whatever might be hungry." His raspy voice claws across the distance between us. "Young Witches should be asleep at this hour, so go to bed before I put you to bed."

My breath hitches and my mouth snaps shut.

He turns, heading back the way he came. With immeasurable dignity, I stick out my tongue in the direction of his retreating back.

Attawitch, Momaw's voice whispers.

The minute I get back to my room, I text Arna Jean.

What would you say to a more permanent internship?

Arna Jean Claywell
Benefits? Health insurance?

free snacks . . .

Arna Jean Claywell
listening

Chapter Thirteen

SUNDAY, MAY 1

51 DAYS UNTIL THE SUMMER SOLSTICE

Honey's Helpful Hint, from
Honey Frost's Southern Cookbook
for Recipes Gone Wrong:

Apple seeds and cherry pits contain cyanide.
Cures and poisons are just a matter of dosage.

Sex is fun, but farmers' markets are better than any I've had in my thirty-one years.

Especially on the first morning of May, when the world is blooming and the sun glows with near-summer energy, no sign of clucking church ladies or Widow Witches.

Farmers' markets in Foxe Holler are an institution, filling the town square in front of our small courthouse every weekend. A rural holler might not have a Starbucks, but we're lousy with farms. Jeweled beets, lacy collard greens, strawberries red and glossy, dried lavender, handsewn quilts, jars of preserves with no labels because they came directly from someone's kitchen.

The market is extra rosy this morning because I'm seeing it through new, wide eyes.

On cue, Lazlo gives my hand an excited—and sticky—squeeze as he absorbs the buzz of activity. "Do you think Beauregard and Ms. Buchanan are here, too?"

"Here or church." I return his squeeze and forgo asking how his hand is already glutinous.

The kid's fidgety brain is often distracted or five thoughts ahead. Fresh air helps, just another reason I've made it my mission to take him into town.

We stop at the Cumberland family's stall, where they sell extra goods from their general store. Today it's spiced mushroom scones so dense, I can smell the butter. When I pay, the middle-aged woman—one of the Cumberland triplets, I'm not sure which—who takes my cash gives me the meanest mug, like I've sullied her ancestors. Then I remember—it was *her* son who disappeared just last year. Sonny Cumberland. We're around the anniversary of when the Widow Witch took him. Pitifully poor timing on my part.

My good mood flickers like a weak pilot light, my usual confidence at the market shaken. Even my friendliest neighbors no longer seem willing to be polite and hide their anger over my decision to help the Warlock. Or maybe, with Pastor Webb challenging the presence of magic, the folks who never liked magic to begin with finally feel free to be vocal about it.

Thankfully, Lazlo's too busy stuffing my half of our shared scone into his cheeks to notice the chilly treatment. "Yooh ge todu diss evur wookend?"

"*We* can do this every weekend." Momaw Frost took me to my very first market, and I'll chase that high forever. Being able to share this with Lazlo, the buzzy *hello*s and handshakes—

"You charged me three dollars a pound two weeks ago, Earl. Not five. Three! Do I look like a tourist who took a wrong turn at Mammoth Cave?"

Ah, right on time. I quickly locate who we came to meet.

Instant relief caffeinates my veins. Even though my favorite Bookwitch looks to be at war with Mr. Earl over Granny Smiths.

Lazlo and I hustle over before things get messy.

Mr. Earl crosses his arms, watching us approach. "It's five now. For you *and* your friends."

The younger Claywell whirls around, her long braids spinning with her. Her eyes flash behind golden octagonal glasses that glimmer against her dark skin. Like her older brother, what she lacks in good eyesight she makes up for in lanky limbs.

"Honeydew! One sec." She turns back to face her victim. "What the hell kind of underhanded malarky is that?"

Lazlo gives a wicked little chuckle at her vocabulary.

Mr. Earl sneers. "What, can the Witches and magic among us not conjure up enough money to support your local farmers? Look here—that Warlock even has a Farewitch babysitting."

"No—*I'm* babysitting *her*," Lazlo says, tugging at my hand.

My confidence resurfaces. "Mr. Earl, I've bought apples from you for how many years?" And I'm the sole supplier of the honey bourbon bread pudding for his insomnia. The man doesn't want me baking in some revenge espresso.

He looks away. "That's when you ran the Apothakery for your neighbors. Now you're the Warlock's Farewitch. Not mine."

Heat wraps my neck. "I'm not *his* Farewitch. I'm everyone's. I'm simply trying to help someone who has not asked for help before. Perhaps you can be generous and allow me to use *my* time as I choose."

But—is it really mine? Or does a Farewitch's time belong to her patients and customers and neighbors first?

Arna Jean pushes her frames onto her head like sunglasses, but they drop right back onto her nose. "And we won't be up-charged for mediocre apples with *worm spots*—"

"Have a pleasant day," I tell Mr. Earl, ushering both Arna Jean and Lazlo from the stall before apples become projectiles. I'm not going to let this ruin my morning, but that doesn't mean a girl can't hope his fruit rots.

"Apples aren't even in season!" Arna Jean calls over her shoulder.

When we're alone between stalls, she adjusts her hoodie. It's sleeveless, with a Technicolor galaxy framing a massive flipped middle finger. It reads: *Cosmic Bitch.*

"The minute I mentioned I was going to help run the Apothakery while you're away—*well.* Forget apples, that man should grow some manners."

"The Apothakery missed you," I say by way of a greeting.

My friend rolls her eyes, making a *psssh* sound. "*You* missed me."

"Nonsense. Millennials don't miss Gen Z. Those are the rules."

My idea to have Arna Jean reopen the shop while I'm still at the Manor won't fix everything, but it might assuage my regulars. It's a start.

She's only six years younger than me, but with her innate magical finesse, social media fluency, and genius—double major in economics and math, minor in marketing and two or three languages—not to mention her scary-accurate vision boards, it all makes me look like a jaded old crone. Not unlike how I see the Warlock, I suppose. If he'd had an Arna Jean all these years, someone younger to keep him on his toes, he might be an entirely different person.

Or still just a cranky grump.

"Also, how did I never hear your brother got the postman job?" I'm not *that* obsessed with my day-to-day grind. Am I?

She waves a manicured hand. "No one knows. That's how quiet he is. Foxe Holler will have a library before you find Rett out on the town, or out of his uniform. He has not a single dating app. A square so square his only hope is to multiply by himself."

"Was that a *math joke*?"

"Are those *clogs*?"

I look down. "They're practical for standing on—"

"*And* farmeralls? I was gone way too long. When's the last time you did a fit check?"

"A what?"

She lets out a displeased hum. "Never mind. I knew it. You're lost without me."

“How kind of you to grace me with your presence in my hour of need.”

“My people will invoice you my appearance fee.”

“Do all Witches talk as fast as you two?” Lazlo says.

We both jump, startled. Arna Jean looks down. “Your interns are getting awfully young.”

“I’m Lazlo,” he replies, giving her a toothy grin.

“Nice to meet you, Lazlo. I’m Arna Jean. You can call me RJ.”

I shift on my feet, restless, and can’t resist asking any longer. “How was your postgraduation world tour? How was the food?” For a couple years, I got a taste of what the world was like outside the Holler. Just enough to whet my appetite.

She shrugs. “Danced in Berlin. Hiked in Corcovado. Made strudel in Salzburg. Ate my weight in roti in Bhubaneswar. Kissed some people in . . . a number of places. It’s easy to be lots of different people the farther away you go.” She inhales, a big two-nostril effort, like she’s picking up the smells of sunshine and good dirt, the soul of the Holler. “But home is home.”

“Glad to hear Webb and Fudge didn’t greet you with angry signs.”

“Oh, I ran into Fudge’s crotchety ass the minute I got home. That lady believes too much in Jesus and not enough in moisturizing. I like to watch her face add a new wrinkle for every piercing I get.” Her eyes narrow. “Is it true you’ve been pissing off Webb and his church ladies? I hope you’re not doing all that labor for free.”

I catch her up as best I can. By the time I finish, I’m not so sure my plan is a great idea anymore. By helping the Farewitch who’s helping the Warlock, she’s stepping into the middle of trouble. I just don’t know what kind yet.

Two nights ago, I ran bangs-first into the chilling reminder that the Warlock is a magical being who could pluck me off the vine of existence. *Go to bed before I put you to bed.* I shiver. Though, it might only be at the memory of his deep voice. Despite the cold edge of his attitude, something about being half naked in front of him really changes the taste of any fear I might have.

"And the Warlock does pay me. Well." Hence why I was able to even hire Arna Jean temporarily.

Her brown eyes churn with mischief. "I bet he does."

I choke on water I'm not even drinking. "It's not like that—he's not—" My hands go over Lazlo's ears. "Are you accusing me of sleeping with a man to get something I want? Shame on you."

She snorts. "Please, you're too tired to ever bring someone home, or you're too busy to fight insurance over birth control. Either way, we both know you're not getting any."

There's a fragile little bubble of quiet and then it pops and we're both cackling like we're storybook Witches plotting over a bubbling cauldron. Maybe that's where the stereotypes come from. People are just afraid of women laughing.

Ears free now, Lazlo looks more confused than ever.

I wipe the joy from my eyes. "Are you *sure* about this? If the Widow Witch decides this year's victim is in line for my cornbread, I don't know if the shop's wards are strong enough to keep her out." Now that I've seen her power in person.

"I can handle the shop. Lucky for you, Bookwitches make terrific entrepreneurs. This Holler could use less blind faith and fear and more concrete hustle, more belief in numbers and evidence. Right now, all you need to worry about is healing your patients."

Plural. "Not sure I'm healing much these days."

Her expression softens. Besides Silas and Nurse Carolina, she's the only other person who knows the truth about my mom. "Self-pity looks as terrible on you as those clogs."

"Ouch," Lazlo says.

"Ignore the town, ignore the gossip. *You* came to *me*. Trust your gut."

She's right. As always. If the Warlock can ask for help at . . .

whatever age he is, I can do it at thirty-one. Lord, I've missed her. "Thank you. For taking care of the Apothakery."

"Because? Say it out loud."

I take a deep breath. "Because I can't do it alone and I need help."

"Gold star. Look at you, breaking one bad generational habit at a time. For the record, I would've said yes no matter what. My travel funds are dry. And we make too good a team."

The tight grip of anxiety inside my chest eases. "Because you're also a shamefully chronic workaholic?"

"Because I can't resist a challenge." She winks.

"Warlock Knight is . . ." As inflexible as cooling caramelized sugar. ". . . a challenge, all right," I mutter.

Arna Jean tilts her head. "Who?" she asks. Like in the span of thirty seconds, she completely forgot why I'm asking her to manage the shop in the first place.

"The Warlock," I repeat, words slow like the unease creeping across my neck.

"Right." Arna Jean shakes her head, like nothing's amiss. "Oh, your kid is gone. We should probably find him."

Lazlo is not, thank Jesus, gone.

He's just gotten bored and run back into the market. We easily catch up and stay a healthy distance behind him so he can explore. This kid could marathon the Dollar General a few or fifty times and still have energy. So far, no one's broken anything, glass or limb, and no one has food poisoning. A triumph, in my book.

Arna Jean lets her gaze wander across the stalls as we walk, no doubt keeping a lookout for the best ROI in produce. "Did you ask Mr. Knight if it was okay to bring the kid?"

"Of course," I huff.

"Did he agree?"

"Of course not." In fact, he expressly forbid it. But I brought Lazlo anyway. Maybe *because* the Warlock forbid it. Ms. Zeen white-knuckled the kettle at hearing my idea but agreed to keep my plan secret. Even she knows the boy needs some long-overdue social interaction. "*If you can't be good—*"

A wicked gleam appears in her eyes. "*Be good at it.*"

"I'll make sure the kid doesn't witness any R-rated situations."

For Witches, May 1 is also Beltane, a celebration of the oncoming sunshine of longer days and the warm results: sun-ripened fruits and vegetables all summer long. Beltane is flavor forged in heat, and thus an especially good holiday for Farewitches.

This year, though, Beltane just reminds me I've blown through three weeks like a bucket of movie-theater popcorn. The calendar on the wall of my bedroom now counts down toward the solstice, the Warlock's supposed End of Times. Fifty-one days. Fifty-one chances for the right recipe.

Arna Jean shrugs. "The sexy bonfires don't happen until the sun sets, anyway."

Beltane is also a celebration of growth—and fertility.

"That's exactly what I told his Governess but *she* didn't laugh."

Foxe Holler's bonfires aren't very sexy or fertility forward since many of the town's young Witches move away to put down roots in larger towns and cities. It's a miracle Arna Jean came back. These days, our celebrations are often organized by whichever older Witch is craving tradition. Carolina's had the last few, though I'm usually too busy with the shop to attend.

"Everyone is mad at us," says a small voice.

My eyes drop, along with my gut. Lazlo's reappeared at our side, looking much less excited than before. I follow his gaze.

At their stall, Farmer Kelsey and his missus are scowling at us over their okra and pole beans. Guess he won't be throwing his nephew at me anymore. Praise be. But I did want some of his tomatoes. It's fried. Green. Tomato. Season. And old Sam the beekeeper—who always gives me free clover honey like I'm a kitchen fairy in need of an offering—didn't even wave earlier. The Widow Witch took his son-in-law a few years back, but everyone in town knows Sam never cared much for the arrogant fellow's gambling problem.

The flame of my good mood sputters. I can't show Lazlo the wonderful parts of Foxe Holler *and* hide him from the whispers and stares that come with the bad parts.

This is a problem. But lately, what isn't?

Some folks get their gossip at church, but I get mine here at the market. That is, I used to. Now I can't very well get gossip from a town that's too busy gossiping about *me*.

But Lazlo is a clever nine-year-old . . . I've been trying to drag answers out of the Warlock when I should be asking the person who's had a front-row seat to his guardian's problems for almost a year. Any details about the man's past could help clue me in to his illness.

"Lazlo," I begin carefully, "has Mr. Knight ever—"

"*Murdered* anyone?" Arna Jean butts in. She shrugs off my glare. "What? The Holler doesn't know any version of your Warlock beyond"—air quotes—"primeval monster."

"He's not *my* Warlock."

"What does *pri-mee-vul* mean?" Lazlo asks.

Arna Jean adjusts her beanie on his head. She gave it to him earlier, saying he looked like an old woman had dressed him (Ms. Zeen had). "Antique. Old. Ancient."

The boy beams under her fussing. "He's super old."

I lean in. "How old, exactly?"

"Forty," Arna Jean guesses.

I cross my arms. "You've never even seen him!"

"Yes, but when I picture your Warlock, I'm getting a strong sense of handsome in a tortured-Austen-hero type of way. So yeah, forty."

"*He's not my Warlock.*" I look back to Lazlo. I try again. "Do you remember what you liked to do before you came to live with Mr. Knight?"

His eyebrows pull together in a flustered line. "I don't know."

My stomach sinks like a janky elevator. This is a scab my brain can't stop picking.

I don't like to use my memory affinity on kids. If they're too young, they don't fully understand how my magic works in tandem with their memories, and that feels invasive. But with Lazlo, I might need a glimpse of his memory for any real answers. He's already an orphan, so he doesn't have a rosy past, but what if I find something even scarier? A big black hole, no evidence of the Warlock at all, just like the rest of the Holler?

"Can you try to remember for me? Even something small?" I urge.

His face scrunches. "I played outside a lot. I was good at hunting for bugs. Went to school. Um . . ." More scrunching. "Dad read to me a lot. They used to . . . My mom cooked! She'd make lots of . . . I can't remember—*oh my goodness*."

Our heads swivel at his shout, geriatric necks cracking.

Pointing to a stand up ahead, he's full bounce now. "*Dog* treats!"

My snooping into the Warlock's past will have to wait. I hand the kid some cash from my overalls. "Go for it."

He hesitates. "Alone?"

Good point. What if folks start giving him more than just unkind glances? I'm not sure I could be responsible for my actions then.

Arna Jean gives me a reassuring look. *He can handle it.* "Come get us if you need anything, kid."

Lazlo throws back his shoulders and sprints ahead. Anything for Beauregard.

I watch him, trying to feed off his bravery. "If we ask him to carry our groceries, is that considered child labor?"

"Nah, builds character." Arna Jean holds up her tote of our slim produce pickings. "He's a strange little guy, isn't he?"

"He and Mr. Knight are on the same family tree, that's for sure."

But how did Lazlo's next of kin just so happen to be a powerful Warlock he'd never met before? Arna Jean's instinct isn't wrong, though. I'm chewing on what concrete facts we have, and if the town thinks the Warlock is murderous and merciless, where is the actual *proof*?

"What do the older folks know that we don't?" I think aloud. "Everyone's looking at us like we defaced the Jesus billboard at the town line."

"*Heaven Sent, Repent*? *Hell Is Real, Are You?* That's my favorite."

I nibble my bottom lip. "We're missing something."

"I'd say you're missing quite a lot, Miss Frost."

Reluctantly is an understatement for how we turn around.

Pastor Oris Webb stands behind us. The beige-ness of him, from his washed-out skin to his khaki ensemble, is out of place against the vibrant market produce. In one hand, he's carrying a bag full of yellow apples. In the other, a stack of paper. He *never* takes an interest in the market, and he picks today of all days to show up, the one time I take Lazlo into town?

Not good.

"Peace be with you," Webb says in greeting.

I recover fast. "It's rude to eavesdrop."

His Windex-blue eyes find my friend. "Good morning, Miss Claywell."

"*Miss* is outdated," Arna Jean says. "*Ms.* is just fine. And we're late for a thing."

Next to Webb, of course, is Gertha Fudge, still in her Sunday finery. She's half his height but looking up at us with twice the disapproval. "Not for church, certainly. I never see you Witches at service." Her gaze rakes over Arna Jean's piercings, which run the length of both her ears. Then the hoodie. Peeved wrinkles crack her sneer.

"I reckon you won't see us there next week, either," I say.

Webb grins but the mirth doesn't spread past his mouth. "Come now. One can't be too busy for the Lord."

"Amen," Ms. Fudge mutters.

"Excuse the interruption," Webb continues. "Open ears, open heart, yes? I listen for those asking for help."

"And what, pray tell, do you believe we're missing?" I don't *not* trust the minimal information the Warlock has shared with me, but I also know to compare sources. My mom didn't raise a blind-faith Witch.

Webb's head tilts just so. "You're trying to find fault with one Warlock, one man. That will only get you so far. The true heart of the corruption is magic itself."

Arna Jean steps closer to me, closing rank. "So says the man without any magic himself."

"*My* magic keeps your congregation feeling well enough to attend church," I say. "I doubt you'd like to lose your generous collection-plate donations."

Webb smiles. "Do we even need a Farewitch if we trust in the healing power of faith?"

My annoyance quickly blends with bitter anger. "The Holler's last mayor never had any magic. Was his early death just a sign he wasn't deserving of that same grace?"

"Does it matter? The previous Farewitch couldn't heal him. Ewing Summer tolerated Witches and magic, and it did him no favors. We need a hierarchy of authority in Foxe Holler, and I intend to deliver it."

"Is that why you're trying to postpone Beltane this year?" I snap.

Webb moves his bag of apples to one shoulder, then divides his stack of paper between a few of the folks who look like they came with him from church. "Not trying. Succeeding," he says as he and his followers begin passing out what I can now see are flyers.

"Succeeding?" Arna Jean asks.

Webb nods. "If you came to service, you would've heard. Just this morning, the town council agreed to cancel the annual bonfire."

Arna Jean and I snatch a few of the flyers. I blanch. They're barebones and to the point:

Can't Spell Warlock Without War

Farmers Against Fare-Weather Fare-Witches

Below each slogan is the same invitation to a candlelight vigil tonight instead, for all the partners and husbands the Widow Witch has disappeared. Held at the church, of course.

Sure enough, when I check my phone, there's a voicemail from Silas. I don't need to listen to it to know how the town council meeting went.

My eyes flick back to a third flyer: *Where Is Our Mayor?*

Before we can even ask how, Webb is already explaining.

"Folks were eager for a change. Someone merely suggested that perhaps these particular traditions could attract the Widow Witch. After all, each year you Witches celebrate Beltane, the Widow Witch comes. And the fire department is always eager for an early burn ban."

"Aren't *you* on the town council?" Arna Jean asks. "Why does the church get to have a voting representative when the mayor's office doesn't?"

A crowd has formed now, folks more interested in entertainment than groceries. With deliberate unhurried movements, Webb shakes a few hands around him as he answers.

"If our mayor is in absentia and not available to make decisions, to do what's best for the Holler, then that responsibility falls to the town council."

Agreement and curious murmurs hum in the air.

"Where *is* your mother, Miss Frost?" Webb adds, speaking more to the crowd now than to me. "It seems odd our mayor so rarely shows her face to the folks she claims to serve."

The expressions around me turn concerned and suspicious. Not for the first time, I wonder why my mother insists on keeping her illness hidden. Sometimes it feels like the two of us will suffocate underneath the need to look like we're *doing just fine.*

Then Webb's cleaner-fluid stare narrows on something past me.

Lazlo.

Alarms go off in my head. My instincts tell me to grab the kid and leave. Now. But I also don't want Lazlo to think something is wrong, or that he's not welcome in his own town.

"Is it true the Warlock has a young ward now?" Webb asks.

"He doesn't have any magic," I blurt. No way am I letting Lazlo get caught in the middle of this mess. Webb smiles, and a beat too late to do any good, I realize that's exactly the answer he wanted.

Ms. Fudge, who's been fanning herself with a flyer, perks up. "No magic? That boy should be in a home free from the threat of it, then."

"I doubt he'd feel comfortable anywhere else, since he's seen how you all treat neighbors," Arna Jean huffs. "A girl can't even buy apples anymore."

"*Insolent Witches.* There are plenty of decent, good country folk in this Holler, and we've got half a mind to—well, to report you."

Half a mind, I agree. "To *whom,* exactly?" My mother? Sheriff Fowler?

"Your board of magic, that's who," Fudge sputters.

"The Eldercraft," Webb says.

The what? Last I checked, Witches have covens, not bureaucracies. Local community instead of formal authority is our whole thing. At my confused look, Arna Jean leans over to me.

"The Eldercraft supervise higher magic. They're the main governing body for Warlocks. They're usually some of the oldest Warlocks, I think. With the most seniority and power."

Now I remember. My mom once mentioned they visited the

Holler when the library burned and the investigation couldn't reveal if it was Warlock or Witch magic.

My friend turns back to Fudge. "But only Warlocks. The Eldercraft don't oversee Witches. So report as many of our magical misdemeanors as you like. They won't care. They don't even bother with the Widow Witch."

Fudge slams her cane into the ground, but the earth is damp from recent rain, so it's more of a squelch, like a blade in a bloody, gurgling throat. "You know, a Bookwitch seems awfully useless without a library. Just like your piercings, girl. Pointless and trashy."

Arna Jean leans forward, her voice a threatening whisper. "*You should see my tattoos.*"

The old woman balks, puffing air so hard she could be mistaken for a grounded zeppelin.

Nevertheless, Fudge will have some Dickensian story about the little neglected orphan in a haunted house spreading through the Holler by tomorrow. Just what we need.

Sure enough, as I glance over at Lazlo, a woman behind the stall refuses the cash. Lazlo starts back our way, carrying a heavy expression of disappointment.

Any of my unease suffocates in the heat of my anger.

It's only then do I register the woman's face—that's Sonny Cumberland's wife. Or she was. Ellie's not a Cumberland by blood, but she helps her mother-in-law at their general store. She's the one who told me I was no longer welcome to shop there. Recognizing her doesn't make me any less mad, but it does keep me from walloping her with a bag of her own dog biscuits.

Maybe the market was *not* the best place to introduce Lazlo to the town.

Before Lazlo is back within listening distance, I step toward Webb and Fudge. "Lazlo is well taken care of. Your concern is unnecessary."

I've never had a dad, but Mr. Knight seems to have all the makings of a good father figure. I *know* he'd do anything for the kid.

But what if someone does start asking questions, poking around the Warlock's business? What happens if this Eldercraft does get involved?

Webb presses his palms together, as if in prayer. The crowd hushes, like they never left the church's sanctuary that morning.

"Foxe Holler always helps those at risk, especially those in danger because of magic. This is no longer just neighborly concern, Miss Frost. For you Witches, this is a warning. *Good* magic is *no* magic. So be smart about your allies."

He means the Warlock. Farewitches have historically been neutral, and to folks like him and Fudge, I've gone and picked a side in a game I didn't even realize had sides. *That* might be what they're truly afraid of.

"The Warlock is a *patient*. Just like any one of you. Not a threat."

"Is that what he told you?" Webb says, a terrible delight crossing his Play-Doh features.

Arna Jean visibly shivers, and I feel my gut become a wet pile of ash. The smoke alarms in my head grow louder, and the warm open air of the market becomes stifling.

"Powerful Warlocks don't get sick, Miss Frost. They get *cursed*."

Chapter Fourteen

SUNDAY, MAY 1 (STILL)

51 DAYS UNTIL THE SUMMER SOLSTICE

Honey's Helpful Hint, from
*Honey Frost's Southern Cookbook
for Recipes Gone Wrong:*

A festival for honoring the beginning of summer, Beltane is also a time for celebrating love and fertility. With bonfires, vibrant greenery, and other symbols of heat and the oncoming summer, this is also a holiday for welcoming change—and growth.

"Girl, you sound like Momaw with a bridge to burn. Slow. Down. He *what?*"

"He canceled the Beltane celebration, and he's got these godawful flyers," I whisper into my phone, even though the first floor of the farmhouse is empty.

Lazlo and I made it back to the Manor without any more trouble in town or the Warlock catching us, but Sunday supper was a stoic affair. I wasn't in the mood for conversation after what happened. I debated telling the Warlock about Webb, but I would've had to confess to our forbidden jaunt into town. After I made a quick batch of elderberry turnovers, the fire I kindled for a fight at the market smoked out in my chest, and I went to bed early.

Not a lie. I *did* sit on my bed—and waited to hear the others retreat to their rooms.

Then, barefoot to be silent, I snuck out into the house, Webb's sneer from the market clawing me from any rest.

Which is why I'm slinking through the Manor after dark. On a hunt.

Ignoring the Warlock's rules against wandering is becoming my favorite sport. I refuse to believe bad is the default in people, especially in Foxe Holler. Momaw certainly didn't. So if the Warlock is actually cursed, as Webb claims, this house is the best place to find the truth. Even if I have to peel answers out from under the country-chic wallpaper, panel by tacky panel.

My mom hisses through the phone. "*That man.* How far does he really expect to get with this propaganda?"

Ever since I smuggled Wi-Fi into the Manor, I can call the outside world from most dark corners of the house, and a girl can't snoop properly without her mom. I'm not sure what I'm looking for exactly, but I turn down halls I haven't walked before, peek through doors I've never opened. Nothing but empty rooms and shadows.

"But what did Webb mean about a curse? Does he think the Warlock is lying to me about his illness?" Silence. I check my cell's connection. "Mom, I can hear you holding your tongue."

"I'm thinking."

"You're not thinking, you're agreeing! With the spider!"

"The spider—who?"

"Just because he doesn't look sick doesn't mean he isn't. I've seen it. His magic is weakening."

Already, my toes are numb, like the floorboards are made of ice. Even a May evening shouldn't get this cold. Definitely regretting my choice to wear nothing more than my favorite oversized T-shirt as a pajama top. The Warlock told me the soil around the house stays colder—a clue I should've paid attention to? I suppose a curse could siphon the warmth and life from a house and thus its owner. Or vice versa.

After he revealed he was dying, I thought about the possibility of a curse, then dismissed it as Witch's magic. Maybe I was too quick to shrug off the idea.

"You think he looks *fine*?"

"Mom." I move deeper into a darker hallway. There aren't even any windows, so I get no help from the moonlight. I try a few of the doorknobs in hallway. No luck. All locked.

"Fine as in fine, or fine as in *fine*—"

"Mom."

"Hun, I'm stuck in a hospital, I need entertainment. Listen . . . how much do we *really* know about Warlock Knight? No matter what age he looks like, he's had time to make enemies. Curses happen, even to Warlocks. Maybe it's not so bad, a mild one, like his coffee goes cold quickly or something. But Lord, that would be terrible . . ."

My chest tightens. That strong taste of thyme, the Widow Witch vanishing with a snap of the Warlock's fingers, the intense power in his stare . . . If the Warlock is cursed, it won't be simple. Like a good crème brûlée, under the armor of his crusty surface, there's *no* flavor of him that's mild.

In the periphery of my vision, a locked door I definitely already tried cracks open.

Curious.

I slip into the room before the house can change its mind on me. It's dark, but not dark enough to delay my cry of surprise.

Vines have consumed the entire room.

No, not just vines. That beaded succulent plant that looks whimsically chic in the daylight. But these particular stringy green strands cover the windows, choke the light fixtures, and buckle the hardwood floors like relentless tree-root systems under sidewalks. I try to wedge open the door again, but it gets stuck in a thick, Medusa's-head bunch of the pearls.

There's a slight slithering sound. I hope it's barn snakes. Something tells me that would be less terrifying.

But I'm not that lucky—it's the vines. They're *growing.*

"Mom, I have to go. I have a succulent situation."

"What did I tell you, just shave in the right direction—"

"G'nightMomIloveyoubye."

I stuff my phone into my bra and study the ravenous greenery I've waded into. The endless vines undulate like a pulsing heart. But the house opened *this* door, so this is the room I want. Granted, this is the same house that tried to boil me. But there has to be something in here worth hiding.

Tiptoeing into the room, I'm careful not to step on any writhing stalks, but the plants move out of the way on their own, making tiny lily pads of clear floorboard for me. Not soon enough, I finally spy an old chest underneath the vine-curtained windows. Before the sentient plants strangle my nerves, I hop over to the chest and fling it open, bracing myself.

The vines don't react. The house is taking pity on me for once.

Piles of framed photos, faces paused in time, stare back. As before, the same woman with glossy dark hair looks up at me. She's slightly older, but her elegant laugh lines are still there. Unlike before, this photo is in color, so there's no mistaking the hazel eyes.

The Warlock's mother.

There are hundreds of photos in here. Like someone went through the entire house and removed every single memory until not even a ghost of this family remained. That photo in the library, the house must've . . . plucked it from here? For me?

One question solved, another pops up. Freaking dandelions over here.

Just then, a vine shoots out and wraps around my ankle. It yanks, hard.

I go down, hitting the hardwood in a riot of noise.

The framed photo cracks, glass shattering. I don't even get the chance to scream before the vines are on me, dragging me across the floor.

Soon I'm covered, only an eye here and a hand there peeking out of the carpet of greenery trying to suffocate me. I try to scream, but a vine wraps around my mouth and I'm too caught up in a tornado of panic to think anything else beyond *I'm going to die in nothing but a T-shirt like some pitiful Winnie-the-Pooh.*

At least I told my mom I love her—Mom! My chest flares with heat, heart racing. What'll happen to her if I don't survive?

Suddenly, a dry cracking sound echoes in the infested room. I glance down at the vines mummifying my body. They're shrinking, shriveling up.

No—rotting.

I scramble away as soon as I'm free, portrait forgotten, and sprint the hell out of that room.

And slam right into Warlock Knight.

He catches me around the waist with a gloved hand and hauls us free of the doorway just as a writhing vine launches for my calf. Then he raises his free hand toward the vines and snaps. Just once.

The door crashes shut, sealing the rotting vines inside.

After the chaos, the hall is starkly soundless.

As I finally take a few non-strangled gasps of air, the Warlock studies me with, let's say, extreme dissatisfaction. "Ms. Frost. You could not underestimate my surprise."

Too much in shock, I still haven't untangled myself from him. Did he just *maim* his own plants to help me?

"Don't flatter yourself," he answers, seeing the question on my face. Curiosity wins out over his anger, and he looks to the door like it's a puzzle. Not a fun one. "That *rot* was not me."

Withering, Ms. Frost. Withering.

I force myself to take a few deep breaths. "What—"

"*Senecio rowleyanus.*"

"What did you call me?"

"That's the name of the plant. String of pearls."

I must be imagining things, because then the Warlock says a very odd thing in a very odd, soft way that makes my toes go all tingly. "Anything bruised beyond your pride?"

He's asking . . . if I'm okay?

No! I'm a blushing disaster!

"I'm stellar." And definitely hallucinating, because I swear his arms tighten around me a fraction.

But in the next moment, he unthreads his tall frame from mine, his gloved fingers lingering half a second too long. Goose bumps skitter up my bare legs, and I almost miss his warmth. He's still in gardening clothes, but barely: gloves, but no shoes, untucked shirt like he was getting ready for a shower to clean off the soil.

"Why have the plants taken over like that?"

A scowl is visible on his face in the dim hall. He brushes imaginary dirt from his sleeves, like *he* was the one about to be a succulent's secondi. Rude. "Why shouldn't they? I don't need the space."

"The room is a death trap, that's why!" I sputter. "This isn't just some rebellious rutabaga, *sir*. I was almost a midnight snack."

"If only someone had warned you not to roam at night."

I see tonight's forecast is grouchy with a heavy chance of sarcasm.

"Unlike the danger of the house's illusions, the plants here are very real. I warned you not to upset them."

"*Me* upset *them*?" I'm about to unleash a helluva rant on this man.

Then his gaze falls quickly down my body and immediately back up, such an unconscious flick I might have missed it.

Oh. Right. Embarrassment tingles up my spine. Caught. Half naked. Again. And not just in an old oversized shirt, no, that would be too easy on me. It happens to be the one with an illustration of fried chicken pieces forming the shape of Kentucky on the front, with the proclamation *Gettin' Lucky in Kentucky!*

He smirks. "You're *lucky* they weren't very hungry."

I guess this is a lesson about not purchasing clothing at a random gas station in a small town like Hell for Certain, Kentucky. The ferocious scolding I had for him dies in my throat.

"Not that I don't trust you, Ms. Frost"—heavy, *heavy* chance of sarcasm—"but I think it's best I escort you to bed."

I'm flustered, but my brush with death makes me feel bold. "Is it, now?"

"Back to bed. Back to your *room*." He blows out an agitated breath. "You know what I mean. Follow me."

I fall into step next to him, only because I don't want to be left alone in the dark, even if my pride takes a hit. "Thank you."

He looks at me like I've lost my mind. But he was here when I needed someone. "You have nothing to thank me for. My magic didn't save you. I just closed a door."

Something he's great at. "It wasn't *my* magic." *Right?*

But then, what was all that? The Warlock has influence over the house and his plants, but both are sentient on their own—and antagonistic. The house opened that door for me, but the vines attacked the minute I pried too far into the past. A headache pulses behind my eyes. Note to self: Always stay in bed.

One thing is clear. Something, or someone, is most definitely cursed in this place. Hell, it might be me.

"Am I going to regret asking why you went into that room tonight?"

I almost laugh. My reasoning feels silly now. "The house unlocked the door for me. There was a trunk of photos, and I thought if I found—never mind. One of the portraits was the woman from the photo in the library."

There. I leave my answer between us, a palm up. *Take it.* Open up, give me something.

With his eyes straight ahead, his next breath is a rough inhale. "That's my mother, Margaret Cho. She was a Chinese exchange student traveling through the States when she met my father, a farmer here. She already loved working outdoors with plants and the earth, so she stayed."

The honesty throws me and I forget to feel victorious at cracking his decades-thick wall. Parents make him much more . . . human. That's the black hair, then. I see his mom in his face, his cheekbones, but his dad in his taller frame.

"Deadly succulent rooms aside, why am I really not allowed to explore the house?"

"Because it prefers to keep to itself."

"You mean keep *secrets.* Like what happened to your family." A chill whips up my bare thighs and I inch closer to him. "Like how Lazlo ended up here—"

"That's enough."

His tone is thorn-sharp. I want to pry. Each day I'm here, I want more of a glimpse into the Warlock's past, secrets and all. I know I'm getting closer to breaking through the hard, crystallized exterior of this particular crème brûlée.

"Why were *you* up this late?" Whatever the reason, I'm glad he was. "Don't know if anyone's told you, but the house is a real prick at night. Do you ever sleep?"

"Less and less," he says, studying me like I'm to blame.

Of course. The entire reason I'm even here. "Did the elderberry turnovers improve how you're feeling at all?" Elderberries are full of antioxidants and good for inflammation, but a Farewitch can amplify their ability to strengthen a weak heart. I resist the urge to ask to see his tongue color. He'd probably fire me for that one.

"Nothing yet." His eyes dart to me, gloved hands clasped tight behind his back. I must look a frightful mess, because his tone softens. Barely. “But the purple hue reminded me of my mother’s ube spoonbread. My grandmother’s recipe. Po Po was from Hong Kong.”

Another detail! Tonight’s adventure might’ve been worth it just for this conversation.

“I tried to sell ube cornbread at the shop once. Honey and cinnamon on top. You’d think folks had never seen the color purple before.”

“A shame that some prefer their food the color of Scrabble tiles.”

I hum in agreement. “It’s too easy to like what’s familiar.”

Just when I think we’re getting close to the stairs, we turn another corner into an identical dark hall. I swear, this house’s favorite game is *maze*. That, or it’s delaying the end of our conversation.

“I noticed you were in town all day,” he says after a beat.

I think that’s a question. “I was meeting my friend Arna Jean. She’s a Bookwitch. She’s going to help run the Apothakery since I’m staying here longer.”

“Good. For your Apothakery, I mean.” Then: “Is that why you took Lazlo to town without my permission?”

So much for skirting that indiscretion. Why did I believe I could fool him?

“Lazlo likes the unfamiliar, you know. Learning, and exploring. Not that I want to threaten Ms. Zeen’s job and incur her wrath, but have you thought about sending him to school? He doesn’t have magic, so why not let him be any other rowdy kid in a classroom?”

A wisp of indecision tugs at his mouth, right before his face hardens. “No. Magic or not, the town would treat him as *my* ward and he’d be fighting the hatred attached to my reputation. It’s simply safer for folks to not know him at all. I can’t . . . explain it any other way.”

I won’t argue with him, not after seeing that behavior firsthand at the market.

Baby steps. “I don’t know what his life was like before he came here, but he lost his parents, and he'll need interaction with other kids, somehow."

"Believe me, I wish the situation were different. But the fewer opportunities the town has to scrutinize him, the better. Certain people could . . . They would use him against me."

"The Widow Witch."

"Among others."

We finally reach the stairs to the second floor, and stand near the first step at an impasse. Almost like he doesn't want to go up to our rooms yet. Probably the insomnia.

As I move for the stairs, he says, "You were quiet at dinner. And you didn't eat."

"Oh—ah." I didn't expect anyone to notice. That he did does a weird thing to my chest. Hopefully the foyer is dark enough to hide my cheeks. "Just puzzling some things out. My brain gets a bit loud sometimes."

Between handing the Apothakery to Arna Jean, then Webb and Fudge, that *sometimes* is turning into *all the time*. And my recipe earlier this week—blueberry buckwheat pancake bread with whipped ricotta lemon frosting—did nothing for my mom's condition. Every day I spend with her in that fluorescent box of a hospital room, the shrill sounds of beeping instead of the soft hum of an oven, guilt clings to me like wet dough.

Going to bed right now means I'll have to be alone with all those worries.

Abruptly, I turn my back on the stairs.

"Would you like to have a drink?" I ask the Warlock.

Chapter Fifteen

MONDAY, MAY 2

50 DAYS UNTIL THE SUMMER SOLSTICE

Honey's Helpful Hint, from
Honey Frost's Southern Cookbook for Recipes Gone Wrong:

Make sure to gradually warm up your honey if you're going to introduce it to something else; otherwise, it will seize and become rigid and uncooperative. A little bourbon doesn't hurt, either.

In the kitchen, a single lamp glows between me and the Warlock. The warm light melts over the island counter, like butter in a perfectly hot skillet. The drink I have in mind requires rich coffee, so I leave some brewing in a French press and prep my other ingredients. The multitasking is such an automatic response for my hands, I don't think my brain is ever set on any other mode.

As I work, the Manor is extra silent, even for a forlorn skeleton of a house.

The Warlock's expression is unreadable—impressively more so than usual—as he leans against the island. Though the lean looks a few steps shy of collapse. Now that I've got light, I can see how rough he looks. Hair tousled, shoulders bent, eyes matte. He's exhausted. Saving me from those plants took more out of him than I thought.

"Would you like to sit?" I ask. "The coffee'll take a minute. Don't worry, you can still flee the room from a seated position." I try to calm my rambling jitters in his calculating silence, but the man is an intimidating hoverer.

"You're not sitting."

"I never sit."

"I've noticed." His eyes study the ingredients. "Did you invite me only because it's ill-advised to drink alone?"

"*Ha.* The Frost women don't believe that. *Never drink without food.* That's our rule."

"So you *are* capable of following rules."

He came for drinks and snark, apparently.

Best get this over with. "I'm sorry," I blurt.

He raises an eyebrow, as if I'm such an annoying little olive fork jammed into his side, he'll need me to be more specific. I swallow the bad name I'd like to call him.

"About the poking around. I'm not trying to ignore your privacy, or make the Manor think it needs to go on the attack."

"The house is not as scary a devil as you think. For now."

This is more of an apology than I would've gotten a couple weeks ago, so I'll take it.

"Are you and the house one and the same?"

"No. And yes. The house listens to me, responds to my magic. But it decides whom it allows inside, and what it shows us. It likes to play tricks. To a fault. And it does enjoy mimicking my emotions and moods." He sucks in a breath. "I haven't been around other people for a long time. Or lived with them. Not that this is an excuse."

"We're not as scary as you think," I say. He doesn't have a retort for that. "Can I be frank with you, Mr. Knight?"

"We both know you don't need my permission for that."

Well then. "You're not sick, are you." I don't make it a question. "You've been cursed."

His lips press together, teeth grinding.

The silence before was nothing compared with the suffocating vacuum enveloping us now.

No no no.

I was hoping Webb was only trying to crawl his way into my mind and lay eggs of doubt. But the Warlock's face confirms my fear.

How the hell did I miss this? He's an *expert* on curse magic, made it his field of study. I should've trusted my instincts all those weeks ago, when I first considered the possibility of a curse. But I tossed the idea because I was so sure that a Warlock wouldn't bother getting involved with Witch magic.

The night hits me then, and I slump against the counter. I'm only going to drain myself further trying to keep up with the Warlock's secrets.

"The curse *makes* me sick," he finally says, voice dark and low. "Those were the terms of the Witch who cursed me. Over the next year, my magic would diminish, my body would weaken, and eventually, well, death."

"On the summer solstice?"

He nods.

"That's why you don't want me wandering." Bad health, bad control. Bad house.

"One reason, yes. I'm no longer capable of managing the Manor's behavior as I used to, so I can't guarantee your safety."

The Witch who cursed me.

"The Widow Witch!" I realize. "*She* cursed you, didn't she? Is that why she hasn't—"

"First, no, I have no idea why she hasn't stolen someone from the Holler yet this year. That has nothing to do with me. Second, the details change nothing."

"They change *everything*. You hired a Farewitch. To cure an illness. Not lift a curse. You need a Hedgewitch, or a—hell, why did you even think I could help in the first place?"

"In my research, I've found evidence of Farewitches lifting curses that mimic illnesses, especially if the curse involves physical symptoms. Vague evidence, but it exists."

"But that depends on the Farewitch and her specific affinity, the recipe, the patient . . ."

"Yes, perhaps it was an optimistic hypothesis."

"A long shot, you mean."

"This past year has been nothing *but* long shots," he snaps. "I may practice the Language of Small Wishes, but I've studied curse magic my entire life, well before this. I should not have had to burden anyone else with it. Not Ms. Zeen, not Lazlo—" He bites down on the boy's name. "And not you. This is *my* nightmare, one I should have been able to handle. *Alone.* But I couldn't. So illness or curse, you are my last option. I have never lied to you about that."

"Wish magic, curse magic—none of that's my specialty. I'm a Farewitch. What exactly do you want me to do here?"

"What you've been doing all along. Hunting for a recipe that will help my body fight a physical ailment."

"And if I don't succeed, do you have a plan for Lazlo, for after the solstice?" *If you die.*

Silence.

That answers that.

Webb's threats from earlier triple in size at this midnight hour, but I refuse to let the current of doubt pool in. "What can you tell me about the Eldercraft?"

Pause. "Why? What makes you ask?"

"At the market today, Oris Webb seemed keen to report you to them. He doesn't like the idea that a Warlock is the guardian of a kid without magic. Do the Eldercraft forbid that or something?" Is there any kind of precedent for that? I suspect they'd be all over this town if they thought one of their own kind was harming children.

The Warlock's eyes fall closed, tight. "Why is that man concerned at all? We wouldn't know if Lazlo has magic. Warlocks don't manifest their power until their teens, and then they often leave home to train with a mentor anyway."

A part of me is relieved to hear that. I don't think I can handle two Warlocks at the same time. Again, I'm surprised by how little I know about Warlocks. Witches sometimes leave home to study, if no one in their family can mentor them. But there's often at least one other Witch who's familiar with their magic. Maybe mentorship is a longer goodbye for Warlocks, since they live so independently from one another and rarely settle in one spot.

An extra dose of gratitude for a Witch's network of covens and communal magic winds through me. Though, it would help to have someone holding the Widow Witch accountable.

Opening his eyes, the Warlock pushes himself off the island to fully face me. "Don't take Lazlo to town again, Ms. Frost."

My arms fold over my chest as I try to muster some intimidation. "Do you know why the turnovers were elderberry and not apple today, sir?"

"Now hardly seems like the time to discuss pastry, Ms. Frost."

"I'll rephrase: Did you know folks at the market wouldn't sell us apples and treated us like crap?"

His frozen irritation melts. "Lazlo didn't say anything."

"*Because he wants to go back.* Rude folks or not, he enjoyed being there, and he doesn't want you to take away that privilege. But Webb and his slimy followers are itching to shun magic from the Holler, more than ever lately. Not just higher magic, but Witches, too. Webb can't get the upper hand on the Widow Witch, so he'll come for you first."

"I doubt the preacher and his congregation are coming to burn me at the stake. I can handle being disliked. I'm just fine with it, in fact."

"Right. Only Witches burn, after all." It comes out before I can stop it, and his mouth clamps tight over any rebuttal. Good. The obstinate man needs to be humbled. "Webb seems ready to do anything necessary to smother magic, even if it means using a kid to get the Eldercraft involved."

"See, this is *exactly* why I forbade you to go—"

"My *point* is that sooner rather than later, someone's going to need to extend an olive branch, but you've spent all your time fighting enemies, you forgot to make friends—"

"*I know!*"

The shout comes out of nowhere, echoing around us.

The breath leaves his rigid body, and a gloved hand runs over the misery twisting his face. For a moment, I see the vulnerable younger man he used to be, before the walls went up. Have I actually *unsettled* him?

As his head hangs, he says, "Lazlo's not supposed to be here, he's not . . . but he can't go back. I know he needs more. More than me." His next breath is a shudder. "They can't take him from me. I don't know what would happen . . . They simply don't understand."

Who? Now he's not making any sense. Webb? The Eldercraft? But *there*—there's that weird flash of guilt again, piercing his hardened stare. I can almost hear the *Please*.

I'm not really sure what makes me do it.

Lunging forward, I wrap my arms around the man in the most unexpected and awkward hug in Witch-Warlock history.

My head fits just below his chin and he smells *good*, like an entire herb garden, thyme and the earth and summer and—I jolt backward. Before he can decide whether to hug me back. This is more mortifying than the animal cracker incident by a factor of light-years.

"That was . . ." He swallows, hard.

Oh God. Please don't finish that thought. "Sorry. I should have asked you first." I wonder if he might combust. "But I'm not sorry for taking Lazlo to the market."

"Right. Well." He clears his throat. For several seconds. "His time here is not a result of pleasant circumstances, so I appreciate your effort to make it better."

I hope I have. Clearly, I'm still missing crucial ingredients to the recipe of how Lazlo ended up here. But this is progress. Finally, I have a sense of the man, not just the Warlock.

The coffee ready, I turn back to my recipe. Every Frost woman has a preferred version of it. I like to use honey instead of sugar, and mix a heaping tablespoon with coffee to help the liquid gold warm up. Next, a healthy pour of Woodford into a big mug. Then the coffee mixture. The last touch: I whip cream with a hand mixer so it's denser than anything in aerosol form, and pour it across the back of a spoon over the coffee so the cream floats like melted marshmallow.

"Kentucky Coffee." I pass the Warlock a full mug and pour one of my own.

My first sip sends the chill of the night's events skittering away. This drink might not be tied to any memory for him, but there's magic in dopamine stimulation. It's the nectar that gets me through any all-nighter. And after tonight's entertainment, the beverage program is needed.

But before I can warn him, the Warlock takes an ambitiously large swig and falls right into a coughing fit.

"Sorry, it's got—"

Cough—"Bourbon, yes"—sputter—"I'm aware." Sniff. He thrusts the mug back to me. "Next time, try to cure me first before you kill me."

He's got whipped cream on his upper lip, a fascinating dollop of sweetness that's—not relevant. "I meant what I said. It does you no good if folks keep thinking the Warlock of Foxe Holler is a monster who preys on innocents and sunshine. I know the town has its bad apples, but most of your neighbors might surprise you with kindness."

Except Gertha Fudge. But she doesn't like anyone.

He clenches his gloved hands. "I'm not sure the truth would do me much good."

His words gnaw at me. He's been isolated up here so long, at some point, the town embraced convenient reputation and bulldozed over actual fact.

"Do you know what *would* be good for you?" I grin over my mug, steam curling into my nostrils.

He finally licks the bit of cream from his lip. I try not to stare. Really.

Then those hazel eyes flick back to me, and in them, something has changed. "I have some ideas," he says, voice low.

I nearly choke on my next sip. My skin flushes with a tingling haze, like the unmoored heat from sitting in front of a fireplace for too long. The bourbon is kicking in.

"You're flushed," he rasps.

I hold up the mug in defense. "Coffee, bourbon."

"Honey."

"Yes?" I cringe at the eagerness in my own voice. But this is the first time he's used my name and I'm woefully unprepared for what the sound does to me.

"I mean, there's honey in the drink. I can taste it."

"Oh. Right."

Bourbon has *definitely* kicked in.

That's when it dawns on me. The Warlock and I are sharing a drink. At night. This is the closest thing *I've* had to a date in a long, long time.

Not sure if my mom would be thrilled or terrified.

"Having allies," I say, clearing the embarrassment out of my throat. "That's what would be good for you. If I agree to keep digging through your library for a cure to this . . . curse, you have to let your neighbors in. Lazlo needs friends. He needs to know the unkind folks don't outnumber the kind ones in the Holler."

"Fine. How?"

How indeed, especially if he won't leave the Manor. But folks have been willing to come here. Arna Jean is proof that the right people will bridge the distance. Everyone deserves a friend like that in their corner. No matter how dismal they are at accepting one . . .

We've got less than eight weeks until the solstice, the Holler's holiest are out for blood, the Warlock is withering under a curse, and now I need to turn a scary bedtime story into a friendly neighbor.

But what people pleaser can say no to a challenge?

After a hearty swig of bourbon and coffee, I slam my mug on the island. "I have an idea."

Chapter Sixteen

SUNDAY, MAY 8

44 DAYS UNTIL THE SUMMER SOLSTICE

Honey's Helpful Hint, from
Honey Frost's Southern Cookbook
for Recipes Gone Wrong:

Ancestral blood bestows the Witch,
therein becomes the seed of power.
Rare and scarce is a Warlock's gift,
the starving never last the hour.
—The Witches' Book of Wisdom

An ungodly number of children crowd the kitchen of Knight Manor.

Momaw Frost always said, when everything's going wrong, bake cookies. But inviting folks to a full-blown Mother's Day cookie bake might not be what she meant. *Maybe* I didn't have to make an irresponsible amount of cookie dough and tell everyone to bring their favorite maternal or parental representative (and cookie cutter). *Maybe* I didn't have to serve banana Fluffernutter sandwiches and Shirley Temples.

Invited might be the wrong verb . . . Preyed on shameless curiosity?

Today, the gossip network of Foxe Holler is working in my favor. With help from the Kentucky fried coven group chat—and Ms. Buchanan, the chatterbox—we've successfully inveigled parents to bring their kids to a cookie bake. Turns out, if the food is free and the mess happens elsewhere, folks become less wary of a definitely-not-haunted farmhouse and the spooky neighbor they've never met before, no matter what Pastor Webb is preaching.

It's time the Warlock of Foxe Holler make his debut at a community event. Then, a certain boy can actually make friends that aren't poodles.

This is how we ended up with a rugby team of kids at Knight Manor.

"When you said we'd host a handful of neighbors . . ." Warlock Knight frowns at me over the full kitchen table. Between us, kids roll and poke and strangle mountains of cookie dough. Everyone is most definitely eating more than they're shaping. Especially Lazlo.

"I meant a Southern handful," I say, placing doughy stars onto a baking sheet.

"Clearly," Ms. Zeen crows over the buzz.

"If I had been honest about the number, you would've said no."

His frown deepens. "Correct assumption, Ms. Frost."

"Honey's a baker, Mr. Knight," Carolina says as she helps one child form an octopus. "Bakers have an entire concept based on calling thirteen a dozen." For once, Carolina's free of her scrubs, though she could've used them in this demolition zone of a cookie operating room. She's here with an entire trunk of the Vázquez family tree. Ms. Marrow would've been here, but she's visiting her daughter out of state.

Arna Jean looks up from coaching a girl on how to frost glasses onto her gingerbread person. Today's hoodie declares, in a rainbow spectrum, *SCRYING IN THE CLUB*. "Which is why I audited the shop's books each summer."

"I'll be offended by that later." I'm too busy sprinkling flour onto sticky dough. No meltdowns over torn cookies, please and thank you.

A child screams.

Warlock Knight finds the missing dragon cookie cutter just before the tears can start.

I restrain a grin. As with Lazlo, the Warlock's gruff moods that rub against my nerves like steel wool fade into mildly scratchy sandpaper around children.

A few parents look over at the scream, but it's only out of habit now. When they witnessed Witches strolling into the Manor without fear, they seemed satisfied the magical beast of Holler legend wasn't hungry for children. Sure, folks were on edge at first, eyeing the gargantuan ferns and palms like they could sense the flora is teething. But after some food and a lack of any murder, everyone relaxed. Their doubt is dwindling with our supply of cookie dough.

My plan might actually be working.

It doesn't escape me that most of the folks here today also happen to be regular customers of mine. Promising. I just hope the house will be on its best behavior. The grannies on our guest list won't survive a stumble over an ornery rug.

"You'll be pleased to know, Honey sugar, young Ms. Claywell is doing a mighty fine job with the Apothakery," Ms. Buchanan says. She drops a morsel of dough for Beauregard, who's lounging strategically between her and Lazlo.

Down the table, Arna Jean raises a container of sprinkles and her phone like twin Bavarian steins. She filled orders this morning, then closed up to join us, and she's been taking video of the chaos when the light is just right, *for content,* she explains. The Apothakery has a small online following now, *you're welcome,* according to her.

Two of my other favorite regulars are here as well. Noxie from Shirley Street, whom the church ladies refer to as *a real hellcat,* must not be too distraught over her husband's missing-toe incident Silas mentioned to skip a cookie bake. Though she's always pale and morose, so it's hard to tell. Next to her is Eva Mae, whose warm brown skin shifts between pregnancy glow and absinthe. Her nausea keeps her close to the bathroom.

As my neighbors debate the Manor's interior design—"Look at this wallpaper, surely one does not need a fern on every surface . . ." —I whip up some ambrosia salad in ten minutes flat and place it on the island. I step aside to safety as folks descend on the customary Southern offering for guests. They're not vultures in a horseman-of-the-apocalypse kind of way, more the kind of scavenger that feeds on purse candy and coupons.

A sudden rush of appreciation threatens to make me as mushy as the coconut cream pie I made earlier for Noxie's cat allergy. Here are neighbors who came all the way up here, despite possible retaliation from Webb and his followers in town. Heaven strike me well and good if I ever let them down.

Even if I have to sacrifice extra hours of sleep here and there. *Extra* extra.

Back at the table, I refill frosting bowls and roll out fresh dough, trying not to sneak glances at the Warlock, who's been conned into helping Carolina's little niece Anna shape a mermaid.

"I wish I was better at cookies," Anna says. "Can you do that kind of wish?"

He's nearly on his knees now so he can be at eye level with her. "Nonsense. I've never seen a better mermaid. And I've met real ones." He winks.

The moment the kids found out the Warlock practices the Language of Small Wishes, there was no stuffing that biscuit back in its can. In Foxe Holler, most folks are only familiar with Witches' practical magic, so all morning, kids have been pleading to see his power at work.

Anna gives a tiny smile. "But she's globby. Like a walrus."

"She's just abstract," Lazlo says, leaning over to inspect.

The kid was up at dawn this morning trying to iron the tiny waistcoat he's wearing, until I swooped in before anyone lost an eyebrow. I'm right—he's been lonely. Now he's feasting on the activity and attention.

"And Small Wishes don't work like that," Lazlo adds, accidentally drenching his lap in sprinkles. "Mr. Knight says, *You can't wish for solved problems, only problem-solving.* Like *I wish the dough was colder*. Or cold hands work, too. That's what Honey told me."

My heart seizes at his smile, which is sweeter than the marshmallow mess that is a Fluffernutter. I can't with this kid.

This kid, who just has one guardian left. Maybe I was a little harsh on the Warlock last week. Why should I assume a Farewitch can't fix a curse like any other affliction? Especially a curse that acts like a physical ailment? Any good Witch knows how finicky magic is.

It's taken three decades on this earth, but I've gotten good at managing mine. I know the cost for me is more than just the energy needed for standing and stirring. Bigger recipes, more complex memories, need more energy I can't just make up with a snack or cup of coffee. A solid day of baking demands a full night's sleep. The inflow and outflow are as familiar to me as the Apothakery.

But I'm not sure I'll ever know this Manor like I know the shop. The Warlock and his house churn with ingredients that are galaxies outside my comfort zone.

"Is your mom really the mayor?" comes a voice at my elbow.

I can't recognize whose kid he is under all the flour. "She is. Mayor Frost baked cookies with me like this when I was your age."

"Told you," Lazlo says with all the proud satisfaction of a kid who knows he picked the right parent for a career-day presentation. He gives Beauregard a *Good boy* and a treat.

Eva Mae looks up from decorating a horseshoe-shaped cookie. "You know, I haven't seen Mayor Frost in months."

"Perhaps she's avoiding Pastor Webb. I would," Ms. Zeen says, nursing a cup of English breakfast next to Ms. Buchanan. Those two haven't stopped whispering, heads bent, since the kettle went off. It's hard to imagine, but maybe Ms. Zeen is also a smidge lonely.

"I can't believe that man," Carolina seethes. "Managing to get my

Beltane bonfire canceled because of some bureaucratic nonsense. Do I have some words for him—"

"When children aren't present," Eva Mae chimes in. That girl was born fifty.

Ms. Buchanan smacks the table, startling a few of the kids. "He won't let us sing any of the good hymns anymore. He cut out 'All Is Well with My Soul' last week for another rant about the dangers of magic."

Arna Jean rolls her eyes, positioning bottles of sprinkles for a picture. "He can't be more dangerous than Noxie's aim."

"RJ!" Eva Mae scolds, stifling laughter. Even Ms. Zeen blows on her tea to disguise a grin. I catch Noxie's slightly off-kilter smile. She's eerily quiet, this one. Like the skeleton hanging in the Halloween-decoration corner of any suburban basement.

Ms. Buchanan nods at Noxie. "If anyone's in need of the Widow Witch's *services*, it's you, girl. That fellow was rotten right out of the pack. I know the options are thin here in the Holler, but get yourself a new one." She turns her sharp eyes on the Warlock. "I know a few eligible bachelors yet."

"And ineligible ones," Carolina quips.

The Warlock busies himself untangling cookie cutters, doing his best to ignore the attention. Far from the safety of his gardens, he's tried to camouflage his tall presence all morning, to no avail. So far, this community event has conjured even more questions. Ms. Buchanan is plenty old enough to have known his face before he withdrew from town. Even Carolina would've seen him; everyone passes through the hospital at some point. I think. Yet it's like everyone is meeting him for the very first time.

When he doesn't take the bait, Ms. Buchanan makes me her next target. "Where is the elusive Mayor Frost, sugar? Skipping a Mother's Day cookie bake? Your mama can't hide behind her work forever."

Eva Mae nods in agreement. "Her neighbors hardly see her."

My heartbeat jackhammers. The Warlock is watching me intently. He frowns.

"She's incredibly bossy," I say, stumbling. "Busy, I mean. She and I celebrated Mother's Day yesterday." That's the truth, at least.

My heart clenches with another truth. Watching all these kids baking cookies with their parents, grandmothers . . . I'm missing my mom extra hard today. Every chef needs her sous-chef.

"Besides, you'd have to make an appointment to visit her office, but her number two is notoriously hard to reach, so I wouldn't even bother."

Sorry, Silas.

"Ladies, I reckon we should pay Marigold a visit soon," Ms. Buchanan declares.

My neck flames up. "Oh, that's not necessary—"

"That does beg the question," Eva Mae ponders.

No, no questions begged!

Eva Mae turns to me. "Why doesn't Marigold just run the Apothakery again? Especially with Arna Jean's help. She'd probably enjoy the baking more than the politics."

Too many eyes land on me, blinking with expectation.

Could be the heat of the ovens, or that I can't remember what I've eaten today, or the Warlock's stare, or this chatter about my mom, who's dying a little more every day—I'm suddenly hot. Sweating under my apron.

It's all *too much*. I need a minute.

"That's the oven timer," I chirp to the backdrop of absolutely no timer. But before they question my hearing, I bolt toward the AGA.

Taking deep breaths, I busy myself making a fresh pitcher of sweet tea. Slowly, my cheeks cool and the surface of my skin stops fizzing.

Calm yourself, girl.

Momaw's voice soothes the turmoil in my mind, but only for a moment. She had similar symptoms as my mom, though she was older, already a grandmother. But like me, my mom started managing the shop years before her mom actually passed, ever since Momaw first began declining. How would I survive not having my mom around?

Right now, a cure feels very much like a wish in the dark.

Thyme tickles the back of my tongue.

"This is utter bedlam, Ms. Frost."

"*Bedlam* is a strong word," I say, turning to face the Warlock. The kids are so besotted with his magic now, they're snapping for fun, mimicking him. "And I've told you twice now not to use magic just to create rainbow frosting. We can make that, sir."

The one rule Ms. Zeen and I agree on is, as it happens, the rule the Warlock is dismal at following. *No magic.* Not while his curse is supposedly squeezing the life from his body like a voracious juicer. If he expends any magic, it's for the Manor's wards.

"The children's wishes are too small to harm me," he grumbles in protest. "The cost is minimal. A headache tomorrow, at most."

Lies. Since splitting my time between the Warlock, my mom's research, baking for my regulars . . . I'm fluent in faking energy. Every granted wish leaves him slightly paler, and he needs more and more time between each one. He doesn't think anyone notices, but I do. If he keeps this up, the thyme smell around me will become permanent. Which wouldn't be so bad. But still.

"You're going to exhaust yourself and I need to be able to measure your health when you're eating my recipes. *Without* competing variables."

However, I can't deny seeing him show an interest in something other than being a brooding recluse . . . It feels *good.* Even his gloves were clean this morning, like he put on a fresh pair just for today.

I can't help my satisfied smirk. "And you said a cookie bake couldn't be done."

"I said *shouldn't* be done. Forgive me for assuming no one would want to visit this tomb of a house."

"But?"

"But," he sighs, "against all odds, no one appears distressed by the presence of a Warlock at a children's confectionary social."

My triumph doesn't last long. It's good news, but it conjures that same feeling I had seeing Arna Jean's confused look at the market. This unease that the memories folks have of the Warlock are all based in rumor, the lore hovering only on the surface like the frothy broth on top of simmering soup. I wonder, when our guests leave the Manor, will they still think of him as the beastly old monster with treacherous magic? Will they even remember the man currently wiping tiny flour handprints off his elephant ear plants?

"I admit, it's nice to see Lazlo laughing so much," the Warlock says, saving me from my garbage disposal of thoughts.

I don't say a word, lest I break the spell. Let it be known I, Fare-witch Honey Frost, got the Warlock of Foxe Holler to use the word *nice*.

Sweet tea made, I fan myself with a dishcloth. With so many bodies in the hot kitchen, I'm lightheaded, my temples warm with sweat.

He eyes me. "You should rest a moment. You haven't eaten all day."

"I'm fine, I'll eat when everything quiets down. Speaking of, Eva Mae's insomnia is flaring up and I need to whip up—"

"Ms. Frost, not three minutes ago you poured Lazlo a mug of Moscato and Ms. Buchanan a glass of chocolate milk. I insist."

Oh dear.

To be honest, I've been enjoying this too much to stop. The buzzy kitchen reminds me of the Apothakery, which keeps my brain from lingering on the laundry list of problems to solve.

"Tell you what," I say. "I'll eat something if you take off your gloves."

He looks at me like he's been stung by an annoying bee. I smirk. I'm going to win this. He'll never—

Finger by finger, he peels off his gloves.

What. Is. *Happening.*

Even Ms. Zeen looks over, as if she senses something terribly wrong. The universe is collapsing, that's what.

Forearm muscles tense, the Warlock looks almost . . . relieved? I've never once seen his hands and they're . . . normal. Dirt hides under his short nails. So he *does* take them off when he's gardening alone. And no wedding ring. For those (me) at home wondering. Not that it matters. Purely for fact-gathering purposes.

"I expected claws," I blurt before I can bite my silly tongue. And if he did have them? Claws are probably good for digging up dirt for new flowers.

"Warlocks don't scratch, Ms. Frost. We bite."

My face warms, and then I'm thinking about the drink we shared last week. I eyeballed my ceiling well into the witching hour that night because I couldn't stop picturing that silly dollop of whipped cream on his lip.

"Now if you'll excuse me," he drawls, "I'm going to locate one of those godawful marshmallow sandwiches for you."

As I watch him go, I feel ready to tip sideways. Maybe I do need a snack.

For the next hour, I wash sticky hands, rescue cookies from the floor before Beauregard pounces, and lead supervised treks to the bathroom so we don't lose a kid Willy Wonka–style, just in case the house decides to try something.

Occasionally, I make eye contact with the Warlock across the room. Okay, a lot more than occasionally. Our chat left me feeling very . . . *very.* I take an aggressive bite of the Fluffernutter sandwich he brought me whenever he looks over. He just smirks, looking entirely too pleased with himself. I can't take my eyes off his hands.

Slowly, the sharp pang of missing my mom goes from *needle* to *dull fork tine.*

Soon, a sugar high hits all parties under four feet tall, and it takes me and Arna Jean twenty minutes to corral the kids outside to work off their fidgets. A few parents make the great sacrifice of offering to chaperone, and the Warlock joins them, though I suspect he just wants to escape for fresh air. Can't blame him. One can take only so many shrieks measuring decibels close to the pain threshold.

The rest of us tidy the kitchen. While I sweep up sprinkles Ms. Zeen will find until Christmas, I snatch pieces of the ongoing conversation at the table.

"How old do you think I am?" Carolina is saying. "Hedgewitches have longer than normal lifespans, not Hearthwitches. Trust me, I wasn't born when this farmhouse went up."

Eva Mae accepts a cup of tea from Ms. Zeen. "Blanche says we're the first folks inside in decades."

Ms. Buchanan snorts. "Blanche also says she remembers the Civil War."

"And you don't, Beulah?" Arna Jean asks.

"Hush your mouth."

Governess Zeen turns to Carolina. "Speaking of Hearthwitches, the Widow Witch might have broken through our warding the other day if not for the protection spell you placed on Ms. Frost. Remarkable spellwork."

Mention of the town's least favorite seasonal tradition sends the jovial mood into the deep end of unease.

Carolina huffs. "Can you believe I actually offered to make one for Gertha Fudge, since she seemed even more anxious than usual this spring? She slammed the door in my face!"

Eva Mae sips tea with one hand and runs the other over her tummy. "She tried to convince me to stay inside until the baby comes. Lectured me about how all the *soulless magic* in the air was no good for *a lady in the family way*."

Ms. Buchanan scoffs. "Pastor Webb's got her stirred into a frenzy this year. He's up to something."

As I clean, I mull over what Ms. Buchanan said earlier. Noxie is someone who could use the Widow Witch's unique curriculum vitae. So it doesn't seem a stretch to assume that in her long life, the Widow Witch has taken some terrible husbands—and created a few grateful widows.

"We'll have to put poor Gertha's mind at ease, bless her heart," Carolina says. "Honey, have you been kidnapped, tortured, maimed, drawn and quartered, or encountered any bodily danger while staying here?"

The copper pots rattle above the island, but the ladies don't notice. "Not yet."

Ms. Buchanan *tsks*. "I am curious about that boy, though. You mean to tell me this Warlock was charming enough to catch at least one young lady to have a baby?"

I accidentally drop the stack of empty trays I'm juggling, and the clatter ricochets right over Eva Mae's halfhearted, chastising "Beulah!"

"What? If he's a bachelor, I need escorts to Gertha's ridiculous church luncheons. Woman boils my blood but she makes a damn fine pineapple upside-down cake. And she lets me bring my Long Island iced teas if I don't cause a fuss."

Attempting to digest the topic of the Warlock's procreation habits, I struggle to gather the rebellious trays. And I can't even blame this ornery house for my clumsiness this time.

Ms. Buchanan smacks her lips at me. "Hang in there, sugar. Learning a new kitchen is like learning a new car or man. The mechanics are the same but all the buttons are in different places, depending on your model."

Oh Lord. I want to jam my head into the hottest door of the AGA. I compose myself long enough to say, "Lazlo is an orphan."

"Mr. Knight was his next of kin," Ms. Zeen explains.

Carolina leans forward, lowering her voice. "I heard the Widow Witch used to leave widowers behind, too. Not just widows."

Eva Mae fidgets. "Lord, I am *not* letting my husband raise this baby alone. I love him, but Hatton's cornbread isn't always done in the middle, if you know what I mean."

Ms. Buchanan nods. "You'll be fine, dear. Your Hatton seems like a good fellow."

"But she's never *not* taken someone before. What is she waiting for?"

I'm with Eva Mae, and I don't even have a husband to worry about. The Witch just changes her routine without any sort of ulterior motive? If she doesn't end up taking whatever unfortunate marital soul is next on her list, I worry that could give Webb's claim at the market credence. How would we prove the Witches of the Holler *don't* attract the Widow Witch's ire?

"The Witch will do what she has always done," Ms. Zeen says. "As she pleases."

Ms. Buchanan jabs a bony finger into the table. "If I were a betting woman—"

"You are a betting woman, Beulah," Carolina says.

"Hush—I'd bet the Witch is busy trying to balance something that's gone crooked. And if anyone's capable of causing an imbalance of magic, *well*."

She means a Warlock is responsible.

While the others don't know what I do about the Warlock's curse, he says the Witch's attention on him doesn't have anything to do with her absence this year. I might believe him. He's not a husband, and if taking him would've met her quota, she'd have done it already.

But would she truly have flattened the farmhouse the other day if Carolina's protection spell weren't in the way? It seems an extreme reaction, for a Witch all about balance.

"At some point, her bad reputation was bound to catch up to the rest of us Witches." Carolina snaps the head off an unsuspecting shortbread cat. "Whether Gertha's encouraging Webb or vice versa, they'll use whatever ammunition and red tape they can to challenge our other gatherings. A Witch won't be able to light a candle without a siren going off."

"Why *does* Fudge hate magic so much?" I ask. The youngest of us here don't have the full history the older women of the Holler do.

"Besides the fact that the Widow Witch took the woman's husband?" Ms. Buchanan shares a glance with Governess Zeen.

Ms. Zeen nods. "Leaving her with young children to raise on her own?"

Well, yes, besides that, but I'm too sheepish to let my sarcasm fight with theirs. Everyone knows Fudge lost her husband to the Witch, but that was decades ago. Why does she have a fire under her bony ass *this* year? Is it just Webb's influence? Or is it just that, for a small town, sometimes a deviation from the norm is more terrifying than the predictable devil next door?

"Gertha's family had powerful Hedgewitch magic, but she never inherited any," Carolina says. "That magic doesn't play by lineage rules, like other lower magics. Made her furious, I think. She's always envied her own ancestors."

"But Mayor Frost—even Ms. Fudge can't deny Honey's mom is a good Witch," Eva Mae says.

Ms. Zeen frowns in my direction. "You'll never convince that woman magic isn't poison. Even if it's just Farewitch magic." Her eyes unfocus, like she's fighting off a memory. If only I could grasp her hand and peek into what haunts her.

As if. She'd probably stab me with her sugar spoon.

Her words nip at me, though. *Just Farewitch magic.*

Webb and Fudge scoff at the practical magic of local Witches, then demonize a Warlock or any power that threatens their hold over the town. Maybe if my magic were meaner, stronger—like the Widow Witch herself—and I was willing to pay any price, I could do more. Like heal my mom. But then how long until someone thought I was *too* powerful?

My nervous energy climbs. Could also be the blood sugar–spiking marshmallow sandwich. Some fresh air would do me good.

On the back porch, gray clouds hang heavy above me and a breeze winds through my overalls. Leaves turn over, pale bellies up to a darkening sky. A storm is rolling in. The rain will be good for the garden, for the health and blooming of even the most stubborn plants.

Behind the Manor, kids squeal and chase one another as parents look on. Soon, the kids cajole a very stiff Warlock into dancing in a lumpy circle, which might be alarming if any of them besides him had the magic needed to form a summoning circle. Then, in a truly shocking turn of events, the Warlock lets the kids explore his gardens. His *gardens*. His private sanctuary.

Either he's sipping tea with bourbon like Ms. Buchanan, or he's actually trying to support my plan, to rewrite years of rumors and suspicion. I'm sure it helps that Lazlo looks the happiest I've ever seen him.

I suck in the crisp air, pushing away my worries, and the scent of blooming flowers coaxes my muscles to relax. The gardens are an entirely different kitchen, the Warlock his own kind of chef, but the smells are just as sweet.

For once, I'm not thinking about the next recipe. I don't want to be anywhere else beyond *this* view in *this* very moment.

"You look like you're high on something, girl." Beulah Buchanan plops onto the iron bench by the door.

Governess Zeen sits beside her. "She always looks like that."

I rehinge my jaw. These two must brainstorm different ways to tell me to fix my face.

"Congratulations, Ms. Frost," the Governess adds. "Not once in the time I've known him has the Warlock ever let anyone tromp through his gardens."

I'd smile, but that somehow sounds like an insult coming from her. It's a talent, really. No wonder she and Ms. Buchanan are friends.

"Today was still wholly unnecessary," she continues. "He didn't hire you to alleviate his tensions with the Holler."

Ouch. I know I'm not here for cookie bakes, but after so many weeks of failure, I'm going to ignore her. A win is a win. Ms. Buchanan elbows the Governess. "C'mon, Letha. Your boy Lazlo needed this. Too many folks in this Holler are afraid of fun."

"I suppose Mr. Knight will appreciate being part of the community, at least for one day."

I try not to look too satisfied. "Even grumpy folks are worth the hard work."

"I hope you still believe that come the solstice. That you believe in him," she says, her attention on the Warlock in the distance. "He certainly believes in you."

This shouldn't be news. The Warlock obviously thinks I can cure him. But somehow, her words make me feel like my heart has the hiccups.

Ms. Buchanan sniffs, lowering her voice. "He believes in you as well. Gertha would listen to you, you know."

"Listen but not forgive. Me or Mr. Knight," Ms. Zeen answers. "The folks of Foxe Holler are quick to forget their neighbors when they need someone to blame, and blame is easier to cast for those of us without magic."

"You don't owe the town—or anyone—anything, Letha."

I pretend not to listen, but I haven't been able to get Ms. Zeen to tell me anything about herself, so maybe a friend can work a different kind of magic.

"He doesn't think so, either. But I do." The Governess sighs. "He never wanted this. One mistake, and it's cost him everything, or it will. I'd hoped he learned from his parents, after—" She cuts off, eyeing me.

I'm caught.

What was *that* all about?

Ms. Buchanan looks back up at me. "And you—you push yourself too much."

Her words have a knack for cueing the beginnings of my fatigue. I shrug them off. "I'm a Farewitch. I like to try hard." *Otherwise, I'm failing.*

"Sugar, you have to care for yourself so you can care for others."

"With respect, ma'am, that doesn't work in every scenario."

The old woman gives me the meanest side-eye. "You've gone above and beyond for the Warlock and that boy, two people you barely know. Even for a Farewitch. Why?"

Ms. Zeen is watching me, my shifting gaze, my complete inability to not follow the Warlock and Lazlo with my eyes at all times. "Hmph. I know that look."

That's when I realize something truly, inescapably terrible.

"Because I care about them," I whisper. A helluva lot more than I bargained for.

Ms. Zeen *tsk*s. "Poor dear."

Before I can respond, Carolina appears at my elbow. "I have the spell you asked for, Honey."

Right. The next part of my plotting. Which doesn't include getting attached.

Tearing my eyes from the gardens, I give the Hearthwitch a grateful smile.

And I try, oh so hard, to remember it's a *good* thing when someone can say goodbye to their Farewitch.

Chapter Seventeen

THURSDAY, MAY 12

40 DAYS UNTIL THE SUMMER SOLSTICE

Honey's Helpful Hint, from
Honey Frost's Southern Cookbook for Recipes Gone Wrong:

Sometimes the recipes you don't make are more important than the ones you do.

Thursday morning, I'm deep in the library's stacks, fueled with coffee and a plan.

I left everyone molasses baked oats on the stove so I won't be bothered for a few hours. Lazlo mostly sticks to me like an adorable, pokey burr, but today he's slept in, and now that the cookie bake is over and the Manor is calm again, I can finally put Carolina's spell to good use.

Calm-ish. The house's silence is never a *true*, empty quiet. Ms. Zeen's clacking heels or Lazlo's laugh will float around corners, and the Warlock is only ever a glower away, watching to see what trouble I cause next. Like a heartbeat, the farmhouse thrums at the edge of my attention. It's comforting to know someone is expecting to see me every morning.

Usually, I take my time in the stacks, hunting through shelves, grabbing any volume that looks exceptionally old. Which is a lot. The sheer collection of texts, magical and not . . . folks would be ecstatic if the Warlock opened his library to the public.

But today, I'm hunting for a single specific book.

Soon, the locked enclave of books looms before me. The hum of anxiety in my mind fades into a literal buzzing vibration. It's coming from the locked stacks. A soft purr, as if the books behind the iron bars are whispering to me, encouraging me to explore.

It's surprisingly easy to break in. That is, with the spell my favorite Hearthwitch, Carolina Vázquez, gave me for tricky locks.

The gate swings open.

There's no sign at all the cage was ever out to grill me like a kebab. But I don't want to test the time limit on the house's docile mood, so I immediately go for the book that caught my attention days ago. Dessert first.

The *Foxe Holler Yonder.*

The first thing I learn is, I'm right: The archival volume contains whole issues and clippings, from a single year of our town's history, twenty-five years ago.

The front page doesn't disappoint: The library fire is the only article above the fold.

The Foxe Holler Library burned shortly after midnight and was a pile of ash by sunrise. As far as authorities know, the fire has claimed the lives of two victims, who likely gained entry after the librarian locked the facility at the usual closing time . . .

It's got facts but not much journalistic investigation. There's one mention of the mayor—Ewing Summer, my mom's predecessor—refusing to comment on accusations and community suspicion that a Witch or Warlock and "rogue" magic were responsible. Instead, he mentions plans to raise funds to rebuild. Which never happened.

No wonder Ms. Zeen got so worked up on Sunday. Since I was only about three when it burned down, I never got the details first-hand. Lord, I hope the two folks who died weren't *related* to the Governess. I've never even asked if she has family.

The rest of the thin volume covers news from the year and community announcements. But for the most part, the saved articles are of dismal affairs. Deaths and crop problems, almanac predictions that proved accurate, missing animals, storms and vicious floods. Similar to the town's rumors about the Warlock.

I flip back to the library fire. There. I spot a tiny line of ink, faded with time, under a black-and-white photo of the smoldering shell of the library. I missed the caption before.

The Foxe Holler Library the morning after the fire. The victims of the fire are believed to have been a couple, survived by a child.

The *Yonder* doesn't mention names, which is odd for a small town. This is the only article about the fire. No follow-up pieces with any identities released to the public. A dead end.

My mind thumps along with my erratic heartbeat and my skin succumbs to a chill, even though noon should be approaching. I begin to feel like I'm not just perusing archives, but holding someone's personal and very depressing scrapbook. Someone keeping track of all the terrible things they couldn't prevent.

Or the terrible things they've done.

If Arna Jean were here, she'd be able to sense the emotions hiding within the pages. Whether they were violent or more melancholy, full of guilt. But I don't want to risk taking the book out of the farmhouse, so I banish the thought of bringing her even further into my messes.

The rest of the restricted books are underwhelming, so I shift my attention to possible recipes and cures. I expected these locked bookshelves to imprison dangerous spell books, family ledgers of misdeeds, bestiaries. All number of Warlock-y texts. *Warlock Knight's Big Bad Book of Grudges Old, New, and Permanent.* I'd read that one.

Instead, I just find the contents of any family's basement: photo albums of grainy memories, property deeds, birth certificates with tiny footprints, farmers' almanacs, tickets to performances gone by, blueprints the house has rebelliously outgrown.

And handwritten recipes. Some are even in elegant Chinese characters. Finally, tucked between other handwritten recipes, I stumble on a particular list of ingredients, the delicate cursive script winking up at me.

Now we're getting somewhere. A plan takes shape.

Back in the kitchen, an hour slips by, and then I'm putting the finishing touches on my idea. A kiss of cinnamon and a first-snow dusting of powdered sugar—

"Have you slept at all since Sunday, Ms. Frost?"

Turning from the stove, I find Warlock Knight at the kitchen island. Dewy sweat mists his forehead and the prominence of the sun spots on his cheeks tells me he's been gardening all morning. May seeds will sprout vegetables, fruits, and blooms for months. He's in his element, and it suits him.

It suits him *very* well. My face heats even though the oven's off.

As his bright hazel eyes study me, I yank my traitorous gaze back under control before the need to accost him with sunscreen wins out over any common sense I have left.

"No time. We're on a schedule. Farewitches rarely rest."

"So I've noticed." He sets his gloves on the island. We've reached an agreement since the cookie bake: I promise to eat some of everything I make, and he removes his gloves in the kitchen.

The tiniest bit pleased with myself, I slide a cooling skillet onto the island.

Ube spoonbread, from what I'm positive is his grandmother's very recipe.

Like its name suggests, spoonbread bakes as a lump, like a soft scone. No slicing—just spoonfuls from a communal skillet. It's best served with friends. I wait for some trace of recognition on his face. Or applause—either works.

But he frowns. And *frowns.* Wrinkles sprout across his features. His fingers twitch toward his gloves. I can't smell the spoonbread anymore, like my taste buds ran for the hills.

"Where did you get the recipe for this?" His voice is low and terse.

"Your library."

"You mean you stole it. From the restricted section. After I told you about my mother, my family. After I asked you not to trespass."

"*Ordered* me, you mean," I retort.

"Fine. Ordered. Which you disobeyed. You're my employee, a guest here, and I've implored you to respect the boundaries that I maintain to keep this Manor running—"

"*Walls.* You have walls. Not boundaries."

"Do not debate semantics with me, Ms. Frost. We're having an argument."

I throw down my oven mitt. The soft, puffy sound is dreadfully unsatisfying. "I've had enough lectures from the men of the Holler lately; I don't need one from you. You insist a crucial resource—part of our agreement, *sir*—is off-limits, and I want a reason. Now."

"*Because* is a good reason. Those archives are restricted *because.* That is where they stay out of the way, where they have been for decades, where they belong."

I might have stayed angry if his voice didn't waver on *belong.*

My thoughts go lumpy, like bad batter, and my mistake hits me like a lobbed frozen pound cake. The locked bookshelf in the library isn't a treasure chest full of cookbooks for my entertainment. They're family artifacts. He lived alone in this house before Ms. Zeen came along. How long, is the question. How long can someone grieve, and grieve alone, before the walls begin to feel like home?

The purple of the yam now looks terribly like knockoff Play-Doh. Food can conjure the best memories. Or the worst.

"What do you need so badly from that bookshelf anyway?" he mutters.

"The recipes in there are old. I doubt a Farewitch has ever looked at them. One of them could save you."

Does he care?

Cold hazel eyes rise to meet mine. "Could they also save your mother?"

That sends the remaining teaspoon of my good mood down the sink.

He knows. He knows and he's going to fire me now for sure.

Somehow, that makes my mom's situation all the more real. I nod weakly. "Maybe. I can't know if I don't try."

"I'm assuming a Farewitch, like a Warlock, can't cure herself with her own magic?"

"Theoretically, it's possible. But we have to be focused for a recipe to be strong. If I'm feeling off, the magic won't work. Think of it like taking a test with a fever. I can do it, but I'm barely gonna pass. C plus material."

As I explain, he just listens, no advice or false encouragement. He looks like he might want to ask more questions, but decides against it. I'm grateful we're not lingering on the topic.

A sigh crawls out of him. "I wouldn't have blamed you for leaving after three weeks. Hell, three days."

Just say *Thank you for staying*, infuriating man. "Well, you are paying me, sir."

"Is it enough?"

"I can manage my finances fine, thanks."

"That's not what I—" He cuts off, some decision crossing his face. "During your interview, I was cross with you. I was . . . unnerved by your memory affinity. But I would never make light of you. Your magic."

I think he just complimented me.

Nah. From him, even a neutral statement would sound like praise. "Do Warlocks ever inherit magic like Witches?"

"It's possible. But it's sporadic. Higher magic often skips generations. We don't have direct lineages like Witches. Our parents can be ordinarily human." His jaw clenches, then releases. "To a fault."

Strong power, but inconsistent. Whereas a Witch's lower magic is more practically bound, but guaranteed in a family. Balance.

"Hence why some might perceive Warlocks as immortal. We've had more opportunities, thus more collective time, for our magic and population to expand."

"And consume." The words jump out like popovers before I can stop them. But something about the Warlock makes me feel like I can speak plainly.

Throughout history, men learned they could take midwifery skills, herbal knowledge, and folk remedies and monetize everything. All while they imprisoned or killed Witches for following the same practices, just outside formal institutions that didn't allow women in the first place.

He nods. "Warlocks have often played a shameful role in the history of Witches."

"Some have," I clarify. "The ordinary men are always the most dangerous, though."

"Don't let Oris Webb intimidate you. You're a talented Farewitch, Ms. Frost."

Maybe he *is* trying to compliment me. "And you're better with people than you think. You certainly don't seem like a man who's lived in a creepy farmhouse forever."

"Some days, I feel like I have. More often than not, lately."

That's my opening. Before his walls close ranks, I say, "I don't think I've ever heard you call this place *home*. Only *house*. *Manor*. *Estate*. Your *parents' home*, maybe, if you slip up."

"When I *slip up*?"

"*Mmm.* When you tell me something you clearly haven't told anyone in a long time. Or ever. Right after you do, you talk a little too fast, like you've been running."

"I do not run to anything. It's terribly demeaning."

"You'd rather run away, right?"

His gaze narrows. "I don't think we know each other well enough for you to say something like that."

Crap. The verbal sparring was so tempting, so natural. Maybe I do need a nap.

"Does anyone know you well enough to say something like that?"

"As in, from my childhood? *Ages ago*, I believe you said during your interview."

Did I say that . . . ? Surely not. "I wasn't trying to imply you were old . . ."

"You did already assume I was more than three hundred."

Recover, recover. "I didn't mean—"

"Is it the gray hair?"

I'm too nervous to stop rambling. "No! It's more pepper than salt—"

"How old do you think I am, really?"

Oh boy, back up. *Retreat.* "No thank you."

"*No thank you?*"

"Not a fan of that question. Sounds like a trap."

The Warlock of Foxe Holler *snorts* at me. His stern exterior fractures, lips twisting to the side. He's . . . *teasing* me. And I fell for it.

"Relax, Ms. Frost. I started getting gray hair at eighteen."

The eggshell tension between us cracks just long enough for me to see him fighting a smirk that, hell, might even be a smile.

The silence that follows is a half-and-half mix of comfortable and heavy, an Arnold Palmer of possibility. Neither of us moves to leave. Minutes ago, we were arguing over spoonbread, and now we're . . . this. Something has shifted.

I muster some of Momaw's *umph* and stumble right out on a skinny little limb. "My mom keeps her illness hidden, so she doesn't get many visitors." Deep breath. I'm at my quota for keeping secrets. "Would you like to visit the hospital with me?"

His wish magic can't cure disease, but maybe the decades of

research he's got on me have unearthed other valuable information. Just maybe, there's something he'll see that I can't.

His eyes darken with indecision.

Then his face disappears into a shadow as he looks away from me. "I don't leave the Manor, Ms. Frost. You know that."

The small spark of something delicate and hopeful behind my rib cage pops like an overtaxed light bulb. A silly little wish. "Right." It was way too brazen a request anyway.

Turning back to the stove, I barely catch the frown on his face. It's different this time, not angry, but . . . regretful.

Like it's the first time he hasn't enjoyed telling someone no.

Chapter Eighteen

FRIDAY, MAY 13

39 DAYS UNTIL THE SUMMER SOLSTICE

Honey's Helpful Hint, from
Honey Frost's Southern Cookbook
for Recipes Gone Wrong:

Hands are a cook's best tools. Keep them busy and they'll stay out of trouble. Nothing like the bustle of a kitchen to shake off the demons of the mind.

Friday the thirteenth is a lucky day for Farewitches.

After all, a baker's dozen promises an extra something special. Who's mad at a bonus bagel, one more cookie?

It takes just thirteen minutes for Marigold Frost to prove me wrong.

From the hospital bed, my mom shakes her head, a bobblehead in one direction. "If he's been cursed by the Widow Witch, he's fu—well, you're shit out of luck."

"Stellar, Mom. Much appreciated."

"That's not an invitation to blame yourself. Curses aren't easy magic. He's got a better chance begging her to release him, and he should be prepared to bargain away a testicle or two. Or a treasured family heirloom, maybe his entire estate. Perhaps all three. Or four, as it were."

I slump back against the stiff pleather of the hospital armchair. "I don't think reasoning with her is his problem." I leave out the part about the Witch nearly demolishing the farmhouse. "If appeasing her were an option, he'd have tried." And the begging type, the Warlock is not.

Still, something has felt odd about the Warlock's curse since he confessed, and I hoped my mom might be able to help me puzzle out the inkling. No such luck.

She looks me up and down. "I hear the nurses keep asking when Honey Frost's next *culinary class* is."

A bittersweet feeling settles in my chest. Teaching kids who don't care if cookies have magic, only if they taste good—turns out, I don't hate that part. But the problem with being a Farewitch, whether at the Apothakery or Knight Manor, is that there's never any time or space to think about becoming anything else. I'm stuck in the life but trying to lead multiple lives, like some crumb-coated James Bond. Call me Double-Oh-Flour.

"Carolina said her niece Anna took home three tins of cookies, and you know what, now that girl is going around the hospital selling them for three dollars a pop!"

My mom has always been able to tell when I'm not myself, and bless her, she never fails to cheer me up.

"Entrepreneurial. I like it."

"You certainly left an impression on the town, girl."

"Good or bad?"

"Depends who you ask. The church ladies and Webb say you're responsible for the miseducation of innocent children. But the kids think you live in a fairy-tale castle. A haunted fairy-tale castle, but the allure is there."

The gossip feels like it should annoy me, but I can't muster the energy. After little to no sleep last night (that did *not* involve fitful dreams of the Warlock), I jumped out of bed at dawn to answer a frantic phone call from Carolina.

Cardiac event—stable now but—she didn't want you to worry. You and Silas need to . . .

Ears numb, I didn't hear the rest, and my skin buzzed all the way into town, like I was wearing a jacket of horseflies. I didn't blink until I parked, and I know I didn't take a full breath until I saw my mom was upright in her bed. Shaken, but alive.

"I'm glad you're engaging with the town," my mom continues. "I trust Silas with the day-to-day, but there's no substituting the relationship folks have with their Farewitch. The recipes aren't as important as the conversations."

"So you've told me."

"Are you still hunting through grimoires?"

"The Warlock's library is massive, Mom. If I can't find something in there to help you, then I'm a disgrace of a Farewitch."

"I was the Farewitch once, too. Trust me, if you're not careful, you won't get any time for rest or pleasure until you're too old to enjoy it."

"But—"

"That's why I don't want you to miss me. When the day comes, mourn me for five minutes, then get on with your life."

My shoulders tense with a chill. The air-conditioning is on extra North Pole the closer we get to June. And the solstice. "Mom, leave the catastrophizing for the church ladies."

But my protest is as weak as she is right now.

Her wild halo of hair isn't even braided this morning, and her under-eye bags are a full set of luggage. An oily sheen hides her irises, like bad store-bought whipped cream, and the veins in her hands pop against her pale skin.

"I'm just being realistic," she says, her mayor voice surfacing. "Magic has limits and costs. Witches can't conjure what we want out of nothing."

"But this time, I know I'm close—"

"We're always *close,* Honey." She slaps a weak hand against her blanketed thigh. "Listen to me. You need to start enjoying your life. Not trying to prolong mine."

"I see we're all cheer and pep this morning." Silas strolls in with a huge thermos of coffee he brews at home. The only coffee shop in town is the diner. Or the gas station.

My mom huffs. "Being mayor means being honest. You have to know what you're up against. Like your Widow Witch problem. She's been a force of chaos since before your great-grandmother Meemaw Hazeleen Frost was in nappies."

"Speaking of stubborn patients . . ." Silas looks in my direction. "How is the Warlock?"

"Stubborn as molasses," I say. But with the right ingredients, could be made sweet.

"Any luck on the culinary side of things?"

"We're apparently bankrupt in the luck department."

I've brought them up to speed to brainstorm. Operation Save the Warlock. Save the Mayor. We're doing a lot of saving. Who in the world gave me the wheel here?

As my mom launches into mayoral housekeeping matters, Silas pulls three ceramic coffee mugs from his satchel. Matching, of course. But I lock the sass inside today. I secretly appreciate this new ritual. It's a sense of normalcy for my mom, who is probably tired of consuming everything via foam cups.

But when he pours me a cup, I can barely touch it.

I can tell my mom has lost more weight. That's the most unsettling thing of all. Moms and Farewitches are supposed to grow latitudinally with wisdom, love, and lots of birthday cakes. Not shrink. What the hell is happening? Not for the first time, I wonder if the Frosts are just unlucky. Wrong soil, sour grapes? Maybe the Warlock really didn't *get* himself cursed. Maybe he was only a man at an impossible crossroads.

His dour expression comes back to me, his reminders for me to eat something when he hasn't even said *Good morning* yet. A sudden warm rush of appreciation fills my belly, confusing the hell out of me.

"Honey!" Mom's voice whisks me out of my thoughts. "Pay attention. Did you hear Silas? He's doing valuable, on-the-ground reconnaissance."

"Sorry." I force myself to be present. When you have limited time left with someone, it becomes impossible to live in the moment and treasure the days left together. The brain thinks only in *before*s and *after*s. Now that's a curse.

"You make me sound like a spy, Marigold, and I don't get paid enough for that." Silas arranges his suit jacket on the back of his chair. New England blue today. "As I was saying, I've spoken with folks in town, and Mr. Knight still isn't polling well, even among the cookie-bake parents. It's as if they've entirely forgotten he hosted them without a single murder. If they were wary of him before, they're wary of him still."

There goes any good mood I was trying to build. "But—how can a town even hate someone they only half remember?" Silas and my mom aren't struggling to remember him right now, and we're well outside the Manor, the Warlock far from their sight. Strange.

"While there are a few outliers with differing opinions," Silas continues, "namely Ms. Buchanan—our efforts to reduce fear and mistrust of the Warlock in town weren't lucrative."

I force down a sip of coffee. "Is this how you sound on your dates? No wonder they end with biscuit dodgeball. I feel like we're on the campaign trail."

He points a finger at me. "We *are* on the campaign trail. To ensure your Warlock doesn't get run out of town. Oris Webb would outlaw all magic in the Holler right now if he could."

"The Kentucky fried coven could've told me that in half the time."

"The what? Never mind, don't tell me. Did you know more than half of the town council goes to his church now? He'll break any tie."

"And ever since Carolina's mother retired, there hasn't been a single Witch on the council, either," my mom adds.

My gut pinches at the thought of what happens if enough incensed sheeple decide they'd rather be on Webb's good side than the side of good. "And he's not *my* Warlock," I mutter.

Silas rolls his eyes. "Well, he *is* your employer and pays your salary, which is a much-needed infusion of cash for the medical bills here."

My mom harrumphs. "If your good looks don't win you my job, your bluntness will."

He leans forward. "Ladies, we are so far past the time for Southern politeness, even Dolly Parton could not sugarcoat our situation."

"You're right, you're right," my mom sighs. "I hear Webb's sermons are getting angrier by the week."

"What's his deal anyway?" I ask. "Why the urgency now? The Widow Witch has been around for ages. If Webb's actually anti-magic, he'd focus his energy there. Not on a disgruntled gardener who doesn't step off his front porch."

"The Warlock is an unknown to Webb, and men are threatened by what they can't control." Mom looks to Silas. "No offense, dear."

"None taken," he says, raising his mug.

"You keep Webb at a distance, you hear? He'll come after you when you're the new mayor. He'll think the changing of the guard is a good time to fight you for territory."

"I'm no stranger to difficult men, Marigold."

And *that's* when I realize why the room is so stuffy, why my clothes itch, why the coffee tastes like watery beef broth, why everything feels *wrong wrong wrong*. Something drastic has shifted in my mom's attitude. A tectonic-plate-level shift.

I send a glare the Warlock would be proud of right at my mom. "You're talking like you're already dead."

The accusation hums between us.

No, no, and no. I will not be the only person convinced there's a cure. Because if my mom has given up on herself . . . that means she's already given up on me. As her Farewitch. As her daughter. Slimy guilt slithers into my core. We've used all this visiting time together to talk about *my* problems. Maybe I am a terrible daughter.

Mom releases a ragged breath. "You shouldn't have to deal with any of this nonsense. I was hoping I could give you another fifteen years before I became a cranky burden."

"You can't think like that. And you know me—great at multitasking. Stretching my bandwidth is my other magical talent."

"I wanted a better life for you, Honey. Less stress. More joy."

"I'll take that on a sticker for my thermos," Silas murmurs.

"But we're Farewitches!" My pulse thrums with the beginnings of panic. This doesn't sound like the mom I know at all.

"And now look at me. I tried to be mayor, something new. And it's nearly killed me."

"Honey's right. You can't think like that," Silas says. "Fate is funny. You might've gotten sick just the same, mayor or not."

He receives two frosty looks.

"The fact is," my mom continues, "the entire basis of a Farewitch's occupation is caretaking at the expense of ourselves. What kind of person bakes all day long and is never allowed a taste of their own work? Their own bite of happiness?"

"People with eating disorders?"

"Lord Almighty, Silas, that was rhetorical."

The hospital room falls into tense silence.

After a loud slurp of coffee, Silas stands. "Those should be by the window, Marigold. Not hiding on your nightstand. The sun is good for them."

He moves a vase of flowers to the room's windowsill. Marigolds. A lot of them. Must've come from a big garden. How've I not noticed them until now?

"Did you bring those?"

He shakes his head. "Not me this time."

"The staff were giving some to all the patients," Mom says. "Someone made an anonymous donation to the hospital this week."

My neck practically lights on fire. Momaw's voice rings in my head. *Silly, silly girl.*

The Warlock has always been honest about one thing: He doesn't leave the Manor. And what do I do? Fault him for it.

What does he do?

The man sends *flowers.*

Oh Lord. I'm *the worst.*

Even as I stew in my chair, a delicate bud of appreciation for the Warlock blooms in my chest. Soon, Mom grows tired enough to nap, and Silas and I leave her in peace.

Outside, sunshine warms my cheeks before a breeze chases it away. Typical Southern spring. Clear skies for a cookout at noon, a vertical bath by three. Already brainstorming recipes, I cinch my corduroy barn coat tight, wishing for my favorite wingback in the Manor's library. Definitely a chicken-and-dumplings kind of day. A dish good for bouts of sadness.

"See what I mean?" Silas says, buttoning his suit. "She's like that all the time now."

"Her morbid pragmatism is normal, but the existential resignation is new. Have her latest tests shown anything new?"

"Nothing definitive. Bloodwork so-so. Her numbers are still off. *More* off. She tried to sign paperwork for me earlier, but her hand was shaking so badly, she couldn't grip the pen. She got pissed. Remind me never to play darts against your mother."

"A temper is a good sign for her."

For once, Silas doesn't have anything to say. The phenomenon is a bit nauseating. The man is meant to be chatty.

"Silas."

"Hmm?" He looks up from his phone.

"What *actually* changed? Don't avoid the question."

"Why do you torture yourself?"

"It's my favorite recipe."

"You want to know? Truly? The cookie bake, of all things. It hit her this could be her last Mother's Day as your mom."

A renewed, icier chill stabs me in the back. I want to vomit. I wasn't even thinking about that possibility—probably because I've refused to accept it.

"Please tell me this is the silence of thinking and not a panic attack."

No panicking. At least, not today. Breathe. Ask for help.

"If this was your mom, what would you do next?"

His face slackens with surprise at my question. "My mom is a lawyer-sommelier in Manhattan who still overnights me care packages of bagels, so I'd be buying a one-way flight to LaGuardia and renewing my New York Public Library card right about now."

"That explains both too much and not enough about you."

"I'm an enigma."

"Wait, you get baked goods shipped all the way from New York City? Betrayal."

"Not important." He grows serious. "You know what is? The quality time has done wonders for her morale. Today was an improvement, if you can believe it."

"Message received. I'm staying in town tonight to help Arna Jean plan the summer menu, so I'll be here tomorrow." Which also gives me a chance to check on the shop. The Bookwitch has a habit of burning sage too close to the paper cupcake liners. Not that I don't already get plenty of Apothakery updates from the Bookwitch's daily posts. She showcases new items every week with the hashtag *#fareforthot*. The latest specialty is a blueberry and yellow corn croissant. "Now if you'll excuse me, I'm going to go sit in my truck and be sad."

He throws on his Illestevas. Even with the somber mood, he looks like an off-duty model. "Between your magic, Carolina's healthcare, and my sunny demeanor, we'll solve what's going on with your mom. You'll have dozens of Mother's Days ahead of you."

"Don't sell yourself short."

He shrugs. "I know when I'm the personality hire."

"Date?" I ask, nodding at his suit. It's Friday night, after all.

"Not tonight. I'm going to sit at home, divinely alone, with a bottle of sauvignon blanc."

"That's a first."

"Follow my example. When's the last time you did something for the first time?" He winks and takes off toward the town square.

As I watch him disappear down the sidewalk, my phone dings with a text before I can think too hard about his question. The screen shows a message from an unknown local number.

Oh no. It can't be.

Hell is surely freezing over.

Greetings, Ms. Frost.
Postman Claywell helped me purchase a mobile cellular device.
Sincerely,
Mr. Knight

My stomach flips. *The Warlock of Foxe Holler bought a cell phone.* For me? Ha. Not likely. And the formality with this guy. *Phew.* But knowing his texts are as on brand as the letter he sent to the Apothakery all those weeks ago is weirdly comforting. At least we've upgraded from *Regretfully*.

So we're doing this, then, are we?

Congrats sir
your new phone can make calls too

even with no cell service you can use WiFi

ask Ms. Zeen to show you

Pending dots dance across the screen. I hold my breath. If he went to these lengths to reach me, I hope everything is all right. This is the longest I've stayed in town to visit my mom, and I bet poor Lazlo is eating nothing but tea and biscuits with Governess Zeen. Or Goldfish. Honestly, the entire Manor is likely to fall apart without my nonnegotiable mealtimes together.

Heavens above, I think I might actually miss the farmhouse.

This is taking way too long. He could have fallen into a ditch in his own garden for all I know. I call the number.

When he picks up, I say, "You don't have to text. Calling is fine."

"Thank God. When do you return? The Manor is too quiet and peaceful."

The sound of his voice does a weird thing to the surface of my skin. "Tomorrow evening. After visiting hours at the hospital—"

"Would you like to have dinner?"

My stomach flips again. Freaking flapjacks in there. Dinner. "Sunday supper?"

"No, Saturday. Keep up, Ms. Frost. Dinner with me. Tomorrow night. Together."

Oh. *Oh.*

All my brain can come up with is: "Are you cooking?"

A maniacal cackle slices through the background. Lazlo. "I haven't thought that far ahead," the Warlock mutters, shushing someone.

I bite my lip.

When's the last time you did something for the first time?

"Invitation accepted. If only to experience what will be your audition video for the Food Network's hottest new show, *Recipes for When You Need to Say Sorry to Your Roommate*."

"You and I are not *roommates*, Ms. Frost." He says the word with derision.

"Oh?" I cling to the familiar mockery to keep from thinking about my mom in the hospital behind me. "Then what are we?"

He scoffs. "I'm not sure. But it's not roommates, sweetheart."

My heart somersaults. Did he just—why am I *smiling*?

There's a pause that might be muffled swearing. "I apologize, Ms. Frost. That was . . ."

"Bold."

"I didn't mean—or intend to imply—"

I can hear it in his voice. He's actually *flustered*. Now *I* feel bold. And like messing with him a bit. "Say it again. Sir."

The silence on the other end of the phone is pure gold. Why do I get such enjoyment from ruffling his careful composure? Whatever the reason, this is a new flavor of something I love the taste of. My rain cloud mood from a minute ago is evaporating.

"Consider your point about my cooking skills well received," he finally replies, his voice low and simmering.

"Alternative show name: *Magical Recipes for the Magic of Friendship*."

"Have your fun, Ms. Frost."

"Oh! *A Knight for One: Solo Recipes for the Reclusive at Heart.*"

"Do you hang up this contraption, or do I?"

I stifle a gratified snicker and hang up before he can hear how pleased I am.

The feeling doesn't last. My grin falls suddenly.

Across the street, so still he nearly quicksands right into the beige concrete of the sidewalk, is Oris Webb, sinking his teeth into a small yellow apple.

Watching me.

I follow his eyes as they skitter to the hospital sliding doors behind me, a question on his pale brow.

Chapter Nineteen

SATURDAY, MAY 14

38 DAYS UNTIL THE SUMMER SOLSTICE

Honey's Helpful Hint, from
Honey Frost's Southern Cookbook
for Recipes Gone Wrong:

There are three rules on a first date:
1. Make your date cook. You'll learn everything you need to know.
2. If you have to cook, stick with the basics. A phenomenal mac and cheese is better than a bad boeuf bourguignon.
3. Don't fall too early.

"You're not wearing overalls, are you?"

The Governess and I are staring at my makeshift rack of clothes.

Unfortunately, the internet does not know what to wear to *dinner with a Warlock* when all you have in your closet are aprons, athleisure, clogs, and a single scrunchy. Prep a five-course meal solo? That I can do. Get ready for a dinner-maybe-date with a man in his own home? Impossible.

Ms. Zeen took one glance at me through my open door and promptly inserted herself into the situation. I think I'm grateful. For now.

"In my defense, I didn't expect to need anything *other* than overalls."

She sighs, clutching an invisible set of pearls like a rural coastal granny. "I might have something you could work with."

I hold back a shimmy of triumph. I knew she must be hiding something other than cardigan sets in her closet. "I'll come, too."

"Let's get a few things clear as moonshine, dear."

"I didn't have you as a moonshine girl."

She frowns. Not a joke girl, either, then. "One. I think this dinner is one of the top-ten worst ideas Mr. Knight has ever had."

"For curiosity's sake, am I more in the one-to-five or the five-to-ten range—"

"Two. I am only helping because Lazlo is excited, and the boy needs something to keep him entertained." She points a tastefully nude, manicured finger at me. "Three. No one goes in my room. Ever. In fact, everyone should make it a general rule to stick to their *own individual rooms*." Her eyes narrow.

Please. No one needs to worry. The last time I put a single toe inside the Warlock's bedroom, I was picked up and removed like a disobedient traffic cone. "Hiding bodies in your lair, Ms. Zeen?"

The older woman pats her French roll even though there's not a hair out of place and she knows it. "If tonight jeopardizes your arrangement with the Warlock regarding his health, *you'll* be the next body." She turns on a kitten heel. "Stay here."

She's gone just long enough for me to get panicky. What if tonight *does* end in disaster? The Warlock is my employer. Maybe he only asked me to dinner to be friendly and this is all a ploy to lodge his gardening fork prongs into my softhearted sympathy. *A ruse to capture naïve young women. Classic fairy-tale monster. Hide your soul!*

Though, if anyone seems like a true beast from a storybook, it's Oris Webb, watching me yesterday at the hospital. I choose to push that memory *far* away tonight.

The Governess returns just before I start spiraling. She holds up a dress the exact shade of pink rock salt.

"I wasn't aware this color was in your vocabulary," I say, earning another scowl. But with a closer look, I see it's not a dress at all. It's a seventies-ish satin nightgown, sleeveless, freed from its housecoat. It looks like it's never been worn. "This is too nice. I can't wear it."

"Take it and let this be the end of it. The color suits your angel food cake complexion."

Even if I've just been insulted . . . she's right. There are no jewel tones in my future. I slip the delicate fabric over my skin. Ms. Zeen has an hourglass figure I don't, so I grab the tie from one of my aprons and fasten it around my waist in a small bow.

Now I look more cocktail hour than sleepover. Better.

We study my appearance in the mirror. Ms. Zeen tilts her head. "Acceptable."

That is a thousand out of ten coming from the old woman. This could be a rare window of camaraderie. Watching her in the safety of the mirror, I ask, "How did you wind up at Knight Manor, Ms. Zeen?"

"The house needed a caretaker, and I needed a house."

I pretend to fiddle with the bow so she thinks I'm making innocent small talk. She'll close up like a clam if she thinks I'm genuinely curious. "You weren't the Governess when Mr. Knight was growing up?"

"No, I arrived long after Mr. Knight was officially a practicing Warlock. He grew busy consulting on curse magic and needed assistance with his research. But he still had dismal manners. Took him years to learn how not to enrage the senior Warlocks of the Eldercraft."

A laugh bubbles out of me. Something tells me she's gotten plenty of pay raises over the years. "And when Lazlo arrived?"

"Mr. Knight, handle the boy alone? Can you *imagine*. Anarchy." She gives me the barest grin. Then it vanishes. Must be some warping in the mirror.

"So you've stayed, all these years? For the Warlock."

"I owed Mr. Knight a favor. Even if he does not agree. Besides, why would I live in town with all the noise and gossip when I can live here, in the peace and quiet?" Her lips purse. "Before you moved in, that is."

I ignore the jab. "Gertha Fudge not your ideal neighbor, then?"

Ms. Zeen breathes the sigh of a weary woman. "Gertha's just angry. And angry women are usually right about something."

Can't argue there. There's a lot of anger going around. "I'm glad Lazlo makes the Warlock happy. Or, less *unhappy*."

"He does. But the boy is only here because of unfortunate circumstances. Mr. Knight would rather he not have needed to come at all."

Right. Lazlo's parents.

"Word of advice, Ms. Frost. The more you avoid growing attached to him, the easier things will be."

My gut churns. Does she mean Lazlo, or the Warlock? "You make it sound like he's going somewhere." I don't specify who I mean, either.

Before she turns away, she tucks in the dress's tag against my spine. A lance of sadness runs right through my ribs. The gesture reminds me of Momaw. "You're going to be late."

Conversation over. I deflate, and don't point out it's hard to be late for a dinner in my own kitchen.

When she's gone and I'm alone again, I wrestle my bangs and fuss over my stress chin acne in the mirror, not sure why I even care. I can't fathom how Arna Jean has the stamina for eyeliner every day. Why did I even agree to this dinner in the first place?

Easy. The more I know about a patient, the more I can connect lifestyle dots and personalize treatment. I wonder if the Warlock will ever let me see another memory, or if I'll have to decipher him like a faded recipe for the dwindling days he has left.

Much too soon, there's a knock, precisely at nine.

With a tissue, I dab the nervous sweat pooling under my arms. Why am I so anxious?

Just. Dinner. *Relax.*

When I open the door, Warlock Knight is at the threshold, loom-brooding as usual. That's about all that's usual, though.

No dirt, no sweaty bandana. He's in a white button-down with a band collar, loafers instead of boots, and his forest-green slacks have a freaking pleat. His black hair rests snugly in a tie at the back of his neck, wild strands tamed away from his face. No gardening gloves in sight, but his hands are hiding, clenched in his pockets. Like he's making an effort to focus.

I stare. And stare. He's looking very much like not *just dinner*. Oh boy.

Oh boy, Momaw Frost echoes in my head.

"Evening." His mouth is a familiar severe line, but I'm glad. I don't know what I'd do with a scowl-free Warlock.

I swallow, throat dry. "I didn't realize I was allowed out in the Manor this late. We sure this is a good idea?"

He raises an unamused eyebrow. "It most definitely isn't. But I'll make sure the house doesn't bother us."

"Right. The only things dangerous here are the books."

"Did you remember to eat lunch, Ms. Frost? Your sarcasm has teeth tonight."

"Are we going to have one of those fun little arguments again?" I run self-conscious hands over my dress, waist to my hips.

His eyes flick down for the briefest second. "Only if you ask nicely."

The tiniest bit of tension dissipates. This feels more like familiar territory. I fall into step beside him and we head for the kitchen.

"So, a cell phone. Miss me that much?"

"Lazlo did." His eyes stay firmly forward as we walk, elbow to elbow but never touching. The farmhouse is suspiciously calm, no mazelike hallways or missing doorways. "How is your mother?"

"Next topic, please."

He glances at me out of the corner of his eye. "I procured a phone because I regretted how we left things before you went to visit her."

"Well, forgiveness depends on what you made for dinner. Redemption depends on the quality of someone's seasoning."

"Actually, I have a small surprise."

"Did you . . . order takeout?"

The surprise is waiting for us in the kitchen, dressed as a tiny maître d'. White bow tie and arm napkin included.

I stifle a pleased chortle when Lazlo bows for us.

"Lazlo made dinner tonight," says the Warlock. "He insisted on serving us in his new restaurant, formerly known as the kitchen."

The boy clucks, chin in the air. "Sorry, we're full. Do you have a *reservation*?"

"Nine o'clock," the Warlock says. "Two people." He adds it like an afterthought, like it's been a minute since he's requested dinner for an even number.

The boy consults his seating booklet (palm). That Sharpie isn't coming off anytime soon. "Hmm. We're very busy. Wait! I see you. Right this way." He leads us to the kitchen table, which someone has dressed with a white linen tablecloth. A pot of fresh basil rests between two place settings, a centerpiece of herbs instead of flowers. Fitting.

But, coming from the Warlock, a bouquet of herbs seems way more intimate than flowers.

My gut squeezes. *Definitely* not Just Dinner.

I take my seat across from the Warlock as Lazlo says, "The specials are a tomato and beet salad, mac and cheese, and Southern shakshuka. And that's all we have so you better order it."

He speeds off to the fridge.

"Ten out of ten surprise," I say, and mean it.

The Warlock meets my gaze across the table. *Our* table. "Don't fret, I'm in charge of anything sharp or fire related. Also, Ms. Zeen is nearby with a fire extinguisher." His voice lowers. "But I'm supposed to deny everything if anyone asks."

Lazlo returns with the beverage program: two frosty glass bottles of Cheerwine. But seeing my mom's favorite drink doesn't ruin my good mood tonight. I just think of her and smile. The Warlock gives the boy a nod of appreciation.

As serious as I can, I say, "Mr. Knight, how do the specials sound to you?"

"We came all this way, we have to try them."

Lazlo dashes away, pleased. With the smells coming from the kitchen, my pulse is quick, giddy.

The Warlock brings out a bottle of Shiraz—it's dusty, older than I am—and pours two glasses. "Lazlo's having an illegal amount of fun cooking for you."

I sip the wine. It's fantastic, of course. He must have a stash hidden in some pocket of the farmhouse. I need to find *that*. "I reject the idea fun can be illegal."

"A twenty-year-old me would have agreed. The Eldercraft . . . not so much." He hesitates. "I wanted to apologize in a way that would mean something to you. Anything less would be insincere. You came here to do your job and I haven't made it easy."

The basil bouquet, the wine, the tablecloth. Two candles flicker between us. Two! Did he really go to all this trouble to say *sorry*?

"I hope you didn't find new clothes just for me. For dinner, I mean."

"Don't think me that industrious. Lazlo found these items at the back of my closet. You should be grateful I'm not in a waistcoat or a bow tie. Or both."

I bite the inside of my cheek to stop a giggle. Really, what's gotten into me? Have I been on so few dates recently, I've forgotten how to do this? But this isn't a date. So it doesn't matter.

"Probably for the best." I give my best non-date shrug of indifference. "You don't have the Adam's apple for a bow tie."

"I'll have to burn my collection, then."

I grin over the lip of my wineglass. "If it makes you feel better, I borrowed this dress from Ms. Zeen. All I had clean was a single apron and a pair of knee socks."

He coughs roughly, sputtering. You'd think a wizened old Warlock could handle his vintage.

Just as he recovers, Lazlo appears with the appetizer. "Tomato and beet salad, *right from the garden*." He levels A Look at the Warlock. "*He* didn't want me to mention that part, but Ms. Zeen said he's too modest."

Then he scampers back to the other side of the kitchen.

Not *just* tomatoes. Heirloom tomatoes and glistening beets, hues of rusty red and poppy orange and indigo purple, like a sun is setting across the sky of my plate. The first bite is pure sunshine. Simple. Maldon salt, young basil, balsamic vinegar, olive oil.

Half my dish is already gone when I stop to speak. "You are too humble. Ms. Zeen is right. But don't tell her I said that."

The pink tint on his cheeks is gone so quickly, I might've imagined it. "Ms. Zeen has an aversion to the disruption of any historically proven routine."

"Something in the water around here, huh."

He raises an eyebrow.

Twirling a beet in pooled olive oil, I add, "She told me you were a real helligan when you were younger."

"Ms. Zeen is . . ." He stares hard at his tomatoes. "She's a formidable and welcome force of good in the midst of my mistakes."

"Her power comes from her cardigan sets." Swear on my cast iron, I get the smallest smile out of him. It only makes me want another.

"I think she only wears those shoes of hers so I can hear her coming and won't be startled," he says. "I was too used to my own silence before she arrived."

Jesus, and here I thought the place was awfully dead when I got here. Before Ms. Zeen, he would've lived completely alone. For years. What must it have been like?

Incredibly lonely. That's what. I try not to think about it.

The Warlock bites into a tomato as yellow as a Meyer lemon. "Ms. Zeen says you're writing a book. Tell me about it."

Oh, that woman. She *does* listen to me. But only to gather embarrassment fuel. "Ah, it's not really a *book* book." I shrug so it feels less serious. "I'm just compiling cooking tips and life lessons courtesy of the Frost family, gems I don't want to lose. And I wanted my favorite recipes in one place."

He refills my glass. "That sounds like a real book to me."

"My Momaw inspired the idea," I say, perking up. "Her stories about growing up got me curious about food culture here. Like the connection between resources and wealth, culinary heritage. These small towns can't guarantee passable roads, and even then, fresh goods can be tough to source and keep, refrigeration or not. Ironic, given the farms, but a lot of the farmland around here back then went to tobacco. So these hollers end up with cookbooks full of recipes dependent on canned items and what you grow yourself. Even my mom never saw an actual bulb of garlic growing up. It was only garlic powder . . ."

I stop. He's watching me, silent. Not even eating.

"Sorry, I didn't mean to ramble."

He shakes his head. "You often apologize for knowing things. It's a poor habit you should break."

The next sip of wine goes right to my warm cheeks. "It's less book, more hobby. I've been too busy to finish the thing. Although I've been able to test way more recipes here than in my tiny apartment. I'd kill to live in this kitchen."

"You do live in this kitchen, Ms. Frost."

"That's . . . beside the point."

He sighs, but it's halfhearted. One might even say *affectionately irritated.*

"You sent marigolds to my mom." This is my interrogation, after all. "Despite calling them—what was it?—*an uninspired choice*."

"Is that a question?"

"More an observation of a disruption to a historically proven routine."

He buys time with a long sip of his wine. Then, "Why did you hide her illness from me?"

My fork clatters on my plate. How did he turn this third-degree interview into one of his own so fast? "I didn't want you to think I took this job because you might cure my mom. You asked for a Farewitch's help, I answered as a Farewitch."

Thirtyeightdaysuntilthesummersolstice.

"So why spend your time here with me when you could be with her?"

Another question, but one I've battled all my life, really. Here or there. School or Apothakery. Big wide world or home. I opt for the truth.

"Farewitches can't keep trying the same old recipes if they're not working. Some variable has to change. So I need new material. A lot of it. The texts in your library are one of a kind. Some Witches use spells, Farewitches need recipes."

His head tilts, curious. "That's why you need access to the restricted section. Why we were arguing over spoonbread."

"Which you can admit was excellent, by the way."

"It was adequate."

I resist the urge to wad up my napkin and toss it at his skull. Before I can formulate a better retort, he stands and takes our wiped-clean plates to the sink. He returns with a massive cast-iron skillet of bubbling shakshuka.

Eggs swim in the tomato sauce like little suns in roiling lava, and golden-brown biscuits flecked with herbs rest between them. The Southern part of Southern shakshuka. The biscuits are soaking up gobs of spicy sauce, and my stomach growls even though we've just eaten a few pounds of tomatoes between the two of us.

Lazlo follows behind the Warlock, wiggling his eyebrows in anticipation. A bowl of mac and cheese jiggles in his arms. "I made mac, too. It's my favorite."

"You've had dinner, right?" I ask him.

"Oh yeah. I had four bowls of popcorn." His smile blips. "Don't tell Ms. Zeen."

The Warlock adds the side dish to the table and winks at his ward. Or me. I can't tell. "Don't worry. Warlocks are very good at keeping secrets."

When Lazlo scurries away, we dive in.

The new order of fun goes: farmers' markets, *this shakshuka*, then sex.

"Biscuits are super versatile, you know," I say, still battling to get another smile out of him. "Buttermilk cheddar biscuits will fix a sprained ankle. Biscuits and gravy? Broken bones. Biscuits with honey butter?"

"Let me guess, broken ego?"

"Broken heart."

Lovely laugh lines come alive around his mouth just before he stifles the grin. I bite my lip to avoid the temptation to gloat. Doesn't matter. He knows I won, anyway.

Tomato and egg in one cheek, biscuit in the other, I swallow and rip off the next Band-Aid while I'm ahead and have him at ease. "You know what's strange?"

"That you elected to go barefoot instead of wearing your usual chef's shoes?"

"Hey, I wanted to be comfortable but I didn't have anything ni—*not the point*. Lazlo asked me to read his memories the other day. Do you know what I found?"

A shadow falls across his face, his expression darkening.

"Nothing. Couldn't pull out a single memory."

His relief is instant, chest swelling as he breathes again. "How odd."

C'mon, tell me the truth. He's hiding *something* else about Lazlo's history. I'm not on a date with Geppetto—even a Warlock can't conjure up a kid out of thin air. Magic can't create life.

"Like I said, I took him in because he's blood. I won't refuse family. He might be a distant relation, but plenty of folks are related to each other across the hollers down here."

Fine. I'll back off—but only because I can just argue with him tomorrow. It's quickly becoming my favorite hobby.

"Believe me, I know. Makes dating hard, doesn't it?"

He gives me a grave look. "Not a fan of that question. Sounds like a trap."

I can't believe this man. Using my own words against me.

"Is this about my three-hundred-years-old comment from before? Because your gray hair is only at the temples, and honestly, it's sophisticated."

He coughs again, except this time he's not even drinking wine. Maybe I should check on that cough. "Don't flatter me for the sake of pity."

"I'm serious. You could snag someone with those temples."

"I'm dying. I'm not *snagging* anyone."

Oh, right. Lord, sometimes I don't know when to shut up. And he's my employer! "Sorry, I—you're right. I think I'm running on more wine than tomatoes and my mouth sometimes . . ."

"Don't stop on my account. Dying doesn't mean I can't accept a compliment."

Then he's *smirking* at me.

Any coherency dies in my throat. Was he . . . *flirting*? Was that an honest-to-God *flirtation*?

But instead of being appropriately horrified, I can only focus on the single mental image of his sun-spotted cheeks. Those peppered temples.

Oh no.

Before I can process whatever's fluttering in my chest, he asks, "I'm curious. What does a Farewitch's magic cost? To you, I mean."

Grateful for the quick change in topic, I purse my lips around a bite of mac and cheese. "Why? Are you planning to do something nefarious with that information?"

"Just making sure I'm paying you enough."

"Energy," I admit. "I get tired, weak. When I'm making food *with* magic, it's like I'm jogging, not walking. Sleep is the best renewal. It would be nice if I could forfeit some hours of rest for extra research time, but that's not how it works."

We Frost women move through life and to-do lists at autobahn speeds, and I've always resented how the need to recover slows me down. Who doesn't want more hours in the day? But magic always has a system of checks and balances. Every spell has a price tag.

See entry *Widow Witch.*

"Your magic," I begin, thoughts buzzing. "Can I—"

"No, you cannot wish for more energy."

"Not even in the Language of Small Wishes? Something like *I wish I could stay up late without getting sleepy.*"

"Theoretically. But you would still have to sleep at some point, and I won't have you become a walking waif. I can't get better if my Farewitch falls ill. You're already your mother's caregiver as well."

He runs a thumb over the lip of his wineglass, and I find myself wondering what the fine muscles of his hand would look like kneading bread dough. I wrench back my attention.

"Actually, I was in town longer this time to spend more time with her. She's not . . . I thought it was a good idea," I explain. "It's funny, usually she's so *her*, a force. I always feel like a child whenever I'm with her. But lately, it's like I'm skipping ahead now, too fast. Like I'm standing in some generational line of Frosts and soon I'm going to move up a spot. One more spot closer to the front of the line."

I don't know why I'm telling him all this now. Maybe if I open up, he will?

But he just stares at the candles between us, right through the flames and table, the tiled floor, all the way to the house's foundation. A haunted look if I've ever seen one. I suppose in another way, I'm incredibly lucky to have had my mom this long at all.

Finally, he says, "Mothers make tough patients."

A cryptic answer, frustratingly on brand. He isn't making this easy. Before the wine wears off and I lose my nerve, I'll just have to get right to my best guess.

"Did your parents die in the library fire twenty-five years ago?"

The lines of his face, which have been softening all evening, harden back in place. He hasn't admitted it directly, but I'd bet my best vanilla beans I'm right. No one looks like their own ghost is chasing them for nothing less than a tragedy like that. I'm beyond prying at this point, but I think the gaps in Lazlo's past must be related to the absolute craters in the Warlock's.

He takes a long sip before he answers, and I watch the wine pulse down his long throat. Fine, his Adam's apple is actually quite nice.

"That's a gamble of a question."

"Maybe I feel like taking some risks tonight."

His gaze whips to my exposed collarbone, then my lips, then my eyes. I feel way more naked right now than I did in the towel the night of my Bath from Hell. "You're much too clever for your own good," he murmurs.

My neck warms. *Not* what I was expecting him to say.

"The restricted books . . ." he begins, letting out a breath. "Those shelves are full of my mother's recipes, my father's notes. Their letters to each other. There are endless rooms of family history in this house, and I haven't been able to make myself go through any of it."

Oh. Those family photos—the vines that trapped me must have been protecting some of that history. Sans makeup, my own naïveté is the only blush I need. "That's why you have those books locked away. The family memories . . . I'm sorry, I wasn't thinking."

He waves a forgiving hand in my direction, finally freeing himself from his own dark cauldron of thoughts. A long, delicate strand of silence slips between us.

There's a single biscuit left in the skillet. Just as I'm debating whether I'm the kind of person who fights for a biscuit—answer: *yes*—the Warlock deftly saws it in half so we can share. A gentleman, for sure.

Lazlo has run off somewhere, and I don't want him to have to stay up past his bedtime to clean, especially since he cooked. Our plates empty, I stand to take them to the sink but the Warlock stops me. "I owe you a tour of the gardens."

He shared his gardens with the kids at the cookie bake, but I've only seen them from a distance. He insists on bringing me all the herbs I need.

Glancing down, I'm relieved to see I haven't splattered sauce on my dress. "I'm not dressed for nature." In the South, a girl is used to being barefoot in summer. But what if it's chilly and my nipples make a surprise guest appearance?

"Your dress is . . . It's . . ."

"Adequate?"

"Adequate."

I'll take it. After all this time, the Warlock is finally inviting me into his sacred space. For a stroll. Alone. At night.

Am I going to be murdered?

Eh. Probably not. Ms. Zeen wouldn't ignore my screams. Surely.

I follow him out into the moonlight.

Chapter Twenty

SATURDAY, MAY 14 (STILL)

38 DAYS UNTIL THE SUMMER SOLSTICE

Honey's Helpful Hint, from
Honey Frost's Southern Cookbook
for Recipes Gone Wrong:

There are three rules on a first date.
1. Do not trust eggs that float
to the surface of water,
2. someone else's oven, or
3. ~~charming~~ lying Warlocks.

The Warlock of Foxe Holler is a geek for plants.

He spends the next hour showing me all the fruit and vegetables he's growing, the produce and herbs I can grab as long as I don't use *rusty dull sewing scissors from 1979*. He tells me the full genus and species Latin name of each plant, their prime growing seasons, the amount of sunlight they crave. I thought I knew a fair amount being a Farewitch, but this man is a walking almanac.

Silas was right. Horticulture professor, for sure.

Giddiness slips into my step as we wander the garden's organized paths of gravel and grass, eager branches and leaves reaching out to shake my hand. Thick hedges and groves burst with pops of colorful blooms. But not a single plant suffocates; even the smallest bud has room to grow. Ferns and flower beds are tastefully wild, trimmed but never too neatly. The spring air carries flavors right from my nose to my tongue: honeysuckle, lavender, ripe strawberries, hearty soil and mint and collecting dew.

We stroll close but not so close I'd accidentally touch his ungloved hand.

The crisp night air sharpens the edges around us, moonlight tickling every leaf and flower yet to bloom. It has to be almost midnight by now. Even in a small holler where green hills and lively creeks and lush, cave-spotted woods thrive in the isolation, beauty like *this* is rare. Delicate. No wonder the Warlock spends all his time here.

The only other place I've seen him direct this level of care is Lazlo. Not himself, certainly. Again, I wonder, what happens if the Warlock succumbs to his curse? So far, I can tell his body grows weaker along with his magic, but what does dying actually mean? Will he just keel over on the solstice from a heart attack? Something feels . . . off.

Eventually, we stop next to a wall of cornflowers, their blue petals almost purple in the semidarkness. "My plants won't bite," he says, watching my face scrunch up with worry.

I notice he doesn't say *don't* bite. "I've heard Warlocks do, sir."

"You don't need to call me *sir* all the time."

"Only some of the time?"

He looks away, his strong jaw flexing, like he's fighting some internal voice or demon. My cheeks heat when I realize I'm staring, and the cool air across my flushed bare skin is a needed comfort. I can't help it—I shiver.

Even lost in thought, he notices. "You're cold."

"I'm always cold." When I'm not around him, that is. "Frost, remember?"

"Make a wish."

"What? No. Absolutely not. What did we talk about? No magic. Not until you're well again." It's like he doesn't even care anymore if he exhausts himself.

He restrains any protests, but looks me right in the eye when he gives me a grumbled "Yes, ma'am."

"Thank you," I say. "And for sharing your gardens with me."

"They've helped make the years in the Manor go by quickly." His voice sounds like it's in the dark, low and distant.

"Why plants?"

"Plants are better listeners than people."

"Even though they don't talk back?"

His mouth quirks to the side. "What makes you think they don't talk back?"

The half smile flushes my digits all over again, and I wonder if he can see my skin buzzing. "Do you know when you do magic around me, I can taste it?"

His eyes spark. "What do you taste?"

"Thyme."

He studies me for a long moment. "Everyone tastes something different. Or so I've been told. Ms. Zeen says it's pistachio for her."

"What do you taste?"

"Pardon?"

"You. Personally. Surely you taste something. It's *your* magic."

A heavy pause. "No one has ever asked me that."

I don't hide my eye roll. "You don't offer many opportunities to ask you questions."

"Do you have others?"

If he thinks I won't call his bluff, he's going to be disappointed. "When—" I stop. The *when* of it doesn't matter so much as the *who* he was at that moment in time. Everything is relative with time, especially when there's not enough of it. "How old were you when your parents died?"

"Sixteen." He pauses at my look. "A *true* sixteen. I didn't even have my driver's permit."

My lips part, mostly just stunned he told me. Then my heart

catches up, and clenches. The story and pain are familiar. When I was sixteen, we'd just lost Momaw Frost. But still, even with her illness, she was older, and I still had my mom by my side.

For a Farewitch tasked with healing, I sure conjure up plenty of sore memories and deep wounds. He looked content when we were just admiring his gardens, so I tap my chin, thinking. "Favorite plant you grow?"

"Watercress. My mother sowed the plants here. It grows well because of the spring-fed creeks nearby. And it reminds me of where her side of our family comes from."

"What does your magic cost you, when you use it?"

"Too much. Next question."

"How old are you, exactly?"

"*Next question.*"

"Is this a date?"

Silence.

I wait, perfectly content to look up into his hazel eyes for the rest of the night.

Finally, he clears his throat. "I don't believe I know how to date."

Crossing my arms, I enter chef mode. As frustrating, as *confounding*, as this man is, he's no scarier than any new recipe.

"A place to start is liking the person you're spending time with. Do you think we can be friends?"

His scowl works its way back onto his face like stubborn sun spots. "As you've helpfully pointed out, I have forgotten how to have friends as well."

"You're better at it than you think. But friends have to be honest with each other."

"I agree. So how bad is your mother's health? Truly."

The air flies out of me. Point taken. You can't tell someone how to make perfect scrambled eggs if you can't crack an egg yourself. "I don't know." My voice wavers. "Because I don't know what's wrong with her. We think she has a couple months left."

Understanding peeks through his scowl. "Near the solstice as well."

I nod. "I've tried everything, for nearly a year. My grandmother died of something similar. Witches, Warlocks, no one could cure her. And now, my mom—*you two*—are the only people in the Holler I've never been able to help." A hairline fracture cracks my voice.

His eyes roam over me, and I wonder if this is how his plants feel under his careful stare. Noticed. Protected. "Two minds will be more efficient than one. In the library, with my archives, I mean. We'll start with the restricted section."

"Really?" Fragile hope seeps into the word. With his help instead of defiant roadblocks . . . I might be able to do this. *We* could do this.

His lips part, as if he can't decide whether to say what he's thinking. He extends a pale hand, palm upward. "May I see your hand?"

Please! Touch me! Praise be! My sensical side wins out and hesitates, only because I'm still not used to seeing his bare hands. Then my palm meets his, face down, like we're starting some Regency-era dance I definitely didn't practice. Or learn.

Though none of this, here between us, feels like anything I've ever learned.

Gently, he flips my hand so all the little kitchen battle wounds I've accumulated over the years on my palm are visible. He runs one calloused thumb over the inside of my wrist, right over my veins. Static tickles the veil of my skin at his touch. Then wildfire rushes through my blood as I sense his magic reach out to mine, hot but not scalding.

He's reading my magical signature. I think? Some Witches and Warlocks can determine the strength of magic in others, like studying ley lines and energy thrumming beneath the earth. Hidden, but potent. Ancestral, but alive.

"You're absolutely wasted at that Apothakery," he murmurs, eyes on our hands, even though whatever he's seeing has to be more of a sense of energy. "Your magic is strong. But—restless. Unwieldly. Has anyone ever told you that?"

Whatever magic you have, Ms. Frost, it isn't little.

He has. All along. He must feel my pulse pick up. I can practically see my heartbeat thumping right under his fingers. "My mom was supposed to be my mentor. So I've just learned on the job." I fake a smile. "I like to think of it as a work-study program where the work and study are both full-time."

He's not amused. "You need a real mentor, someone who will tutor you properly. Higher or lower, magic should never be left untrained. The consequences—it *needs* direction. Trust me."

"So . . . I should do more than just be a Farewitch?"

His frustrated sigh hangs between us. "*No,* Honey. You should do *less.* Less for people who take your labor for granted, who would ignore your best interests as a Witch." He almost sounds offended, like how I've been treating my time and magic is a terrible injustice.

Surprised, I look up to find him closer than I remember. I'm suddenly shy. Frosts don't *get* shy. And way too warm. Jesus, I'm already feeling swoony enough as it is. And he's still holding my hand.

"I don't even know your name," I realize.

"No one told you? It's Knight."

Ass. "Your *first* name."

"I can't tell you that."

"Is it terrible? Something like *Karen*? Or, God forbid—are you a *Junior*?"

"God, no. Warlocks . . . we don't give our names away. It's akin to giving up some of our power, and I'm weak enough as it is. I won't survive you."

"You won't survive telling me your name?"

A sharp breath leaves his chest. "Sure. That."

"Does anyone know it?"

"Lazlo and Ms. Zeen."

On its own, my free hand rises to his shoulder to remove a stray leaf. Then my rebellious fingers roam gently over his shoulder, grazing the lean muscles through his shirt. Damn a good white shirt on a man. This close, he smells like a bottled botanical garden. Earth. Growth. Life.

His unoccupied hand drops over mine. "That's distracting," he rasps, eyes hooded. He leans down close enough for me to see those pesky, endearing lines by his eyes. "You said you felt like taking risks tonight. What did you mean?"

Oh. Lord. In. Heaven. And below, for good measure. Where's a Kentucky Coffee for courage when a girl needs one?

Forget that. I've got plenty of grit without magic.

"You know," I say through a sly grin, "I would think you were about to kiss me, but given how rarely you've left your house, I'm not sure you know how."

Calloused fingers squeeze mine, skin rough as his voice, but the pressure is gentle. "We'll revisit that brazen insult later." He finally lets go of my wrist to flick away a chunk of my bangs that lost their curl in the warm air and fell into my eyes. "You need a haircut."

"And you need a friend."

His gaze drops to my mouth and he bends down. The tip of his nose brushes mine and I'm really hoping he tastes like thyme, too—

"It's past bedtime for those of us under ten. Lazlo would like to say good night."

Ms. Zeen's disembodied voice cuts the stillness of the night from the back porch.

A low sound rumbles in the Warlock's chest. His jaw clenches. We can't see the Governess, so she can't see us, but the moment is gone. He leans away.

I want to yank him back by his shirtfront, but the molten hazel color has been diluted with cold self-reproach. I know that look on him well now. Guilt.

For one very brief second, he wasn't thinking about Lazlo. And he knows it.

His warmth vanishes as he steps back, putting distance between us. The heady haze of the blooming gardens is gone, only a misty chill left behind.

"I apologize. That was unprofessional," he grinds out. "Lazlo is relying on me to get better. I shouldn't jeopardize your focus and work in the little time we have left."

My heart fumbles. He doesn't think he can have a single evening of happiness. Not while the consequences of this curse affect Lazlo's future, too.

No way. *No way* am I going to let him beat himself up, not when I've seen him happier in one night than he's been collectively over six weeks.

"Sir, you couldn't have known what the Widow Witch's curse would do to you. That's why they're *curses*: They're unpredictable. You can't load guilt like that onto yourself."

His shoulders drop, like they're too heavy to carry. "Lazlo doesn't belong here and I—we *tried* to send him back, but it wasn't possible . . ."

Confused, I stay where I am, toes digging into the grass. It feels like I only made things worse. I'm afraid if I touch him now, I'll lose him. Maybe other relatives were vying for guardianship. Or maybe he just wasn't prepared to take care of a little boy who stumbled onto his doorstep. But who would be?

"The town is right." His expression hardens, painfully unreadable. "I thought the least I could do was keep him happy and healthy and I couldn't even do that."

He means the threat of the Widow Witch, I think, and her assaults on the Manor. "She wouldn't really hurt a child, would she?"

I feel like I skipped a step in someone else's recipe, totally lost. The

Widow Witch cursed him to die slowly over the course of a year. But that doesn't have anything to do with Lazlo, other than the question of who's going to take care of him.

"He loves you, you know," I say. "Unconditionally. So you aren't allowed to give up. Lazlo will be happier if *you're* happier."

"You don't understand."

"*So help me to.* You've given him a *good* home."

He huffs, shaking his head. "Ms. Frost, you've made this house into a home more in weeks than I have in years."

"Well, I did it for Lazlo." *And maybe for you.*

Fervent indecision twists the Warlock's face, a bright heat slipping through his restraint.

He gets a grip on whatever inner battle he's fighting, and that intense gaze finally lets up on me. "I think the chef wants to put on his dog pajamas."

"I—right. Yes. If he's up another hour, he'll inhale an entire bag of Goldfish."

We don't speak as we walk back to the Manor, the buttery kitchen lighting a beacon.

It's an undeniable fact of the universe: A man who can cook is sexy. Spices become pheromones. Was I so hungry, a good meal was all it took to make my knees go wobbly? I'm feeling a helluva number of confusing things. Mostly, surprise.

I *wanted* that kiss. Badly.

Back inside, the warmth of the kitchen infuses my bones, chasing away some of the chill from our conversation outside.

The Warlock and Ms. Zeen urge a yawning Lazlo to bed, and my eyes are greedy for the cozy scene before me. I can't help but think this looks like home. *Feels* like home. Perhaps this smitten sensation isn't just about really good shakshuka.

"That was the best meal I've had all year," I tell Lazlo before he heads to bed.

"I can be tipped in candy," he replies.

"Promise to show me how you made everything?" We clasp pinkies.

He nods. "I could be as good as you one day." His face twists like he's thinking extra hard about his future. "When I'm not walking dogs. I'll be very busy when I'm a grown-up."

Next to me, the Warlock tenses.

"Lazlo, it's after midnight," Governess Zeen chastens. "You can be sure Beauregard Buchanan is fast asleep already."

This gets him moving. He follows her but then halts at the door, heaving a ragged sigh that doesn't match his small body. Then he stumbles, like he's dizzy. The Governess lunges for him, but he turns back, looking for us instead.

"It's happening again," Lazlo says, voice weak, his small hands grabbing for the Warlock.

Or what *should* be two hands.

Instead, poking out of the boy's sleeves are hazy outlines of his palms and digits. The color and texture of his skin have evaporated, as if he's fading away right before our eyes.

My stomach plummets.

The Warlock's sturdy grip finds the boy's shoulders in an instant. "How do you feel?"

"Tired." Lazlo stares at his palms, face pale as bleached flour. The vanishing has stopped at his wrists—and I have no idea if that's a good or bad thing.

"It's going to be all right," the Warlock says. "Just like last time, remember? You'll be fine in the morning. Ms. Zeen will put you to bed. You know I won't let any harm come to you, yes?"

The boy's expression scrunches. His posture slumps like a wilting stem. "But I forgot to serve dessert."

"Even chefs need sleep," Ms. Zeen says. I've never heard her voice so uneven.

The Warlock nods at the Governess. "Stay with him. I'll come relieve you shortly."

I can only stare, motionless with a terrible, hollow yet expanding black hole of a feeling. I think I'm going to vomit up several helpings of shakshuka. I barely notice the Governess and Lazlo leave. All I can see are those small little hands, here then gone.

When the kitchen is empty, the Warlock whirls to face me, eyes wide and pleading.

My heart skips. Stops. Restarts. Skips again.

This has to be a mistake. A trick. A ruse.

But the layers pile into place, a sickly sweet cake of deception.

"Ms. Frost, let me explain . . ." His jaw works back and forth so hard, I think I hear it pop.

Air withers in my throat, and I try to control my breathing, but my limbs feel like they detach for a split second and then refit back into place, a Barbie put together by a toddler. It feels exactly like the moment I learned my mom was dying.

How did I not see it—how did I miss the largest locked door of secrets in Knight Manor? I force out a shuddering breath. My lungs feel like they've stopped working, just to give my heart plenty of room to crack.

My fists clench, nails cutting my palms. I brace myself against the kitchen island, eyes burning into the man who almost just kissed me. "All this time?"

Shame carves lines in his face, that guilt I couldn't place. Until now. He jerks a tense hand through his hair, hair I've daydreamed about running my fingers through, and gives a single grim nod of his head. "Stay for him. As long as you can. Please."

"*You*," I manage to choke out, "are worse than your rumors."

The Warlock of Foxe Holler might be cursed, but he isn't dying.

Lazlo is.

PART TWO

thyme

Chapter Twenty-One

SUNDAY, MAY 22

30 DAYS UNTIL THE SUMMER SOLSTICE

Honey's Helpful Hint, from
Honey Frost's Southern Cookbook
for Recipes Gone Wrong:

If their love language is food, seek forgiveness in flour, not flowers.

My universe has careened right off its tilted lazy Susan.

I've discovered being furious at the Warlock follows the exact emotions a Frost woman battles when a recipe goes wrong:

First, naïve determination. The food will right itself with some salt. Surely, Lazlo's curse-illness-*problem* is fixable. Next, hopeful substitution. I can trade one ingredient for another without ruining the flavor. With my Farewitch magic and the right spell . . . Then, sour despair. If the recipe's already cooking, it's too late to fix. The chemical reaction has started, hot as the fury now in my core. Lastly, avoidance. Stuff the dastardly results into the freezer "for later" but never look at them again.

I don't become angry very often. And when I do, I get sugary, syrupy *polite*. Whenever the Warlock and I cross paths over the next week—unfortunately, it is possible to run out of places to hide in this funhouse farmhouse—I give him my best dead-eyed, saccharine *Yes, sir* and monosyllabic answers. Only when a nod won't suffice.

I half expect him to corner me, to renew his efforts to explain. He never does. He gives me my space, the menace.

You are worse than your rumors.

Those words shadow me, tumbling around my head. I don't feel guilty, do I? Surely not. He probably thinks I would've crumbled under the pressure of healing a child if I knew. A really cute, funny, warm firework spark of a kid. Hence the secret. So I might slightly, kind of understand why he hid the truth.

But I've finally memorized where everything lives in the kitchen, the house has stopped sending me up staircases to nowhere, and my cast-iron skillets even have their own section of the pantry. I've actually gotten snug in this house. *Comfortable.*

Just in time for me to realize I might be doomed.

That's what makes me most furious of all.

While I'm an anger-soaked tiramisu, the energy has to go somewhere, so I get right back to work. My mom and the Warlock and Lazlo are depending on me. Especially Lazlo. Luckily, we haven't wasted time. Now I understand why the Warlock made sure Lazlo always ate whatever I made. Always. (How did I miss the signs? *Foolish, foolish.*)

At least that frustrating enigma of a Warlock kept his word and unlocked the restricted bookshelf. So when I'm not in the kitchen tossing new dishes at Lazlo, my butt print in my favorite wingback in the library gets deeper every day. A week after my worst date on record, Governess Zeen finds me in the library, still tired and determined as ever.

She's wearing a robin's-egg-blue cardigan set this morning that reminds me of Ostara and blooming flowers and bunnies. My bad mood resurfaces at the cheery color.

"Tell me your secret, Ms. Zeen. How do you manage to always look put together?" I gesture at my own stained apron, hiding pajamas from Thursday. Wednesday? "I guess you've had more time to adjust to information *everyone* was aware of but me." My fake politeness doesn't extend to her. She probably dislikes me enough it wouldn't matter.

"Don't be petty. It's unbecoming." She halts next to where I'm folded like clumsy croissant layers in my usual armchair.

"I'm owed some petty. You let me run around naïve and oblivious."

"You would do that anyway."

"Ouch. I thought you and I were making progress, Ms. Zeen. Bonding."

"I don't bond, dear. And it was not my secret to divulge."

My cheeks go pink. She knows exactly how to manipulate a Farewitch. But isn't her world crumbling around her, like mine is? "Right, because you owe the Warlock a debt or loyalty or whatever, but that's a secret, too. Am I *keeping up* now?"

"I warned you about growing attached."

"Everyone is *always* warning everyone else with vague, moody threats. It's the brand and it's getting old. I'd appreciate a little more specificity next time, if we can manage that."

You've made this house into a home.

The Warlock's voice comes back to me. Traitorous brain.

The fire in me cools a smidge. That's all Ms. Zeen was trying to do, too. Carve out a home, a life, for someone who might not get to enjoy it much longer. It's not her fault the Warlock got cursed and now Lazlo is suffering for it. She's always been here for the kid. And for the Warlock. Watching out for them. They do both need constant supervision.

The Governess clasps her hands and I get the urge to correct my posture. "Mr. Knight has left an apology muffin in the kitchen."

"*Another?* Jesus." His brown butter sage ones smelled divine. I almost gave in and ate one of the devils.

"You shouldn't have taught him to bake. Lemon poppy seed this time, I believe. With thyme? He was mumbling. Could've said *add time* on the oven."

"He thinks he can make everything all right just because he knows my favorite flavor of baked goods—"

She snatches the cookbook in my lap and shuts it with a loud *SMACK*. "So you found out what he was trying to spare you from. What now? Would anything be different if you'd known about Lazlo sooner? Would the knowledge have changed your approach?"

Lord, she moves fast. I don't even have an answer. She's not wrong. I'm still trying to cure an illness because of a curse. The only difference is my patient's ability to ride tall roller coasters. What's changed here is me. How I choose to move forward.

"So that's it, then. You've come to knock me out of my sulking."

She stares down her nose at me. "I'm here to remind you that the more time you spend *sulking*, the less you spend with Lazlo. Cook for the boy all you please, but that doesn't do him as much good as authentic attention."

"Low blow." I sit up from my slouch. My pajamas are frumpier than I remembered. "It's hard to look at him," I admit in a soft voice. "When my mom got sick, I was there for her, physically. But mentally . . . If I didn't look too closely, her illness wasn't as real. Or at least, that's what Arna Jean told me her therapist would tell me."

"Does every young person have a therapist now?"

"You should try it, Ms. Zeen."

"My emotions are quiet, just the way I like them."

"Healthy."

She places her hands on her wide hips. "Lazlo is even worried about you, and you know that boy has the attention span of a toddler."

My heart clenches. "Lower blow."

"Those are my specialty." She returns my cookbook. "From one stubborn soul to another: The sooner you begin to live outside the rules of your recipes, the better—"

CRASH.

A shattering sound ricochets from down the hall. A boy screams.

Ms. Zeen and I exchange a look. Then we're running.

I was wrong, I think as I sprint through the farmhouse. *This* feeling is worse. If my stomach turns just thinking about Lazlo's illness, it downright Ferris-wheels at the sound of the boy's terror, dragging my heart with it.

I'm faster than Ms. Zeen in her kitten heels, and burst into the foyer.

Right into a tornado.

At least, it feels like a tornado.

The front doors are wide open, slamming in gale-force winds that whip sideways and tear through even the largest potted plants. Any furniture toppled over a while ago. A jade vase falls from the air and smashes right at my feet in the time I take to blink.

Warlock Knight stands in the eye of it all, black hair whirlpooling around the sharp edges of his face, arms thrown up, holding something at bay with his magic.

Or someone.

Ms. Zeen runs into my back and says what I'm already thinking: "The Widow Witch."

Except this time, the windstorm isn't outside the Manor.

The Warlock spots us, his entire body tense, muscles straining with the effort of whatever power he's using to keep the winds corralled.

Shivering, I struggle to catch my breath. The winds aren't just strong, they're *frigid*. My hair tangles into knots of blonde, bangs flying off my forehead. Whatever wards he's so proud of must be crumbling. This time, his magic isn't going to be enough.

The winds grow faster, whirring harder. A window cracks and shatters. Something sharp slices my cheek, and the pain narrows to a bright sting.

Then, as quickly as the deafening storm appeared, it stops.

The air stills. I can finally take a full breath.

Outside, the sky breaks open, and rain patters against what windows are still in place. Scattered detritus litters the floor, and the foyer shimmers as the changing light dances off glass under our feet. The wallpaper's peeling, but that was already a problem. Did the wards hold their own after all?

The Warlock looms where he was, looking between his hands and the door. Perplexed. Concerned. Then his face drains of color. "Where's Lazlo?"

Panic clutches my lungs. We were so occupied with the Widow Witch's attack—

"Here!"

Lazlo appears from where he was sheltering under a staircase, also still in pajamas. His windswept hair could easily just be bed head. He spots the state of the foyer and his eyes go big. "Wasn't me."

My chest seizes with the same relief that passes over the Warlock's face. "Don't come any farther without your shoes, Lazlo," he calls.

The boy halts.

"Mr. Knight." The Governess points across the foyer, where carved into the hardwood under a window are still-burning and very familiar scorch marks.

YOUR TIME IS MINE.

Just like her first attack, in the kitchen. I'm getting real tired of this Witch's inability to leave a voicemail.

In my house slippers, I tiptoe over broken ceramic and splintered wood and uprooted plants toward the Warlock.

"You look like death," I say when I reach him, my voice loud in the stillness after the storm. It's the first real thing I've said to him in a week. Sweat mists his temples and his skin could double for a translucent onion, but I force down my distracting concern for him.

"Nice to see you, too, Ms. Frost. I'm glad you've done away with the counterfeit civility."

"It's a Southern skill."

"I prefer our arguments." His stare travels over me, like of all things, *he's* concerned for *me*. His attention lands on my cut cheek. "You're hurt."

"Very hurt," I murmur, the Widow Witch and her storm far from my thoughts.

"So is my front door." His voice is low, the words just for the two of us. He reaches up and wipes the blood from my cheekbone, his thumb gentle where it lingers on my skin.

I cross my arms. She already bestowed her curse. Lazlo's dying. "What the hell does she want now?"

"Not a husband, clearly," Ms. Zeen says. "She still hasn't taken a single soul in town yet, according to Beulah."

And it's nearly June. So why is she up here in the hills, trying to topple the farmhouse? Why not go tithe the husband she's overdue to collect?

"A more pertinent question is, how have the wards held for so long? They should have . . . gaps by now," the Warlock replies.

"Why wouldn't they?" I say. "*You're* fine. Your magic should be, too."

"It should, shouldn't it?" Another one of his ominous answers. Then, "I think we should resume our discussion from the garden, Ms. Frost."

Right *now*? I'm still puzzling out how we almost kissed a week ago. And Ms. Zeen and Lazlo are in full view! Maybe this is the real reason Frosts don't partner up. The true scourge is our inability to make romance anything but awkward. Besides, an almost-kiss can hardly be called romance—

"About your power, your Farewitch magic," he clarifies.

Oh. Right. "You think—no. I can't be the reason the farmhouse is still standing."

My thoughts jump to the string of pearl plants determined to swallow me. Even if my magic infuses the house with protection like at the Apothakery, we're talking simple stuff. Farewitch magic can't hold off the Widow Witch.

Whatever magic you have, Ms. Frost, it isn't little.

His focus is unrelenting, like I'm a vexing map to someplace without an *X*, promise and power hidden in the core of me. It makes me feel . . . I don't know. Unsure. Cautious.

Powerful.

I brush off his hand before the villain can make me feel any better. His shoulders slump, in what must be disappointment.

But as I take in his gaunt expression, I can't help but think he looks awfully sallow and mortal for a man who *isn't* the one dying from a curse.

"I think we need some help," I say.

Chapter Twenty-Two

SUNDAY, MAY 29

23 DAYS UNTIL THE SUMMER SOLSTICE

Honey's Helpful Hint, from
Honey Frost's Southern Cookbook for Recipes Gone Wrong:

For the best bread, remember:
Bake Really Early At Dawn.
It's nearly impossible for a bad day to take root if you start with freshly baked bread.

Have you redecorated?" Arna Jean says before the doorbell even exhausts itself.

I wince as a yard of wallpaper peels off from the wall behind her with all the grace of a lazy banana. "Just some spring-cleaning."

A light bulb in a sconce bursts by our heads.

I wipe a hand over my face. "Don't ask."

With the recent remodeling courtesy of the Widow Witch, the Warlock hasn't yet replaced any of his demolished plants. At least the front door is upright again.

Silas arrives right after the Bookwitch.

Initially, the Warlock refused my demand to get outside help, so he and Ms. Zeen spent the last week in the library with me. We dug through the archives of records and grimoires with six hands instead of just my two, looking for anything resembling a recipe or potion—anything a Farewitch could work with. I haven't forgiven the Warlock for lying, but I rally and compartmentalize, for Lazlo's sake.

Even before the Warlock confessed to me about his curse over our midnight drink, something felt off to me. I'm tasting that same doubt now. We know Lazlo will succumb to this illness by the solstice—he'll physically just fade away—unless we find a cure.

So why does this illness still feel bigger than what a Farewitch can fix with food?

Whatever magic fueled the Widow Witch's curse is way out of my league, so after a week in the library with no success, I gave the Warlock an ultimatum today: We tell a couple friends the truth and get some real help and expertise or . . . I didn't give him a second option.

He finally agreed, but probably only because he thought I'd just scry up a brainstorm with a coven, not invite actual guests over to the Manor. He might be livid. Which is partly why I did it. Even when I'm mad at him, I can't get enough of annoying someone whose reputation rivals the Grinch.

Arna Jean and Silas answered my call for help tonight, and I've never been more grateful to see their faces, flummoxed as they are.

As Silas scrutinizes the ambitious modern art installation that is the foyer, his lips pucker. "Will there be wine?"

"Do I look like a girl who deglazes her pans with water?"

Arna Jean peers too closely at my tousled bangs and roots. "You're clearly a girl who skips wash day."

"Y'all should be grateful I'm in overalls and not pajamas."

"No blends," Silas says. His sigh sounds like exhausted agreement. "Lead the way."

The three of us return to the kitchen just as Lazlo says, "We have a doorbell?"

No one answers.

The Warlock and Ms. Zeen are too busy eyeing Silas, whom they haven't met since he wasn't at the cookie bake. Well, eyeing for Ms. Zeen. Wishing death with his corneas, for the Warlock.

I breeze over their chilly non-welcome. "This is Silas Key, the mayor's assistant—"

"Associate," Silas corrects.

"—assistant associate."

"Hope you don't mind the late RSVP," Silas says with his usual confidence. "Honey invited us for Sunday supper."

Warlock Knight's stare hovers on him before landing heavily on me. "Did she."

I've promised him no more surprise guests and voilà, here I am. *Not as scary as you think*, I mouth, hoping he can read lips.

Silas turns to me, unbothered, and holds up a signature white box with gold lettering. "We brought you a host gift. Alas, no flowers this time."

"Modjeskas!" I cry.

The Warlock is less impressed. His hazel eyes narrow even more, if that's possible. "*You* brought those flowers for Beltane."

"From the mayor," Silas explains. "A gift for her daughter."

I don't think the Warlock believes him. "Kingcup? Really?"

"It's also called the—"

"The marsh marigold, I know. Bit of an uninspired choice."

Silas smiles without his teeth. "Prickly. You and Honey must get along so well."

I glare at the Warlock. Arna Jean bumps my elbow, whispering, "Does the entertainment have a two-drink minimum?"

Silas casually steps around the Warlock. "We'll give these to the lovely lady here. Beauty before age." He hands *my* gift box of marshmallowy caramel sin to Governess Zeen, who doesn't seem to know what to do with her hands, or flattery in general.

"We only made enough food for four," the Warlock declares.

"We have plenty," I counter. "A Southern four is a metropolitan eight."

"We'll have to set additional places at the table—"

"I don't mind!" Ms. Zeen dashes into action, grabbing utensils and napkins.

"How kind of you, Ms. Zeen," the Warlock mutters.

Lazlo sandwiches himself next to Silas. He holds up two sticky palms like trophies. "You can judge the food and pick a winner. I made the dessert." Wink.

Bless that kid and his de-escalating smiles. I'm relieved his little hands haven't faded again, more, since the other night. "Silas, this is Lazlo, and Ms. Zeen. And this—"

"Mr. Knight." The Warlock gives Silas one of those weird, curt man-nods. He doesn't extend a hand. "The Warlock of Foxe Holler," he adds, like a threatening doctorate degree.

Silas looks him up and down. "Oh, I thought you were the gardener."

A throaty peal of laughter escapes Arna Jean before she can smother it. To be fair, Silas does look like the kind of guy who owns a manor, and the Warlock . . . does not.

"I can be both," the Warlock says. It's almost a growl.

Before imminent disaster, I usher everyone to the table. Fingers crossed the house doesn't catch on to the Warlock's attitude and start emptying the knife block.

As I carry over a massive skillet of cornbread, Silas pulls out Ms. Zeen's chair for her. She looks even more flabbergasted. With the table full, Lazlo pats the seat next to him, and I oblige, Arna Jean on his other side. Across from us, Silas sits next to his new best friend the Governess, and to my right—

Ms. Zeen does a double take. "Sir, not once, in the decades I've known you, have you sat at the head of a table in this house."

"Tonight I do," the Warlock replies.

At the exact moment I drop a thimble of yellow butter on top of the steaming cornbread, a commotion clatters in the front hall.

A minute later, a tall and lanky man drags what is possibly a body into the kitchen.

"The door unlocked for me," Rett Claywell grunts in greeting.

The Warlock glowers up at the ceiling, as if he can scold his own house. "The wards are intended for *everyone*—"

"Our microwave!" I bolt up to help with the heavy package. It took so long, I forgot about it.

"And the Spam—who orders a whole case of Spam?"

"A Witch whose favorite postman is now Reginald Claywell."

"He's the only postman," Arna Jean drawls at the same time Lazlo goes, "*Reginald?*"

I pat the box. "So *extra* favorite."

Rett levels a dry look at his sister. "Thanks for your support."

She rolls her eyes. "You know, most folks lie about working so they can go out and *not work*. You told me you couldn't hang out because you were napping, not pulling a late shift."

Her brother rights his uniform, fingers nervous. His shy soul probably didn't expect a whole kitchen full of stares. He doesn't get to escape, because Silas rises and saunters over with an unfair amount of elegance and offers a hand. "Claywell, right? I've been meaning to introduce myself. Silas Key."

Rett gapes at Silas, expression icing over in utter panic, as if all the vocal cords have eloped from his body.

Silas drops his hand. "Are you all right, Mr. Claywell? Not a hands man?"

Arna Jean and the Governess watch with such investment, this might as well be a hot-air balloon crash. I elbow Rett. He can handle every mail route in the Holler but not a handshake?

The postman collects himself. "You're fine. I mean, just Rett. Rett is fine."

"Nice to meet you. You're doing the Holler an invaluable service, keeping people in touch with the world. It's a goal of mine to make sure there's not a resident I don't know."

"Townsfolk who vote being of particular interest," I quip.

"You can't shame him, Honey," Arna Jean says. "He's had literal biscuits pelted at his head in the middle of the dinner rush at Kitty's Kitchen."

Silas scoffs. "Correct, but not the point. It depends on the constituent. Mr. Claywell delivers my *New Yorker*s. Even during that four-day ice storm last winter."

What in the scuppernong pie— "The Apothakery didn't get mail for two weeks!"

Like an oven timer, my brain dings with the obvious.

Rett's shyness under Silas's attention, asking me to set up a meeting. Oh yes. Things click *very* well. This is perfect. I still owe the postman for his help making deliveries to my regulars.

"Stay for dinner, won't you?" I ask Rett. "We're strategizing."

"Excellent idea," Silas proclaims. "We just set the table."

"We set it twenty minutes ago," the Warlock grumbles.

Rett steps back. "Oh, no, that would be unprofessional." His glasses fog with heat from his cheeks. "Also, as a rule I don't eat in my uniform in case I were to spill—"

"Fabulous, we'll put on some music," Silas says, and pulls out the chair right next to him.

Rett sits. I think his knees tremble. Poor fellow seems more shaken by Silas than the fact that this is the first time he's met the Warlock face-to-face, too.

I do introductions, and finally, we eat. Bobby Hebb's jazzy vocals fill any awkward hushes. There aren't many, because Lazlo's blessed our two newcomers with a question spree.

"Oh, no, my brother's routes keep him too busy to ever be at home long enough," Arna Jean chimes in.

Rett swallows a hunk of cornbread. "*But* I get to see all the dogs in the Holler when I'm delivering mail."

Lazlo turns to Silas. "What about you?"

Silas takes a leisurely sip of some chardonnay I found. "No pets, I'm afraid. I'm running across the Holler most hours of the day, when I'm not behind a desk."

The boy nods. "You look like a lint-roller kind of guy anyway."

Arna Jean's cheeks bulge with a stifled snort, and I even have to flash A Look at the Warlock for smirking. Though I'm barely holding it together myself.

"I feel like I should be offended somehow. He must get his bluntness from you, Mr. Knight," Silas retorts.

The Warlock huffs, interrupting the chatter. "Okra, Ms. Zeen?" He snaps and the dish of okra floats through the air over to the Governess, even though Silas has his hands extended. He does the same thing with the wine, another snap sending the bottle to Arna Jean, conveniently out of Silas's reach.

I raise a *What the hell?* eyebrow at him. Thyme dusts my tongue. The flavor will, frustratingly, go well with the cornbread. But as the taste dissolves, so does my irritation. I don't think I've seen him use magic since the Widow Witch destroyed the foyer. The minute there's a chance for peacocking, he's tossing it about to levitate side dishes? Has he been conserving his power for some reason?

Putting the thought out of my head, I turn to Silas. "So, Silas," I begin in my sweetest voice. "I may have promised a neighbor you'd take a meeting."

Empty-handed, Silas turns to me. "You did not."

"Don't hate me. We're trying to be friends, remember?"

Silas heaves a sigh. "Which scheming neighbor did you trade my time to?"

I take a large bite of cornbread. "A truly conniving fellow."

Rett sinks down in his seat as Silas mutters, "Can't be worse than Samson. Or any ex of mine, really."

The Warlock perks up at that, glancing between the two men.

"Say hello," I tell Silas, nodding at Rett.

And dammit, Silas's smile is as charming as one can expect from a person with media training. The man dodges social blunders like biscuits. He really would make a good mayor for the Holler. If anyone might be able to wrangle Oris Webb's fanaticism and public smearing of magic, besides my mom, it could be Silas.

Rett fiddles with the napkin tucked into his collar. "I asked for some direct engagement but I didn't think Honey would take me this . . . literally."

"How did you think you'd reach him?" Arna Jean asks her brother.

"A . . . letter?"

Silas stares at Rett with sincere curiosity. "Old-fashioned. I like it."

"What's wrong with letters?" the Warlock asks. When his eyes meet mine, his lips twitch once before he glances away from me.

"How about we meet in the middle with an email," Silas says. "Unless you'd like to meet over coffee?"

"No!" Rett catches himself. "I mean, that won't be necessary. I just wanted to . . . uh, start a conversation. We need to expand the mail routes. Folks living farther out want to stay involved with the community, but some can only trek in once a week to the post office."

Silas's expression sobers, the mayor-in-training taking over. "Can you add those houses to your own routes now?"

"I'll need a second mailperson," Rett admits, like he isn't happy about it. I get it: Asking for help is as tricky as Julia Child's pâté de canard en croûte. "This Manor isn't even officially on my route. But it's on my way most days, so I make the stop."

"It's not on your route?" the Warlock asks, his expression matching Ms. Zeen's when Silas gave her flowers and pulled out her chair.

Rett looks offended, as if the woes of the postal service are a personal burden on his soul. "*Everyone* deserves access to mail."

"The town council votes on something like that, so you'll face resistance from Pastor Webb," Ms. Zeen says to Silas. "He likes the town to orbit close, and around the church."

"How do you know Oris Webb so well?" Rett asks her.

I nod. "And Gertha Fudge."

Ms. Zeen purses her lips. "Believe it or not, the Holler existed before the lot of you were born. Gertha hasn't always been angry. And Webb hasn't always been a preacher. He wanted to be mayor, you know. But Marigold got there first."

"So his pissy vibe isn't just because he's anti-magic," Arna Jean says. "He's also anti-Honey."

Great. "I get the sense the man is just afraid of women in general."

Ms. Zeen huffs. "As he should be."

My skin starts to itch. This crap heats my blood like a sous vide. Why does every grudge in this town have to be personal? "Webb can't claim to protect the safety of his neighbors, then pick and choose who that means. He can't tolerate a Witch but hate her magic."

"Can't he?" The Warlock's expression hardens. "Gertha Fudge despises magic. But Webb wants to control it. They have two different agendas, but both are a good example of why, for some, the edge of the Holler is the safest place to be. Isolation is often the best protection."

In a town where folks like to remember Warlocks—and if Webb has his way, Witches, too—only for the bad, maybe it is better to be out of sight. But if I really believed that, I wouldn't still be here after all these weeks at the Warlock's kitchen table.

It's why I've invited my friends tonight in the first place.

"I would like to know why Webb has chosen to act on his clearly deep-rooted obsession with magic now," the Warlock adds. "The previous mayor had no magic and might not have posed as much resistance to an anti-magic town council."

"And I don't remember his congregation ever being so vocal,"

Arna Jean says. "Why would his followers have their come-to-Jesus moment now and go after magic while we've got a Witch in office?"

A Witch who is, lately, never actually in the office. Our home is changing right out from under my mom and she's not well enough to stand up and fight it.

Which is the perfect time for a man like Webb to weave doubt and make his move.

"Webb and Fudge have folks scared," I say. "Even a cure can look like poison to folks who don't understand magic."

Silas's tone is harsh. "I won't stand for exclusion, because of magic or otherwise. Even if his church ladies would sell their pearls to help him finance his own ark, Webb is just a man."

I wipe my hand down my face, despising Silas's confidence but also immensely grateful for it. No wonder my mom keeps him around. "Just a man is plenty dangerous."

Arna Jean snorts. "Especially one who says things like, *We've always done it this way*."

A dark promise hangs in the Warlock's eyes. "I've handled my fair share of bigoted fools over the decades. New face, same soul. I'm not afraid of Oris Webb."

At that, Lazlo finally comes up for air after devouring his dinner. "Can we visit your shop soon, Honey? RJ promised she would give me free desserts."

"Hey, I said *one* free cookie, kid."

Ms. Zeen stands, folding her napkin. "On that note, I believe it's time for bed for those of us too young for small-town politics."

With much protesting from Lazlo even as he's yawning, Ms. Zeen escorts him from the kitchen, leaving me with a Bookwitch, the postman, the mayor's number two, and one stiff Warlock, his unreadable scowl back in place.

Eventually, the clink of forks hushes. That's when I tell them everything.

The Widow Witch, her curse, Lazlo's illness. How we have mere weeks until the solstice. All of it. The Warlock doesn't interrupt, even to fill in any gaps, and instead just scrunches his face as if he's getting a cavity filled.

When I finish, my friends' mouths are open.

The Warlock levels a stare at me. "So this dinner wasn't for idle chitchat, then?"

Mid–slice of cornbread, I point the butter knife at him, golden glob of fat dangling on the end. "Hey, I told you we were getting help. And the Holler runs on chitchat. If you don't appreciate that, then that's how you end up thinking isolation is safer than friends."

His voice is sharper than my knife. "Is that why you hide your mother's illness?"

Silence. The wine on my tongue turns to pond water. Even Arna Jean doesn't have a sarcastic remark.

Then, Rett, quietly: "Mayor Frost is sick?"

My cheeks warm and I force-swallow my cornbread. "If the town knew I couldn't cure my mom, how long would they trust their Farewitch? Folks are already in a tizzy because I'm helping a Warlock. And now, if Webb found out, he'd just use that to prove that Witches and their magic don't do the Holler a bit of good."

"How would Webb find out, though?" Arna Jean asks. "Carolina, Silas—we haven't said a word. I've never held a secret this long."

"He might've seen me leaving the hospital," I admit, an encounter I was trying to forget.

The Warlock goes eerily still, which is impressive, since he's usually part statue anyway. "This man was watching you? In what way?"

"Like he knew I wasn't just there bringing cookies for the nurses? I don't know, it's a small town, people accidentally follow each other all the time—"

"This man was *following* you?" The Warlock looks ready to float a wine bottle right into someone's skull.

Thankfully, Silas jumps in. "One thing at a time. If Webb knew the truth about Honey's mom, why would he be spreading his latest rumors about her?"

Right. I've been getting updates from the Kentucky fried coven group chat all week. "Oh, you mean the fun ones about how Warlock Knight is now hunting Farewitches?"

The Warlock chokes. "*What.*"

Silas cringes. "At the last town council meeting, Webb suggested the mayor's lack of public appearances is because you're blackmailing Honey into helping you in exchange for her mom's life."

"Christ," he groans.

Arna Jean chortles into her wine. "I know, ridiculous. Marigold Frost doesn't have the patience to be kidnapped. Especially by a Warlock."

Silas steeples his hands, elbows on the table. "So the Widow Witch renovates your foyer—very MoMA, I don't hate it—but still hasn't come after anyone in town. *Why?* Why is Webb taking action the one spring the Witch isn't causing trouble? If he and Fudge are all in for a war against magic, the Witch's behavior would be their greatest ammunition."

"Maybe it's not about the Witch," Rett says. "What if he was planning all this before she changed her behavior, and instead was just trying to take advantage of the mayor being gone?" He turns to me. "Your mom only stepped back from the public eye within the last year, right?"

"Yeah. Her health wasn't bad enough to move her into the hospital until last August."

"So *after* the Widow Witch came last spring. Maybe this year, Webb was still counting on the Witch to make her usual appearance, but when she didn't show up—"

"He had to fill the role with *something* to make magic look bad," Arna Jean says, drumming the table as we all follow her conclusion.

"If magic looks out of control, then someone will need to step in to control it."

The Warlock confirms what we're all thinking. "Webb needs a villain more than peace."

"I bet the church ladies are all in cahoots with Webb on this, too," Rett says.

Silas eyes him. "Is *cahoots* a paying tenant in your vocabulary?"

The postman fidgets in his chair; his leg won't stop bouncing under the table. "I listen to historical murder mysteries on audiobook while I drive. The accents keep me awake."

"That is . . . delightfully unsurprising," Silas says. "And Beulah Buchanan might know for sure. She tells me something juicy about the other church ladies whenever I stop by for one of her Strong Island iced teas."

Reaching over, he moves Rett's cupped hand from the goblet of his glass to the stem.

"There. This way, you won't warm the wine with your body heat."

Rett's eyes go wide behind his glasses. Arna Jean rolls hers. "Barf."

"What, the sommelitism or the abysmal flirting?" I say.

The shift of the tension in the air is a much-needed relief, and my spirits lift for a hot second. Then plummet when Rett says, "So your mom *and* the little guy are sick."

"Cursed," I amend, taking a gulp of my own wine. "Lazlo, that is." I can't even bring myself to think of his round, innocent face right now. "Fatally so."

"Forgive my lack of magical knowledge, but is he disappearing or dying?" Silas asks.

"I can't be entirely sure," the Warlock says at the same time I say, "Does it matter?"

Fading away physically sure seems like a kind of death to me.

The Bookwitch levels a heavy stare at the Warlock down the

length of the kitchen table. "Does Lazlo *know* he's sick because of a Witch's curse?"

I didn't even think to ask that.

"To a degree," the Warlock answers. "He understands he has an affliction, and that Ms. Frost is here to help. That the sooner we find a cure, the better."

We slump into silence once more. As I study the Warlock's tired face, I can't keep from noticing how he's starting to resemble a sickly Victorian child. Has he slept at all this week? I doubt it. Lazlo is his greatest joy and his greatest regret, and every time he looks at the boy, the conflicted shame in his eyes drowns the love I know is there.

I must be staring for too long, because Silas claps his hands together. "Right, well. Outsiders, pariahs, and lost causes need to stick together, so what can we do to help?"

"We could use help in the library, going through the archives," I say.

The Warlock crosses his arms. "I've spent months already combing through texts, but perhaps if we work together, we can find something I missed."

I raise a brow at his reluctant teamwork. "There are more grimoires in this place than bats in the attic, and we need extra hands and eyes. We're looking for any information about curing physical afflictions caused by curses. Ideally with food or herbs, potions, something a Farewitch would use."

Arna Jean whips out her phone. "I can reach out to a few covens in larger cities where there might be more than one Farewitch. See if they have a record of anything like that."

Silas nods. "If we ask around town, some of the older folks might remember if your grandmother ever cured anything like this when she was the Holler's Farewitch."

"Oh, Ms. Marrow might have some ideas. Herbalism is her forte."

As my two favorite extroverts trade ideas, Rett leans in. "And if we don't find anything helpful before the solstice? What then?"

The conversation comes to a halt.

With a screech of his chair, the Warlock stands. "I'm going to say good night to Lazlo," he says in a tight breath. "I trust Ms. Frost can handle things from here."

He heads for the door, and damn my willpower, my eyes track him as he leaves. Just before he turns into the hallway, he grips the frame of the door, and without his gloves on, it's easy to see the blue veins pop against the pallor of his skin, his fingers stiff with tension.

His bare hands hook into my thoughts, pulling with them a feeling I can't ignore, that there's something else I'm not seeing right in front of me.

When the Warlock is gone, Silas tops off my wine. "I feel like we're missing a crucial *previously on*. You two stare at each other like you had a terrible one-night stand."

Arna Jean props her chin on her hand. "Or you *didn't* have a one-night stand and that's the problem."

Rett sniffs. Loudly.

I rub my tired eyes, grabbing my glass. "*Nothing* happened. Mr. Knight and I . . . we're colleagues. That's it." Sip. "Not even friends." Sip.

The wine might be making me sentimental, but I'm suddenly warm with a flush of gratitude that these three are here tonight. *Friends.*

The Warlock could use a friend.

"There's another thing," I say, thinking back to the farmers' market. I didn't want to bring this up in front of the Warlock. "For some reason, our neighbors have a hard time remembering Mr. Knight. The real him, from the cookie bake."

The neighbors we invited then ate food I made in his kitchen, and with my affinity, that should've helped leave an impression of the Warlock on a prefrontal cortex or two. But he's a blur, wet ink smudged too soon across everyone's memory.

"I noticed that when I spoke to folks in town," Silas says. "It's like new memories of him were written over with the stories of his old reputation."

The word *erased* swipes at the back of my mind. "Or not written at all."

Arna Jean studies me. "But you can always remember him without any problems."

Can I ever. His scowl is there, under my eyelids whenever I close my— *Focus.*

"But I live here. Just like Ms. Zeen and Lazlo. It makes sense, especially since the Warlock and his magic are tied to the house."

"It must be your food," the Bookwitch declares. "You always feed us, and if I'm not at the shop, I'm here. More than Silas and Rett but they're here more than other neighbors."

"Whatever the reason," I say, "right now, the folks who dislike magic outnumber those who do. If this all comes to a head with Webb and the Widow Witch—or both—we need neighbors on our side so we're not facing them alone."

Silas salutes. "Say no more. Canvassing and community outreach are *my* magical affinity. Webb has flyers, I have a handsome face. If you gave me time, I could even get the Widow Witch to vote."

Before I can smile, Silas's words sink in my gut as I remember:

The Warlock never told me why the Widow Witch cursed him in the first place.

Chapter Twenty-Three

MONDAY, MAY 30

22 DAYS UNTIL THE SUMMER SOLSTICE

Honey's Helpful Hint, from
Honey Frost's Southern Cookbook
for Recipes Gone Wrong:

~~***Dear Ms. Honey,***~~

~~***I've kidnapped your notebook.***~~

~~***Please order more sweets and Goldfish.***~~

~~***Love, Lazlo***~~

sorry

I'm in a staring contest with the refrigerator.

Waiting. *Any time now.*

Maybe it's just leftover confidence since Sunday supper last night was more wine than supper, but after working through my thoughts with friends, a renewed energy greases the cogs in my head. I trusted my magic enough to take on a Warlock's request for help, and that hasn't changed.

I sense him before he says a word. My blood thrums at my temples when I think about how sensitive my body is to his presence. Turning, I lean against the closed fridge.

"Mr. Knight." Glare.

The Warlock stands at the island. Sunken eyes, black hair like overgrown weeds, stains of either soil or ink or magical spellsoot on his fingers.

A cough of thunder shakes the windows. A storm's been gathering, the sky shifting from lemon to artichoke to eggplant and back again, all against a hovering chartreuse glow. No rain yet, though, and no sign this is unnatural weather courtesy of the Widow Witch.

"You left me a note," he says in greeting.

"Yes."

Silence. ". . . It was a grocery list."

"Yes."

"I see."

"I figured anything less vague would seem too friendly," I explain. He doesn't need to know I just couldn't think of what to write. "Arna Jean is coming by soon, to help with research in the library. She's bringing me the Frost grimoires from the shop's attic. Did you find anything useful in that almanac Ms. Marrow sent over? She says she sourced it from a Warlock."

His bare hands tense at his sides. I long for the days when his hands were his biggest mystery, when I was blissfully unaware of the stakes. "Nothing of use, yet. Warlocks are very good at spellwork, but ask one to record anything in legible handwriting, and you're out of luck."

"Don't you have some extensive network of Warlocks you could reach out to, from all the clients you've helped over the years? Call in some favors? The Eldercraft must be able to connect you to folks who could help, if you're willing to give them the details."

"Of course, let me just consult the Master Magical Folk Rolodex."

Sarcasm, really? "*Rolodex?* You aged yourself more in four seconds than in . . . ?"

"Valiant effort, Ms. Frost." A half smirk creases his cheek. "Only Ms. Zeen knows my exact age, and that's because she's in my will."

If that's an effort to lighten whatever's hanging between us, I ignore it. "I found a few promising journals in other languages in the library this morning, but they'll need translating. Which could take a while." Luckily, we have Wi-Fi. Because of *me*. "We should talk about what we're going to do if we run out of time to exhaust your archives."

Or if the answer isn't there at all.

"How's Lazlo?" I ask.

"He wasn't feeling well. Ms. Zeen forced him into a nap." The truth hides in the line between his brows. Lazlo gets a little bit weaker every day we edge toward the solstice. "And your mother?"

I bite my lip. "She's the same. This storm coming has her feeling off. Bad weather messes with our magic. Wonky air pressure. No good for baking."

I hate it, but I do feel a smidge lighter. It's nice to let the worries filter out so I don't have to hold them so tightly myself.

Before I lose my nerve, I say, "You never told me why the Widow Witch cursed you."

There's an edge to the set of his mouth, but it's not his usual virulent scowl. I wish it were. Show me some fight. *I'm* still in the mood for fighting. The least he can do is keep up.

"We're not discussing this today, Ms. Frost."

"Another secret, then?"

Frowning in a way that tells me I already know the answer, he braces his hands on the island, elbows locked, arms rigid. His voice falters. "You will hate me."

Gooseflesh rises on my skin. Do I really want to hear this? Do we ever really want to know everything about a person, or only the good parts? I could stop, save myself what might be a flavor of heartbreak I don't have the palate to swallow right now.

But even if I don't always know my heart, I'm a Farewitch, and I know my gut. I'd rather understand the real him than simply like the surface layer.

"Then you're in luck, because we already don't like each other," I say.

He takes a ragged breath. "My last birthday was a noteworthy one, but I was not aging gracefully, not after wasting years rotting away in this place. So I sought out the Widow Witch. I thought she'd delight in watching me ask for help."

"With what?"

"What everyone wants on their birthday. To make a wish. A powerful one I could not do on my own."

The Widow Witch can do *wish* magic? I suppose of all the types of Witches, a Hedgewitch's power is the most similar to a Warlock's higher magic. "What did you wish for?"

"What would you wish for? What would anyone?"

Oh.

"Time," I breathe.

"I asked her for a second chance at making my last twenty-five years worth something. Correct mistakes, make new choices." His expression hardens. "I should've known better, but I had age and no wisdom. The Witch is a herald for magical equilibrium, but she balances the scales with her own sick creativity. She granted me the wish, but on her terms."

More low thunder rattles the windows. I know where this is going, but I don't want to believe it.

"I got a second chance at childhood, but not because she sent me back in time to rewrite my past—instead, she *handed* me a new childhood. Like I'd asked for some party favor. A boy with no memory appeared on my doorstep."

Lazlo.

He won't meet my eyes. "Every time I look at him . . ."

Memories of our night in the garden rush into what little headspace I've got left.

We tried *to send him back, but it wasn't possible . . .*

"Lazlo doesn't belong here because he *literally* doesn't belong here." The realization feels like remaking a beloved childhood recipe, only to discover it isn't as good as remembered. "And her terms?"

"Take care of the boy. Make him happy. Simple. But it was only after Lazlo arrived that she told me the full truth. This wasn't a wish, it was a curse. Lazlo would succumb to an illness by my next birthday. I had a year to try to cure him. If I even could. So now this boy was—*is* dying and I haven't been able to do anything about it. I have no idea where he came from, if he came from anywhere at all, or how she managed it. All I know is, he's of my bloodline and—"

He cuts off. Swallows.

This time, he doesn't hide his face, as if challenging me to give up on him and run, far from this house and its ghosts. Lazlo is pure light after decades of dark isolation . . . yet a constant reminder of the Warlock's choice, his desperation. His true loneliness. And he's been living with this vicious onus, his own personal beast, for nearly an entire year.

He always told me I was his last chance. My stare falls to his hands, pale and clenched.

My bloodline.

His struggling wards, the house's erratic moods, his grim-reaper complexion lately . . . "It's not just him, is it?"

It's brief, but he hesitates before he answers. "Our shared bloodline tangles things somehow. As Lazlo's health worsens, so does mine. And as I weaken, the Manor feels the consequences as well."

An oven timer goes off in my head. "*That's* why you wore gloves. You thought there was a chance you'd start disappearing, too."

Reluctantly, he nods. "I figured if he was fading, I would eventually."

"So if we don't cure Lazlo by the solstice . . ." I almost can't say the words. Every part of the sentence is terrible. "Hold on—after all of that—you *are* dying! Or you will."

He manages a half smile. "Aren't we all dying, all the time?"

"Jesus." Of all moments to be sardonic. My brain chugs along as it lays a track of a timeline. "But that means you stopped leaving the Manor *before* your deal with the Widow Witch. I thought you stayed here to avoid her."

"Like with Witches, Warlocks and their magic are strongest on their own land, their home. I've always kept to the Manor for that reason. Though when Lazlo came along, I did theorize that anchoring myself here could somehow help his strength."

Was I really this oblivious to what was going on in my own kitchen—his kitchen? I feel like I need to run the last two months through a colander and scrub them of dirt. If only I'd paid more attention to what my patient *wasn't* telling me, I might've caught on earlier.

The Warlock takes a deep breath. "Lazlo and I might be connected by blood, but right now, your focus is *his* health. If you find a cure for him, we shall hope it works for me, too. So does any of what you've learned now really matter?"

A moldy taste runs down my throat. The Holler knows the wrath of the Widow Witch, but this is a special kind of cruel. Part of me wants to slap this man with a sheet of puff pastry for attempting such an arrogant bargain. Another part wants to just put aside my anger, grab Lazlo, and squeeze him tight. Maybe the Warlock, too.

"No. I suppose it doesn't," I say lamely.

The unyielding stress of our timeline hasn't changed. If we don't cure Lazlo of this illness by the solstice, the Warlock's birthday is going to be a very bad day all around.

If Oris Webb manages to ask enough questions to get the Eldercraft involved, they might remove Lazlo from Mr. Knight's care before we ever get the chance to cure him. I doubt they'd take kindly to a Warlock who struck a bargain with a dangerous Hedgewitch, much less let him keep custody of a kid with no magic. Especially if that kid . . . isn't supposed to be here.

If if if.

If I had kissed the Warlock, would all this be easier to handle? Or that much harder?

I cinch my apron tighter. Hell.

Shouldn't I be livid? If there were ever a moment to take a rusty pair of sewing scissors to his gardens, we have arrived. Instead, I'm just relieved I've finally got some answers. He's right. The recipe might be different, but our oven temperatures are still set at the same relentless heat. There's no time to be upset when Lazlo needs help.

"Why did the Widow Witch even agree to grant you a wish in the first place?"

"I promised her a future favor, as payment. Which I refused to honor when I discovered she'd cursed me instead."

Further upsetting the balance of magic and power. "Bet she loved that."

A brooding look takes over as he retreats behind that gruff facade. "As far as I'm concerned, she began this feud."

"Can you blame her? You thought you could just *wish* your way out of a midlife crisis. All this mess, because you wanted to be younger?" *Men.* Good. Lord. Unbelievable.

"Younger is not what I wanted—you can't think me *that* vain."

I scoff. "I'd love to go backward, before my mom got sick. To spend more time with her, learn how to be a great Farewitch. Hell, just a good one. But life doesn't work like that." He warned me I would be mad, but I want him to be mad, too. Not withdraw into himself.

My attitude works. He straightens to his full height and faces me, and my favorite glower returns. That's more like it.

"This *mess* was not intentional. I never would have made the wish if I knew a child—whatever his origins—would be affected. Or anyone besides me, for that matter. Wish magic is my craft, and that is why I turned to it to solve a problem. You would have done the same, Ms. Frost. You told me so when you arrived."

My mouth closes on a retort.

What are you looking for in all those books?

A happy ending. A second chance. They all have one thing in common. Time.

What would I give to carve out more time for my mom? A lot. Too much. Everything.

Fine, so maybe it isn't about being younger. We spend away all our time and then somehow want it to still add up to something. Suddenly, I feel small, a silly little Farewitch. How the hell did I, Honey Frost, end up at the top of the Warlock's emergency contact list?

I tear my gaze from his. If I keep staring into those hazel cauldrons of self-contempt, I'll never concentrate. "What moment in your life were you trying to redo? Your parents' deaths?"

"No. Deaths are fixed events in time. I simply wanted to go back to when someone kind offered me help I should not have refused."

Even if I don't want to, I understand. Accepting help is almost harder than asking for it.

I cross the gap between us so I'm right up in his face. With our height difference, it's not as intimidating as I hoped. "For future reference, lies by omission are still lies. *Sir.*" To drive home my point, I poke a single finger into his hard chest.

Before I can blink, he snatches my hand in an unyielding grip. I swallow. Probably should *not* have literally poked the beast. But then he threads his long fingers through my stiff ones, loosening my hand, like roots threading up through soil to find the sun. We're *much* closer than I realized and I can see his worry lines, which are way too endearing for their own good. He holds my fist against his chest, gaze burning into mine, like he wants to set something on fire. Maybe me. In the best way.

Out of nowhere, a small voice tiptoes into our argument. "Are you fighting about me?"

Lazlo watches us from the kitchen doorway.

My face probably matches the Warlock's exactly, a cocktail of surprise and distress. He composes himself first.

"Ms. Frost cares a great deal for you, Lazlo. She's teaching me how to be better. But sometimes, I'm not very good at listening."

Disbelief swallows the rest of my anger. Something in my chest shivers and I refuse to believe it's my heart.

Lazlo glances to the windows. "Ms. Zeen says a big storm is coming. Do you think Beauregard is okay? Dogs don't like thunder."

The kid would know, given how often Ms. Buchanan stops by so Lazlo can play with Beau. She and Arna Jean are always stopping by for chatter. Neither likes to text.

"I'm positive," the Warlock says, looking grateful for the change in topic.

"But it's gonna be *nasty*, Ms. Zeen says, and Beau doesn't like loud noises or even lightning. Can we go check on him? *Please.*"

"Not right now. We need to stay inside, but we can call Ms. Buchanan from here."

"We tried, but Ms. Buchanan doesn't answer numbers she doesn't know, and what if the storm knocked out her power? *Please.* Honey and I can go—"

The Warlock rubs his temple. "I said no. We need to remain within the Manor's wards."

"*Why?*" The kid crosses his arms. Definitely a habit he picked up from me. Whoops. He does his best to stare down his guardian from a height of four feet. "They don't even work."

"Lazlo, we are not free from the Widow Witch. I know you think the world of that dog, but there are decisions adults have to make to keep you safe—"

"But it's boring that way, and you never let me go *anywhere*—"

"Because you're important, Lazlo, the dog is not!"

I cringe. Lazlo's face goes white as eggshell, scrunched with hurt.

The Warlock understands, a moment too late. "Lazlo, I didn't mean—"

But the damage is done. The first tears fall down the boy's cheeks. His tiny hands fade in and out, translucent, his emotions unmoored and his focus floating away.

"Honey's right," he mumbles between tears. "This is why you don't have friends."

He bolts out of the kitchen, leaving it feeling twice as empty.

The Warlock hangs his head, black hair curtaining his face. He's still holding our tangled fingers. Like a lifeline. "Have you ever seen someone cause two different arguments in as many minutes? I'm a disaster."

My chest seizes. Stupid heart. "One summer, Arna Jean tried to introduce vegan butter to the Apothakery. You don't know the meaning of disaster."

Some tension in his jaw unlocks. "You're right about Lazlo. About everything, frustratingly. In case I have not made it clear, I'm terribly . . . glad you're here."

His thumb runs a delicate circle over the soft triangle between my own thumb and forefinger, and I have to suppress a shiver. My mood lifts despite our crap situation.

"For the record, I still think you're keeping secrets."

"I'd be disappointed if you didn't."

"I *will* figure it all out."

He smirks. "I'll be disappointed if you don't." Then he brings our clasped hands to his mouth and brushes his lips over the oven scars on my knuckles.

I can't stop the second shiver that hits me. It's not a kiss. But in a way, it's a helluva lot more. Warmth pools in my cheeks. My mouth is definitely open. We're still fighting. Right? But if this is mad, what's *not*-mad like between us? Sudden sneaky daydreams send the warmth in my face right down my neck, to my chest, then belly and down, down, down . . .

A throat clears. "Mr. Knight, the postman is here with mail."

The Warlock's eyes squeeze shut, his nostrils flaring. "On Memorial Day, Ms. Zeen?"

"He's precocious."

"That's probably for me," I whisper. "I ordered more Modjeskas. Forgot. Sorry." My words coast against his lips, a breath away.

With an inscrutable look, he steps aside. I take my chance and flee the kitchen before I get too caught up in his . . . everything.

By the time I reach my room, I'm fanning myself with the mail Rett left, even more confused and flustered.

Glancing at the mail, I see there's a notice about the Memorial Day potluck in the town square later today, weather permitting, and—*blegh.*

One of Webb's stupid flyers leers up at me. This one's doubling as a notice for Gertha Fudge's next church luncheon.

Magic Spells Trouble: Senior Safety in Foxe Holler.

An idea hits me like a shiny brand-new 4x4.

Before I can change my mind, I grab my truck keys and a cake I made earlier from the fridge, and hightail it to my Dodge. Above me, it's not even noon yet and the clouds have the sun cornered. The impending storm weaves a charge through the air.

Silas suggested some of the oldest Holler residents might remember if my grandmother ever cured something like a curse when she was a young and new Farewitch herself. If they do, they might also remember a time before the Widow Witch started taking husbands. When she was just a Witch, with her own wants and desires and ambitions. And weaknesses.

If anyone knows *anything* about the Widow Witch that could possibly help me fight her curse magic—it's the person who hates her the most.

Chapter Twenty-Four

MONDAY, MAY 30 (STILL)

22 DAYS UNTIL THE SUMMER SOLSTICE

Honey's Helpful Hint, from
Honey Frost's Southern Cookbook
for Recipes Gone Wrong:

Remember to soak your raisins. A little liquor makes the wrinkles disappear. But don't forget—sometimes age can be the best ingredient.

There's a tiny house poised in the shadow of Foxe Holler's church at the center of town.

Just the way Gertha Fudge likes it, if I had to guess. The house's white paint is as crisp as its landscaping. Even the flower boxes under the windows are perfect. The entire place looks like it belongs in *Southern Living.*

In what is either a terribly clever or terribly terrible idea, I ring the bell.

The front door opens, a screen the only barrier between me and a very grumpy church lady. "Go away." Slam.

The thin screen door shakes in its frame. I rub my temple. Cue the wine hangover. But I didn't make the long drive into town only to give up because a woman half my height dismisses me like a crying toddler in church. I try again, holding down on the doorbell so long, the front door begrudgingly cracks open again.

One dark eye stares out. "I said go away, Witch. I don't need any magic souring my doorstep today. No thank you, Jesus."

"If I recall, you don't think Farewitches are a real threat. What was it? No need to worry over *violent scones*?"

The crack widens. "That was before the good pastor showed us the truth. There can be no good Witches because there is no good magic."

I notice she doesn't mention the rumor about the Warlock imprisoning my mom. Then again, how does Fudge have the energy to keep up with half these rumors?

"Witches have been around the Holler a long time, ma'am. If magic were bad on its own, why is the Widow Witch the only one of us ever causing problems?"

She huffs through bold red lipstick. A white silk housecoat and robe set contrasts starkly with her dark skin. For a grouchy old lady, she has an envious amount of style.

I'm fighting a futile battle. This isn't about logic. This is about faith. "Ms. Fudge, do you really believe what Webb is preaching? Why place so much blind faith in a man who scorns his neighbors? Doesn't sound very Jesus-like to me."

I think I have her.

Then, "Doesn't matter what I believe, girl. The Widow Witch took my husband, and that's enough for me."

"I know, Ms. Fudge, and I'm real sorry—"

"But did you know my husband was the *first* she took?"

Crap. No one ever mentioned that little detail. She moves to shut the door, so I step closer, nose to the mesh screen. I don't want to be insensitive, but there are two lives at stake. Three, now that I know the Warlock's health is tied to Lazlo's.

I take a deep breath. I need answers, and Fudge might be able to give them to me. "I came to talk about the Widow Witch."

"Go bother Beulah Buchanan instead," she snaps.

"I want to talk to *you*." I smile as innocently as I can. "You know everything that happens in this Holler, right? Or should I trust Ms. Buchanan's word first?"

Her eyes narrow. "If only you were as clever as you are ornery."

"Don't you think it's odd Webb is so determined to make all magic the enemy, not just the Widow Witch? She sent a storm after the Warlock the other day, in his own house. Whatever Webb is telling you, they're not allies conspiring against you."

"I don't know anything about that. The only storm I see is brewing over our heads right now. The sky is sick. Go home. I haven't lived this long because I laughed at floods."

Time for the cavalry. I reveal the offering in my tote bag. "I brought rum cake. A Frost family classic. Great for arthritis, I hear. With raisins." *Take the bait.*

The door opens an inch. ". . . Did you soak the raisins?"

"Of course. Not a wrinkle in sight." Gertha Fudge could use a rum soaking. She might be more pleasant then.

"What kind of rum?"

"Mount Gay."

She finally relents, and swings a hand around the screen door. "Hand it over."

I do as I'm told.

"My father always kept Barbadian rum in the house," she says, sniffing the cake. "I like rum cake with a little of my pineapple jam on top." Back behind the screen, she gives me her reluctant attention. "My arthritis makes me cranky sometimes. Gets worse with a storm."

That might be an apology? "I understand the Warlock's history with this town is a lot more complicated than—"

"You *don't* understand, girl. Not this history. Not the Knights."

"Hear me out, Ms. Fudge. I'm here as your Farewitch, *your*

neighbor. I came to ask about the Widow Witch, what you know about her. I'll take anything you can tell me. *Please.*"

She clucks at me. "Here's what I'll tell you: If anyone's capable of enraging the Widow Witch, it's Knight. His fight with the old bat has been a long time coming. That boy's been rotten and on her bad side since before you were eating solid food, girl. Nothing more dangerous than an undisciplined Warlock. Don't need any fancy Eldercraft to tell me *that*."

A Witch won't argue there—wait.

Gertha Fudge remembers the Warlock.

"You knew him when he was younger, didn't you?" *That's* why her anger feels personal.

"Everyone was a child once, girl. Terrible business with his parents. No one should meet the good Lord so soon." Then she shakes herself out of that thought, jowls shivering. "Take that little boy and leave that tomb of a farmhouse. Some folks are just meant to be alone."

"I don't believe that. And I don't think you believe it, either."

"Didn't your mama ever warn you *a giggling girl and a gaggling hen always meet a terrible end*? Go cluck somewhere else, girl. It's Memorial Day and I'm resting."

"Ms. Fudge, you're retired."

"What, so I don't get a holiday?" she huffs, shaky hands gripping the rum cake. "Stop trying to play with magic bigger than you. Go back to your shop and just be a Farewitch."

Ms. Zeen's voice comes back to me. *Angry women are usually right.* "Honestly, Ms. Fudge, I think all this loathing of magic is because you're scared, not mean."

The tiniest morsel of surprise peeks through her expression, just before her face hardens into weathered stone. "You're in luck, girl. 'Cause I can be scared and mean at the same time."

The door slams in my face, the frame shaking with the force of her spite.

A clap of thunder cracks through my bewilderment. Right. I need to get back to the Manor before the hills turn to mud.

On the way back to the farmhouse, I expect a maelstrom, but the clouds only grow darker. Whichever way I look, the horizon promises storms. The sky threatens to weep but never does. In my rearview mirror, Foxe Holler hunkers under a blanket of sickly gray.

When I near the edge of town, a text pings my phone. I don't check it, my eyes on the narrow country lanes, but my pocket buzzes with a cacophony of texts. Then, an actual phone call. That's when I get worried.

I pull over at the town's gas station to check my phone, and I see Silas's text first.

Silas Key
Tornado moving toward town, stay put
Your mom is OK

My breath catches, nervous system officially in fight-or-flight mode. Just as I'm about to call the Warlock, he calls me.

It's not his voice on the other end. Ms. Zeen's normally stoic tone is shrill in my ear.

"Slow down, Ms. Zeen—"

"*Lazlo is missing.* His favorite sneakers are gone. And his coat. Even his little umbrella."

My stomach rolls like dough in a bread machine, my thoughts cycloning back to earlier. He was so upset with Mr. Knight—

Do you think Beauregard is okay? Can we go check on him? Please.

Oh no no no.

Surely not. Even if he did, how could the kid get all the way from the Manor to town? A bike? If he's on foot, maybe I can intercept him . . .

I clutch the steering wheel, head bubbling with worst cases. "Does the Warlock keep any functioning portals around the Manor?"

A frantic sentence comes through the phone. I have to kill the Dodge's engine to hear.

"—not for ages," Ms. Zeen's saying. "I suppose something could've been left open; there was always a tricky one in Mr. Knight's study—"

"Does he know Lazlo is gone?"

"Not yet, but only because he's busy futzing with the wards. He thinks the storm is—"

"The Widow Witch." Of course. "Stay there. Double-check the usual hiding spots. But try to act normal. I'll find Lazlo."

As soon as we hang up, I pull up the group chat.

kentucky fried coven

Everyone OK?

Carolina Vázquez
We're moving patients to safer rooms
Hospital's fine but in a panic, text y'all later

Arna Jean Claywell
shop is safe and secure, I'm headed home
got too much delicate crystal sitting around

is this the WW? finally?

Ms. Marrow
I think we're on the edge of it out here.
We needed the rain but Lord, not like this.

Can anyone here portal?

Ms. Marrow
Sorry, dear. Not me. Not after Mammoth Cave.

Arna Jean Claywell
portal? no one portals anymore
that's old witch magic

Damn. I call Arna Jean.

She answers on the first ring. "Hey, I'm almost at my apartment. You seen my fool of a brother by chance? He was delivering mail in this chaos."

"RJ, you shouldn't be outside at all!" And her apartment doesn't have a cellar. But even six years her senior, I've never been able to tell the Bookwitch what to do. "Can you meet me at Beulah's house? You might get there faster. Lazlo—I think he went to see her."

"You *think*? Are y'all trying that free-range parenting?"

"RJ!"

"Beulah isn't even in town right now. She was taking Beauregard to visit y'all, before the storm got bad. I saw her at the shop, an hour ago, maybe? She came by to grab something sweet for Lazlo."

Shit. If he's not in town and he's not at the Manor . . . Shit shit shit.

"Honey!"

"Yeah?" I squeak into the phone.

"I said, I think I know where your kid's gone."

I start the Dodge's ignition and careen back the way I came. "I'm on the way."

Chapter Twenty-Five

MONDAY, MAY 30 (STILL)

22 DAYS UNTIL THE SUMMER SOLSTICE

Honey's Helpful Hint, from
*Honey Frost's Southern Cookbook
for Recipes Gone Wrong*:

**A Warlock's curse at three,
and the Devil's fire at four,
but when the witchkind sing,
their hymns spell death at the door.**
—"A Cautionary Rhyme for Young Warlocks"

I'm not sure where it all goes wrong.

One minute, the tornado is on the horizon, kissing the edge of the Holler.

The next, it's shot through the town square and heading right for Knight Manor.

Not far from the gas station, I intercept Arna Jean. Winds threaten to upturn the more anemic carports we pass as I floor it out of town and up into the hills. The sound of a train in the clouds grows louder, chasing us, the skies a dark bruise everywhere we look.

We abandon the truck just inside the Manor's gates, and I follow Arna Jean into the overgrown maze of greenery bordering the property's long drive. The farmhouse itself is a ghostly monument in the distance as torrential winds and overcast light smudge any familiar shapes into blurs.

The old tobacco barn I never paid much attention to until now looms just beyond the unkempt tree line, in a clearing that was likely once wide-open farmland. As we hike toward the barn's open-mouthed entrance, all I can think about is how *small* Lazlo is; he's likely to just float away in the storm.

This feels like all my fault.

Finally, Arna Jean and I stumble into the barn, its skeletal structure just barely keeping the wind from tearing my friend's glasses right off her face.

A dog barks.

Luckily I missed lunch, because I almost vomit with relief.

There, nestled together in a mound of damp hay, are Lazlo and Beauregard. Next to them, Ms. Buchanan perches on the top flat beam of a rusted disc harrow. Everyone's hair looks like it's been through a blender, but otherwise they seem unharmed.

"Honey!"

Before I even see him move, Lazlo is by my side, his little hands making fists in my shirtfront.

My arms go around him and I squeeze. And squeeze. Arna Jean was right. "How—" I start, but just then, the barn shakes, groaning under the stress of the gale.

Ms. Buchanan wraps her arms around Beauregard to keep him still, no leash in sight. "I don't mean to alarm anyone, but I gather we don't have time to get up to the farmhouse."

I lock eyes with Arna Jean and see the same thought in my mind shivering across her face. Now would be a great time to be any Witch other than a Bookwitch or Farewitch.

The old woman reads us as well as any tarot deck and wags a finger at me. "I'm no Witch, but even I know magic can't protect a foolish girl from a tornado."

But before anyone can panic, Arna Jean shouts something about shelter, pointing back to the entrance.

There. Canted, in-ground doors just outside the barn. A root cellar.

Somehow, in a handful of seconds, Arna Jean and I corral Ms. Buchanan, her poodle, and Lazlo into the cellar at the front of the building. I seal the doors behind us as best I can.

By the meager light of a tiny camping lantern Lazlo brought with him, I count heads in the musk of the underground cellar. Judging by the short aisles of old wooden shelving, this place was once used for storing perishable food goods and canned stock.

Another endless minute later—it could be an hour, it could be just seconds—the tornado hits. The Widow Witch has arrived, and she's angry.

The barn groans, along with the sound of glass shattering somewhere. I taste electricity on the air. I don't recall that lovely side effect during the Widow Witch's previous attacks.

A horrendous cracking noise rips through the air outside the cellar. There's the sound of what has to be wood shrieking as it splits, and then a crash as something large falls against the cellar doors, like heaven felled a giant beast right onto our little plot of earth.

The doors bulge inward but don't give way.

Our heads turn skyward, and the last thing I see is the gold flash of Arna Jean's octagonal glasses before Lazlo's lantern coughs out and the cellar sinks into darkness. As Ms. Buchanan begins panic-humming church hymns, I wade through the dark emptiness toward where I last saw my little runaway. I'd take the most stressful day at the shop over this.

The root cellar is small, so I find him quickly and hold him to me again, tighter, like he'll just evaporate through any gaps in the cellar if I can't see him. Soon, the chaotic thrall outside is right on top of us. One hand in Arna Jean's and the other in Lazlo's, I hold my breath.

Please don't cave in. Please don't cave in.

Ms. Buchanan stops humming long enough to grumble. "As God is my witness, I'm not going to die in a root cellar. I should be nursing a Long Island iced tea on my own porch. That's the way to go."

Not helping, Beulah.

"It's okay, Ms. Buchanan," Lazlo says. I feel him move around me, closer to the old woman. "We'll keep you safe."

The poodle yips.

Then, all at once, my ears ring with a sudden, unholy silence. The noise stops.

The cellar doesn't crumble inward.

When the world outside seems stable, all my terror about losing Lazlo comes tumbling back. I aim my full attention at him. "How in the *world* . . . ?" I gasp, not even able to finish. If this is what being a parent is like, no wonder the Frost women are big fans of *one and done*.

When Arna Jean said the kid's favorite place to take Beauregard for a walk whenever Ms. Buchanan visits is down by the old barn, I almost didn't believe her. I was willing to bet the old woman's precious poodle had not once set paw in a barn. Shows what I know.

"I ran after Beauregard," Lazlo says, zero regret in his voice.

"We pulled up to the Manor just as the boy was running out," Ms. Buchanan chimes in.

"I was going to go visit them, I wasn't running away, promise, I just didn't tell anyone—"

"Then the thunder hit us and my poor old Beauregard lost his marbles. In the frenzy, he ran right off without his leash down the drive. I caught up with them just a few minutes before you two stumbled in looking like feverish hill people."

Of course. The dog ran off to the safe place he remembered, and Lazlo followed, without question. Jesus, I'm not sure how Ms. Buchanan trekked her way down here, with her bad ankles and dislike of sweating.

The only downside to finding Lazlo is that now my brain has

plenty of energy to focus on our other big problem: the Widow Witch. If she wants her curse to inflict as much suffering on the Warlock as possible, she'd let him watch Lazlo perish on the solstice. Why would she hurt the kid now? Has she decided to trade marital disasters for natural disasters?

Arna Jean pulls out her phone, turning on the flashlight. "No signal. Phone lines are down, or we're too far underground."

In the white-blue halo of her phone, Arna Jean and I try pushing against the cellar doors. Even Ms. Buchanan joins in, arthritis be damned. The doors don't budge. Now would *really* be a stellar time to have someone like a Tombwitch in our friend group. They're good at unearthing things, intentionally or unintentionally buried.

"One of those big oak trees probably fell right across the doors," Ms. Buchanan determines. "We're going to have to wait for the fire department to get over here. If they weren't swept away, that is."

Lazlo gulps, and Beauregard whimpers.

I send a useless glare through the dark. The old woman has terrible bedside manner. "Save your battery," I whisper to Arna Jean.

After surviving a literal tornado, are we really going to rot away with dwindling air, forgotten in a cellar? Someone has to know we're here. See Ms. Buchanan's car. Ms. Zeen! She knew I was coming from town. But will she tell the Warlock? She doesn't even know I found Lazlo yet. The chances she'd leave me missing are low, but not zero.

There's nothing to do but wait until someone realizes we're down here.

The air gets muggy real quick. We only know how much time passes because of Arna Jean's phone. I left mine in the pickup. Right now, I'd give anything for one of the Warlock's silly formal texts.

Despite everything, Ms. Buchanan won't stop muttering about the church ladies, and how *Blanche wasn't going to cancel the Memorial Day potluck, even with the forecast.* She's spoiling for a fight. Or a distraction. At least she's keeping Lazlo entertained.

After a full hour goes by, even Ms. Buchanan is too tired to complain or argue with imaginary neighbors.

Beauregard pants next to Lazlo, whose hand is glued in mine. "I'm sorry I ran off," he whispers to me.

My heart cracks at his small voice.

"You don't have anything to be sorry about. I'm sorry Mr. Knight and I didn't listen."

I hear the softest sniffle. "Sometimes I get mad and . . . I don't know."

"Lonely? Mr. Knight does, too. Then he says things he doesn't mean."

"I don't think he does. Get lonely, I mean. Not really."

"Trust me, he does. And he doesn't want you to grow up like him."

A hobbling clutter comes from our left, along with a strong whiff of perfume. "Mr. Lazlo," Ms. Buchanan says in the darkness, "I wanted to thank you for keeping my Beauregard safe. I don't have the strength to chase him myself."

"You're welcome," Lazlo mumbles from where he's slumped against me. He needs cheering up, and Ms. Buchanan can sense it.

"You know, my boy, I have a few simple pleasures in life as ninety comes along . . ."

"Like her evening bourbon," Arna Jean whispers from somewhere on my other side.

". . . and Beauregard is the most important. I adopted him when my memory went spotty. He even follows me into rooms when I forget where I'm going. I hoped a big dog would keep folks from bothering me, but he isn't too good at being scary yet. We're working on it."

I feel Lazlo's huff of a tiny laugh. "His tail wags too much to be mean."

"Remember, my boy, there are lots of things more dangerous than storms out there. Like vet bills. Or memory loss. Or the Widow Witch."

"Or Gertha Fudge," Arna Jean mutters.

Ms. Buchanan shuffles away, presumably to bother Arna Jean. If she can find her.

When we're again alone as we can be in a root cellar, Lazlo tugs on my elbow. "What happens when you cure me?"

When. Not if. Bless him. "What do you mean?"

"Will you still live with us? Or will you leave?"

I don't answer. His question makes me feel like spoiled milk. Sour, useless, clogged with clumpy unpleasantness. A pang of hunger hits me so suddenly I can feel my heartbeat in my stomach.

I wish the Warlock were here with us. I miss him. But that thought feels very Big Wish tier, not Small, and the man's magic doesn't work like that anyway.

Or it *shouldn't.*

A sudden commotion beyond the cellar doors shatters the silence.

I hustle to the doors, Arna Jean's chunky heels behind me, the two of us tripping over what I think are old canning jars. We get as close as we dare, in case the old doors might still collapse inward. Slowly, I begin to make out a pair of voices, right outside. Three voices? Three male voices. Arguing.

"There's no way the three of us can lift that tree—" The exchange is muffled but heated.

"Speak for yourself, I do my calisthenics four times a week."

"—have you seen us? At least I lift heavy boxes."

Arna Jean's voice travels from the left. "Is that my brother?"

An indignant shout from the surface: "You are not *hitching* to my truck. Her name is Stamp of Approval and she's a United States Postal Service vehicle, not a trailer. That would ruin my bumper—"

"That's him," she mutters. "Jesus, I've always hated that name. Like some kind of racehorse in the Derby."

"If you gentlemen won't take your argument elsewhere, kindly back up or shut up. I need someone to make a clear wish."

My heart flutters. It can't be . . .

"I wish you'd be useful and move the tree."

"I am not a *genie*, Mr. Key. What did I say? *The Language of Small Wishes.*"

"I've got it," says someone who sounds like Rett. "I wish I could tell my sister her perfume is too loud."

Arna Jean huffs. "It is *not*."

All at once, there's the sound of something heavy lifting off the doors, and the clatter echoes through the cellar. With much heaving, the doors at last fly open. The dim sunset makes me squint as I blink away the darkness.

Then I'm staring up into a familiar set of hazel eyes.

Chapter Twenty-Six

MONDAY, MAY 30 (STILL)

22 DAYS UNTIL THE SUMMER SOLSTICE

Honey's Helpful Hint, from
Honey Frost's Southern Cookbook
for Recipes Gone Wrong:

A giggling girl and a gaggling hen
always meet a terrible end.
—Meemaw Hazeleen Frost

Warlock Knight peers down at me.

A visibly held breath leaves him as he looks me up and down. "Are you hurt? Lazlo?"

My usually steady chef's hands are shaking. "In need of some of Ms. Zeen's calming tea, but no worse for wear."

"You're in luck. She came along."

"Lazlo first?" I ask, still in shock he's here, he found us. Found me.

"Indeed, hand him up. I don't think that cellar is long for this world. The stairs are nonexistent on our end. Mind the splintered wood."

Once Arna Jean and I hand off Lazlo through the hole that was previously the cellar entrance, the Warlock gives him a quick fierce hug, though his eyes stay on me over the boy's shoulder. He whispers something to the kid I can't hear, then passes him off to the safety of Governess Zeen's waiting arms.

Next goes Beauregard, Ms. Buchanan insists, and he launches right into a flustered Rett, whose glasses slide askew with a slobbery lick. Then we free the old woman herself, somehow without dislocating one of her hips, and finally the Warlock and Silas haul Arna Jean to the surface.

It begins to rain.

My turn.

Before I can insist on climbing out myself, the Warlock hauls me right into his arms. Under the thick haze of thyme, he smells like wet, clean earth, and I try very hard not to press my nose against his neck. The cold drizzle has me damp to the bone, and I relish the warmth from his large palms at my waist.

"All field trips are to be approved by me, Ms. Frost," he murmurs. The words would carry an edge if it weren't for the teasing quirk of his lips.

"To be fair, you would've said no."

He raises an eyebrow, like we're just having a Good Old Normal Bicker, not standing in the wreckage of a tornado. This close, I notice his cheekbones, already sharp and high, jut out more than usual.

He clears his throat. "It took me longer than I intended to find you. We had to figure out where you'd gone, and I couldn't expend magic on a tracking spell in case we needed to—no one could get here to help because the streets were impassable in the squall and the fire department was putting out other literal fires . . ."

He's ranting. He never rants. He doesn't even realize he's still holding me.

"So everything went awry when I left the Manor. As I suspected."

His chest expands under my hand. A fortifying breath. "Thank you. For finding Lazlo."

The low timbre of his voice leaves my ears humming. "Thank you for the rescue."

"Give your regards to our postman. It was his wish that moved the tree."

Only then do I notice the massive crater a toppled oak tree's exposed roots have left behind. *My wish was for you,* I want to say. After every secret I've wrested out of the man, I don't want to be anywhere else. But right on time, worry crowds into my head.

The bags under his eyes are the same color as the evening sky. If he refrained from a simple tracking spell to conserve power . . . Now that I know his health and energy decline right along with Lazlo's, I wonder how he even managed the magic needed to power Rett's wish, especially after bolstering the Manor's wards before the tornado hit. He's pushing his body and his luck.

"I'm surprised to see you three working together," I say, in lieu of letting my anxieties get the best of me.

"I might have gotten off on the wrong foot with them. Especially Mr. Key."

"Oh?"

In response, his hands squeeze my waist, pulling me closer against him. Maybe my nerves are on high alert, but I can feel exactly where his thumbs press into my hip bones, moving in unconscious circles. I'm defenseless against the oncoming heat under my skin, and that's even before his gaze tracks a brave drop of rainwater as it crests over my cheek, down to my lips—

"Mr. Knight!"

This time, it's Rett who interrupts us. We break eye contact long enough to see the postman waving at us from a dozen yards away. The rest of our group is already halfway back to the property's gravel drive.

"Mr. Knight, you've got . . . company." Rett says the word like *ants* or *insufficient postage.*

We step apart and follow Rett back through the trees, toward the Manor's gate. Whatever moment the Warlock and I were caught in is gone, embrace over. But the entire walk back, he doesn't let go of my hand.

We emerge from the overgrown brush and onto the gravel drive.

My truck is right where Arna Jean and I left it, blocking the path up to the farmhouse. Parked at a slant just below it is Stamp of Approval. Ms. Zeen and Lazlo hunker with Ms. Buchanan and Beauregard in the back of the empty mail truck, out of the drizzle.

"Peace be with you, Miss Frost. Glad to see y'all are safe."

For the love of—not *now.*

Pastor Oris Webb stands on the other side of the large iron gates, one side of which is holding on to its hinges with something stronger than even Gertha Fudge's faith. His truck sits in the road, engine running, headlights shining right at us through the rain. Blinding. Downed trees litter the area.

What did Fudge say? *A home free from the threat of magic.*

This looks all kinds of bad.

The Warlock and I stop just inside the Manor's gate, facing Webb. Silas, Rett, and Arna Jean remain behind us with the rest of our group in the mail truck.

"Mr. Knight, I presume?" Webb asks.

With my overalls and the Warlock's sour expression, we're nailing the Holler Gothic look, like some Grant Wood knockoff. These two have never met in the flesh, but based on the Warlock's glower, he knows exactly who this beige man is.

"Pleasure to meet you." Webb levels his attention on the Warlock's hand, tight around my own. And smiles. "Not a moment too soon, it seems. A Witch and a Warlock make quite the damaging pair."

"Couldn't get your followers to come out during a literal tornado?" I ask. A confrontation at the farmers' market is one thing, but accosted on our own driveway? Not today. "I'm sure you have bigger concerns right now than bothering us."

"Please, indulge me. This tornado rent right through the middle of town, phone lines are down, and I've come all this way to talk, as a representative of us folks without magic."

The Warlock goes rigid against me, his grip tightening on my hand.

Why is the Widow Witch causing destruction all over town when the Warlock is up here? As far as I know, she doesn't have a vendetta against *all* of Foxe Holler. She's never used a widespread storm to take a husband before. She's too efficient. During a normal spring, she comes for one person, and no one else is caught in the cross fire.

Then again, this hasn't been a normal spring from the beginning.

"Did the Widow Witch finally take someone, then?" Ms. Zeen asks from behind us.

"By some *miracle*," Webb says, "no one was harmed. Yet. But our church is a wretched, pitiful thing. Service will need to be relocated for the foreseeable future. We have lost yet another focal point of our community to magic. Just like our library."

The tension in Mr. Knight's body pulses right into my own muscles. If we hoped to convince folks there's no such thing as bad magic, that chance has shriveled up. The universe has some wretched timing. Almost perfectly so.

"Judging by your barn, Mr. Knight—what's left of it—even you can't escape dangerous magic."

In the aftermath of the tornado, it didn't even cross my mind to check if the Widow Witch left her usual scorch marks, her familiar threat burning in the earth. The chill of my fear begins to dissolve as my suspicion brews.

Webb needs a villain more than peace.

I step forward, trying to look formidable, but it's hard when my bangs are going this way and that. "You can't blame all magic for this, or all Witches in the Holler. Not even the Warlock."

"Whether higher or lower magics, neither bodes well for regular townsfolk. Someone always ends up hurt. Especially the innocent."

"This is the Widow Witch's doing. Blame her," I press.

Sickly glee skitters across Webb's face. "Excellent point, Miss Frost. The Widow Witch seems particularly interested in Mr. Knight this year. Why is that?" When I don't immediately answer, he peers toward the mail truck with greedy curiosity. "I'm glad to see your boy is well, Mr. Knight. It would have been a shame, had he been swept away."

The Warlock does a double take toward the mail truck, but his doubt isn't quick enough.

The preacher notices, a spider eyeing a tremor in his web. He *tsks*. "In a time of crisis, you didn't know where you own boy was? Any sensible parent would agree carelessness is a form of neglect."

"He was safe," the Warlock rasps, his thumb jittering in tight circles over my palm. "He *is* safe. His well-being is always my first priority."

"Can a Warlock be a caretaker if he's fighting threats, as well as capable of violent, unpredictable magic himself? Can the community trust Witches if a Witch herself is the cause of such mayhem? In our time of modern medicine, perhaps we don't need Farewitches at all. We have the healing power of faith, and what's meant to be, will be."

I can't take any more of this. "And when someone's on her deathbed, is that the miracle healing power of faith, too?"

Webb sets his stare on me. "No need to insult me with subtlety. You might be a Frost but you are a Witch first. All magic is rotten, and it will poison our souls to the core. You've seen it yourself, have you not?"

This boiled chicken tender of a man surely isn't accusing the indomitable Marigold Frost of being her own illness? Then realization creeps down the back of my neck. *He knows.* The truth about my mom, where she's been. Her illness and my inability to cure her.

"Don't worry, Miss Frost. I have *bigger concerns* than your mother right now. Farewitches don't frighten me. So I'll keep your secret. For now."

Not out of the goodness of his heart, that's for sure. If the town keeps believing the Warlock is the villain in my mom's story, magic is the villain, too. And Pastor Webb wins.

"Besides, Mayor Frost wouldn't have much of a chance charming the town council now anyway. Before summer is out, I'll make sure you Witches don't have a single holiday left on the community calendar. And by the time next spring rolls around, there won't be a single Witch left in the Holler."

"How dare you—"

"I *do* dare," he snaps. "The only *good* magic is *no* magic. This will be safer for everyone. It's a real shame, of course, that a storied institution such as your family's Apothakery could be a victim of all this mess. But if I were you, Miss Frost, I would seek out other employment."

I didn't think my mood could get much worse, but here we are.

"You don't get to decide what Ms. Frost can and can't do." The Warlock's voice is halfway to a growl.

Webb pulls something from his pocket then, and I almost recoil. But it's just another one of his golden-yellow apples.

"I'll get to the point, Mr. Knight. After today, it will be clear to the Holler that the Widow Witch, for whatever purpose drives that devil, is after *you* this season. The longer you remain in Foxe Holler, the more you put the town at risk. The neighbors you've ignored for so long are concerned, especially for the well-being of that young boy."

"The Witches won't see it that way," I say. His congregation might buy this, but surely the rest of the town can smell the manure. *Some* of the town.

"Perhaps not. But I'm sure the Eldercraft would. In fact, I know they would be acutely interested to know if a Warlock was putting a child at risk. They've been known to bar a Warlock from using his magic for much less, haven't they?"

"You have no jurisdiction with the Eldercraft," the Warlock says, growing paler.

He might not, but Webb's tied to all of this somehow. I know it. I just can't see how.

Webb yanks the stem from his apple. "We'll test that theory, won't we? You are no proper caretaker for a child. Not when a Hedgewitch has made you her target. Wrap up your affairs here, or I'll have the Eldercraft at your door. If removing you from the Holler could expel the Widow Witch as well, then the town will see me drag you from that mausoleum of a house myself."

"Good luck with that," I say.

"I don't need luck, Miss Frost, when I have faith."

Webb takes a large bite of apple. Juice drips down his chin.

My ears buzz, the only flavor on my tongue bright red rage, like I've bitten a live wire. Before I know I'm moving, I place myself between Webb and the Warlock. "*Leave.*"

Webb sneers. Then his smile dissolves.

His apple, once the buttery gold of a chanterelle shroom, begins to decay right in his hand. I watch in morbid fascination as the flesh withers and bruises like it sat under a hot sun for a month, in seconds. He drops the rancid apple—it hits the earth with a gooey *squelch*—and his mouth twists in disgust as he spits out the bite he took. Instead of crisp apple, a hunk of woody, purple mold lands on the ground. A tiny worm crawls out of the half-chewed hunk.

Lazlo's voice carries from the mail truck. "Metal."

Webb spits again, this time at my feet. Impossibly fast, the Warlock lunges at him, but I turn and catch him, my hands pushing against his chest to hold him back.

The pastor wipes his mouth, revulsion warping his face. "Like I said. Rotten." His chalky eyes don't blink. "You have three weeks, Mr. Knight. Either the Eldercraft will come for you, or they will come for the boy. It's your choice."

He retreats, heading back to his truck.

Only once Webb is driving back the way he came do I notice the Warlock is still pressed up against me, his body tight with tension. No, he's *leaning* on me. "Sir, are you all right—"

He sways on his feet and collapses.

Chapter Twenty-Seven

TUESDAY, JUNE 7

14 DAYS UNTIL THE SUMMER SOLSTICE

Honey's Helpful Hint, from
Honey Frost's Southern Cookbook for Recipes Gone Wrong:

Food is not a reward. Starving yourself just makes you hungrier.

"You're suspiciously quiet in those clogs."

Warlock Knight stands in his gardens, staring up at nothing in the evening June sky. I pause mid-creep behind him, trying to see if I can spot what he's hunting for. "Scouting for your next archnemeses, sir?"

At least he's on his feet, a rare sight this past week. So far, I've resisted ambushing him in his bedroom to force him to eat, and kept my worrying to the kitchen.

The house is more unruly than ever, which makes it tough for Arna Jean and Rett to focus on their research in the library. We haven't had a proper working lamp in days. And whenever I leave the house, usually on an errand to borrow grimoires from the other Witch families, the wards seem to blip and disappear for a breath. There's always a pop in my ears, like we're all hurtling down the Appalachian mountainside.

Not a good sign for warding, if I had to guess.

As Mr. Knight loses a grip on his power, his energy and magic draining, Lazlo's little hands fade in and out at random to varying degrees. I feel like it's getting harder to keep track of all the edges of our catastrophe map. Sooner or later, we're bound to fall off.

"That tornado was not regular Hedgewitch magic," the Warlock says as I join him. "Something isn't right."

We've had no more trouble from the Widow Witch, but this period of peace just leaves behind a bitter flavor of anticipation. What is she planning? Her latest attack wasn't sitting right in my gut, so I went back to check the area where the old barn once stood: no scorched message.

"I agree, but we should be more afraid of Oris Webb right now."

Ever since his threats at the Manor's gate, Webb's anti-magic sermons in the town square have increased, and Silas tells me he's gotten more of the town council to listen to his ideas about finding a way to limit magic from the Holler, starting with his church. According to the group chat, more than just the church ladies follow him around now, passing out flyers. Gertha Fudge used her latest luncheon to rant against *sinful sorcery*.

The Widow Witch's tornado was the very devastation Webb and Fudge needed to further sour Mr. Knight's reputation and turn folks against magic in Foxe Holler.

And if Webb succeeds and casts out the Warlock, he'll come for Witches next.

"I suspect he'll think twice about showing up here again, with such a *rotten* Farewitch in residence," the Warlock says. "He's more afraid of your magic than mine."

"We still don't know if that was me. I already have my affinity." I'm a Farewitch, not a . . . whatever that was. A Greenwitch type of thing? But rot is death. So, Tombwitch? I could ask Carolina or my mom, but with everything else going on, I don't have the headspace to think too hard about how Webb's apple met its maker.

"Where is it written a Farewitch can't have more than one affinity? You'll be ripening all your own produce in no time."

His words shiver in my chest, like I've swallowed a handful of frozen blueberries. I've been thinking of this power as decay, but he thought only of growth. Life. A powerful thing and powerfully good.

He turns to me, holding up a plump, bright red cherry tomato. "Try this."

I'm not going to be the embarrassed mess I was the last time he offered me food, so instead of accepting the tomato like a normal person, I open my mouth and look up at him with wide eyes. It takes him the most adorable moment to understand the challenge. His Adam's apple bobs as he stares at my mouth. I'm half bluffing. He won't do it, I know it.

But after some internal argument, he places the tomato right on my tongue.

This time, no gloves. My teeth graze his bare fingers. Sweet acidity bursts between my molars as a shadow crosses his face. "Careful, Witch." His voice rumbles low in his chest.

I give him my best satisfied grin. He called my bluff, but somehow, I still won.

He thrusts a basket in my direction, and the spun-sugar-thin thread of tension between us snaps. "I thought you might like to use these tonight."

As I pick through his offering of earth-toned carrots, I suppress an undignified squeal. But summer harvests are my love language.

"Thank you," I say, and head back inside before I do something silly. Reckless.

I get to work scrubbing our vegetables. The Warlock hauls in more baskets: peppers, tomatoes, green beans, rhubarb, and sweet onions. He unloads the spoils into the sink next to me, rolls up his sleeves, and starts cleaning. I try not to stare at his forearms, but the sight of his muscles flexing so very close to my own skin . . . I'm lightheaded and I just need a snack.

Is there anything *wrong* with being roommates? Do I even *want* to know if this man can be something more than a friend to a person? A voice in my head shouts *Yes* but I'm pretty sure that's just the overachiever in me who likes a challenge, and she needs to be quiet right now.

I'm overthinking this. The stress of our impending deadlines is gobbling up all the oxygen meant for my brain. We've been scouring, translating, nearly ripping apart every grimoire we can find, hoping to find recipes and spellwork a Farewitch can use. The Warlock said he came across evidence Farewitches might be able to lift some curses, and even a rumor contains traces of fact. The Holler taught me that.

Somewhere, a Warlock or Witch has written down a spell or potion or recipe or *something* that a Farewitch can turn into a cure for someone dying from a Hedgewitch's curse.

While the Claywell siblings are researching so I can keep baking, Silas has his eyes on Webb in town and during council meetings. With Carolina watching my mom at the hospital, I can focus on curing Lazlo, and Ms. Marrow sends me herbs and other flora that might help.

When he's not helping me in the kitchen or the library, the Warlock is putting his new phone to good use and has conversations well into the night with other Warlocks. Not friends, of course, but a few he trusts to not immediately run and report him to the Eldercraft.

Now we've got two weeks. Two weeks until the solstice. Two weeks until Webb comes knocking, which won't even matter if one of my recipes doesn't work on Lazlo before then.

Events have ballooned way beyond May Honey's expectations.

When I sneak another glance at the Warlock at the sink, deep purple smudges collect under his heavy-lidded eyes, and the fatigue in his posture tells me we've gone from blanket of exhaustion to full-body poncho.

"Any sign of your magic returning?"

Ever since he freed us from the cellar, his well of magic has been empty. I don't quite have the gumption to ask if that's a stomach kind of empty that will eventually be full again—or a permanent empty.

He huffs. "I'm about as magical as your KitchenAid mixer. I couldn't grant you a lit candle right now."

Comforting. Maybe it's time to get Carolina over here for a thorough audit of the wards. If there are any left.

"What I'd like to know," the Warlock says, "is how Oris Webb can acquire an audience with the Eldercraft. They're not a customer service hotline. Even Warlocks have trouble getting their attention, unless something is very wrong."

"Would they really remove a child without magic from a home with magic?"

Would they take Lazlo from the Warlock?

His brows pull tight, and his hands pause mid-scrub. "If a guardian is dangerous or uses magic for harmful purposes that put the child's safety at risk, yes." His jaw locks, unlocks. "Oddly enough, Oris Webb knows what he's doing."

Great. Now I wish I'd never asked the question.

I refocus on snapping the ends off green beans, head hammering with a familiar near dizziness. My hand dripping cool sink water, I run my palm across the back of my neck and try to ignore the emptiness in my belly. Hungry, but no appetite. Not after this conversation.

"Are you having lunch?" the Warlock asks, reading my thoughts. He's getting way too good at that lately.

"I'll grab something later while I work."

"A bowl of cereal is not a meal, Ms. Frost."

"Do you run the FDA behind my back, too, sir?"

"You hardly ate anything last night."

"I've been distracted and—and I'm an adult, *thank you*. I can eat what I want."

"We don't need three of us in this house wasting away. We'll outnumber Ms. Zeen."

"Not if you take care of yourself," I fire back.

"And you? How have you spent your twenties? Trying to appease your mother by running the family Apothakery?"

Where is this sudden interrogation coming from? "I *chose* to come back."

"Because of your mother's illness."

"That's—that's irrelevant. I love being a Farewitch. It's not a chore."

"You'll hate it before you're forty if that's the only way you spend your days."

The *nerve*. "Don't lecture me."

His voice lowers. "I lecture you *because* I'm older."

I whirl to face him, hip propped against the sink. A slap of my palm shuts off the faucet. "Are you really telling me *to listen to my elders*?" I've had enough of this.

So has he. Before I can move, his hands are braced against the lip of the sink on either side of my waist. My entire world is suddenly the space between his arms and chest. I stuff my hands into my apron pockets, not sure what they would do if I let them free.

"I spent my youth like you, hunting obsessively for solutions I thought I could will into existence," he rasps. "I ran ragged. Don't make my mistake."

"Unlike you, I don't have the luxury of watching out just for myself. I have my mom to think about, her health and the Apothakery."

"Having a job doesn't replace having a life."

"What does *that* mean?"

His voice sharpens, feeling like fingernails on my skin. "You don't sleep. I hear you at all hours of the night. The Manor echoes with you, constantly. It's *maddening*." His eyes drop to my mouth, and that one small look sends my pulse racing. "Then, you never rest. Even your relaxation is productive."

"Looking up recipes *is* peaceful for me."

His eyes work down my form and back up, and yup, I'm suddenly very much anti–tall men. "And you don't eat. You're thinner than when you arrived."

My face goes hot with . . . with *something*. Fury. Embarrassment. This man tenderly fed me a tomato fifteen minutes ago. *Tenderly.*

"Of all the ridiculous—I'm a Farewitch! I eat plenty. I've just been stressed. *Everyone* is stressed. We're trying to save multiple lives, remember? So forgive me if I'm just not hungry. I'll eat once I've accomplished what I need to do. I don't like to break my concentration."

"You can't go through life treating food as a reward. You're not a dog. As much as Lazlo might prefer that."

My skin buzzes with the urge to flee, but only animals on the defense retreat. "I'm trying to run a business *and* take care of a parent. I am an only child, an only daughter. I. Am. Busy." I enunciate each word."

"And do you ever finish the list of things you have to do?"

Irrelevant. "I enjoy something I want when I've earned it. That's how I stay motivated, and that's how I appreciate something in *peace*. And—and you're my employer! You don't get to offer advice on my health."

His next words are startlingly soft. "But as your friend, I do, and I think you've gotten too used to starving yourself."

"*Excuse me?*" Blood whooshes in my ears. "Do you want me here or not?"

"Do I—" He runs an agitated hand over his face, like he can't decide if this should be a lecture or a scolding and I'm making the choice difficult.

"You know what? Don't answer that. I don't care." I can't think when I'm tucked in his body space like this. My hands spring free of my apron and push against his chest. "Move."

He steps away, no questions asked. "Ms. Frost, you know very well I don't have the energy to fight with you. Quite literally."

Before I can feel disappointed his body heat is gone, I point to the door. “Then get out, because I feel like fighting.”

“It’s *my* house.”

“It’s *my* kitchen.”

He throws up his hands in defeat. “Yes, ma’am.” Then he’s gone.

Immediately, I open the fridge and scream into it. The cool air is heaven on my hot face.

How dare he. *Howdarehehowdarehe.* I’ll stomp through his gardens and squish every last delicate vegetable under my clogs. Rip the petals from his flowers. The mental image is incredibly satisfying. I shouldn’t care if the Warlock is upset with me.

So why do his words sting so much?

Momaw’s voice trickles through my mind’s dam of anger. *It only hurts if it’s true.*

I cradle my head in my hands over the sink, staring at the stupid vegetables that the stupid man nurtured and grew and cared for in his stupid garden.

My frenzied thoughts sharpen as I gather ingredients. Do I eat? Ha. Do I ever.

Weisenberger stone-ground yellow grits. Burners click to life. Water boils. Shrimp dance in a sauté pan on the stove. I stir my grits until they bite back like al dente pasta, and then fold in cream, cheddar cheese, and butter, of course. Buttermilk and paprika, freshly cracked black pepper, too. No bland grits in this house. The soundtrack at my fingertips is always the best way to channel the angry thrum under my pulse, the growl in my stomach.

As I stand over the hot stove, temples sweating, my mind fogs for a second, but then the dizzy sensation is gone. Maybe I’m hungrier than I realized. But that doesn’t mean the Warlock is right.

Finishing touch: I add molasses to the sizzling sauce. The salty bite of the grits will wear it well. Everything sharp needs a little sweet.

In under an hour, I’ve rage-cooked something gorgeous. Sautéed buttered shrimp with Southern cheddar grits. How a person can create something from nothing and have immediate, delicious evidence to prove it—this is the real magic in the world.

I plate the plump shrimp onto a pillow of grits, ley lines of butter creating a glorious foundation. Then I plop down at the kitchen table and eat every. Last. Shrimp. The grits, too, for good measure.

Utterly full and warm, I slump back and stare out at the Manor's kitchen. *His* kitchen. Mine? Who cares. I can't remember the last time I've eaten a full meal I made just for myself. It's divine. For about twenty minutes.

And then it isn't.

The fuzzy feeling starts in my neck, like I'm wearing a cheap scarf. Sniffles spread through my nose. My sinuses stop up, head stuffy. It's way too warm in here. Did I leave the oven on? I clear my throat but it feels like I'm swallowing my lymph nodes. My eyes grow watery. Am I crying?

Then my chest tightens, and I realize I'm not breathing fully.

My internal smoke detector starts screaming. I shuffle to the main staircase, but my limbs are heavy and the hallways are as warm as the kitchen. I want to shed itchy layers, but all I have on under my apron are my overalls. With an embarrassing amount of effort, I at last reach the third floor and pause to catch my breath. My gut turns over and my lower abdomen clenches. I can't decide if I need to sit on a toilet or lean over one.

Then I catch a glimpse of myself in a hall mirror. Skin splotchy red like a McIntosh apple.

What the hell is wrong with me?

Somehow, I stumble to the Warlock's rooms. Knock. "Mr. Knight." No answer. I knock again, taking a wheezy breath. "Sir, please."

Thank the Lord, his voice comes through the door. "We're fighting, Ms. Frost. I'd like to be mad at least until tomorrow morning."

I rest my forehead against his door. I need to sit down. Or bend at the waist. Or go completely horizontal? Air. I need air. Or him. Same thing.

Smothering my pride, I croak, "I need your help. I don't feel so—"

The door flies open, revealing alarmed hazel eyes. My voice must sound as bad as I feel.

"Ms. Frost, what's wrong—why are you *swollen*?"

Chapter Twenty-Eight

WEDNESDAY, JUNE 8

13 DAYS UNTIL THE SUMMER SOLSTICE

Honey's Helpful Hint, from
Honey Frost's Southern Cookbook
for Recipes Gone Wrong:

You must put your pie dough in the fridge and let it rest. Otherwise, the butter that makes the core of it special will get too warm and your crust will dissolve into a mess.

"*Honey Hazeleen Frost.* What in heaven's name is going on?"

My eyes flutter open. I'm in a narrow bed. Morning light peeks through the vertical blinds, and my forehead pounds with a headache. Did I fall and hit my head?

Marigold Frost sits in a wheelchair next to the bed. She's in a hospital gown, her long gray hair unwinding from her braid, looking thinner than the last time I visited.

"When they brought you in, you were half delirious and swollen like a plump Christmas pig."

"Lovely." My voice comes out as a dry rasp. Memories rise, foamy as feeding yeast: Warlock Knight, pressing a cool rag to my forehead . . . "How did I even get here?"

"That Governess—" She cuts off, clearing her throat through a phlegmy cough. Not good.

As she collects herself, I notice the table under the little television. There's a prickly cactus—definitely Arna Jean. The Bookwitch likes her houseplants as self-reliant as possible, to survive long periods of neglect when she falls deep into a reading phase. Or is that what she said about her relationships?

Tucked next to it, almost hidden, is a young thyme plant. Odd.

When I dare to check my phone, the Kentucky fried coven group chat is responsible for no fewer than fifty new texts, the other Witches checking in on me because of course they heard I'm here, too. Arna Jean is mostly threatening to sneak me in some airplane bourbons. The screen quickly hurts my eyes, and my stomach stirs, growling.

"I can't tell if I'm starving or need to hurl."

"You upchucked everything when you got to the hospital last night. About tossed my own supper when Carolina told me my *only child* was in the emergency room."

My headache doubles. "Mom, I'm fine. You should be resting, in *your* room." *Save me from this cross-examination, Carolina.* "If someone sees their mayor in a hospital gown, the rumors will have you dead by morning, killed by the Warlock, and the town will panic. More."

"Fine? *Fine?*" She crosses her arms. Blue veins pop under her skin. "Doctor says you had a wicked allergic reaction. Shellfish allergy."

I let out a disbelieving snort. "You're saying I've been in the hospital for *hours* just because I needed a Benadryl?"

A fire I haven't witnessed in a *long* time lights in her gaze. "Listen, little girl. You're downright lucky it wasn't a lot worse. You could be dead! Because of *food*. My own daughter. A *Farewitch*. What happens if you ever get *really* sick? Who will take care of you when I'm not around?"

My headache triples. More memories wiggle back, nauseating, slimy little things: trouble breathing, stomach pain. Even though I've been asleep, I'm tired and cranky, and I don't need another lecture right now.

"Is that what happened to *you*? You overworked yourself and then had to drag me back to town to fill your shoes because you didn't watch your own health?"

The words are a low blow but I've been thinking them for a while now. At some point, we'll have to talk about this, but not now. When she's better. Or maybe when I'm stronger.

At last, my mom's frail fists unclench in her lap. She pats my blanketed leg. "You scared me is all, girl."

I squeeze her offered palm, a truce. Her grip is much too weak.

"Here, I brought your favorite." She pulls out a pack of Lemonheads. "Can't fathom how you stand these things."

"The sour brings out the sweet."

"Just don't tell Carolina. She already caught me with Cheetos this morning."

I pop a candy into my mouth, hoping it'll help what is probably terrible breath.

"Shellfish? I'm a Farewitch. In the South. I can't be allergic to an entire food group."

"Get you some EpiPens, you hear? Carry them at all times. It's a protein allergy, so each reaction is worse, and before you know it, you're swollen up like roadkill—"

"Well, look at you. Glad to see you're alive," Silas says as he strides into the room. "Those bangs, phew—we'll work on them."

His suit is black today, and I wonder if he wore it just in case the shrimp took me out and we needed an impromptu memorial service.

"You know, no one carried *me* to the hospital when I overdid it on shrimp on my thirtieth in New Orleans," he says, placing a full cardboard coffee tote by the cactus.

Mom jerks a thumb at him. "He agrees with me. You need to take better care of yourself."

I scowl at him. Conniving, up-to-no-good gossips.

He shrugs. "Your mother is, for once, being sensible about rest and recovery. I didn't have the heart to sabotage the therapy."

"I mean it. Who would take care of Foxe Holler? There's no plan B Farewitch in a town this small."

And why not? Arna Jean can't help me forever, and that girl is not made to be anyone's understudy.

"At the moment, the Holler might not go for plan A, either." Silas hands me a coffee, charcoal black, the way I take it. He's redeemed. For now. "Once they heard the mayor's daughter was at the hospital, Webb and his followers posted up outside. He still hasn't mentioned you, Marigold, but they're going on again about evicting the Warlock from town. Claiming if magic can make a Farewitch sick, it'll make all the patients sicker, that kind of nonsense."

When my mom sighs, the sound rattles in her chest. "They just want someone to blame so they can fundraise to repair the church."

Silas shakes his head. "It's more than that this time. Carolina and I have done our best to dissuade the crowd, but we can't just rip the signs from their hands."

"They have *signs*?" I say.

"*Magic Is Poison, Not Food.*" He takes a sip of coffee. "*Farewitches Are Still Witches.*"

My temples throb. "Okay, that's enough—"

"*Neighbors Not Necromancy.*"

"Oh, that's a good one," my mom says.

"Right? Clever."

"I get it!" I exclaim.

Just then, another person bursts into the room at the same moment my addled brain realizes Silas brought *four* coffees, not three.

Warlock Knight halts when he sees I'm awake.

The candy slides whole down my throat, choking me. I must still be caught in a crustacean-induced delirium.

The Warlock of Foxe Holler is here. In town. *Outside* of Knight Manor, the one place he told me he never left. But he did. He left the safety of his wards. To come *here.*

I'll kill him.

His eyes dart over me, and that intense curiosity is almost more unsettling than his usual frown. I'm glad I'm not hooked up to any heart monitor because the beeping would betray my pulse for sure. What looks like relief flickers across his face, but I'm probably imagining it. He likely just wants to gauge if I'm well enough to finish our argument from earlier. I'm ready for him. I swear to all in heaven above, if he so much as lobs one *I told you so* at me—

"Done terrorizing the hospital?" my mom asks him, breaking this silent spell.

"Had to take him on a walk earlier because he wouldn't stop pacing," Silas tells me, like the Warlock isn't even there. "Worse than Ms. Buchanan's frenetic poodle."

My mom nods. "And as weak as it is, his magic is making all the machines in here staticky." On cue, the lamp in the corner gives an annoyed flicker.

Warlock Knight finally remembers how to move. "Did you know they have this monstrous thing in the vending machine called a *Cow Tale*?" he asks, approaching my bed. "Even worse, something called pig ears—"

"Pork rinds," Silas corrects.

"Regardless, you have your choice of any part of the animal." He holds up . . . snacks. A Warlock is hand-delivering me junk food. "I don't even recognize vending machines any longer. Back in my day—"

Silas cuts him off. "Don't finish that sentence."

"Right." The Warlock drops the snacks next to the coffee. "I've evaded Nurse Carolina. She's still cross with me."

My mom rolls her eyes. "Can you blame her? Every time you walk by an elevator, it switches directions."

The Warlock grabs the last coffee and folds himself into the empty chair at my right. His cheekbones are sharper than usual, gaunt. He hasn't slept. Probably hasn't eaten. I *almost* feel guilty. Almost.

"Ms. Frost, this is twice in as many weeks you've made me engage with the public. I cannot be expected to live this way."

Despite our tennis match of harsh words last night, he almost makes me smile. "Did it occur to you it might be more of a hazard to my health to drive me here in your condition than let me fight anaphylactic shock?"

"It did," he muses, completely serious. "But I don't have a working portal at the house and Ms. Zeen doesn't have magic, so alas, here we are. We had to take two vehicles since you were horizontal, but we only have two-door pickup trucks apparently, so I followed Ms. Zeen in the Dodge with you—"

"You drove my truck?" You've got to be kidding me.

"—then I took a wrong turn at one point—that's unimportant. Regretfully, we'll have to drive back."

"Let me know what I owe for gas."

"I'll deduct it from your paycheck."

Lord does it feel good to be back to our normal . . . whatever *this* is. "Mr. Knight, this is my mom, Mayor Marigold Frost. Mom, this is—"

"Oh, we've spent the last twelve hours together in this hospital," she says. "Believe me, we've met."

I swallow. "Outstanding."

Given the Frost family's history with Warlocks, my mom is sitting on years of resentment, yet here she is chatting with one at my bedside. Both cranky and stubborn. Oddly alike. No—*sick*. Neither feels good, a lot of the time.

"What did you talk about for *twelve* hours?" The new question has the benefit of keeping my focus safe from paralysis. The Warlock is here—*here!*—in town.

My mom looks around the room, anywhere but at me. "You sure you don't need another Benadryl? Another nap?"

"*Mom.*" I won't be distracted.

"All right, all right."

She looks to the Warlock. "We have a theory. One I've been toying with since your Momaw got sick, but Mr. Knight's knowledge of curse magic has helped me rethink how we're approaching this. And confirmed some suspicions."

That doesn't make me feel any better.

My mom meets my stare head-on, and in her mayor voice, which I'm realizing sounds exactly like Momaw's voice in my head, she says, "Our magic is killing us."

Silas blows out a low whistle. I sit up so fast, my head whooshes. "I'm going to need you to elaborate."

My mom tugs at her unwound hair. "Farewitches turn magic and intention into cures. All for our community. So our profession means we have to know lots of people well, but no one gets to know *us*. Your Momaw ignored her own illness as long as she could to keep working, stay moving. My entire relationship with her centered on the Apothakery."

She falls into a coughing fit, but waves off my concerned look and downs some water Silas hands her.

When her voice returns, she continues. "Me? I've got the knees and back of an eighty-year-old, no friends my age, and I've missed how many milestones with you? All for what? I've never even left the Holler! And you and me, girl? I'm going to die before we ever get the chance to spend time together as grown women. Our magic spreads us thin, isolates us. From romantic partners, friends, neighbors. It's wearing us down to nothing, slowly but surely."

I whirl to the Warlock. "You think *loneliness* is killing the Frost women."

He levels his full severe attention at me; he's never been one to sugarcoat anything. "Some magic, especially inherited through bloodlines, can cause premature aging, the effects delayed but exponential over time. Like a protein allergy, as it were. Your family's brutal hours, no rest, burnout. Isolation. This isn't a curse, per se. It's more of a . . . decay that feeds on stress."

In other words: Rot. From the inside.

"But . . . we're Farewitches," I say lamely. "It's what we *are*."

Sadness sweeps across my mom's face. "It's just what we *do*, Honey. Not who we are. I'm not sure when it started, but the Frost Farewitches began keeping their distance from neighbors, friends, any loved ones. To protect them, maybe. To protect ourselves. Now we're barely keeping the line alive with each new generation."

I always thought the Widow Witch was the reason Frost women didn't take husbands, but that only explains romantic partners. Not our scarcity of deep friendships. I have community, customers and neighbors who like me, and I *know* them—but does anyone really know *me*?

The protesting folks outside the hospital right now point to no.

"You've been on bed rest for months," I point out. "Why hasn't that offset the problem?"

"Has she? Been resting, that is?" Silas asks, the question clearly not for me. "When she's not stressing over being a backseat mayor, she's worrying over her daughter."

"Also, the isolation of being hospitalized," the Warlock adds. "Keeping the town at arm's length to preserve this secret has hindered recovery, not enabled it."

Silas nods to me. "*Theoretically*, if a Farewitch uses her magic less, could the side effects, these symptoms, be managed?"

"If this is caught early enough to change certain behaviors," my mom says, wrangling a sheepish look. "I thought giving up my post as Farewitch might save me from the effects. Reverse them, even. But no luck. I think the decades I put into being a Farewitch catapulted me past some point of no return. But it's not too late for a younger Witch."

Of course. My mom, always looking ahead to the last step in the recipe. She didn't just transition to mayor to help a friend. She was trying to break a cycle, showing me that years later, I might be free to choose to become something other than a Farewitch, too.

"It's only a working theory," the Warlock says. "While your family's . . . affliction isn't a by-the-book curse, there is always—"

"—a cost to magic," I finish, voice soft.

He nods. "Two Frost women could be a coincidence, but I'd—your mother—would like to not have our hypothesis proven correct by a third."

Me. Rotting away. Slowly but surely. "But," I start, stop. Start again. "Why does the cost have to be so *high*?"

"Our power is tied to the land. *This* land, Foxe Holler. It can only support so much magic. Recent generations of Frosts might have kept the family small, to avoid the Widow Witch, but a small holler means fewer Witches in general."

"Or one Farewitch," I say.

He nods. "Witches take on more and more responsibility, but without extra help, especially as younger generations move away to larger cities. So the labor grows but the Witch population doesn't. Whether this stress is uniquely devastating for Farewitches, or Frost Farewitches, I'm not sure, but the fact remains: You will literally work yourself to death."

There's no plan B Farewitch in a town this small.

The answer has always been right in front of me. But I've never been good at paying attention to negative thinking.

When my mom speaks again, her voice is a feeble thing. "You have a job to do for your community, but you're also your own person. Your life is *your* time. There's balance in there. Somewhere."

That kind of balance feels impossible.

YOUR TIME IS MINE.

My throat tightens, a flush crawling under my skin. The rising June sun has got the room feeling like the inside of a toaster. This is *not* how this is supposed to go. I'd cure my mom, save Lazlo and the Warlock, and keep the Holler happy and healthy. I'd be proud, knowing I always give everything I have to folks who depend on me.

I swallow the doubt before I can taste it. I can solve both problems. There's enough time. There has to be. I'll work harder. I've had twelve hours of sleep; I can do anything. After everyone's okay—then I can focus on my problem, on what living as a Farewitch means for me. Only then.

But . . . isn't that exactly why I've been angry at the Warlock? For trying to make more time appear out of nowhere, even if it meant making a messy deal with an ancient Witch?

An ancient Witch. *That's it.*

We've spent all this time asking the Holler about the legend but never the legend herself.

"We need help," I blurt. "From a Witch who knows way more than we do about magic, especially lower magics. Someone who's been tied to the Holler and its history for so long, she might be able to tell us how this . . . decay started for the Frosts. If there's a fix. Or at least a way to undo the damage that's been done." I glance at my mom.

"The only creature old enough to know anything about generational magic and afflictions this undefined . . ." The Warlock's expression flips from exhausted to defiant. "*Absolutely* not. This is the *Widow Witch.* Oris Webb is a zealot but he isn't wrong about the danger she poses. She has a depthless well of magic, thrives on recompense, and she will use whatever torments you to feed on your desperation. Then she will ask the impossible in return."

"But she's still a Witch," my mom says, catching on to my thinking.

"Coven or no coven, Witches help Witches. Maybe she'll help me," I say, never breaking the Warlock's gaze.

My mom heaves a sigh. "As your mother, I should tell you not to do this, but . . ."

The Warlock leans forward, his elbows digging into the tops of his knees. "I haven't spent the past year behind wards avoiding her just to go make a house call."

"Your archives haven't helped. We've exhausted the network we've got." I jam a finger into my hospital mattress for emphasis. Flimsy, underwhelming emphasis. "We're officially out of options. Lazlo has two weeks." *You have two weeks, you inane Warlock!* "Besides, it's not like she can curse you again."

"I'm not worried about—this isn't about *me*."

"Then don't do it for you. Do it for me."

With a furious puff of air, he turns to my mom. "Are all Frost women this ornery?"

"Afraid we just bake that way in the oven, dear."

"We're not confronting the Widow Witch, Ms. Frost. End of discussion." An edge cuts through his low voice, sharp as my good knives.

"Beginning of discussion. Mom, Silas, give us a second?"

Miraculously, they're civil and agree. Silas wheels my mom from the room. Then it's just me and an agitated Warlock.

Chapter Twenty-Nine

WEDNESDAY, JUNE 8 (STILL)

13 DAYS UNTIL THE SUMMER SOLSTICE

Honey's Helpful Hint, from
Honey Frost's Southern Cookbook for Recipes Gone Wrong:

A family recipe is a creed. The paper becomes an heirloom, the measurements a history, the ingredients a story. If you doubt yourself, trust the recipe, and if you doubt the recipe, throw it out. But always trust the handwriting.

"You got lost in your own town?"

The Warlock's indignant scowl at me feels like coming home to a favorite smell in the kitchen. "Everyone should be *grateful* I didn't end up in Tennessee. Ms. Zeen is a wonderful Governess but a terrible navigator."

I conjure my best incredulous look. His face softens. At least the man knows he's difficult. "Dare I ask when your license expired?"

"License?"

Bless his heart.

He changes the topic before I press the matter. "You know, I've been thinking on it, and Mr. Key and Governess Zeen could run a high-end boutique for sophisticated professionals."

His comment is so unexpected, I manage a genuine smile.

"Governess and Son's Boutique of Sophisticated Wares. Or how about Tailored and Timeless Tradition—For Two."

He grunts out what might be a quarter of a laugh.

I won't have it. That was stellar stuff. "C'mon, you know you've got one. Let's hear it."

"I practice the Language of Small Wishes, Ms. Frost. Not alliterations."

Fine. I'll quiz him later. "You like theories. How is your magic upsetting a hospital's electrical grid when your reserves are totally empty?"

"To be frank, I have no idea. I must be leaving some kind of echo. Like my magic is still a part of me but inaccessible. I can feel it slowly returning. Or perhaps—do *not* change the subject, Ms. Frost."

I taste just the subtlest amount of thyme in the air. Proof he's still the Warlock I know, that he's *real* and here. The solstice hasn't caught up to him yet.

The thyme plant catches my attention. Its little buds turn toward the sunbaked windows, eager and hungry. A spot of greenery and life but practical, sentimental at a distance. His sneaky thoughtful gesture only confirms my plan. If there's even a sliver of a chance the Widow Witch has an answer—that she'll hear us out—I'll take it.

Then I remember: "You left the Manor."

He looks to the window, his stare hiding in the shadow of his dark brow. "I did. It was neither easy nor wise."

"But you *can* leave. I mean, now that you have, there's no undoing having left. Right?"

His gaze darts back to me, anchoring me to the bed. "Like I said. Not. Wise."

I try a new approach. "Our magic is connected to the land, and your health is connected to Lazlo's. So if the Eldercraft take Lazlo, what happens to you? Or if Webb forces you from the Holler, what happens to Lazlo?" That is, if we've cured his illness before the solstice.

"All signs point to nothing good." The words are scratchy, stiff.

It's either the Widow Witch and the solstice, or Webb and the Eldercraft. Every straw is short here.

I don't think I'll like the answer, but I wrangle my grit and ask it anyway. "There's always a cost to using magic, so what did leaving cost *you*?"

No answer. No sharp or wicked retort. He just takes a slow sip of coffee.

"*Sir.*"

"A price I have come to the alarming revelation I would regretfully pay again."

The inscrutable admission hangs between us. What am I supposed to do with *that*?

Then, out of nowhere, he says, "Posh Practicals for the Positively Professional."

I dissolve into immediate laughter. The weight of a cast-iron skillet falls off my back, and I have to wipe my eyes before I can speak. A smirk tugs at his mouth.

When I'm coherent, I try to look serious again. "Sir, at some point, you're going to have to stop writing checks you can't cash."

"Careful, you might invite questions about your age with words like *checks*."

"*My* age? If you keep expending energy you don't have, you'll be flat on your face before the solstice at this rate."

"I can make my own decisions, Ms. Frost. I'm your *elder*, remember?" He drags a hand through his hair. "I don't leave the Manor because I've built up years of warding there, and not just the powerful but temporary defenses typical of Warlocks. This magic doesn't wipe clean every time I cast a new protection spell. It layers, like . . . croissant dough or baklava. Lasagna."

Just like with my shop. Like a Witch's warding. "Are you speaking to me in cooking metaphors?"

"Unfortunately, I'm trying to get on your good side."

"It's working, but I'm not going to tell you that because we're still fighting. I'd like to be mad at least until tomorrow morning."

His gloveless hands dent the coffee cup between them. "Prying into your health was out of line. I apologize."

He's staring up at me through his eyelashes, looking way too forgivable. Damn him. I *am* in a hospital room, after all. It dawns on me that I might not have gotten so upset and cooked an unhinged five-star meal if anyone else had spoken to me like that. Because I'd have to first trust their opinion enough to believe it. And I care what the Warlock thinks about me as a friend, not just as a Farewitch. If he can't ask me uncomfortable and honest questions, how can I expect uncomfortable and honest answers from him?

"You're right, though. If I'm not going to end up like my Momaw or my mom, I'll have to take better care of myself. Especially if the Widow Witch might not help us." We can't craft extra time out of nothing, but maybe I can take back some of mine I've been too quick to give away. "Thank you, for being there last night. Shellfish allergy, apparently."

"No gumbo in our future, then?"

Our future. I try to ignore how those words make my gut float. Probably lingering shrimp.

"Think about it, sir. When a Farewitch can't figure out a cure, we look to the source of the illness. The Widow Witch cursed you—we should've confronted her from the beginning. If we convince her to remove her curse, we won't have to keeping hunting for a cure. And now my family's problem gives us one more reason to do just that."

He doesn't look convinced, but I'm ready with my next argument.

"Curse or not, Webb is using your feud with her to drive his campaign against all of us with magic now, not just Warlocks. Do this for the Witches in the Holler. Hell, if you manage to help save the town's mayor—and the only Farewitch family—you might make friends." Against all odds. "If they see you take the fight to her, your neighbors won't feel like they're standing up to a powerful Hedgewitch all alone."

"I'd never leave this town to defend itself alone." His attention shifts to the window and back again, the same way he's always watching the sky from the kitchen, constantly monitoring the farmhouse's wards and—

Oh.

"You have other wards!" I blurt. "Not *just* for the Manor. But in town—" My brain's firing on all burners. "Why didn't you tell me—*were you just going to let me prattle on*?"

"Sometimes, Ms. Frost, I just like to watch you run your mouth for a while."

Ass. "How many? Where are they? The Apotha—?"

"No, your family's magic protects your shop. It's mostly public spaces. The school. The town square. But they're not as permanent as the Manor's wards, and I can't cover the entire town, or individual homes. All of that would require too much of my magic."

"So the church . . . no wards?"

He nods. "I have to pick and choose. The Widow Witch knew exactly where to strike."

My new bite-sized hope dissolves. He's as much a prisoner of the Witch's fearmongering as the rest of the town. But why let the town accuse him of being such a force of bad magic when the exact opposite is true?

"How long?" I ask.

"After the library burned, and once I learned proper warding. Then, ever since." New regret I haven't seen before spills into his tired eyes. Not as raw as when he talks about Lazlo, but older. Worn down, from years of chafing against it. "I felt I owed the Holler something after—after."

That sounds . . . demanding. Exhausting. "What did the town do before that? The Widow Witch started stealing husbands well before the library fire."

"To be quite honest, I don't know. My wards clearly don't keep her at bay completely, but they slow her down. Perhaps, when she began this tithe of hers, it was easier for her. Perhaps without wards, taking partners required less of her own magic."

As a Hedgewitch obsessed with balance, she'd want to ensure even her kidnapping was energy efficient. And here I've been living with the Warlock, completely unaware of his efforts. What does that say about me? We've *all* been taking him for granted.

He reads my face easily. "This makes me no less a coward, hiding away all these years. Wards are not the same as rebuilding. My own mistakes have been plenty destructive."

"The library."

He nods. "My magic was new to me, but if my spellwork had been good enough that night, I might've been able to do *something*. Anything would have been better than nothing."

He doesn't need to finish. To stop tragedy, save the people inside. *His parents.*

Taking a breath, I tread over the glass bridge of tension between us. "Anything *is* better than nothing. If we confront the Widow Witch one more time, we could make it the last time."

"You smell like lemons," he blurts.

Hot sunshine jolts my veins. "Excuse me?"

"Your candy," he murmurs, nodding to my hands.

"Oh, right." I give the Lemonheads box a little shake. "You know what I wish I had right now?"

His breath hitches, just barely. "I'm not sure I'll survive this answer."

An odd response. But *he's* odd. And I think I've come to like that. "Crappy hospital Jell-O. Neon. Something guaranteed not to upset my stomach."

When a smug grin crawls onto his face, I realize my mistake.

"No way," I snap. "Do *not* try and use magic for a wish."

"Respectfully, Ms. Frost, I can tell it's slowly returning, so what better time to test my rate of recovery—"

"I forbid you—you'll just exhaust yourself! Don't you dare—"

He snaps anyway.

Nothing happens.

He scowls, snaps again. Absolutely nothing. Not even the barest smudge of thyme. Then a look of flustered shock slaps across his face. His eyes sweep over me, intensity crackling under raw distress and what might even be mortification.

No one has ever looked at me like *this*. Humbling, for sure.

But as quick as the look appeared, it's gone. Not gone—smothered.

"You okay?" I ask, cautious. I warned him.

"Yes," he croaks, clearing his throat. "I just . . . You're right. I've expended too much energy lately. And with Lazlo not well . . . It'll take a moment to fire up. When it's ready."

"Must be an age thing," I quip.

"Hush. It's a Warlock thing," he mutters. He runs a hand through his hair again, thumb lingering on the gray at his temples. "Need I remind you, with age comes experience, Ms. Frost."

There he is. "To be fair, sir, not if you've been a hermit. Let's be rational. Unless you're seeing Governess Zeen . . ."

"She would be a fine match. Not for me, but someone . . ."

". . . and you don't date or invite strangers or any guests over—"

"You're a wicked little Witch. I'm taking my thyme plant back."

"—logically, when's the last time you've actually had—"

"*Careful, Honey.*"

I bite my lip, keeping a laugh to myself. I'll pester him later. My name on his tongue is an awful distraction. "Any chance you'll tell me your name now?"

He doesn't answer. He's actually thinking about it. Stressfully. As if I've asked him for his firstborn child.

Then, "No," he answers, voice rough. "Not . . . today."

"Someday? When?"

"When it's important."

"What does that mean?"

His jaw clenches. "You'll know."

Worth a shot. I'll figure it out somehow. There are plenty of rooms in the Manor I haven't broken into yet.

"Listen, I'm sure you were just as charmingly exasperating twenty-five years ago, but I'm glad I get to know *this* you," I say. "You aren't only made up of the mistakes you made. A Farewitch helps people, and you're worth helping. We're doing this."

He sighs. Deeply. Like he just lost a debate with himself. Takes another ragged breath. "You truly want to hunt the Witch hunting us?"

"I thought you knew me by now, Mr. Knight." My smile thins. "This might be our only chance to save your life."

"Lazlo is my life. I just want him safe."

"Then do this for him, too."

Reluctantly, he nods. "Fine. For Lazlo. For the Frosts." He rummages in his pocket and pulls out a plastic yellow tube the length of a pencil. "For you. *Bottled epinephrine.*"

But there's no time to gloat over my win.

The impending summer solstice is too much of a merciless calendar on the wall.

Chapter Thirty

THURSDAY, JUNE 16

5 DAYS UNTIL THE SUMMER SOLSTICE

Honey's Helpful Hint, from
*Honey Frost's Southern Cookbook
for Recipes Gone Wrong*:

**The body can only handle
one mystery meat at a time.**
—Mayor Marigold Frost

Eight days later, I'm outside the one door in Knight Manor that frightens me most.

I raise my hand to knock but pause, stiff as cold butter.

The Warlock and I leave at dawn. It's now or never, Frost.

My brain whirs like my mom's old Breadman. The last week was a blur of preparation.

Sunday supper became a strategy dinner. Rett delivered the traveling equipment we ordered; Arna Jean packed me with various tiny charms and mysterious herbal tinctures she collected from Carolina and Ms. Marrow. Silas . . . made me call my mother. At some point, all of us were in the library, ransacking the archives one more time for anything we missed.

The Warlock's magic hasn't returned, and the Manor has been feeding off the man's anxieties all week as the solstice looms. The kitchen cabinets are *extra* grumpy. At this rate, the house might suck the next visitor through the floorboards of the front porch.

But no one has tried to talk me out of my plan. Everyone knows we're out of fixes buried in books or baked in breakfasts. *Trip* sounds like a vacation. *Expedition deep into the forgotten parts of the Holler to find an infamous magical being who casts dangerous curses and has a personal vendetta against the Warlock.*

That's better.

My fist still frozen, the door opens before I can knock.

Governess Zeen stares back. "Please cease your loitering. I could hear you breathing from inside."

I crane my neck to glimpse her room. What mysteries does Letha Zeen's personal space contain? Old harlequin romances? An entire closet devoted to cardigan sets?

She places her stout figure in the doorframe, blocking my view. "Are you lost?" she asks in a voice a local might use with a tourist. Not that the Holler gets tourists.

I steel myself. The Widow Witch will be much more frightening. Probably. "I, uh, wanted to thank you again for protecting Lazlo while we're gone. And for watching him while I was at the hospital. And for letting me borrow that dress—"

"You're rambling, dear."

"Sorry."

"Stop using that word. Just promise me we'll avoid a repeat of last week. When Mr. Knight gets panicky, you know the house is a dreadful copycat."

Oh, I can tell. Asking me to elude anaphylactic shock is a . . . surprisingly thoughtful gesture coming from her. I'm almost touched.

"Don't look at me like that. We're not friends, dear. Good night."

"Wait," I say before she can close the door in my face. She looks like she *really* wants to. "I wanted to—say hello? Or goodbye. Whichever. Before tomorrow since we don't know . . ." Deep breath. "Why *aren't* we friends? You've hated me from day one."

Ms. Zeen somehow looks down her nose at me despite being inches shorter, even in kitten heels. They match her black-and-white houndstooth cardigan today. “I don’t hate you. No matter how hard I’ve tried.”

I must look pitifully confused, because she sighs, smoothing nonexistent wrinkles from her skirt. “I have always voiced concerns about Lazlo’s sheltered routine. I’ve fought Mr. Knight’s stubbornness for *years*. You’re here mere weeks and he acquiesces to your ideas. Why is that?”

My shoulders fall. “I don’t know. My magic doesn’t involve any kind of persuasion. Even if I had a recipe for persuasion, I wouldn’t bake it.”

“That was a rhetorical question, dear.”

“Oh.”

“*Why* are you outside my door, Ms. Frost?”

“I wanted to get your advice.”

Of all things, this is what sends genuine surprise skittering across her face. “My advice?”

“The deal Mr. Knight made with the Widow Witch last year—did you know?”

“*Ah.* When did you figure it out?”

“He told me himself.”

“Curious. My money was on you discovering it first.”

There’s not much left in my own shock tank these days, but Ms. Zeen bet on *me*? This iron Mary Poppins *bet on me*.

“I didn’t find out until after he’d gone through with it. Otherwise I would have forbidden him from it. Make no mistake, we began hunting for a cure long before he hired you.”

And I wouldn’t be here if they’d succeeded.

If there’s one person who can forbid the Warlock from doing anything, it’s Governess Zeen. No wonder he skipped permission and went right to forgiveness.

“He made a mess of things,” she huffs, “but that *mess* was Lazlo. However shortsighted that bargain, Mr. Knight has been happier in the last year than I’ve ever seen him.”

I feel like there’s a prologue to this story that I’ve skipped.

Ms. Zeen has been the Warlock's gloved right hand—assisting with research, Manor upkeep, Lazlo—all these years. *Why?* Then I remember the crumbs of our last conversation.

"You told me you owed him a favor."

But it's more than that. This loyalty smells almost like debt.

She glances down the hall then, as if the house is listening. A melancholic shadow crosses her face. "How much do you know about the library fire?"

My brain limps to keep up. "You were *there* that night. Weren't you?"

"More than there. I was the librarian."

"*What?*" There *is* still some gasoline churning in my shock tank.

Her nose becomes a sharp beak as her nostrils constrict with a tight inhale. A decision. "I won't repeat myself, so you best listen."

My shoulders snap back. I try not to salute.

"Twenty-five years ago, Mr. Knight's parents broke into the library intending to use the empty building for hazardous spellwork."

"Why didn't they just call on a Witch in town?"

Folks who don't have magic can still utilize a few basic spells if they have the intention and right tools. But beyond that, spellwork doesn't amount to much without corresponding magical energy to power it. The only reason they'd dodge asking a Witch to help is—oh no.

"Chaos magic," I breathe. *Hedgewitch* magic.

Ms. Zeen nods. "The Widow Witch granted them a wish, years before. For a price, of course. But only with time did they realize the price was too high. When she came to collect, they tried to escape their bargain, counter the magical imbalance with stronger spellwork . . ."

She doesn't finish. I know what happened next.

The library burned up like a toothpick rocking chair.

"Mr. Knight followed them that night. But he was young, his own magic was new to him . . . He would've given his own life to save his parents. So I pulled him from the inferno before it could take him, too."

Of course. The missing paragraph was right there, hiding under my bookmark, all this time. How did I look at Ms. Zeen every day and read her as anything *but* a librarian?

"His parents weren't bad people," she murmurs, her hands clenching the hem of her cardigan. "Just human." Her exterior cracks, stern eyes glistening. "But I couldn't save them. Or wasn't brave enough to. All on my watch—"

"Ms. Zeen, none of that is your fault."

She gives a terse jerk of her head, dismissing my words. "If I had just intervened sooner, Mr. Knight might not have grown up alone. Or made his own fool bargain with that Witch years later. We might not be here at all, gambling another boy's childhood."

My throat constricts. After losing so much, no wonder he disappeared into this Manor and never dug himself out.

"I tried to defend the Knights, for their boy's sake. He was barely sixteen . . ." Her expression hardens again, back to the Governess I know. "But the Holler didn't handle the fire well. Tensions grew, sides formed. Magic versus the church. The beginnings of what you see now. Oris Webb's father was the pastor then, and he was a nasty fellow, always blaming magic and looking for enemies."

No wonder Oris Webb has been strategically harboring his vendetta against magic. It's his family legacy.

"I'm guessing it didn't take much for Gertha Fudge to exile you from the Holler's good favor. And the church," I say. She'd already lost her husband to the Widow Witch at that point.

Another grim nod. "Tolerance for magic got better under Mayor Summer, but the damage was done. I tried to live quietly, take up as little space as possible. I stomached ten years of that nonsense. Then my dear friend Ambrosia Frost passed."

Dear friend? My grandmother? Even I sometimes forget how small Foxe Holler is. Momaw Frost probably baked the Governess plenty of cures over the years. Shoot, Ms. Zeen likely knew my grandmother longer than I did.

"Her death . . . I decided I wasn't going to waste the rest of my life shrinking myself to fit into a place that made no room for me. Mr. Knight was the only other person who'd lived through that fire, and I knew he was alone, up in this empty house. So I thought, if we both had to suffer in silence, we could do it together. He never blamed me, didn't care about my history with the church or the library. He gave me a room and a job and never asked me to leave."

My mouth is definitely open. Attractive, I'm sure. I somehow have more questions than I did before. If Ms. Zeen knew my Momaw, then surely the Knight family made it down to the Apothakery while my mother was the Farewitch. Or did they keep to themselves even then?

One mystery meat at a time, my mom says. I need to be focused on tomorrow, not twenty-five years ago.

"Can you tell me anything more about the Widow Witch?"

"Ask Beulah. She's older than Gertha, and Fudge won't give you a straight answer, anyway."

"So I've learned." I make a mental note to visit Ms. Buchanan before we leave if I can. "Why *is* Fudge so pissy all the time?"

I know why she hates magic—the Widow Witch took her husband. And I know why she dislikes Ms. Zeen. But none of this explains why she hates a man who hasn't stepped foot in town in two decades.

Ms. Zeen pulls me from my thoughts. "Sometimes, dear, when folks think old women are grouchy, we're just weary. We've been tired for years. No one is perfect. As there is a cost to magic, there is a cost to caring for someone. You just need to find the good folks who are worth the cost and hold on to them." Her expression shifts. "Be cautious tomorrow, Ms. Frost. Some folks despise magic because they have none. But some resent it whether they have their own or not, simply because *others* have it, too."

"So which one is the Widow Witch?"

"It doesn't matter which your enemy is, dear. It just matters which one you are."

Chapter Thirty-One

FRIDAY, JUNE 17

4 DAYS UNTIL THE SUMMER SOLSTICE

Honey's Helpful Hint, from
Honey Frost's Southern Cookbook
for Recipes Gone Wrong:

Don't let expensive taste become the enemy of good flavor.

"You've known where she lives this whole time? And we're just going to *drive up to her house*?"

"Not quite. Electricity, batteries, anything mechanical won't work where she is. This land yacht would never make it."

"Now wait just a molasses minute here—"

The Warlock pokes his head out of the passenger window. "Pull over here."

Pull over is a courtesy. We haven't been on an actual road in hours. Even the gravel and dirt paths gave out miles ago.

I park the Dodge in a slightly less overgrown clearing. We hop out into still-as-death humidity, the truck's settling engine the only sound. Checking the sneaky tall grass and cattails around us, I'm grateful I swapped my clogs for these boots, but summertime is the worst season to take a hike in the South. Mosquitoes. Ticks. Chigger bites like chickenpox. *Snakes.* The wild and unkempt vegetation hides exactly what a person should be wary of.

Shoulder to shoulder, we stare into the depths of the woods past the tree line. The greenery is so thick, the morning sun won't be following us in. "I suppose I have an abysmal chance of convincing you to stay here while I try to negotiate with the Widow Witch to help your mother?" he asks.

I half turn to him, real slow, and raise a brow.

"Right. Forget I asked."

"This is my idea, remember?" I shake my head, *tsk*ing. "If only you had a driver's license, you could've martyred alone." Or if he, you know, still had any of his magic.

On the surface, he's physically *up*right, but that's about all he has going for him. I can't tell if the sun spots on his cheeks I like so much are evaporating with his color, or growing more pronounced as the rest of his skin flips through a Pantone swatch for shades of oatmeal. I think he'd make Oris Webb look tan right now. Every few minutes, his fingers subconsciously fidget, as if he feels an urge to snap, the phantom pull of the Language of Small Wishes.

If this comes down to a fight between an infamous Hedgewitch and a Warlock who can't snap some hospital gelatin into existence, I don't feel great about our odds.

"If we're expecting to find her in just a day or two," I grunt, hauling my gear onto my back, "why is my pack so heavy?"

"The extra supplies are just for an emergency. If we don't reach her den after a couple of days, we'll have a larger problem on our hands." His words are soft, as if to not wake something. "Beasts roam these woods, sometimes orphaned familiars whose Witch or Warlock has died. They're attracted to her energy."

Of course they are.

His fingers clench by his sides. "Don't go far from me, Ms. Frost." Then, with stubborn confidence, he goes headfirst into the woods.

The temperature sinks fast inside the trees. Gooseflesh pricks my skin like a rash, and soon our breaths frost over. It feels like November, not June. Unnaturally cold. Hedgewitch territory. Staying close won't be a problem.

We trek without speaking. My lungs and thighs aren't used to these dips and swells in elevation at the foot of the Appalachian Mountains, and the Warlock appears to be listening for something. There's an occasional rustle of a critter, but nothing else. Soon, he's moving slower than me. Every step of his demands effort, and whenever he takes one of his shuddering, ragged breaths, I listen to make sure I hear him exhale again.

I've lost track of how far from town we are, but I don't mind the quiet. Small towns always have a quaint quiet, but that's not the real silence. *Out here,* in this forgotten piece of empty, is true stillness. Something . . . primordial. The nothingness before existence.

Ahead of me, the Warlock carves paths for us through curtains of foliage. He's in his sturdy gardening clothes, his bandana a welcome bright spot of color. My attention sticks to him like epizoochorous seeds. I'm following a man into isolated woods, alone, to confront his greatest foe, all on the chance I can persuade said foe to help a fellow Witch save her mom, herself, and any Frosts who come after us.

Oh, and maybe release the Warlock from his curse while she's at it.

We trek until we're both sweating, even with the chill. The passing hours feel both too short and too long. This hiking crap is *exhausting.* I'm grateful I listened to Silas and swapped my usual overalls for a durable yet lightweight set. His other advice yesterday was less helpful: *Don't die tomorrow. Your mother will be unbearable.*

Eventually, we take a break by a meandering, glassy creek. The Warlock refills our bottles from the creek as I unpack some provisions: dried fruit and nuts, hard cheese, apples, dense molasses bread, wild turkey jerky. Then a box of Lemonheads, a bag of mini marshmallows, and one half of a cherry Pop-Tart?

"Uh . . . question."

"Lazlo wanted to help pack our food."

"Ah."

"I packed our other meals."

"Bless you."

We dig in.

"How do you know where we're going?" I ask between bites, after I've restored some energy.

"Memory. Warlock's intuition." He chews on an apple as he paces the clearing, eyes tracking the ground. He finally stops his odd shuffling at the bank of the creek, where his focus lands on the crisp surface of the water. Satisfied with something, he extends a hand back to me. "We should keep moving."

I've already packed our food and water. Hesitant, I approach and take his offered palm. He pulls me flush against him, to the water's edge. Which I'm now noticing is oddly still for a creek that should be bubbling, on the move with rainwater from the mountains. Too perfect.

"Stay close for this next part, Ms. Frost."

"If you want to hold my hand, just ask."

He smirks. Wickedly.

I have zero time to regret being a smart-ass because he lifts a long leg and simply *steps off* into the water, taking me down into the depths right along with him.

I don't even have a chance to hold my breath.

My body flinches, bracing for a rocky creek bed. But my brain stutters when we don't land in the chill of mountain runoff. Instead, we sink right through the creek, as if swallowed by a looking glass.

Our bodies leave solid ground and my gut floats into my rib cage. The only sign we're passing through water is the mist kissing my cheeks. The sudden drop, the unnerving weightlessness—I rode a log flume once and swore never to do it again. I upchucked perfectly good corn dogs. What a waste of allowance money.

I cling to the feeling of the Warlock's hand in mine. Solid. Solid. *Solid.*

Then in half a breath, we're standing on a stony and uneven surface.

Unmoving. Gravity returns. I remember to breathe. Open my eyes. A damp darkness envelops us completely.

"Did we just fall through the earth?"

Give a girl some warning. I hope my nails leave vicious little impressions in his palm. This kind of magic is way beyond Farewitch territory.

"Yes and no. That creek is a window. I just had to find the right place to open it."

My eyes adjust. Around us, boulders and sharp rock formations stick out like the canines of some giant creature. Nooks and gaps hide shadows blacker than my cast iron. A gaping dark hole yawns open up ahead.

"Welcome to the path to the Widow Witch's holler."

We have just days until the summer solstice, or Litha, when Witches normally prepare feasts to celebrate the longest day of the year and welcome the extra hours of sunlight. And we're in—

"*Caves?*" I groan.

"Not a spelunking fan?"

"I was just envisioning something less . . . Batman." I blink away water from my bangs. "Are we supposed to be *wet*?"

"Ah, no." He shifts on his feet. "This portal operates with its own magic, but having mine would have made the transition . . . smoother." He clicks on a flashlight from his pack. "Shall we?"

As we hike through the cave system, soggy darkness sucks any warmth from my core. Ironically, the Frosts are not intended for the cold. Bread does not rise in icy air. I cling to the thought of fresh steaming bread as we trek through the dark, like some hapless couple in a fairy tale. Except we're not a couple. And if this is a fairy tale, the villain is just around the corner.

After endless near tumbles on loose rocks, I feel myself growing less intimidated and more irked. The Widow Witch doesn't have a side porch entrance? "If electricity and batteries don't work inside her holler, we're going to lose our light at some point, won't we?"

The Warlock's eyes glint in the flashlight. "Yes. She allows some power and magic to flow within her own home, but not in the territory around it. To ensure another magical being can't sneak up on her. In a sense, she's created a massive electric fence. My magic always itched up against the buzz as I got closer."

How often has he done this? Did he come back at all before now to try to fix things? I haven't felt any static pushback yet, but my Farewitch magic isn't constantly *on* like his would have been.

"You know, when Lazlo disappeared during the tornado, I thought maybe he was showing early signs of being a Warlock, too. That his magic was peeking through enough for him to portal somewhere."

The Warlock takes a long time to answer. "He's too young to know. But when it's time, our power does often manifest with heightened emotion or stress. The transition for a new Warlock can be unpredictable. It's easy to lose control." He peers into the darkness ahead of us. "Look out for anything that moves. The Witch has her own beasts roaming around."

I don't ask for clarification. When death comes for me, at least it'll be too dark to see it. Gotta think positive.

My eyes adjust hour by hour. The piercing teeth in the caverns are only stalactites and stalagmites; the wide mouths opening to consume us are just branching tunnels. Mazes like this riddle Appalachia, stretching for miles underground, across state lines. An endless, connected root system, most parts hidden and unexplored. For good reason. If the Widow Witch isn't our biggest threat, getting lost will be.

My boots slip on the moist limestone rock, losing traction, and I keep sliding right into the Warlock, who's annoyingly balanced. The farther we go, the wetter it gets. Underground streams snake around us, pools of water collecting like mirrors across the ground.

"Not mirrors," the Warlock says when I make the observation.

No—more *windows*. Much to the horror of my stomach. Arna Jean was right: The older Witches love their portals.

For what feels like hours, the Warlock proceeds to guide us *through* the cave pools, in no discernible pattern. One minute, we're on an uneven tunnel path, and then he steps right into a pool like he's simply changing lanes on a highway, pulling me with him.

"Shortcuts," he explains between jumps.

Men and shortcuts, honestly.

Each blind jump into a cave lake feels like that first steep drop on a rickety state fair coaster. At least it's too dim for him to see the green color of my face. At last, we finally stop to rest in a vast, echoing chamber.

It has to be night by now. Hell, I can't tell. In a cave, it's always midnight. I'm too exhausted to care. I go horizontal fast, reclining on one of the two sleeping mats we brought. We switch from flashlight to stationary battery lantern.

Stark shadows dance across the Warlock's face, so I can't get a grasp of his expression when I catch him staring at me.

"I'm famished," he says. "You?"

"Too tired. Give me a second. I'm no vernal poultry anymore."

"Please, you're not even old enough to run for president."

"I will be by the time we get out of this cave. I think we're going in circles."

"Then that means we're on exactly the right track."

I shift to see him fully. He sits next to me, elbows resting on raised knees, back propped against a hunk of limestone. "How are you coping so well in the dark? Aren't you half plant? You've got no sunlight down here."

"I have my own sources of sunlight." He casts a sideways glance at me. "Remember when you asked me why I liked plants so much?"

"You said they're better than people."

"Better *listeners* than people. But I love them for their resilience. They can grow in terrible environments. Even here, in this cave. Leave trees alone and they'll grow for centuries. And that's before any attention or care. Plants will outlive me, you. Everything." His voice grows ragged. "They're certainly not frightened by the passage of time."

"Well, don't let me stop you. There's some liverwort over there that looks lonely."

"Unfortunately, you're easier to talk to."

"A *compliment*? You feeling okay?"

"Don't torture me right now, Ms. Frost." He drags a hand down his face. "I've made a colossal mess of things. You'd still be safe at the Apothakery if it weren't for me."

True. The thought is oddly . . . bland.

I don't like seeing him this way. Anxious. Spread thin. Fighting wars on two fronts. At least he's got an appetite, normal hunger cues. "Do you know why my apple butter is so good?"

"Because you make it?"

"No. Well, yes. It's the vinegar."

"Vinegar?"

"Just a touch. The sharpness heightens the sweetness."

"We both know if anyone has the potential for sweetness in this situation, it's you."

Don't blush, don't blush. "What I'm saying is, everyone is their own sugar *and* vinegar. We're both. Some days there's more of one, so we just have to try to balance it out."

Hazel eyes, sunken in severe sternness, grab hold of me. "We never finished our discussion. After I told you the truth about the deal I made."

"Are you asking if I hate you, like you promised I would?"

He presses his lips together. Waiting.

I've been wondering myself, but my brain's brooding feels like a ruse. The beating muscle in my chest already made a decision, the minute I saw my mom in that wheelchair.

"I was angry, sure. How could someone make that deal, not knowing the consequences?" I can hear him holding his breath. "But what if the Widow Witch offered me the same thing, a second chance at making different choices when they mattered most, a way to save my mom? Even knowing how that bargain went wrong for you . . . I would take it."

And I'm not ashamed to admit it.

"Ever since I took over the shop, I've felt like I'm already seventy, skipped over a whole life someone else lived. A different Honey. A happier one. So I understand why you did it."

"And I know that feeling," he says. "Once Ms. Zeen and I understood there was no home to send Lazlo back to, I was selfishly glad. If I couldn't rewrite my own past, I could ensure *this* boy, however he got here, would have happy memories."

My thoughts swirl into a mess of marbled cake batter. Anyone would love Lazlo, but the Warlock's guilt still seems older, deeper. Stuck in his bones. A reason is *there*, at the edge of my mind, like a crumb caught under a gas burner, sparking and smoking until it sets off an alarm.

"Why did you lie to me?" That's what bothers me, more than any secret itself. "I thought you might've trusted me enough to tell me."

He takes a labored breath. "Would you have taken the job knowing that your patient is a child, and what would happen if you failed?"

An answer sticks in my throat. I'd like to think so. But this is exactly why I didn't tell him about my mom. I didn't want to concentrate on the illness, or an inevitable sad finale. I wanted the attention to be on the possible. The hope. The tomorrow.

I hate that he lied. But I understand why he did.

"It wasn't my initial aim to withhold the truth. But then you showed up at the Manor, smiling, and you were so unbelievably bright and—" His mouth clamps shut.

"I don't hate you," I finally say. "You hate yourself enough for the both of us. But I don't forgive you, either. So I'll let you keep apologizing for another decade. That ought to do it."

He almost grins. "You assume I'll still be around then. Could you really tolerate me for that long?"

I hope so.

Before I can answer, he's rustling through his pack. My fingers are crossed he's going to pull out an atlas of this cave system that will point us in exactly the right direction. It'd be called something like *Incorporeal Deadly Lairs of Magical Folk and Other Appalachian Caves.*

"If I have a decade of apologizing to do, I best get started. Consider this the first apology of many." He hands me a thick square of wax paper.

Sandwiches. He pulls out *sandwiches.*

In the lamplight, I can't see what kind. Screw it. I take a huge bite, suddenly ravenous. Then pause. No way in hell. How did—I take another bite, to be sure. Well, butter my biscuit.

The flavor slingshots me back to growing up, my mom plating a quick dinner for me on busy baking days. I haven't tasted this blasphemous yet flawlessly sinful combination of pork and fake cheese since childhood.

"A Spam and Cheeto sandwich? Are you serious? How did you know these are my . . ." *Favorite* is too disappointing a word. My religion?

"Your mother told me at the hospital." Cough. "She likes to talk."

The soft and meaty Spam is the perfect mate to the salty, cheesy crunch, and the Cheetos are so processed, they don't get soggy smooshed up against the Spam. *Happy* is a pitiful word for what I feel right now. Because of him. "You're like a Spam Santa."

Once we've both devoured half our sandwiches, he says, "My mother always made Spam scrambled eggs for breakfast."

I grin at the thought of a little Warlock, when the Manor was full of life. "My Momaw was orphaned young, like you. She used to make meals for her foster siblings. She could turn a single can of Spam into twelve sandwiches. She said you could hold up a slice and see the sunrise through it."

The Apothakery's warm yellow kitchen melts into my thoughts. My smile slips. I stop mid-chew, my throat dry, struggling to swallow. When was the last time my mom cooked in that kitchen? Will I be able to stand in there again, completely alone, if my mom isn't with me? The next bite of my Spam-Cheeto-childhood sandwich sticks in my throat. That does it.

I burst right into a mess of tears.

The Warlock is next to me in half a second. "If the sandwiches are bad, just tell me—"

I snort, still crying, my nose producing a hideous noise I didn't even know it could make. Lord, I did not expect to see the day I willingly set down a Spam and Cheeto sandwich. "They're perfect." I wipe my eyes. "They just taste too much like home."

He sits next to me, but doesn't try to comfort me or distract me. He just gives me the space and the peace to work through it.

When I'm no longer sniffling like a toddler, I say, "You were right. I'm not holding it together as well as I thought."

"Your mother is dying. You don't have to be fine."

I shake my head. "It's not just that. I set impossible standards, and when I don't meet them, I punish myself and withhold the rewards." I had hoped I would've learned this lesson by my thirties. "But they're not rewards—they're just things that make me happy."

"You can't cure everyone, Ms. Frost. Even in a small town. The magic is a burden of responsibility. You're the Holler's Farewitch, not its fail-safe."

"Great bedside manner." I hiccup. "But I love my job."

I think I do.

I loved the idea of the shop. Making a name for myself, not just as a Frost, but as Honey. Maybe I might've enjoyed all this if I'd gotten the chance to train, take my time.

With a little time, it's easy to fall in love with something.

"Then you'll be excited to return after a break from it," he says.

My skin itches at a sting buried deep. I'm the Farewitch, *I'm* supposed to be the deliverer of cures and truths. "My Momaw always said our brains work against us. The magic we've got, the power, makes us think we can do anything. So when we fall short of . . . *anything*, we're always disappointed."

"Sounds like I would have liked your grandmother."

I grin. "She'd've hated you."

At my smile, a bright sheen of hunger flickers in the look he gives me. The darkness must be playing with my bravery, because I ask him something I'd never ask him if he could fully see me right now. "Who was the last person you loved?"

"Besides Lazlo and Ms. Zeen?" He doesn't hesitate. "My parents. They were kind people. Complicated. But good folk."

Deep lines of tension around his mouth emphasize his exhaustion. But there's a fresh pain there, too. Like he polishes it every day, as much a part of his routine as watering his plants.

"I'm sorry about your parents."

"Ms. Zeen gave you additional context, I take it."

"She cares a lot about you. And not out of obligation. Or because she *owes* you. It's important you know that."

"I do. Very much so."

"And you know you can love people without guilt, right, sir?"

My words hang in the damp air between us. He doesn't answer this time. My hands tremble with the sudden urge to reach for him and . . . I don't know what. The possibilities are infinite. Reckless. *New.*

He swallows. Hard. "You have to stop calling me *sir*."

"Tell me your name, then. *Sir.*"

"I can't. Not yet. I told you, it's like giving away—"

"Power or control, I remember. But you even know my middle name now. How is that fair? Are you worried you'll regret telling me?"

"No." The word is sharp, decisive. "I'm worried I won't."

His voice is like gravel, hard as the cave floor beneath us. I almost shiver, and I don't know what to do with the way he's looking at me. At my mouth. The cave has to be playing tricks on us. We inhale the cool cave air together, faces inches apart, his breath on my lips.

Our lantern goes out.

Everything vanishes into pitch-black nothing. That battery was freshly charged, too. Which means—

"That would be the Witch's way of telling us she knows we're here," he confirms.

Closer to the Witch, closer to the solstice.

Abruptly, he stands and spreads out his bedroll *several* feet away from me. Away from whatever . . . that was. I'm sure my cheeks are as pink as Spam.

"We'll switch to a manual flame lantern soon. We should sleep. This will likely be our only chance to rest."

Right. Sure.

Head and heart buzzing, I stretch out on my own roll and try to sleep. I really do.

But for hours, I'm wide awake, the Warlock just out of my reach.

Chapter Thirty-Two

SATURDAY, JUNE 18

3 DAYS UNTIL THE SUMMER SOLSTICE

Honey's Helpful Hint, from
Honey Frost's Southern Cookbook for Recipes Gone Wrong:

Long past the farm, down in the Holler
there is a sideways place
where the friends are foes,
lost in the creek and deep in the caves,
there is a sideways Witch
with a soul of shadow
who goes by the call of woeful Widow.
—"Song of the Widow Witch"

Strong hands stir me awake.

My eyes stay shut in protest. I *finally* fell asleep. Just a few more minutes.

"Ms. Frost, wake up."

That man's voice again. I recognize it. Why isn't he asleep, too? It's way too early for this nonsense.

"You have to fight through the lethargy."

Why won't the universe let me sleep? I. Am. *Tired.*

"*Honey,* can you hear me? Wake up."

Ah, I see. We're playing a game. I can do pet names. "Of course, dear," I murmur. With some drool, I'm sure.

"*Of all the times*—you are the most vexing woman—do not make me empty our water bottles on top of your head—"

"Let me sleep, darling." I'm going to run out of patience. And endearments.

The next thing I register is that my soft bed is gone and I'm upright on two feet, swaying with sleepy eyes. The Warlock's face is not the worst view to wake up to, even if it's rather tense. And sallow. He's hauled me to my feet, my cheeks cupped in his palms. "Are you all right?"

I bat at his hands. "Congratulations, you saved me from a nap." Now I'm tired *and* flustered. His thumbs were doing these nice—

"A nap courtesy of the Widow Witch."

My dreary eyes go wide. *Now* I'm awake.

We are *not* where we fell asleep.

We're still in a cave, but not any kind I've seen before. Our bedrolls are gone, and we're standing in a meadow. The green earth beneath our feet covers the entire expansive footprint of a gaping cave chamber. Stalactites hang from the uneven ceiling and stalagmites sprout from the ground like stony trees. Pools of cave water glisten, and trickling waterfalls echo around us. Pinpricks of light glow and wink out everywhere I look. *Fireflies.*

Farther into the cavern, dusky sunshine filters through the air.

I can see.

There—the roof of the chamber is open to the surface above us. Shafts of light banish the deeper shadows, the brightness dancing off the cave pools. A larger, rushing waterfall pours in from the surface, filling a massive cave lake. And there, in the middle of the lake on its own tiny island, is no lair or fortress. Just a small cottage. Candles burn in the windows. Smoke kisses the air above a chimney.

A *cozy* cottage.

The entire place is a storybook grotto.

A footbridge springs like a Slinky over the lake to connect the cottage's island to the nearest grassy platform, not far from where we're standing. "This is where she lives?"

He nods, solemn. "She transported us here while we were sleeping."

"Why the hell would she help us find her?"

"Either she's eager to see if we've come to bargain," he says, "or she likes to play with her food."

Even though I'm only subsisting on last night's Spam sandwich, my appetite evaporates.

We don't get long to contemplate her motivations.

Right as we step toward the footbridge, bone-white hounds emerge from the air, like mist taking shape. They're twice as large as wolves, practically horses with paws and dagger-sharp canines. And they're all missing their eyes.

The hounds surround us, going by scent.

"Run for the cottage," the Warlock whispers.

I watch the beasts creep closer. "Run *toward* the evil Witch's lair. Got it."

The hounds snarl collectively, onyx teeth bared.

"Stay close to the waterfalls; the noise will confuse them. These nightmares will have the upper hand everywhere else," he adds, making me feel a helluva lot worse. I try to suffocate my rising dread before I freeze in place.

That's when the hounds lunge.

I run.

Mental blinders fly up as I focus on the cottage, running faster than I ever have in my short and looking-shorter life. The footbridge inches closer with every leap over a cave pool. I slip once, twice, three times on grass dewy from the waterfalls' spray, though the falls are also the only thing keeping the hounds from fully tracking me.

The Warlock's long legs are on the edge of my vision, barely keeping up. Even after a night's sleep, his body is just as fatigued as it was yesterday. The hounds howl and snarl, narrowing the distance. I hear their massive paws striking the earth right behind me. *Closer.*

But I'm slowing down.

The hounds snap at my ankles, howling for the hunt. The Widow Witch dumped us in her front yard simply because it was time to feed her dogs.

We're almost to the footbridge, but it's too late.

The hounds surround us.

A thoroughbred of a dog pounces. I jump out of the way but slide in the wet grass. The Warlock is there in the same instant, as if to throw himself between me and the hound, but we collide and go down together, our limbs tangling. I land hard on my ass.

We scramble backward on our palms, the Warlock in front of me, his feet closest to the jaws of the hounds. Maybe we can jump off the footbridge, if we can reach it. But if these hounds are her defense on land, what's lurking under the water? My insides quiver, gut tightening with panic. Now is not the time to need a bathroom.

The beasts circle us with oddly human precision. When my arms give out, the Warlock's back hits my chest. His body nearly covers mine as he stays facing the hounds.

There's nowhere else for us to go.

I wrap my arms around his heaving chest from behind and haul him closer. These hounds are going to tear us into shredded cheese, but holding him like this calms my pulse for one brief, sweet second. As he leans against me, torso tucked between my legs, his hands grip the backs of my thighs. "If this doesn't go well—"

"Don't you dare," I gasp between lungfuls of air.

The hound closest to us looks ready to pounce. To devour.

My thoughts tumble. Devour. He's hungry. And I'm a Farewitch—that's it! Using precious seconds, I reach into my backpack and yank out a plastic container.

The hounds lunge just as I chuck the contents of the container over their heads.

Feral and starving, they pounce for the bait, stopping their attack long enough to demolish the food.

Not *just* food. Honey bourbon bread pudding. For insomnia.

One by one, the dogs stretch, yawn, stomp the grass in circles, and plop down, eyelids heavy. The dessert is harmless—I brought it in case my brain was too wired to sleep—but it works *fast*. Soon, the vicious demons become fur-balls no more dangerous than Beauregard.

Our path to the footbridge is clear. For now.

The Warlock's head falls back against my chest. "You're brilliant." Hands still cupped under my thighs, he pulls my legs tighter around him, like he has no intention of moving. "I admit, the dogs are a surprise."

He's shaking. Or I am. I press my cheek into the top of his head, greedy for the smell of soil and thyme that reminds me of the Manor. Of safety. Home.

"We need to go to the gym," I say, breathing heavily. "Do some cardio."

"I have a few ideas—"

He doesn't get to finish. In a matter of seconds, my vision of the cottage and sleeping hounds vanishes in a gray cyclone swirling around us, and then my feet are off the ground and I'm spinning, spinning—

Quick as it begins, the carnival ride from hell ends.

From the air, we drop a few feet to the earth. My ears pop, like we've emerged in some pressurized dome. I stumble to my feet, disoriented but determined to be ready for whatever's next. Beside me, the Warlock does the same, looking up to see where we've landed.

The front porch of the Widow Witch's cottage.

That was the pop—we must be inside her own personal bubble of warding now. Her winds whipped us here like we're paper cutouts. Not far off from how I feel right now, fragile enough to tear. Just as I catch my first full breath, the cottage's front door swings open.

But it's not the Widow Witch on the threshold.

It's Gertha Fudge.

Well, not *quite* Gertha Fudge.

Same dark skin and short frame, which swims in a black kaftan dress. Like Gertha, her white hair, streaked with pearlescent gray, sits atop her head in braids. They could be twins, except the Witch's wrinkled and sagging face is an even older copy of the already-aged church lady. Impossibly, this woman has to be generations older than Gertha.

The Widow Witch crosses her arms. "You sedated my hounds, girl." Same voice, too, but cracked and deep. Old. Tired.

My heart pounds. "They'll be fine. It was only a recipe for sleep."

"Farewitches," she sneers. Her dark eyes twinkle with a wicked bitterness that sends horripilation over my neck. "A crafty one. I'm not surprised you keep her company, Knight." Her gaze at last travels to the Warlock.

He gives her a terse nod. I think he's about to bite a molar in two. "Okolona."

I suppress a gulp. This is the very person who cursed him, the Witch who is the reason he and a little boy are inching toward death. But the thought of Lazlo gives me the courage to look her in the eye. "I'm Honey Frost. Nice to meet you."

Momaw stressed manners.

"You owe us a new foyer."

Manners, *sometimes*. I don't dare bring up the barn or church.

"If you're going to make demands," the Witch says, "you best come inside. I have a sonker cooking."

"Honey is off-limits, Okolona," the Warlock says, his voice raspy. "If a morsel of your magic touches her, I'll—"

"You'll what? With what power? I can't even sense your magic. Not a spark."

He glowers. "Because of *your* curse, Okolona."

The woman gives a throaty chuckle. "Relax, boy. I'm not interested in breaking your toys. Yet."

That doesn't make me relax at all. But we're only here because we're desperate. So I follow a magical being leagues more powerful than myself into the dark beyond the threshold.

The inside is like the outside: wooden beams warped from water damage, walls mossy with age. A large stone hearth that is suspiciously person-sized hosts a blazing fire. Sunlight is minimal and candles are everywhere. Between those and the fire, the cottage is aglow. The place doesn't look much like the home of a dreaded Witch.

Yet it's *frigid* in here. Like all this heat is just for show.

She isn't lying: A cast-iron skillet rests deep in the fireplace, baking. Goopy fruit and its juice bubble up around a golden-brown cake-batter crust, threatening to spill over. A sonker uses riper fruit than a cobbler. I hate to admit it, but the thing smells divine.

"Blackberry?" I ask.

She adds a log to her fire. "Huckleberry. It's seasonal."

"Don't accept any food from her," the Warlock says, following right behind me.

An unkind grin twitches at the Witch's mouth. "Would I really poison you two? We haven't had a lick of fun yet."

"We're here for your help," I say without preamble. There's no time to be shy.

She looks past me, her cold eyes narrowing on the Warlock. "You've been busy, Knight. And here I thought you couldn't possibly get into any more trouble. Then again, I've never seen you following a girl around."

"I'm thirty-one, thanks," I protest.

"Child, do you know how ancient I am? You are all children

tugging hair on the playground to me." She hums, almost giddy. "Speaking of children, I hear the Eldercraft may pay the Holler a visit, to drive out a rogue Warlock before he can corrupt an innocent soul. Same town, same story. Foxe Holler never changes, does it?"

I shake my head. "You don't get information for free. Witches like to trade, don't we? You get a question, we get a question." I hope I sound more sure than I feel. I'm the novice here when it comes to age and field experience.

"Well, I like her more in four minutes than I ever liked you in four decades, Knight. Where did you find this one?"

The Warlock shifts closer to me, and I can feel the defensive unease threaded through his muscles where we brush up against each other. "She found me."

"Ah. The good ones usually do."

"Why did you transport us here?" I ask, keeping us on track. Time might not pass here the same way it does in the Holler. What if we've already wasted hours, or days? "Why not let us get lost and die in the caves?"

"That's two questions. But I'll be generous since you're my guest: I don't like when folks meddle in my bargains. A deal is between those who make it." She nods at him. "He asked for time, I gave it to him. A year. No more."

The fire pops. Sparks tickle the walls of the stone. The entire cottage smells of sugary, ripe huckleberry and woodsmoke. Sweet and dangerous.

"That doesn't sound like a very fair deal to me," I say.

"It's my turn to ask a question, girl. Why are *you* here?"

I swallow. "My family's magic is poisoning my mom. And me. I don't know how to reverse the effects. Or even just stop them. But I think you can help me."

"This one's awfully nosey and blunt, Knight."

"I know," he says at the same time I say, "Thank you."

I keep my chin high. "My Momaw said, *You can't spell* honesty *without* honey."

The Witch wrinkles her nose, looking even more like Gertha Fudge. "How disgustingly quaint."

That's it. "You're Gertha Fudge's grandmother!"

"*Great*-grandmother. Don't short me my life experience. But yes. Gertha didn't inherit any Hedgewitch magic. She'll die a normal old woman. But I have a few centuries in me yet. My turn, Witch to Witch, girl. Why are you here helping a *Warlock* who could trade your life for his own gain if he wanted? *Honesty* is not in his vocabulary."

The Warlock makes a sound of objection. "I'm simply selective about when I choose to reveal information."

I ignore his affronted expression. "He's honest when it matters."

She waves a bony hand at the Warlock. "Did you bring this poor girl here so she could make an equally as foolish bargain? Shame on you, boy."

"No deals. No tricks. Only answers," I say. "That was your question. Here's my next one: What exactly happened between you and the Knight family twenty-five years ago?"

Surprise crosses the Warlock's face. Like he's been avoiding this story, running from it for years. But he's going to have to go with me on this.

The Witch eyes him. "How much does she know?"

His surprise shifts to confusion. "As much as I do."

She snorts. "This story begins long before the last solstice." She sticks a wrinkled finger right into the bubbling sonker, then licks off the gooey fruit filling like third-degree burns are a myth. "Once upon a time . . ."

The Brief and Fraught Melancholic Adolescence of a Warlock

Fifty-some years ago, a young woman arrived in Foxe Holler.

The townsfolk distrusted her, simply because she came from afar and looked different from their kin. They treated her like they did a local poor farmer, whose father had been a Warlock. Against their better judgment, as mortals do, the woman and farmer fell in love. A decade passed in peace. Then they had a child.

It's not easy to make a living in a small holler, especially when neighbors distrust you. The parents knew bigotry would fall upon their boy if he ever displayed his own magic. So they asked a powerful Witch for help. For a wish. A profitable farm, a comfortable life for their boy. Desperate parents will do anything, damn the consequences.

The Witch granted them everything. Security, wealth, friends. And they prospered.

But magic has a cost. Unpaid debts upset balance. The Witch asked for a humble payment: If the boy ever manifested magic, he was hers to mentor. The naïve fools agreed, thinking their child would turn out just like them, as all parents hope. No magic. Just another ordinary boy. Years went by. The boy grew up in the easy comfort his parents didn't pay for, and became a spoiled young man. But on the cusp of sixteen, his magic came forward.

When the Witch came to settle the debt, his parents refused to honor their deal. They were afraid embracing their son's oddity, what made him too unique, was a death wish in a small town. So to cheat their way out of the bargain, they toyed with spellwork they didn't understand.

But with no magic themselves, their desperation was their own curse, and it killed them.

For the first time, the young man was on his own.

The Witch offered her guidance, one more time. But he refused any gesture of help. All he wanted was to brood and lock himself away where his magic could grow wild and arrogant, unrefined and irresponsible. Just like him, and the Warlocks before him.

Which is exactly what he did.

As the Witch spoke, Warlock Knight moved to stare out a set of bay windows that overlook the back of the cottage. Where no one could see his face. How much of this did he already know?

"Debts or not, your intention was never selfless," the Warlock says. "You only wanted a mentee to mold, young power to manipulate."

The Witch looks over at me from the hearth, where she's now tending her sonker. "Don't let him fool you, girl. This one has loved growing enemies before he ever loved growing plants."

"I was *sixteen*, Okolona," the Warlock snaps, turning to face her. "I wasn't thinking about enemies, I was grieving." Anger burns in his words, as deep and simmering as the sonker. "My parents made poor choices, yes, but you dropped them into a damn maze with no way out. They didn't even have any magic to defend themselves."

The fire in the hearth flares up, roaring with the Witch's rising voice. "But you did, boy. You could have been the best Warlock of your generation, but that opportunity passed."

His head hangs as her words settle on him. He seems to have come to the same conclusion. "I followed them that night," he says, his words carrying half the fight they had before. "But the magic they were exploiting . . . I only remember there was so much light. Heat. My power was brand new, volatile, and if I'd had more control, I could've saved—"

"*You didn't kill them*," I interrupt. Raw power in his veins, but missing the experience to do anything with it? That thought will take him nowhere good, fast. Not many Witches can thwart a Hedgewitch, and someone without any magic at all, misusing powerful spells?

A shudder racks his taut shoulders. "I might as well have."

The Widow Witch snorts. "Good Lord, you only children. You always think everything is about you."

I round on her. "You had to know the Knights would never actually be able to pay such a steep price. He was their son."

The fire twitches behind her so she's more silhouette than woman. "The price was steep because their request was steep. I cannot expend magic without paying a price, and if a price is not paid, the imbalance grows. The weaker *I* become. If I spend magic for souls who do not restore the balance with their own payment, I lose the privilege of my own power."

"But no one's forcing you to bargain with desperate people. It's predatory."

"Is it? Because of my magic, the Knight family prospered. It's why *this* one grew up in a grand farmhouse."

"You made it a prison," the Warlock croaks.

"Your sense of fairness has gone cattywampus, boy. *Your* parents came to *me*. I don't horde my magic only for myself. Nor do I expend it for free. They learned both lessons."

"But it's not only about balancing the debt with you, is it? You wanted to punish me for your feud with them, even after the fire."

The hearth flares. "Because you were ungrateful and *spoiled*. You were the town's first Warlock in generations, born *here*, your magic tied to the Holler. Made stronger for it. But all that potential just left you with more power than humility."

He runs an agitated hand through his hair. "*Everyone* has an ego as a teenager."

"But you grew older, and still you hid away. What has your magic done for your town, helped anyone in your community, before or after the fire?"

Doubt tears through the anger on his face. His eyes flick to me. Haven't I been telling him the same thing the last two months?

"Regardless, they're dead," he mutters. "None of this matters anymore."

The anger on the Witch's face shifts to disappointment. "What a shame." From a bowl, she grabs a raw huckleberry and squeezes it between two crooked fingers. "That farmhouse gave you all the time and space to grow, yet your heart is still the size of a huckleberry."

She bursts the berry with a squishy *pop*.

"That's true," I say.

The Warlock shoots me an affronted expression, which I ignore. I might be a guest in a conversation decades in the making, but I don't like feeling akin to a pot on a back burner.

"But it's not the only truth," I continue. "He left the town, but he never left its people."

Her sharp attention lands on me. "Pretty words, but you're biased, girl."

The Warlock scoffs. "I know I grew up with comfort my parents didn't pay for. But they made that deal for *me*. Only once I came along, not before. Their intention was selfless. Even if I didn't grow up to be."

He stalks back to my side, confidence renewing his stern if ashen expression. A welcome sight, over the shame.

"Your garden, Okolona—I can see it's dying. Which means *you're* dying. That's why you agreed to grant my wish a year ago. I'd owe you a favor, and you planned to ask for my help."

She purses her lips, her sonker forgotten and bubbling over.

My jaw slackens. "*That's* why you haven't taken a husband this season." *She doesn't have the magic.* The smaller, concentrated attacks on the Manor make sense, but how in the world did she manage that tornado?

An idea goes off like a kitchen timer in my head. "How about a deal?"

The Warlock whirls to me. "*What?* Frost, what the hell are you doing?"

I'm not sure, but I'm doing it. I look at the Witch head-on. "I'll make you a recipe. A cure. In exchange, you'll tell me all you can about my family's affliction. Whatever information you've possibly got. If I can reverse the effects for my mom, I want to know."

Momaw Frost is rolling her eyes from the grave. That's three people I've promised to save now, but it seems every godforsaken person in the Holler is dying, so what's another?

Violent interest gleams in the Witch's eyes. "Is that all?"

"And you lift your curse on Mr. Knight before the solstice. You let him live."

She hums. "It has to be one of *my* recipes. From my books."

"Fine."

"And if the recipe you choose doesn't work?"

"Then we lose. The Frosts don't come to you for help ever again, and the Warlock succumbs to his own illness on the solstice with Lazlo."

The Witch smiles, revealing charcoal-black teeth, canines sharp as nails, just like her hounds. "You have two days. I'll return then to taste what you've made. Don't try to leave—my grimoires and anything else you need are here."

Standing, she snaps. The sonker disappears from the fireplace and materializes on the kitchen table. The flames behind her cackle.

I stick out my hand, hoping the nervous spasm in my fingers isn't visible.

She stares at my hand like it's odd magic she's never seen. "No one's ever brave enough to touch me, girl."

"I was raised to be polite." My voice might be trembling like my hand.

The Warlock looks ready to murder me. *Manners,* I mouth in his direction.

"Very well," the Witch croons, toxic glee spilling into her features.

We shake on it. Her magic jolts through me and I hold on to her hand as long as I can. The energy there . . . it's not violent. It's weak, dying, like the Warlock said. But there's also something else underneath the centuries of power and knowledge.

Melancholy.

She drops my hand as a cloak appears and drapes over her shoulders, like limp roadkill. "Oh, and the hounds need to be fed every four hours."

"Or what?"

She vanishes.

Then it's just me and the Warlock, all alone in the Widow Witch's cottage.

"For the undeniable and permanent record, Ms. Frost, this is the worst idea you've ever had."

I swallow, flexing my hand where the Witch's magic still tingles, a dull static buzz of worry pulling at my chest. "That's what you said about the cookie bake."

Chapter Thirty-Three

SATURDAY, JUNE 18 (STILL)

3 DAYS UNTIL THE SUMMER SOLSTICE

Honey's Helpful Hint, from
Honey Frost's Southern Cookbook for Recipes Gone Wrong:

Memories are the best recipes, and a recipe is only as good as its ingredients.

We've got forty-eight hours to cure a formidable Hedgewitch of Holler legend.

No big thing.

We split up to cover more ground, and the Warlock shuffles outside to look for ingredients I might need, muttering about the state of the garden.

I immediately pilfer the kitchen. Cornmeal, dark potatoes, molasses, ears of corn dangling from the rafters. And moonshine. Plenty of moonshine. The fridge, an icebox that predates the first Roosevelt, holds an entire zoo of game and unlabeled jars whose contents jiggle. I don't open those. Okay, so the pantry might be more woefully barren than the Manor's when I first moved in.

But the Witch wasn't *totally* lying about the cottage having what we need. I find what I'm looking for hiding above the kitchen: a low-ceilinged loft, each wall a bookcase stacked two rows deep. Her library of grimoires and magical texts.

The first few books I grab snap closed on my fingers. But my frustration pricks more than the pain. When I threaten to start cracking spines, the assault stops. For now.

Déjà vu wallops me. I've traded one tetchy library for another.

Then I get snooping.

After a while, I hear the back door. When I peek down through the loft's open spiral staircase, I see the Warlock carrying an armful of odd metal tools that look less for gardening and more for torture.

He peers up at me from below. "Good news. The Witch's garden might be dying, but it's coughed up a few wilted herbs you might be able to use."

"And the bad news?"

"The garden is more dangerous than the hounds. Don't go outside without me. The Witch has amassed an impressively nasty collection of anthropophagous plants."

"You mean carnivorous?"

"I do not."

Right. No midnight pee trips to the outhouse, then.

"Care to tell me how you plan on finding the recipe that will cure whatever's eating away at her wretched soul, in less than two days?"

"I already know what recipe I need," I call down. "I just have to find *her* copy of it."

"Of course you do."

"I'll try not to be insulted by the lack of faith."

"How—" He lets out an *Ah*. "You saw her memories when you shook her hand."

"*Manners.*"

"Like I said, too clever for your own good." The words are low and deep in his chest.

Not going to lie, that voice has my breath shallow.

The satisfaction doesn't last long.

Using my magic to peek at someone's innermost headspace

without asking makes me feel as slimy as whatever's living in the icebox. The Witch's memory was old, dark, and out of focus, but it appeared for me without prompting. Like it was waiting to be discovered.

"If you know the end product, can't you simply deduce the ingredients?" he asks.

I snort. Oh, my naïve little Warlock. "It has to be the exact ingredients and amounts from her own dish. *A recipe is only as good as its ingredients.*" Another Momaw-ism.

My chest seizes. Momaw would know where an old Witch keeps something important and personal. The closest thing I have to an old Witch is . . . an old Warlock.

I peek over the loft so I can see him fully. "Innocent question: Where would an ancient magical being hide a precious memento? Something priceless?"

He frowns back up at me. "Not every Warlock hoards valuable treasure or gold. Common misconception."

I roll my eyes. "I said *priceless*, not *valuable*."

"Is this a riddle?"

"Not all Witches like riddles. Common stereotype. Shame on you."

"When someone says *innocent question* before a question, it's usually not innocent."

Ridiculous man, I think he's *stalling*. "Don't make me come down there."

His eyes travel across my face in a slow way I'm not prepared for. Definitely stalling.

"I wouldn't hide it," he finally answers. "I'd keep it where I could see it every day."

I shuffle back into the loft before he can see the heat in my cheeks. This man would barely look at me when I first moved into the Manor, and now I wish he'd stop. Who gave him the right to have such good focus.

"I'll be outside," he calls up. "Try not to set the cottage on fire."

"Not without you," I singsong back.

Something clangs down below and I hear him swear before he disappears outside again.

I spend a chunk of our precious time gathering all the cookbooks and grimoires I can find. Luckily, nowhere near the number in the Warlock's library. It wouldn't kill her to have a single armchair up here, though. Does the Witch never find herself in need of some sitting?

I start reading. The hours and light from the cave's open ceiling drain away. Eventually, I make a nest of books and blankets at the Witch's kitchen table, a hunk of old oak as cracked as she is. The kitchen fireplace keeps the cottage lit, and I sit as close as I can to the flames. It's June and this place is *freezing*.

I don't see the Warlock until long after sunset. When he comes back inside, I'm oddly comforted to see him covered in dirt again. "Hounds?"

He drops into the chair across from me. "Ferns. With a bad temper."

The bags under his eyes are twice as noticeable as they were this morning. Gaunt shadows cling to his face. He's starting to resemble the Witch's hounds. But I have to trust he knows what he's doing, the way he's trusting me. The way he's believed in me all this time.

I just hope that come the solstice, believing in him doesn't mean losing him.

"We are *not* sleeping in the Witch's bedroom," the Warlock declares close to midnight.

We spent the evening in silence, me deep in the Witch's books while he studied a small plant field guide he brought in his pack. Dinner was the last of our packed food. He gave me the rest of the marshmallows. I think they remind him too much of Lazlo. With the gloaming now a true darkness, growing winds test the strength of the windows and the place is cold everywhere except by the fire.

Prompting the Warlock to make his latest bold statement.

"Or any room with locks, and I'd rather not find out what made the claw marks on the cellar door." He nods to the fireplace. "We can roll out our mats in front of the fire. That's safest."

"Yeah. Yes. Good idea." There are literal icicles in the corners of the room. But in front of the fire . . . *together*? When I made our deal with the Witch, I didn't register that staying here means having two nights to account for. Two entire sleeps. Maybe I'll just find some coffee and pull an all-nighter—

He unfurls our bedrolls. Next to each other. Then stretches out on his, feet facing the fire.

I flit around the kitchen, busying my hands with absolutely nothing. Against my best efforts, I keep remembering the hooded look he gave me back in the cave. *Lord.* I'm almost willing to take my chances in the Witch's bedroom. I've had some unremarkable sex, but have I ever just *slept* next to a guy? The whole night? What if my body chooses this moment at thirty-one years old to begin snoring?

But it's either *this*—a giddy yet terrified sensation—or face another too-dark corner of this hell-cottage.

So be it. I plunk down on my own mat right next to him.

Without a word, he throws a single blanket over us and rests his head on a bunched-up jacket. This close, I can see him swallow, the threads of muscle pulsing in his neck.

I'm saved from those unhelpfully distracting thoughts when an empty pot on a shelf above the sink gives a sudden jerk.

Out springs a bright ebony flower, glowing as if lit from within.

The Warlock perks up, head lifting. "A Midnight Bloom. I've never seen one in person." Despite his wan face, his voice is reverential, full of boyish wonder.

I smile in spite of this entire crap situation. Even with our looming deadlines, this man finds time to be awed by plants. A minute later, the flower closes in on itself, the beauty of its petals just for the souls who find themselves awake in the emptiest, loneliest part of the night.

"Beautiful," I whisper.

"And cumbersome to grow and keep alive. Okolona doesn't have the patience."

"Someone here did." I think of the vicious garden outside and its beasties. "Oh! *That's* why."

"That's why what?"

"I've been trying to figure out why you even entertained my early idea that plant toxins were causing your illness, since you already knew you were cursed, not just sick. You thought there was a chance the Witch had used something in that garden to cast the original curse, that the cure could've been in the ingredients."

"See, Ms. Frost? I didn't completely waste your time." He leans back against his makeshift pillow. "We should sleep. Even the hounds have stopped howling."

I nod, but his eyes are already closed. Spine rigid, I lean against a leg of the kitchen table to stay half upright. We're fully clothed, but I feel like a cartoon animal whose fur has walked away. *Now what?*

"Are you well, Ms. Frost?" he murmurs.

"Mm-hmm."

He cracks open an eye at me. "Your breathing says otherwise."

"Just nervous. About the solstice. And the outhouse. It seems hungry, if that makes sense? It keeps groaning." *Rambling liar.*

"Sleep, then. You might need the energy to fight a ravenous latrine tomorrow."

"You enjoy telling me to rest, don't you?"

"If I didn't, you wouldn't."

I hate that he's probably right. "I'm going to read for little bit longer. She's got so many books, I don't want to miss anything."

Next to me, he throws one arm over his eyes against the firelight. The other is nudged up against me, his shoulder at my hip. Comfortable. Like we're an old married couple nestled together on a chilly night like we have in countless previous lives. I don't hate the idea.

"Good night, Ms. Frost," he whispers, unable to fight his fatigue.

His breathing slows as I flip through another of the Witch's grimoires.

The fire crackles, the house creaks. It's deceptively peaceful. I'm not sure how long I focus, a few minutes or an hour, but I start reading the same pages over and over, my eyes crossing. Research is impossible with this man burrowed against me. If he would just snore or something, break the moment, shatter my body's constant awareness of him and this absurd urge to curl into him . . .

That's it, I give up. Unable to keep my eyes off him, I track the rise and fall of his chest, the lines of his collarbone where his shirt has edged lower. He shifts in his sleep, burrowing even closer into my side. The movement sends a shiver right through my core but I don't feel chilled at all. Quite the opposite.

I could wake him up. We only have so many nights together before the solstice . . .

But his shifting reveals something that catches my eye.

The book he's been referencing since we've arrived is tucked beside his bedroll.

Careful not to wake him, I snatch it up, greedy for something that will take my thoughts off him pressed against me. Can't hurt to peek. It's not like he's been hiding it.

I'm not quite prepared for what I find.

The plants, I'm expecting: black-and-white sketches, colored-pencil drawings, green watercolors. It's definitely his own field journal of flora.

What I don't expect is that everything is done by hand. The pieces are more aesthetic than textbook, capturing beauty, not just herbal or medicinal function. Detailed handwritten notes line the margins. This isn't a guide he purchased. It's one he's created over years, researching and gardening, learning by doing. His own grimoire.

A formidable Warlock, a green thumb, and a talented artist. I guess when you spend decades alone, you pick up some hobbies. I take my time flipping through the pages, his art and notes meditative.

But when I reach the last page, my spine stiffens.

Tucked at the very back of his journal, hidden but protected, is a loose piece of paper that's way too familiar. Only a few words dot the page.

Butter
Coffee
Good olive oil
Tea for Z
Buttermilk

In my handwriting. Except for one last item—*Goldfish*, scrawled in the shaky, horror-film font belonging to someone under ten. Lazlo.

It's one of my grocery lists. But not just any list. It's the note I left him to get his attention right before the tornado, when I wasn't sure who was avoiding whom.

What in the world does a Warlock want with a shopping list?

My heart does a goddamn cartwheel right through my chest, up my throat, and back down to my belly.

Where would an ancient magical being hide a precious memento? Something priceless?

I wouldn't hide it. I'd keep it where I could see it every day.

The most careful I have ever handled something in my entire life, I return his journal as if I've never disturbed it. Definitely not sleeping tonight—*of course*.

I slip out from the blanket, praying I don't wake him. Despite telling me he rarely sleeps well, he's a sound sleeper tonight. Maybe the Manor keeps him up, where he's surrounded by memories of his parents. A prison, indeed.

Immediately, I miss the warmth, but thanks to him, I know exactly what I'm looking for now. Or rather, I know where to do the looking.

I tiptoe down the hallway at the back of the cottage to the very last door. Closed, of course, but after three months in Knight Manor, I've gotten good at opening doors I'm not supposed to.

The door isn't locked.

Either the Widow Witch doesn't think anyone will try to get in—or she doesn't care what crawls out. Tension pools in my shoulders, begging me to turn and run. But I can't second-guess myself. This room can't be worse than a flesh-eating garden. Right?

When I throw the door wide, the smell of decay blankets the Widow Witch's bedroom.

I don't want to risk using a lantern and disturbing any . . . thing that might be hiding in here, so the glow of the fireplace from down the hall will have to do. The firelight splayed across the floorboards is enough to reveal dusty curtains over a single window and a bed with pillows clustered to one side, bookended by two nightstands. A room barely lived in.

As quietly as possible, I rifle through the nightstand on the side with no pillows. Empty. My hope sinks. This spot was my best guess. It *has* to be here—hold on. *There.*

Shoved at the very back, forgotten like a Bible in a motel.

A thick spell book.

The outline of a Midnight Bloom flower is etched into the leather cover.

Not just any spell book. A gardener's grimoire. I know the moment I grasp it in my hands, smell the soil in the pages. This is it.

Just as I open the cover, an icy pain seeps into my fingertips and up my arms, into the core of me, an IV of Arctic Ocean. Every breath feels half frosted, an icicle that's melting and refreezing inside my lungs. Then the numbness begins, a frigid tingling claiming me one extremity at a time, like I've fallen through the frozen surface of a lake, sinking right into the subzero temperatures beneath.

An absurd, savage laugh catches in my throat. I'll need to revise my headline.

FAREWITCH FROST FOUND FATALLY FROZEN!

I start shaking. My thoughts tremble with me, my uncertainty jostling whatever good sense I've got left.

What made me, a dollar store hillbilly Farewitch, think I could stroll into a Warlock's life and fix a problem I don't understand? I can't even cure my own mother, and she couldn't help hers. By the time I take a break from work, Mom will be gone. And if she's not here, what's the point? The Warlock and I aren't so different after all. He lost the two people who raised him, and I'm almost two for two. We just chose different distractions to keep us too busy to fall apart.

The cold trickling under my skin throbs as my heart tries to manage a few last pumps. It would be easy to let whatever curse is on this grimoire have me. So easy. *How funny.* I touched another forbidden book, but this time I met frost instead of fire. The Witch defends herself with what she's suffered, the cold frostbite of grief. The Warlock's house fought back using the pain he knows: heat and fire.

The Warlock. Right. He'll be so peeved if I die. He'd probably say something like *Now who's going to make my apple butter?* I miss that scowl. I miss *him*. And the Manor's kitchen. It's not yellow, but it's the sunniest kitchen I've ever had. He called his home a prison, but I miss *all* of it. Every persnickety room. Maybe more than I miss the Apothakery.

My mind slows with my pulse, leaving me with a single memory.

Me, the Warlock. Close together. His gardens. August? He tucks a sprig of thyme behind my ear. I can *almost* smell it. Warmth flushes my cheeks. My real cheeks, I think. But I'm not wearing my apron. Something isn't right about this memory.

No. Not a memory. This never happened.

But I want it to. Or at least, I want the *chance* to make it happen.

Ice kisses my neck. It would be so easy to choose this cold numbness that dulls the worries of the outside world. But I've come awfully far to cower at spiteful grimoires, magical tantrums parading as protection. What if I don't let the Widow Witch and her grimoire win this time? How many more wonderful things would I get to learn about the Warlock, about Foxe Holler and my friends?

How much more would I learn about myself?

Just as I think *I don't want to go yet,* the Warlock in my false memory puts his lips on mine. Fire floods my blood, searing every pathway to my heart.

I take a gasping breath. Heat courses through me, the ice in my limbs thawing.

The illusion's hold on me vanishes and my eyes flutter open.

I'm back in the cottage. No daydream, no nightmare. My blood pumps back into my extremities. I can move, I can breathe, I can think. I'm *alive.*

The grimoire is still in my hands, but I've broken its hold on me. That was a helluva nasty spell to punish prying eyes. One formed with years of grief and despair.

I shudder. Even on my worst nights, I haven't thought about giving up like that. When I run my thumb over my lips, there's no taste of thyme.

There's no time to ponder the illusion. I came in here for one reason, and I intend to leave in one Honey-shaped piece.

The grimoire's brittle pages crackle as I pry them open. Dust puffs up and I hold in a sneeze. Thinking about the Warlock's journal, I check the back first.

Thank you, Mr. Knight.

The recipe isn't labeled. Grease spots and dried flour stain its surface, a history of countless evenings and meals together, connection over shared food. The best kind of love story.

A handwritten note runs across the top of the page. Like a riddle or puzzle.

If it walked, crawled, or flew . . .

There you are.

Chapter Thirty-Four

SUNDAY, JUNE 19

2 DAYS UNTIL THE SUMMER SOLSTICE

Honey's Helpful Hint, from
Honey Frost's Southern Cookbook for Recipes Gone Wrong:

Witches fall in love, too.
—Beulah Buchanan

What I think is Sunday morning arrives.

Probably. In this cave, only diffuse sunshine sifts into the cottage, and the warped window glass sculpts shadows into odd shapes. Time here feels adjustable. Untrustworthy. The fireplace and the Warlock's nearby body kept me blessedly flushed until morning. When I wake, the fire is just embers, the bedroll next to me empty.

He's already outside. So I get to work, too.

I jostle between dicing onions and okra, digging through cupboards, and stoking the fireplace to keep it roaring. A few of my knives disappear throughout the morning. The cottage has some kleptomaniac tendencies. I don't need my food tasting like panic, so I try hard to be grateful the cottage hasn't yet attempted to steal *us*.

All morning, my thoughts swim in a sea of fear and what-ifs. Glimpses of my grocery list in the Warlock's journal bob along in my mind, little rafts in the maelstrom.

"The hounds eat secrets," the Warlock says when he comes inside around lunch.

I look up from the icebox where I'm mining for meat. "Excuse me?"

He removes his gardening gloves to grab water. "You have to feed them a secret, and then they'll settle down."

"That . . . is abnormally specific."

He studies the disarray of ingredients and kitchen tools I've strewn across any free surface, my *mess en place*, as it were. "Any success in here?"

The June warmth has left him doused in sweat, even in this grotto. I keep sneaking glimpses of him through the back windows to see what he's up to, but he's always on his knees in the soil beds, his back to me. If things were different, I might relish the domesticity of it all. But every time he comes in from the garden, it takes him longer to work up the energy to go back outside, and his eyes are more opaque than not throughout the day, the hazel dull.

He's stopped eating as much, too. The loss of his appetite worries me more than anything.

"Yes," I say, getting a grip on myself. "I found the recipe. *Her* recipe."

Lord, it better be the right one. It's a bold gamble on my part.

"Already? Where? And nothing's popped out of a settee to steal your soul?"

He almost sounds impressed. Does the Warlock even do impressed?

"The Witch's bedroom," I say, and leave it at that.

He doesn't need to know his journal gave me the idea, and the less he knows about my questionable survival instincts, the better.

I pour us rich black coffee from a pot in the fireplace. "There are ingredients I can't find in the house, but I think I can gather most of them from the meadow around the cottage. I saw mushrooms near where we appeared."

"The hounds like to dig up garlic bulbs, if you're in need of those," he says between sips of coffee. "You'll have to trade them a secret, of course."

"I could use an herb-hunting, canine version of a truffle pig. Lazlo would love us if we brought back a hound."

He rubs a tired hand across his face, his stare finding me through his long fingers. "He loves you already, Ms. Frost."

"My cooking, maybe."

Something about his answer is odd, off. The difference between imitation vanilla and the real stuff. If I could just have a moment to think, out from under all our ticking clocks . . .

The Warlock finishes his coffee and hauls himself to his feet. "I'll be outside. If you hear howling, assume it's me."

"Was that a joke?"

"I can be funny, Ms. Frost."

Of course he waits until he's at death's door to be cheerful. Unbelievable.

"What are you doing out there anyway?"

He elbows the back door open. "My best."

Once he's gone, I find a massive cauldron and lug it into the hearth, hoping it's only been used for stew. Then I spend the afternoon collecting ingredients from the cave's meadow, and learn the hounds can sniff out *many* a vegetable. Later, from what must be a non-dying part of the garden, the Warlock unearths carrots, celery, and green beans for me. As the sun sets beyond the grotto, I finally have everything I need.

Working by firelight now, I reserve enough extra ingredients to make us a quick dinner of braised leek and mushroom soup. But as the Warlock and I eat, my fear turns every spoonful of flavor into dishwater.

What if we fail?

Too soon, the Midnight Bloom appears as we're unfurling our bedrolls once more in front of the popping fire. We're both exhausted and wide awake, anticipating tomorrow, and as we stare at our bedrolls, the Warlock finally breaks the tense silence.

"Ms. Frost, if this doesn't work tomorrow . . ."

"Then don't take it personally," I say, forcing a grin. "But it will."

"It might not."

"Then what? You and Lazlo keel over on a random Tuesday?" The soup from dinner bubbles in my gut, slowly turning to acid. Failure isn't an option. "No thanks."

"It wouldn't be a *random* Tuesday. It would be the solstice, my birthday."

"We wouldn't even get to have a cake," I protest. Everywhere I turn, my measuring cups are portioning time left. Can't we pretend the bad isn't a possibility until it actually happens?

"Ms. Frost."

"Or a party! You know how disappointed Silas will be if there's no party."

"*Ms. Frost.*"

"*What?*" I snap.

"You're . . ." He eyes me, lips in a tight line. "Delightful."

His sullen frown somehow eases. He's actually smiling. *At me.* My heartbeat picks up as his words settle into my bones.

"You're tolerable." I step away to lean against the kitchen table and breathe. The cottage feels extra cramped tonight. My hands itch to be busy. But he's already washed all the dishes, the scoundrel. "We should go to sleep."

Now said scoundrel is standing in front of me, his back to the fireplace. Awfully close to me. "Should we?"

The blood leaves my face, thrumming everywhere but where I need it, like my brain, my good judgment. All I can focus on is how the backlit glow of the fire sears the edges of his silhouette. He's giving me *that* look again, where his gaze hangs heavy, anchoring me.

The silence is too loud. Panicking, I say the first thing that comes to mind. "Do you ever think about how, if you'd gotten your wish the way you wanted, we wouldn't have met?"

"I prefer to believe I would meet you in any timeline, Ms. Frost."

"Like one of those fixed points? Like death?"

"Well, yes. Less morbid, though."

"Less morbid? Careful, someone might think you're flirting."

I mean the words to be funny, to ease this tightrope of tension pulling between us. But instead, his eyelids lower, the firelight catching the sheen of his dark pupils.

"Come here," he says.

The rough edge to his voice sends my heart right into my gut-soup. *Oh Lord.*

Instead of moving, I say, "Why do you keep one of my grocery lists at the back of your journal?"

His lips part, the surprise on his face gone as quickly as it appeared. "Would you believe me if I told you it's because I forgot it was there?"

"Try again."

His next step toward me brings him nearly up against me. "Then you know why."

Without thinking, my nervous fingers come up and begin fiddling with the buttons at the collar of his shirt. What the hell am I doing? What if we do only have until the solstice together? Why torture myself with a taste I can't taste again?

I think you've gotten too used to starving yourself.

In the next moment, he bends down and his lips flutter against the side of my neck. My mind shorts out on me, all excuses gone. He. Smells. So. Good. I'll never be able to cook with thyme again without sticking my head in the freezer to cool down.

"It wasn't hard to figure out how old you are," I manage to whisper.

His warm breath coasts over my skin, lips barely touching me. "And?"

"I *thought* you were having some mid-millennia crisis, but you're barely in your forties. You're a—" The pulse in my throat jumps when his lips brush my earlobe. "You're a baby."

He hums against my neck before leaning back to look me in the eye. "That's the first time anyone has called me a baby."

"That you know of." Of their own accord, my fingers flip aside a few stray pieces of black hair that have fallen across his eyes. "I think you need a haircut, *baby*."

In one quick movement, he lifts me onto the kitchen table so my legs hang off, my knees on either side of his hips. His hands settle firmly at my waist while his mouth returns to its teasing expedition over the skin of my throat. Never kissing, just raw, featherlight madness.

"Listen very closely, Witch," he murmurs against my neck. "I would like to kiss you. Not because of what might happen tomorrow. Not because I haven't kissed anyone in ages. Not even because you're always wearing a frustratingly adorable apron." To prove his point, his long fingers crawl under the strings of the tie at the small of my back, tugging against the knot. "But because I've wanted to kiss you for a shamefully long time."

I try to breathe but it's not going very well. "Since when? Since giving me a tour of your gardens?"

"No."

"Since you fed me an animal cracker?"

His mouth runs over my jaw. "*No.*"

My voice shudders from my lungs. "Don't be shy. Tell me." If he's torturing me, I'll torture him. I'm not one to back down from a recipe I haven't tried before. Something about this man makes me want to let go and lick at fire I can't find in the kitchen.

"Since you shoved that hideous clog in my door and ordered me to clean something."

White-hot sparks ignite in my core, and now my brain is reexamining every interaction after that moment, every smirk that was almost a smile. The man took his time.

"*Ordered* is a strong word . . ." I mumble.

"That's one of the secrets I told the hounds." His fingers dig for purchase under my rib cage. "Frankly, I'd like to do more than kiss you," he adds in a breathless whisper. "But given what pitiful amount of energy I have left as we near the solstice, a kiss might be all I can do."

The cottage is, impossibly, too huge now and there's an appalling amount of space between us. I tug him closer. A growl rumbles low in his throat. I know the sound of hunger more than anyone.

I pull back to look in his face, and shove aside my worries about tomorrow, about the Widow Witch and curses and cures and . . . Enough.

"We can start there, can't we? Go ahead. Ask me."

I've never seen the hazel of his irises so bright, green cocooning rich, buttery yellow. He almost looks like he's not dying. "Ms. Frost, may I kiss you?"

"Yes, but do you remember how? I mean how long exactly is *ages*—"

"*Careful, Witch*," he rasps, but there's no threat in his voice. Only need. He gives the smallest bite to the skin over my pulse at my neck. Then he kisses the exact spot he bit.

I think I combust. Yes. *Please.*

I definitely make some kind of truly embarrassing sound. That's all it takes. His mouth lands on mine and then he's *everywhere.*

One of his hands roams my lower back, holding me against him, while the other cups my cheek, my neck, his calloused thumb deliciously scratchy on the skin of my throat. My fists are so tight in his shirtfront, those wrinkles will be permanent. Our lips move, but we barely take more than a second at a time to breathe. When he at last needs real air, he pauses long enough for me to suck on his lower lip, hard.

He gets the message and palms my backside, dragging me to

the edge of the table so I fit right up against him, chest to chest, my thighs, core, all of it, pressed to him.

Much better.

His lips find mine again, and *good Lord*, this man kisses like he's been starved for years.

My hands and instinct take over. I claw my fingers through his thick hair, something I've wanted to do for *ages*, and he rewards me with a sound I've never heard him make before, a clipped release of breath that's suspiciously like a purr. I give a soft, playful tug to the dark strands, which makes him lean back just enough to give me the most piercing, devilish grin.

When his mouth touches me again, he's found my collarbone this time, teeth grazing the dip and swell of the bone, separated only by a thin layer of my increasingly buzzing skin. Not buzzing—electrified. When his tongue finds the hollow at my throat, a vicious shiver racks me from my ears to my toes.

I definitely combust.

His lips cover my racing pulse point, like he'd swallow my whole heart if he could.

I can't help it—a quiet whimper slips out of me.

"Jesus, Honey," he gasps into my neck, breathing hard.

My arms blanket his shoulders, my legs wrap around his hips, and I squeeze, needing to feel him against me, seeking some kind of relief to the pressure building in my chest, my gut, everywhere.

But there are still too many layers between us. I need to feel his skin on mine.

His hands slip under my apron strings, under the hem of my shirt, his fingers leaving kisses on my spine. Glad we're on the same page. I let go of him long enough to fiddle with the apron's knot—this thing needs to come off. Now. But my fingers are shaking—hell, *all of me* is. My heart rate is spiking so hard, I wonder how in the world I waited so long to kiss this man.

He grabs my hands battling the tie and throws them right back around his shoulders. "Just leave the apron on." His mouth claims the next whimper that slips out of me.

Never mind what I said before. *This* is better than any farmers' market.

And I'm right—he tastes like thyme, even without his magic. The crisp herb bites my tongue, and soon I'm wondering if the rest of him will taste like thyme—

"Thyme?" he pants, pulling back to gulp down air.

Whoops. Said that part aloud.

Somehow, his hands are already back under the hem of my shirt. With each frantic inhale, his hard chest brushes mine and I'm savoring every second of the friction. I can tell he is, too. Or, I can *feel* he is. A hot blush fills my face, and it's not from the fireplace.

Instead of putting him on the spot, I nuzzle my face into the crook of his neck, leaving sharp kisses as I go. "You know, if you'd gotten your wish and started over, you'd be younger than me now."

"Maybe then I could keep up with you."

I find his earlobe and take it between two of my canines. He swears, the sound more prayer than curse.

"Farewitches can bite, too. *Sir*," I taunt in his ear, loving how he shivers on the last word.

"*Honey*," he rasps, voice half gone. "I don't have much left in me."

"That's okay, I'm the better driver anyway."

His deep, heady chuckle rumbles in my veins. To my disappointment, he untangles my arms from around him and pulls back to look at me. His irises are alight, but his brows pull together over sunken eye sockets. "I'm afraid I'm not going to survive you."

A splinter of guilt pricks me. He'd abandon any remaining restraint if I asked him to. But I need him strong, strong enough to survive tomorrow. Or else there is no *after*.

When I lower my gaze to our hands, clasped together against his heaving chest, I scream.

"Your fingers!"

Only then does he take his eyes off me long enough to look down, too. "That is new."

His fingers, the skin, bone—gone. Or nearly gone. I can still *feel* him. But just like with Lazlo's hands, I'm looking at the vague shape of a palm, a ghostly outline of knuckles and digits. Just like Lazlo, full stop.

"You're fading now, too." This time, it's a whisper. I shouldn't be this shocked, honestly. Even the Warlock thought this might happen. My legs drop from around him as I fight for the logical part of my brain, which flew away the moment he started in with his tongue.

Our shared bloodline tangles things somehow. As Lazlo's health worsens, so does mine.

His words tumble around my mind. My pulse jitters, but now for a different reason.

"When you said Lazlo is part of your bloodline," I begin, as loud as I dare.

I let the unspoken question bloom between us.

It's the question that's been chafing against me for weeks now, but the answer didn't begin to emerge for me until our night in the cave. Like the darkness finally expelled the harsh light that kept me from looking closely. Some truths live in the small silhouettes right under our feet. I just couldn't see it yet. Until now.

The real truth about Lazlo.

It takes him a second to register the shift in my face. Then realization cuts through the tenderness of his charmingly ravished expression. As he hardens back into the Warlock I know best, the self-reproach festering in his eyes makes me want to burn something to the ground.

I have no idea where he came from, if he came from anywhere at all.

"He's . . ." My voice cracks. "He's you. Isn't he."

Silence.

Then he meets my stare head-on. "Yes. A younger copy of me, or a facsimile. A reflection. I don't really know. He's real. I know that. He believes he's nine and that his name is Lazlo." A chastened grin. "Ms. Zeen and I never knew how to describe someone who exists now but never existed before. Someone who exists twice, in the same moment in time."

Someone who doesn't have any memories before the Manor. Not his child. Not his relative. Not his future. Not fully him . . . but also in no way could he be anyone else.

A headache knocks at the back of my skull. "How did the Widow Witch even manage this? It's the definition of imbalance. Even a Hedgewitch can't create something out of nothing."

He shakes his head. "She must've been confident I wouldn't cure him in time. She created him, and then he'll be gone. A lateral transaction."

"But you'll die with him. How does that keep the scale even?"

"My best guess is, she's counting this as a long overdue recompense for my parents. They died by accident, if foolishly, and now Lazlo and I will die with . . . Well."

"Intent," I finish. Two people for two people.

"Now you know everything I do. Everything."

I sure do.

If you find a cure for him, we shall hope it works for me, too. So does any of what you've learned now really matter?

More than ever, I want to cling to his pragmatism. We've come this far; now is not the time to fall apart. Too many people are counting on us. On me.

Breathe. I can do this. Make the recipe. Cure the Widow Witch. Save lives.

"Well, almost everything," he adds.

Changed my mind. Maybe I will let the man die.

I cross my arms over my chest, mostly to escape the unsettling sensation of feeling his hands but not seeing them.

But it's no use, because he lifts a hand to my face anyway, his palm a solid presence against my cheek. He's still real. He's still here.

"Before the solstice," he begins, rubbing a thumb over my swollen bottom lip. I must look *great.* Bangs pasted to my sweaty forehead, apron askew, flour filling extra wrinkles from stress and no sleep. He clears his throat. "I want to give you my name."

My pulse quickens, only for my heart to plummet into the earth. Like the silly, delicate thing stepped off an edge and dove right into a bottomless cavern.

Any chance you'll tell me your name now?

When it's important.

I know what's he's doing. He's not expecting to survive, is he? Oh, *hell no.*

"I don't want it," I snap. "Not like this. Next week, next year, I don't care. Because you'll be here to give it to me."

"I won't be able to wish my way out of this. We might not have another chance."

I. Refuse. I shuffle farther back on the table, creating distance between us. Air. Air is good. Of all times, *now* he accepts we can't just wish for second chances, for more time.

"I'm going to write you a letter and sign my name," he tries again. "Open it later. Whenever you want. If you want. Then you'll have it, even if I'm—"

"Don't say it. You can't do . . . *this* right now. It's not fair—" Pressure pricks my eyes as a tight sob lodges in my throat.

"I won't be able to handle it if you cry, sweetheart."

I wipe away a treacherous splotch of wetness on my cheek. "I can't . . ." *Can't be sad over so many people at once.* There's no recipe for this kind of thing. Even now, I can hear Momaw Frost agreeing with me. If I had one more day with her, would I spend it angry? If I have one day left with my mom, will I spend it bitter?

No. I'm a Farewitch. I don't hurt, I heal.

So I try to push away the hurt and the spite. "Fine, a letter," I grind out. "But write it tomorrow. You need to sleep."

"Honey . . ."

"Just go to sleep, Mr. Knight. Please."

He takes a heavy breath. "Yes, ma'am."

Then he does something truly, terribly heinous. As he steps away, cold air claiming the space between us, he brushes my bangs aside and places a single, delicate kiss on my forehead.

And it feels wretched.

It feels exactly like a goodbye.

Chapter Thirty-Five

MONDAY, JUNE 20

1 DAY UNTIL THE SUMMER SOLSTICE

Honey's Helpful Hint, from
Honey Frost's Southern Cookbook for Recipes Gone Wrong:

Leave your ego at the door to the kitchen. You might know more than the recipe but you'll know less than your oven.

Monday arrives like all Mondays before it.

Horribly.

The Warlock wakes before I do, and stops me on my way outside to the outhouse. Judging by his bloodshot eyes, he didn't sleep at all last night. Even so, he still manages to look at me with an impressive intensity for seven in the morning Witch Standard Time.

He holds up a folded square of paper. With most of his fingers faded into a mere outline, it looks like the paper is floating.

My heart floats with it, unmoored in my chest, like a bad egg. Right. The stupid letter. Just in case.

He tucks the letter into the chest pocket of my apron, then dons a shield of stoicism. My apron used to feel like armor, too, once. Finally, I've got his name, resting so close to my heart. So why does he feel further away from me than ever?

Maybe because I feel like I could lose him twice.

Now that I know the truth about Lazlo, I keep looking for the boy in the Warlock's face. The physical resemblance was always clear, but I just can't blend them together in my head. Lazlo is Lazlo. Mr. Knight told me I know everything he knows now, but all this still feels like the Swiss cheese of answers. A loose end, but also a loose beginning. It's like I told him—no Witch can just break physics. Something can't come from nothing.

And Lazlo is a big, lovable something.

But I don't have time to dwell on the details, and Farewitch magic depends on sincere intention. So I archive all the feelings in my sternum and get to cooking.

Too short a time later, the Widow Witch returns.

Poised at the kitchen table, she looks exactly as she did before, not a braid out of place. Since manners have gotten us this far, I don't let her eat alone, and set two extra places across from her. Right where the Warlock kissed me senseless last night.

I hope Hedgewitches can't read minds.

The Warlock is already sitting, slumped, elbows braced on the table so he doesn't pitch over. He looks ready for a coffin.

The Witch scrutinizes the bowl of thick stew in front of her. Sniffs it. Prods it with her spoon. I've never seen someone stir with derision before. "This is no recipe of mine."

"It's Kentucky burgoo. Thick enough to stand a wooden spoon in." My chest swells with satisfaction as realization simmers on her face. "I'm sure you know the saying: *If it walked, crawled, or flew, it goes in burgoo.*"

And made in the hands of a Farewitch, great for the flu. But I don't think the Witch is suffering from something as banal as a stomach bug.

"I know the old adages, child. I spoke them first," she snarls, pushing her bowl away. "I won't eat this."

"*What?*"

"You had to use one of my recipes—that was my condition. I didn't ask you to prepare whatever drivel *you* wanted to make."

I jam a finger into the table between us. "I'm a Farewitch. I don't make what you want, I make what you need."

"*You* serve a community of folks who've been living here since before your mama was no more than too much wine and a bad decision. What you need is to respect your elders and our legacies of spellwork and recipes."

"She won't eat it because she knows it will work," the Warlock rasps.

The Witch lets go of a wicked chortle. "How are you two so disgustingly confident this mush will make me better?"

Stowing my anger, I slide the recipe I nearly died for across the table. Just below the ingredient list is a handwritten note, the basis of my entire plan.

For anniversary.

"Because it's your husband's recipe."

The instant *venomous* look that overcomes her face makes the hounds seem as threatening as cotton balls. Something dangerous burns in her dark eyes. I want to shout *Just kidding!* But I haven't come this far because I'm afraid of angry old women. I've gotten this far because I listen to them.

"The oldest resident of Foxe Holler is Beulah Buchanan," I explain, forgoing the *besides you*. I'm not trying to get incinerated. "She has history to share if someone slows down to keep her company. One story is even about you. You weren't the Widow Witch because you preyed on couples. Not at first. Folks called you Widow Okolona first. *You* were the widow."

Before the Warlock and I left town, I took Ms. Zeen's advice and paid a last-minute visit to Ms. Buchanan. Seems the sage old lady was right.

She wasn't always the Widow Witch, sugar. Witches fall in love, too.

A gamble, sure, but this recipe is our lottery ticket out of this mess. It has to be.

"I'm sorry. About your husband." And I mean it.

"I'm not," she huffs, exactly the way Ms. Fudge does. "Hedgewitches always live longer than folks without magic, and Witches, too. Life and death, past and present, that's the nature of our magic. I knew that meant I'd bury my husband someday."

"That doesn't mean you aren't allowed to mourn him."

"Unpaid debts and magical imbalance might weaken your power," the Warlock adds, "but that's never been the root of your illness, Okolona."

He looks sideways at me, and I nod, confirming our theory from this morning when I told him the details of my plan. Seeing him and my mom, a Warlock and a Witch, put their heads together at the hospital gave me the idea. If a Farewitch can burn out, so can a Hedgewitch.

"We think your grief is poisoning you."

I barely get the words out before the Witch slams a fist on the table. Spittle clings to her lips. "Doesn't matter what you think. You picked the wrong recipe. You failed."

No.

My gut twists. We're *so close.* And I'm *so damn tired.*

The Warlock heaves a terrifyingly ragged breath.

No no no.

"We watched your dogs, didn't we?" I blurt, desperation in my voice. "You owe us. *Try* the burgoo. Or would you leave that debt unpaid?"

She raises one wild, unkempt eyebrow. Picks up her spoon.

The smallest bite of thick gravy vanishes into her mouth and I hold my breath. She swallows. Then closes her eyes.

I *love* it when they close their eyes. Like I said, best feeling in the world.

The cottage grows eerily quiet, like it's well behaved and not the unruly hellion I've come to know. When the Witch finally opens her eyes, they're glossy and wet.

"Where did you find his recipe?"

"It was buried in a journal. Forgotten. Or hidden away."

The lines on her forehead relax, like she's aged backward with just a bite. "I couldn't touch his things after he . . ." She pushes her bowl away. "I should curse you double for rifling through my business."

That's when I lose it.

My chair skids back as I stand, slamming my hands on the table. Frenetic static buzzes in my veins. The bowls of stew begin to mold right in front of us. Once the color of a perfectly browned Thanksgiving turkey, the gravy festers gray then blue with spots and chartreuse fuzz.

Decayed.

My outburst of magic is an accident, but one with pristine timing.

"That recipe is right. I chose *right.* If you don't honor your side of our deal, I'll rot that Midnight Bloom to dust."

The Warlock gives me a heavily disapproving look through his pallid complexion. Harming plants wasn't part of the plan.

The Witch is trembling. "Why would I care about that silly flower?"

"Because your husband was the gardener," he says. "He grew the Midnight Bloom for you and it's the only thing that's lived as long as you have. I'm guessing the garden began dying when your husband did, and the decay is catching up with you."

Her wrinkled lips squirm, as if the words want to fight their way out. "His plants were his children. I tried—I wanted to keep them alive, but I never had his green thumb."

She takes a heavy breath, her voice turning to steel.

"But then *you* asked for the impossible. I can't bend the rules of time so you can rewrite mistakes. Instead, I granted you what I could, and taught you a lesson about what I couldn't."

"But you've already bent the rules," I say, trying to leash some of this fury. "Lazlo is the Warlock, just a younger version. And you conjured him out of thin air."

If anything, Lazlo has felt more real than Warlock Knight at times. The Holler remembers Lazlo. Folks who visit the Manor recognize him. But the Warlock?

A theory itches at me, the tiniest mosquito bite begging to be scratched. Our neighbors aren't just bad at remembering the Warlock. *Written over. Erased.* But *why*? Why is the gap in their memories a canyon? Someone can't be real and a ghost at the same time.

Just like no Witch can make a boy out of nothing.

Life and death, past and present, that's the nature of our magic.

Past and present.

That's it. Why I could never read Lazlo's memories. He's not missing them.

He is one.

"Lazlo is a memory," I realize. "The Holler's memory of the Warlock."

He isn't a boy from nowhere. He's a thought, a feeling, a figment. Real, but not anymore. A *back then*, not a *here and now*.

I turn to the Warlock. "That's why—well, why *everything.* Why your health is tied to Lazlo's, why you're fading just like him. He belongs here, just not . . . now. He—the town's memory of you—isn't in the right time. Which means there's no *you* in the past to grow up into *you* now. So you're fading from the Holler's memory. Right in front of our eyes."

The Witch smiles. "Very good, little Farewitch."

Bless his heart, the Warlock doesn't have enough energy to look surprised. "I see."

He shakes his head. "You brought him here, then gave him only a year to live, unless I cured him of his wasting illness. But if I had managed to find the right cure, and he grew healthy and stayed here, it wouldn't have mattered. The memory of me would still be absent from the past. I'd be fading away here. Gone."

"That sounds about right."

His shoulders straighten with the barest breath of strength. "So there was never a choice. You've—I've—been wasting Honey's time. Does *that* sound right?"

The Witch tilts her head at me. "Do you feel your time has been wasted, child?"

"No," I say, without needing to think about it. "No, I don't."

The Warlock's hard gaze meets mine but he says nothing.

"I admit, I feel as if I should reward the girl for figuring it out, and I do owe you for the burgoo," the Witch says. "So I'll offer you a new deal, Knight. It is almost your birthday, after all. I will let the boy stay here, cured and perfectly healthy, but you have to take his place to balance out the discrepancy."

"Or?"

"Or I can help you send the boy back to his place in time, before the solstice. You get to stay here, because he's grounded once more in the past, where the memory of you belongs."

"But either way, I lose him," he says through gritted teeth.

"In a sense, yes. But don't we all have to lose ourselves a little over time? That's life."

More silence.

He can't seriously be considering her offer, can he? He is. He's thinking about it. *Don't make the same mistake again!* I want to scream. It's the clear path in my head. But maybe it's not so clear in his how he can learn to live with himself as he is.

At last, the Warlock gives me one last glance and faces the Widow Witch. He attempts a deep breath, but his chest barely moves. "You're right, Okolona. I can't undo my mistakes anymore." The low grit in his voice has lost some of its edge. "But I can make a better choice now. I've already started. It will take time and care, but I'm going to save your garden."

The Witch actually stutters. "Impossible. Your magic is gone, whatever help it gave your own plants—gone."

He nods. "I'm doing it by hand. Small steps, first. Some seeds, warm-season plants and vegetables that will start strong. I'll help refresh the soil, feed the land what it's missing. You won't see the benefit for a while. It's the slow way. But the time is worth it."

"It's *old*. There's no life left in it to bring back."

"You'd be surprised how well an old thing can live if it gets a second chance."

I'm awestruck. Proud.

"This wasn't a part of your Farewitch's bargain, Knight," she sneers. "How does this benefit you?"

He manages a shrug. "Consider it a kindness, no price. I'll show you how to maintain it, and we'll work together when I visit. One season to the next. Those hounds shouldn't be your only source of conversation."

"No price?"

"One price," I jump in. He might give away his effort for free, but not me. "On top of helping my mom and removing his curse, you have to stop terrorizing the Holler every spring. Or any season," I add for good measure. "No more stealing folks, bad ones or not."

What feels like an hour passes even though I know it's just a few brief, crucial seconds. At last, she heaves a great sigh.

"All right, children. Agreed."

My chest swells but I'm not sure I'm breathing, and my hands start to shake. I want to cry. Or laugh. Grab the Warlock and kiss him. Again. We did it.

"First of all, your"—the Witch glances at the Warlock's fading skin, which has stretched from his fingers up along his wrists now—"*corporeal* predicament is because of the spell I used to bring the boy here. It's not a curse. So you'll need my spellwork to undo it."

I slump back down in my seat. "*What?*"

She waves a hand at me, like she knows I'm about to raise hell. "Don't insult me, children. I leave curse magic for other Witches. My magic is neither that simple nor fragile enough to break." She sniffs. "Curses always start to smell, anyway."

Somehow, the Warlock looks even more sickly. "Stop with the riddles, Okolona."

"My spell simply created an imbalance, and there's no cure for that except *balance*. The boy must go back to where he came from."

The Warlock shakes his head. "Why in God's name are you only telling me this now?"

She gives him a warning glance. "Why indeed?"

"Because this wouldn't be hard to do a year ago," I say. Now, the boy is more than just a figment or an idea. He's become the Warlock's heart and soul. He's *Lazlo*.

The Witch nods. "After spending a year raising that boy, giving him up is not easy, is it? Your parents failed to respect the consequences of their choice. I want you to understand what you risk losing if you abuse magic. It's as you said. The second chance you want can only come from making a better choice than they did."

With surprising swiftness, she shuffles to a breadbox on the counter and returns with a slip of paper.

"You'll have to complete the reversal spell yourselves, alongside the boy. Do it before the sun sets on your birthday, Knight, and you'll see your next sunrise."

"Will my power return then?" he asks.

"If you want it to, it will," she hums. "Probably."

Helpful.

"And how am I to perform this spell without any magic?" he retorts, but his usual pessimism doesn't have any bite, the words slurring. I frown with concern.

"You don't." She hands over the spell—to me. "She does. This is a memory spell. It will find an errant soul and send it home. That boy is no more than a memory that needs to go home."

My frown deepens. "I don't understand. Incantations aren't the kind of magic I do. I only see memories with food."

She snorts. "And this spell needs someone with memory magic to recite it. It will work."

"I'm just a Farewitch," I protest. A pretty good one, I've realized, but surely there's someone with more power, better suited for this job.

"Perhaps, child. But you're the *right* Farewitch."

After hesitating, I take the spell, the paper like a little white flag in my hands.

"However," the Witch adds, "I can't reverse what is happening to your mother."

The ice in the corners of the cottage creeps in, dampening the already moldy space. My body tenses, like I'm freezing all over again as I wait for her to go on.

"What took your grandmother, now your mother—it's no spell or curse. All of us Witches must pay something for our magic, and your family seems to pay with your health. Your best chance at helping her is with one of your recipes. My advice for you is the same: Learn from her mistake before it's too late for you."

For a brief moment, I drift outside my body, watch myself nod. I'm not surprised, though it still doesn't hurt any less.

The Warlock places an invisible hand over mine. Squeezes with the gentle fingers of someone who handles the most delicate of tiny blooms. The only thing that keeps me from falling apart right here is the void of air where his forearm should be. He's fading faster.

Outside, the hounds begin to howl.

The Witch looks to the window. "If you two are going to make it before tomorrow evening, you best get. Now. Don't you dare ask me for a portal, Knight. Your tab is closed."

"And if we don't make it?"

"Then the world has one less grumpy old man."

Said man lets out an indignant huff that's closer to a growl.

I'm already in motion, packing our things. The task keeps me from thinking too hard about everything I stand to lose. But before I leave, I need to know.

"Why did you start disappearing spouses in the first place?" I ask as I tuck her spell safely into my pack. Her own great-granddaughter's husband, too.

Feral delight sparks in her eyes. "I don't go after partners, child. I go after people who ask me to grant them their desires and then refuse to pay the cost for them. The husbands you see disappearing are just men who have made poor deals with me. Though, bad husbands don't just go away, and divorce was shunned in my time. Those nasty natural causes—men are so terrible at aging, aren't they . . ."

"Where did they all go?" I sputter. *What did you do with them?*

"Oh, they'll find their way back eventually. Maybe." She shrugs. "These days, it's enough for me to just threaten the rotten ones. They run off on their own."

"Then why let folks make all the awful rumors about you?"

"As life gets hard, folks want scapegoats. Bad choices, bad crops, bad kids? Must be bad magic. Blame the other, the different, the unexplainable. In this Holler, the misunderstood often turns into the legend. And the villain. It's easier for folks to have someone to hate, child. Brings them together. Why not the old Witch they already distrust?"

The Warlock frowns. "You're only feeding their fear, then, Okolona."

"And you have family here. Gertha—" I protest.

"Oh, Gertie doesn't want anything to do with me."

"So—did you really kill her husband?"

"Heavens no. He was stepping out on her. She turned such a

blind eye, she couldn't see what she was worth. So I threatened him. Leave town or become one of my hounds. Gertie never forgave me."

I'm starting to like the Widow Witch. Just a little.

Soon, we're ready to leave. I'm carrying most of our gear because the Warlock needs to focus on staying upright. How we're going to make it through those caves and back to the Manor in time, I have no idea. But we have to try.

"Your burgoo needs salt," the old bat says instead of goodbye.

"No it doesn't," I say over my shoulder as we leave. The hounds watch us go with soulful eyes and some howling.

Just before we're out of earshot, the Warlock turns one last time to the Witch. "I apologize, Okolona. For what it's worth. I should not have assumed you were solely responsible for what happened to my parents."

"Neither are you, boy," she calls from her porch. "My problem was with your folks, not you. But if you're ever going to forgive yourself, you have to forgive them, and you can't do that until you understand people make bad decisions even if they're not bad people."

Chapter Thirty-Six
TUESDAY, JUNE 21

THE SUMMER SOLSTICE

Honey's Helpful Hint, from
Honey Frost's Southern Cookbook
for Recipes Gone Wrong:

There is always a cost to magic.

We reach Knight Manor just as the sun begins to sink on the solstice.

I launch out of my Dodge at the same time I throw the thing into park. The Warlock is considerably less graceful with his slide-fall combo from the passenger seat. I haul ass to his side to help him into the farmhouse, and he doesn't even protest at my quip about his rheumatic joints. When I throw his arm over my shoulder for support, I don't get any whiff of thyme.

This is *bad* bad.

After the cave pools led us back to the pickup, I floored it home in a trance, my mind fixated on reciting the Widow Witch's instructions.

Governess Zeen is waiting for us at the front door. "He's almost gone, sir," she says by way of greeting, then swallows a sharp breath when she sees the Warlock.

I don't blame her. Because so is the Warlock.

In the waning summer sunlight, his skin is so translucent, phyllo dough won't be appetizing for a long time. His hazel eyes have gone milky, like the broth of some expired can of soup. With our height difference, he's leaning sideways into me like the world's saddest cake. Appropriate for what might be the world's saddest birthday. The formidable and feared Warlock of Foxe Holler, this man is not.

Ms. Zeen hurries us inside. "He's been asking for you."

Those few words wrench the Warlock's face into a devastating frown.

Still sweaty and dirt caked, we stumble behind Ms. Zeen to the kitchen.

Folks are already waiting for us there. Not just people. Friends.

Arna Jean has her head on her brother's shoulder, and next to Rett is Silas, hands deep in his suit pockets like he isn't sure what to do with them. Even old Beulah Buchanan is here, nursing something amber at the kitchen table. The burnt smell of old coffee hangs on the air, and no one looks like they've slept since we left.

When they spot me and the Warlock's half-faded upper body, they droop like wilting plants. We stumble over to where they're gathered around a fluffy lump of fur by the island.

Beauregard yips his hello. And snuggled up with him on the floor, his back leaning against the island, is Lazlo.

My eyes prick at the sight of him, and the Warlock flinches against me.

Disappearing skin now crawls up Lazlo's neck and above his socks, and his little hands are gone. His unfocused eyes brighten as we come closer, but he doesn't move to get up.

Jesus. I'm not ready for this. But there's no *getting ready* for something like this. Lazlo doesn't belong with us. He needs to go home, *now*.

Wincing, the Warlock kneels next to the boy. "Comfortable?"

Lazlo nods, his head nestled against the poodle like his neck is too tired.

"Did you bring me anything from your trip?" Lazlo asks.

"Of course," the Warlock scoffs. "Cave crystals." With an invisible hand, he brushes a strand of hair from Lazlo's pale forehead, but it looks like a breeze just whipped by.

"You're disappearing, like me," Lazlo says with a shuddery breath.

Everyone in the room goes rigid.

I've been operating on sheer muscle memory since we left the Witch's cottage, my mind too busy counting the hours, the minutes, we have left. So it's only now I let myself think the worst: What if the Witch's spell doesn't work? What if she lied to us?

"I don't feel good today," Lazlo says. "Beau can tell, too. He won't eat his treats."

The Warlock's clenched jaw releases. "Ms. Frost and I are going to help with that."

The boy's eyelids flutter. "I wanted to bake you a birthday cake but Ms. Zeen wouldn't let me."

"I *believe* I said you should rest," the Governess says. "I don't get paid enough to supervise that."

My palms smart under the pressure of my fingernails. I'm not sure what's worse, seeing my mom in the hospital or *this*.

An abrupt banging echoes from the front of the Manor.

Arna Jean shifts to the windows facing the porch. "Oris Webb again," she groans, and tosses up a middle finger through the glass. The banging escalates.

Rett joins his sister at the window. "And half his congregation this time."

Some impressive swearing runs through my head. Webb promised he'd get enough folks to believe the Warlock is a threat to the Holler as long as the Widow Witch's target is on his back. A part of me didn't think he'd actually follow through on his plan to try to pitchfork the Warlock right out of the Holler.

Shouts carry in from outside, like Webb is now giving an impromptu sermon right on the front porch. "No Eldercraft as far as we can tell," the Bookwitch adds.

"Yet," the Warlock says.

Ms. Zeen gives me a dry look. "Glad to see you're back in one piece. Did the Widow Witch agree to help?"

"She gave us a spell to right things for Lazlo. We have to perform it now, before the solstice ends." I share a glance with the Warlock. We can explain the rest later. There's no time.

Arna Jean and Rett join us at the island again as the banging knocks turn into outright pounding. I begin to doubt the strength of the old farmhouse door. Beauregard unleashes a deluge of barking.

"The Manor has wards, right?" Silas asks over the noise.

It should. Even if the house was going haywire the last few weeks as the Warlock was losing his power and control over his magic.

That's when it strikes me—why the house feels off. It's *not* throwing a fit for once. No jumpy floorboards, no humming faucets, no sounds of tinkering from otherwise empty rooms.

The house isn't calm. It's just . . . empty.

My chest tightens. An empty Manor is scarier than anything I've seen here yet.

"Sir," I breathe, pointing outside. "The sun."

Soft light now slants through the back windows, the kitchen turning a dusky lavender. Magic can do a lot, but it can't stop the sun from setting. It's almost gone.

We have to make this spell work. Now or never.

The Warlock's eyes squeeze shut, just before fresh determination sweeps across his features. "Lazlo, can you be brave, for an adventure?"

At first, the boy looks confused, but then a bright curiosity peeks through the uncertainty. He squeezes Beauregard, kisses his muzzle.

Arna Jean swipes a finger under her glasses.

I pull the Widow Witch's spell from my pack and kneel down next to the Warlock. Like it's the thinnest, most delicate pizza dough, I fold the spell into a tiny square and hand it to Lazlo. "I want you to keep this pressed to your chest, right against your heart. Hold it with both hands."

He follows my instructions.

The spell the Witch gave us isn't a verbal incantation, praise be. I was always crap at learning the old Witches' tongues, even with Momaw Frost's lessons. I wish I'd treasured that time with her a little more. The small moments, the small hopes, grant the biggest magic.

But for this spell, I just need to call on the power I already have.

"May I?" I ask Lazlo, holding up my hands. When he nods, I cup his small cheeks. Skin to skin. "Lazlo, I want you to try to picture where you came from. I know it's hard; just try and find the last memory you have of home, of your parents. Who you were before us."

Show us where the Widow Witch found you.

That's all it takes. The spell, my memory magic, and a dash of Lazlo's homesickness.

The memories, blank before now, awaken and begin to stumble toward me as if learning to walk. His eyelids flutter as the images come faster, sprinting. I only catch brief glimpses of those with food. Slowly, understanding and awe replace the confusion and curiosity on his face.

"I can remember things," the boy murmurs. "But not everything—I can't . . ." His chin dimples, unshed tears pooling in his hazel eyes. "I want my mom and dad. *I want to go home.*"

The words are like a wish.

The paper in his faded hands sparks and burns up in a gentle, quick flame. There and gone, the lifespan of a match.

Moving back, I avoid looking at the Warlock. I'll see his heart breaking, and then mine will shatter right along with it. But still, I catch a glimpse of the skin at his collarbone disappearing, over his heart, and I can hear his shaky breaths growing further and further apart.

This spell needs to work. Fast. I can't lose him twice.

Suddenly, a furious wind blows open the kitchen windows. A wave of June air hits us, the smell of a hundred shades of the color green. In seconds, Lazlo's entire body is no more than a wispy outline of himself. Physical, but barely. Beauregard licks at the boy's clothes where his scent lingers.

Then, in the corner of the kitchen, two other translucent figures appear.

The taller of the two is a broad-shouldered man. The physique of a farmer. His arm encircles the waist of the other, a short woman with the Warlock's cheekbones.

Mr. and Ms. Knight.

The Warlock and I get to our feet with Lazlo. The couple remain patiently still, faces drawn taut with anticipation. Like they're eager for the return of something long missed.

"Don't forget to play with Beau," Lazlo says to us. "I mean it."

The Warlock leans down and presses his forehead to where the boy's should be. "I won't. Be good. Especially to your parents."

My turn. For all my fear the Warlock wouldn't be able to make the right choices to save himself, here I am, holding us up. I came here to cure him at all costs . . .

I just didn't expect the price to be so high.

How in the world will this house ever feel the same?

It won't. That's the answer. The Apothakery never felt the same after Momaw died, and it won't if my mom is gone. But that doesn't mean a place can't still feel alive. It doesn't mean the farmhouse can't still feel like home. Finally, I understand why the Warlock wished to go back, to make a second chance worthwhile. He was looking for a home. The last one he really knew.

I kneel in front of Lazlo. "Remember what I told you."

"Goldfish aren't a food group."

"And?"

"And I should make friends."

"Good man. I'll miss you."

"You weren't so bad." His smile is going to be the thing that sends me to tears, I know it.

"I'll see you soon, yeah? I'm your neighbor. Don't forget."

"I won't. Promise."

"And happy birthday to you, too. Goodbye, Mr. Knight."

The boy perks up, hearing his name. As if he only just remembered it belongs to *him*.

My friends in the room make various noises of surprise as they begin to understand.

It was never a question of finding Lazlo's cure.

It was a matter of finding his home.

Lazlo gives the Warlock one last hug and then approaches the waiting couple. The Warlock's parents. *His* parents, too.

They open their arms, smiling. He takes his place between them, the shimmering outline of his form blending with theirs. No longer just Lazlo, but Mr. and Ms. Knight and their son.

Not ghosts or spirits. Memories.

Versions of themselves from when they lived at the Manor, years ago, thumbprints on the surface of time. More echoes or reflections than the true originals. But that doesn't make them any less real. The Widow Witch helped me dust off these last heirlooms of truth.

Unsteady, the Warlock—*my* Warlock, with the gray temples—takes a cautious step toward the memories of his parents.

Margaret Cho Knight reaches for her son, her translucent hand palm up. But the hope on her face isn't intangible. It's as lucent as Lazlo is all the time. And that raw emotion makes me wonder—are there arguments my mom and I should have now, regrets we need to settle in the days she has left? How do we forgive someone who's long gone before their mistakes are?

No. Going backward will only turn what time I do have left with her into a deep well of only potential memories, instead of lived ones. What good is a second chance if we don't learn anything from the first one?

The Warlock takes the tenuous hand of his mother's memory.

She mouths something in a language I don't catch. But I can guess. *I'm sorry.*

"I know. Thank you." He says something else, in what might be Cantonese.

Ms. Knight whispers back to her son, glancing at me as she does. He nods, and an entire conversation happens between them in just a sentence or two. Then the Knights vanish in a gust of wind and glimmering, fractured light.

No one in the kitchen speaks. Beauregard doesn't even bark.

The Warlock stands alone, but very much *here*.

His extremities slowly become visible again, and his body flushes with the normal color of his only mildly pale skin. I think I see his sun spots sprout back onto his flushed cheeks.

Just then, a frantic commotion from the front of the Manor echoes down the halls all the way to the kitchen, and the indistinct shouting we heard outside turns cacophonous. With the Manor void of the Warlock's usual power, and with no wards, the house can't keep the outside world *out* any longer. The front door must have finally given up.

The Warlock comes to the same conclusion. He takes off toward the noise, a renewed energy in his step. Furious energy. The rest of us follow, and we crowd into the foyer at the same time Oris Webb and his cavalcade of followers ooze through the front door.

There aren't nearly as many as I expect. I spot some of the same angry folks who stop to listen to Webb's preaching in the town square. They're hard to ignore, but not because they're a big group by any means. They're usually just the loudest folks, noisy with nothing to say.

The mob quiets in a collective shush when Governess Zeen steps forward. "Gentlemen, we *have* a doorbell, you know," she says, hands clasped primly behind her back. "May we help you with something?"

"This need not concern you, Letha." The preacher looks around, like he can sense the magic on the air. Like he's *hungry*. "The time I graciously gave Mr. Knight is at an end, and we are here to uphold our promise to rid the Holler of dangerous magic."

Murmurs of agreement sound behind him, worried looks darting left and right.

The Warlock stalks forward and lets his voice carry, strong and sure, through his home. "We will belabor the point one last time, Mr. Webb. Magic is neither inherently bad nor good. Just like people, whether your neighbors are Witches or Warlocks or something in between."

"Tell that to the Widow Witch!" shouts a man from the back.

"No, tell that to the Holler's *widows*," cries another.

The Warlock looks out over the crowd, no longer addressing only Webb. "I make no excuses for my past negligence, but I promise you, I will not remain a passive bystander. Farewitch Frost and I have ensured the Widow Witch will no longer torment Foxe Holler. Not in spring, not in any season."

Curious murmuring bounces throughout the room, a white noise of delicate optimism. The mood in the foyer shifts, just a degree, but as any Farewitch will say, a single degree can make a lot of difference.

The only person who doesn't look relieved is Oris Webb.

His pale eyes narrow at us, his lips pressed tight. "And why should the good people of Foxe Holler trust *you*?" he asks. "What assurances do these folks without magic have that they're safe? What if the Widow Witch changes her mind? She's a *Witch*, after all. Who will protect the Holler from *you*, Mr. Knight?"

The Warlock levels his commanding attention on the pastor once more. "Witches will. As they have always done. The Holler never needs to fear them. You, on the other hand—I would recommend extreme caution."

His words puncture the quiet of the room, a sharp-edged cut right through the tension. The whispering escalates. I don't think Mr. Knight realizes how . . . spicy his statement is. Well, *in for a penne,* Momaw Frost would say.

"But what have you done for the town, Mr. Knight? For these people, for our mayor? Or done with her, I should say," Webb croons, turning to me. "Where *is* your mother, Miss Frost?"

He clasps his hands like he's about to pray, but I can see the whites of his knuckles, the tension underneath the milky froth of his false fervor. This isn't faith. This is desperation.

"That's enough." The Warlock's command reverberates like we're in a bell tower. For a moment, he truly does seem centuries old, a force from well before my time. A true match for the Widow Witch, capable of spinning tornadoes across the earth like a children's spinning top.

At this, Webb turns to the crowd at his heels, the foyer his altar.

"When Warlocks and Witches quarrel, those of us without magic are caught in the middle. *We* suffer the devastating loss. How can we protect our youngest in a community where our neighbors attract danger? Our church, an invaluable community center, is gone. What's next?" His preacher's voice carries easily over the nervous murmuring. "Magic is unnecessary at best and fatal at worst. It is a plague of extremes. As children of the Lord, we must not choose the lesser evil, but rather, no evil at all—"

Abruptly, he stops, his mouth still open. His eyes widen at something beyond the crowd. His followers turn as one, and I pop onto my tiptoes to see over their heads.

A figure stands in the threshold of the Manor's open front door. This time, she arrives quietly, but a storm just the same.

The Widow Witch peers out at the faces of Foxe Holler. "Hello, children."

The men in Webb's crowd take a collective step back.

My hands can't decide to be clammy or not. Half of me prefers her over Webb, and the other half wonders if she followed us all the way here or used one of her portals to get here faster. Either way, I feel like she's using us for entertainment.

Formidable in her dark cloak, she has no trouble commanding the attention of the room, even though she's half the height of any of the men. Her sharp eyes spear Webb over the heads of his congregation.

"Oris Webb," she sneers. "Couldn't get the Eldercraft to pay a visit and interrogate Warlock Knight? Or is that perhaps because you didn't contact them in the first place, lest they pay attention to *you*?"

Pastor Webb finally closes his mouth but looks no less dumbstruck.

The Witch doesn't give him time to answer. "You'll be interested to know, Oris Webb, that after years and years of silence, my kin chose this afternoon to seek my help and advice. Her beloved church had been destroyed. While I believe she'd like revenge, for now, I think she'd settle knowing the same fate did not befall another center of the community."

Gertha Fudge. My eyes dart around, but I don't see her in the crowd in her normal place right behind Webb. Interesting. Fudge went to her ancestor about the tornado?

Just then, I remember: We never did find the Witch's scorches in the ground by the barn. And I never understood why she sent a tornado careening through the middle of town, and the church. Not just Webb's domain, but the home base for the folks in town who distrust magic so much, they'll do anything to rid the Holler of it forever.

Only a powerful Witch or Warlock could've conjured that tornado. Or—

Someone truly rotten. The answer hits me right between the shoulder blades.

"*You*," I blurt into the stillness, looking at Webb. "You sent that tornado through town." I can't believe I didn't see it before. "You're a Warlock."

The chorus of shock and alarmed muttering has a rhythm even the church ladies would be proud of. Somewhere behind me, Beulah Buchanan cackles.

Webb huffs in my direction. "Excuse me, Miss Frost? That is a bold claim for a simple Farewitch who is well in over her head."

He's right. The folks here have no reason to believe me, especially if they're already here on behalf of the pastor.

But the Widow Witch—they'll believe her. Because they're afraid of her.

And she knows it. A scar of a frown emerges from deep within the Witch's face.

"Hush yourself, Webb. *Shame on you*, using the magic I granted you with abandon. How far did you think you would get, coveting power like this? What did you reckon would happen once your followers realized you didn't hate magic, you just wanted to control it? To be the only soul with it."

This time, he doesn't deny her, doesn't say a single word in protest.

For the first time since I've known the man, Webb actually looks afraid.

Suddenly, the crowd pushes toward the door, leaving the pastor standing alone. I realize it has less to do with the man's betrayal and more to do with the incensed Warlock currently closing the remaining distance between himself and Webb.

Now I understand how the Holler could believe the Warlock s'mored an entire library.

The Warlock halts in front of Webb. When he speaks, his anger is a low rumble in his chest. "That tornado put people I care about in danger."

For once, Webb's cheeks aren't pale, but a pasty red, flushed with guilt. "Lest you forget the sins on your conscience, I wasn't the one who burned the library. Faith forgives, but Foxe Holler does not."

"I have a library," the Warlock says, looking out to the crowd. "A house, too, with dozens of empty rooms. Anytime the town is in need of a community space, Knight Manor is open. Everyone is welcome. And I mean *everyone*."

I do a legitimate double take. Even Ms. Zeen is looking at Mr. Knight like he's had one too many slices of Gertha Fudge's rum cake. *What in the world is he doing?*

Webb barks a laugh. "You're assuming your neighbors would want to take their lives into their own hands in such a way."

Governess Zeen raises a delicate hand. "I would."

A chorus of agreement rings out behind me.

Ms. Buchanan sidles up to Webb, Beauregard on her heels. "Go home, Oris."

Before Webb can respond, a sharp eruption of light envelopes the foyer.

The Warlock's figure flushes with a glow the exact green of his gardens. The color in his cheeks returns, and when his eyes find mine, the hazel is bright and healthy again.

My tongue tastes that wonderful earthy bite of thyme as his magic returns.

The air hums with the force of his power as he studies his hands. "That's better." Then he looks back to the pastor. "It's time you leave, Mr. Webb. After all, if the Eldercraft visit Foxe Holler, they're looking for a dangerous Warlock, are they not?"

Webb opens his mouth to respond but quickly shuts it again. He turns in a flustered shuffle and pushes his way through the crowd.

Quickly, the Widow Witch blocks his path. He tries to backpedal but runs right into Silas, Arna Jean, Rett, and me.

"Knight is correct," the Witch says. "In fact, they're quite interested in how you've been spending your time, Webb. I promised I'd do them the favor of delivering you. Come with me—though, you don't really have a choice, do you?"

She holds up a bony hand, ready to snap, and gives the Warlock one last glance.

"Oh, my kinfolk sends her regards."

Then, in a supernova of blinding wind, the Widow Witch winks out of existence—dragging Oris Webb with her.

Chapter Thirty-Seven

WEDNESDAY, JUNE 22

Honey's Helpful Hint, from
Honey Frost's Southern Cookbook for Recipes Gone Wrong:

If a recipe goes wrong, embrace it and eat the surprise. If a recipe goes really wrong, start over and learn. If a recipe goes disastrously and irreversibly wrong, now you have a story to share, and that's where the meal begins.

The last of my cast-iron skillets clang as I deposit them into the bed of my truck.

The morning sun tickles my cheeks as a summer breeze blows my bangs into disarray. It's the day after the summer solstice, I have a Spam, egg, and cheese on a biscuit for the drive ahead, and I feel good.

For a moment.

A bedraggled Warlock stomps down the Manor's front steps, scrutinizing my loaded truck with extreme distaste.

"I get one full night of sleep, and a million things happen without me." He plants himself in front of me, his black hair wildly disheveled, like some burnt baked Alaska monstrosity. "Why the devil are we outside at the crack of dawn?"

"Sir, it's eleven."

"Are you sure?"

"Everyone's already left. You missed the succotash scramble."

Silas, the Claywells, even Ms. Buchanan and Beauregard stayed the night in guest rooms, no one eager to return to town. Seems they bonded while we were gone.

"Everyone? I allow overnight guests *one* time, and now we're a hotel . . ." He spots my suitcase in my pickup. His voice drops, rough. "You're leaving."

"That's what happens when I finish a job. Sir."

"For the love of—I forbid you from ever calling me *sir* again."

"You *forbid* me?"

"If the job is done, then our contract is over and I'm no longer your employer."

"Then you aren't allowed to call me *Ms. Frost* anymore."

"Fine."

"Good."

His frown falters. "I—impressive work last night. With Okolona's spell. I wouldn't be here without it, and neither would my magic."

Sure enough, the smell of thyme floats between us. It's bittersweet today. The house is behaving again. Well, as much as it ever behaved. It's certainly not empty the way it felt yesterday, now that its Warlock is himself again. The man is surprisingly sure-footed this morning given he was feverish with fatigue all night as his body adjusted to the magic it was missing for weeks. He refused any help upstairs, and there was a lot of mumbled swearing, and *It's my birthday, I shall not be handled like an unruly toddler, Ms. Frost—*

I'll cling to that rare image of a flustered Warlock whenever I need a mood boost. Like now. The part I've been dreading.

"Any word about Oris Webb?" I ask, delaying the next bit.

"No, but it's been less than a day, and the Eldercraft are usually quite occupied around the solstice. All I've gleaned is, apparently this isn't the first time they've dealt with him. I was so accustomed to being the only Warlock here, it didn't occur to me there could be another."

"So he *is* a Warlock."

"Not as powerful a one as he would've liked to be, it seems."

"Why would he hide that? For so long?"

But this is Foxe Holler, after all. Like the Widow Witch said, Webb didn't hate magic; he just wanted to control its influence. His behavior over the last couple months makes sense now: Demonize magic, remove those with it from the Holler, and then he'd be the only one left with any. If his congregation found out he had magic himself . . . The town has its problems, but hates a high-horse hypocrite.

The Warlock sighs. "Let the Widow Witch and the Eldercraft fight over him. As long as it's not me."

In the quiet wake of the commotion last night, I only realized it when everyone was gone—none of the townsfolk asked what happened to the little boy living at the Manor. Or even mentioned Lazlo. Ms. Zeen and I remember him, but that's it. Almost like someone dug out a small seed of a memory with a powerfully precise spade of magic just for us, so we didn't have to lose everything about the boy.

My heart clenches, but I remind myself this is a good thing. Lazlo is back where he belongs, and even if the town has forgotten he was ever here, soon they'll start remembering their Warlock more and more.

"Now you can add *dodged the Eldercraft* to your résumé," I say.

"You assume it's not on there already." The smirk he gives me falters as his gaze shifts to my suitcase. "Thank you for making Lazlo's time here special. For . . . seeing him."

"Well, my Farewitch affinity is memory magic. I don't lose memories, I find them."

Lord, I need to leave before my voice starts shaking. But I can't seem to get my backside in the truck. There's one thing I keep thinking about.

"Why did the Witch send you *that* memory of yourself? Why not you at sixteen, when your parents—when everything changed?"

He runs a hand through his hair, making the couch-head worse. "Me at nine, ten—those were purely happy memories. It was before my magic manifested, when I only had to be a child. I was a demon as a teenager. Power, but no control. I can't tell you how often I blew up the gardens, or the number of rooms that needed renovating. Okolona wasn't wrong. I incurred too many costs without paying anything back, and I needed a mentor."

A teenage Warlock terrorizing the Manor, the whole Holler? I can picture it.

"Should we be worried we did any irreparable damage to your past?" I ask.

"I'm simply going to choose to believe that the memory of me, the boy we got to know, he was just one chapter of Knight history, already finished a long time ago."

In other words, it can't be rewritten and change the here and now.

"And in my experience, it's best to leave questions of time to Hedgewitches and the Eldercraft. I think they actually have a bureau for that. Though they have a bureau for everything—not important." A fresh scowl leaks into his expression. "So are you? Leaving?"

My nerves flutter. *Why is this so hard?* "You've lived to see another birthday; your debts are balanced. *We won.* So yes, my job is complete. This one, at least."

That just leaves my mom. If it's not too late to save her.

His glower smooths over. "We can keep looking in the library. There could be something we missed."

My silly heart leaps at that sneaky *we*. If the Warlock's archives didn't reveal an answer, does the right recipe even exist? I don't know. But I won't stop looking. All my time, energy, and ovens belong to Marigold Frost, and I'm due back at her bedside.

I shake my head, and it's the nail in my heart-shaped coffin. "Back to the cutting board, as the Frosts say. I've been away from the Apothakery long enough."

I'm nowhere near ready for the heat in his eyes. The misery. Hunger. "This is our goodbye, then?"

This is *exactly* why I wanted to slip out before he woke up. Now my stupid eyes are stinging, probably from the stupid pollen and stupid allergies. At the Apothakery, a Farewitch knows everyone only well enough to say hello, and so the goodbyes never hurt.

"We live in the same town. I'm not going off to war." The laugh I hope comes through isn't there. "And I can't stay forever." I try hard, *really* hard, to smile. But it won't come.

A part of me wants him to contradict me, the fantasy at my fingertips. *Why not?* he would offer. If he did, what would I say?

He only crosses his arms. "I never fired you."

"Then I quit. Keep your severance."

"You've been in my pantry. You've seen too much for me to let you leave."

"Sir."

"Ms. Frost."

"*Mr. Knight.*"

"*Honey.*"

It's not often I find things I'm attracted to more than the smell of baking bread, but I'm losing that battle now. Losing it bad. My core buzzes with the memory of his mouth on me, his hands under my thighs—

I lean back against my pickup, trying to escape his thyme smell. It's stronger now. As if *he's* stronger, but not just as a Warlock. Happier? Does the Warlock *do* happy?

"I have the best shot if I'm working in my own kitchen, on my own stove." A shitty stove compared with his. But I don't say that. "There's no reason for me to stay."

His mouth purses. "No, I suppose there isn't."

My arms itch to surround him, but I don't trust myself to let him go. Everything about this feels sour. Fitting, since my Farewitch magic can rot good things from the inside out. This man's already lost his parents, and Lazlo, who might not have been truly here but who was real in all the ways that mattered. He can't watch me crumble. He can't lose me, too.

Governess Zeen appears and saves me from the intensity of his gaze.

She's carrying a couple of my bags I was about to go back inside for. "What?" she snaps at my flabbergasted look. "You have too much stuff. You'd never leave in time."

And if I don't leave now, I'm really going to cry. "Thank you, Letha."

"We're not that close yet, dear. *Ms. Zeen* is sufficient."

"Right. Sorry." But right before I hop into my pickup, she gives me a stilted hug and I feel like I've earned a rare Girl Scout badge for my apron.

The Warlock remains next to Ms. Zeen, arms crossed and face hard, the Manor a hulking, gloomy shadow behind him. When I looked up at Knight Manor for the first time, I wondered what kind of darkness a humble farmhouse could hide. What secrets. A lot, apparently.

The Dodge hums as I put it in drive. I roll down my window to holler at the Warlock one last time. "Come visit the shop, yeah? Or at least promise me you'll leave the house once in a while."

"I go outside—"

"The *front* yard."

The Warlock's lips twitch. "No promises."

My useless heart shudders. "I . . ." What can I tell him that will change anything? What *wouldn't* change anything? Or everything? "Happy birthday."

Driving away, I watch Ms. Zeen and the Warlock in the crooked rearview mirror until I make a turn and they vanish from view.

Chapter Thirty-Eight

FRIDAY, JULY 1

ONE WEEK LATER

Honey's Helpful Hint, from
Honey Frost's Southern Cookbook for Recipes Gone Wrong:

Like the traditional Southern apple stack cake, there are some recipes best made with other folks, where the magic happens because it happens together.

The Apothakery is hollering.

I sold out of biscuits by nine, apple butter by ten, and cornbread by eleven. There's a rush on our newest menu item, huckleberry sonker icebox cake—fitting for the start of a typical Southern July—and with the holiday weekend coming up and kids out of school, the other favorites today are lemon elderberry turnovers and Fluffernutters.

Since the solstice, the Apothakery's never been busier. It doesn't just open, it *wakes up*.

With Arna Jean officially managing the business side of the shop, I can spend my free hours doubling down on my research to find a cure for my mom. I admit, the noise of bustling customers, coffee percolating—it's a soundtrack I've missed. Just like the hand-chalked signs, Momaw Frost's favorite yellow everywhere I look. And yet.

Something about the shop doesn't fully taste like home anymore.

Even my apartment upstairs feels more like a way station. Less permanent than the room I had at the Manor.

Taking a much-needed deep breath, I shake the farmhouse from my thoughts just as I catch a whiff of perfume under the nutty smell of browned butter and molasses muffins.

Well, look at that. Even the church ladies came back. Through the gossip-scuppernong-vine, word's spread fast that the Widow Witch won't be bothering the town anymore. All week long, customers have given me either a *thank you* or a *real sorry* depending on how well they liked Pastor Webb. *Former* pastor.

As if sensing my thoughts, my phone dings in my back pocket.

kentucky fried coven

Carolina Vázquez
Does anyone know if the new pastor is single

Arna Jean Claywell
no but if you find out will you tell Beulah
she keeps asking me like I would know??
...
honey do you need more yeast from the store

Ms. Marrow
Oh Arna if you're there can you check if they have arsenic?
Sorry, typo. Aspic.

Arna Jean Claywell
that's worse
also RIP to oyster happy hour with Honey

Carolina Vázquez
Does anyone even do oysters in town?
Maybe you can pick up a man for Beulah at the store
Or for Honey :)

A hive of bees takes up immediate residence in my head, and my neck grows warm, itchy. I haven't heard from Warlock Knight in a week. Not a single, drastically formal text message. I can't help but feel silly. With his power back, he's got his own priorities, a million Warlock-y things to do. Deaths to revenge. Ravens to send. Feuds to reignite. Plants to . . . plant.

Signaling to my customers I'll be back in five, I duck into the back.

Alone in the kitchen, I slide down the nearest fridge until my butt hits the floor. The peace and quiet back here isn't helping like I thought it would, and the silence tastes stale. I rub a palm over my chest, like I might be able to restart whatever's short-circuiting in there.

Something in my apron pocket crinkles.

I pull out a square of paper.

The Warlock's letter. With his name. The one I so badly didn't want, that I completely forgot about it. I was so frazzled packing to leave the Manor, did I ever wash this apron?

The man's taunting me still. He knows how nosey I am, how irresistible a folded letter is to me. But if he really wanted me to know something, he'd come tell me himself. Wouldn't he? I lived with the man for three months and he can't text me once. Not that he's great at texting. But still. He's on my mind but I'm not on his?

Maybe I was always just his hired Farewitch. Nothing more.

So I don't want this letter and I definitely don't want to know his name. It's too big a promise, too big a wish to ever come true.

Jumping up, I switch on a burner on the stove and hold the letter inches away, the flame licking at my fingers.

Just burn it.

Although . . . burning a Warlock's handwriting feels like the recipe for creating a curse.

We don't need that.

I flip off the burner and open the letter.

Dear Ms. Frost,

Your first day trespassing in my house, I asked if you could save me. If your healing magic would give me more time on this earth, but ill days. Or if it would give me better days, if numbered ones. You told me the secret to health is time.

I believe you now. You saved me, no matter what happens with the Widow Witch. But I still wish we had more time. With a lifetime of you, I would be better. A better Warlock. A better neighbor. A better friend. A better man. For you. For me.

I am so sorry we didn't have more time.

Regretfully Yours,
Verne Knight
The Warlock of Foxe Holler

My mind shudders, like a faltering heartbeat. Or maybe that erratic thumping *is* my heart, trying to catch up.

His name—*his name*—sounds like a combination of *vine* and *fern*.

It's perfect.

The first tear finds my cheek. I came so close to losing him, and after all that, after we made it to the next sunrise, *I left*. But would I have made a different choice if I read this earlier?

My eyes blur with wet, and before I can hold it in, a half sob contorts my face. I'm dangerously close to completely falling apart right here on the kitchen floor.

No. This wouldn't have made a difference. Not when I'm responsible for everyone else's happy endings first. That's the curse of a Farewitch.

Somehow, my brain is functional, and I gather myself. My heart? Who knows.

I stuff the Warlock's letter into my apron and head back to the front counter just as the shop door dings. Another customer.

A *new* customer.

I go still as Warlock Knight approaches the counter.

Alert hazel eyes. A soil-free Henley. He looks good. Too good. Ms. Zeen is with him, standing off to the side. When the shop grows oddly quiet, I hardly notice, and stay protected behind the display cases. My heart isn't going to be able to handle this. Handle *him*.

"How can I help you?" I squeeze out when he reaches the counter.

"I've been told the biscuits here are decent."

Heavens above and devil below, I've missed the low rumble of his voice. Warm and deep as the sun on the summer solstice.

"They're better than decent. They're stellar." I start bagging a few, hoping the task will distract me enough to keep my voice even.

"I'll take a dozen. How much?"

"How much do you have?"

"Do you accept apologies?"

All right, I admit it. I've missed all of him. I suspect my eyes would find even the mere shape of his shadow in a parade. "Those are a bit weak to the dollar right now."

He swallows. Twice. "I knew if I saw you, or even texted you, I'd say too much. And I couldn't. Not without knowing for sure I could find it."

My nervous fingers tap the countertop. "What are you talking about? Do you want the biscuits or not?"

Slowly, he slides a folded square of old paper across the counter.

"On the solstice, my mother—or, her memory—gave me an idea, a clue of where to look. Not a precise location, but it was enough. I finally went through all of my parents' personal belongings, and there it was, just packed away."

I suck in a breath as my fingers grasp the grimy paper. Stained. Fatty butter splotches. A well-loved thing if I've ever seen one.

"Your grandmother, Ambrosia, lent this recipe to my mother ages ago. A simple neighborly kindness."

I finally unfold the paper, my fingers shaking so badly I'm worried I'll tear it and the recipe inside. As I read through the ingredients and instructions, in Momaw Frost's handwriting, my chest flutters with a delicate hope.

Of course of course of course.

A gift from a Frost Farewitch to the young Ms. Knight, shared freely, asking nothing in return. Like a laugh. A seat at the table. A Warlock's name.

This is it. I know it.

The Warlock holds up a set of car keys. "Tell me what you need. I drive now, you know."

"With an adult," Ms. Zeen calls from the side. "You only have a permit."

He raises an affronted eyebrow, jiggling the keys. "Where are we going?"

Where aren't we going is the better question.

The Warlock and I knock on a dozen doors by suppertime.

We visit neighbors across the Holler to borrow flour, sugar, salt, baking soda, cinnamon, butter, eggs, oil, vanilla, walnuts, pecans, bananas, powdered sugar, and cream cheese. I've already got these items in my own kitchen, but Momaw Frost's note makes it clear, the ingredients don't matter as much as where they come from. The trick to curing a wasting disease that develops and worsens with isolation and burnout isn't about the final product at all, but how the baking comes together. The magic is the process. The process is the magic.

A herald of a Southern summertime, hummingbird cake is not ungodly popular or secretly obscure. Its flavors aren't out of the ordinary, if a little odd grouped together, like a small town of eccentric personalities.

Foxe Holler, this community, is the key.

This means explaining to my neighbors why I'm visiting them in the first place: Marigold Frost is dying. The Frosts can't hide anymore. If we never ask for help, no one knows to give it.

By the time the sun sets, there's only one ingredient missing.

Once again, I find myself on the porch of Gertha Fudge's immaculate little white house. Except this time, I'm not alone.

"Fudge?" I ask for what's probably the fourth time. "*Our* Gertha Fudge offered to take you in?"

Next to me, Warlock Knight nods. "Sixteen-year-old me was equally as stunned."

I swallow my disbelief. "Why?"

A sigh settles deep in his chest. "After the library fire, I didn't have another guardian, so the Eldercraft wanted to relocate me to live with other young Warlocks. But Gertha offered to take me in so I didn't have to leave the Holler. It was the only home I'd known. Instead, I hid in the Manor and avoided the Eldercraft until I was eighteen. That was the end of it."

"What in the world did you say to Gertha?"

He grimaces.

"*That's* the moment in time you wanted to fix, isn't it? You refused Gertha's help and everything went downhill. More downhill."

And he fled uphill, as far to the edge of the Holler as he could get.

"Shunning her kindness was one of my biggest mistakes."

I step forward. "Ready?"

He glowers at the door. A lot has changed since April, but his sullen scowl didn't go anywhere. "No, but you've already knocked."

When Gertha Fudge opens her door, she doesn't immediately slam it, a positive sign this is already going better than it could have. Time to make amends. But based on her unblinking glare, she won't be going first.

I'll start. "Hello—"

"Go away. I'm busy making fudge."

Or *try* to make amends. The Warlock side-eyes me just long enough to mouth what looks like *I told you so.*

Then to my surprise, he steps up. "Good evening, Ms. Fudge."

"Don't *Ms. Fudge* me, boy. Not after all these years. No matter what the DMV says, I can still see well enough to spot trouble miles away." She points at me. "I knew you'd be a problem."

I try again. "We noticed you weren't with Oris Webb and his followers on the solstice."

"What of it? Sending that tornado down on us—not *my* church, nossir. I knew something was out of sorts. That storm didn't have the Widow Witch's flare."

She would know. "We met her," I say. "Your great-grandmother."

The Warlock takes a fortifying breath. "Ms. Fudge, I regret how you and I ended our last conversation. You only had your neighbors in mind, and I treated you unfairly."

The old woman eyes him up and down. "If I didn't know better, I'd say you grew up."

I think I hear a growl, so I grab his elbow, in case the old woman starts throwing hands. So much for positive thinking. "We need your help."

"So I heard. Asking your neighbors for help. *Imagine that.*" Her tone shoves my confidence right through a meat grinder. Looking at the Warlock, she adds, "When someone extends a hand to help you now, do you take it?"

The Warlock glances at me. "I'm learning to."

"You should've learned a long time ago. *Both* of you."

He stiffens. "Save your ire for me. Ms. Frost has been nothing but kind to you."

"Kindness isn't always rewarded. You would know that, Knight."

"Kindness shouldn't be given with the intention of exchange, *Gertha*."

"Why—I will put you right, you hear?" She jabs a finger at him but looks to me. "I opened my home to this boy. But what did he do? Shunned me. The entire Holler."

"Can you fault me? My family was gone. I was too angry to know any better."

"And my own children were grown and gone. We could've looked out for each other. This town's always hated Warlocks, and after the fire, that was your chance to change their minds, to show them you could be part of this community."

"You could have asked me again later, when I was thinking properly—"

"Why would I? Where have you been when the Holler has needed help? You and that Letha Zeen, either of you."

The Warlock's voice sharpens to a threatening edge. "You may criticize me all you like, Ms. Fudge. But never Ms. Zeen."

When I taste thyme, I plant myself between them. Why do people so love to be mad?

Then I remember—she never had a problem recalling the Warlock. With the chaos of the tornado, I completely forgot. "You've always been able to remember Mr. Knight. Not just the rumors, but details about him. His history."

"Because of her bloodline," the Warlock says. "Descendants of Hedgewitches can see through their family's spells or illusions."

Of course.

"You had to be able to tell he was disappearing from folks'

memories," I say to her. "Were you curious why?" Maybe she already knew why.

Her dark eyes burn through her folds of wrinkles. "Knight made it clear, he wanted to be left alone. I was happy to oblige. You know why, girl? *Because he knew he deserved it.*"

"No one *deserves* loneliness. And he's not alone. Not anymore."

He glances at me in that inscrutable way of his. Severe but unreadable. Lord, I don't have time for all these brooding stares and angry pouts.

"My mom is dying," I say, teeth grinding. It hasn't gotten easier to say aloud, no matter how often I have today. "But I have the right recipe, and you've got the last ingredient I need. Momaw swore by your canned pineapple for her hummingbird cake. So I'm asking for your kindness, Ms. Fudge. One more time. Please."

She huffs. Clicks her tongue.

The air stills around us, the porch a delicate bubble of pressure about to pop. Muggy humidity clings to my lungs. This is the final ingredient I need. My last chance to save my mom.

The Warlock breaks the silence first. "I apologize, Gertha."

And here I thought I'd seen it all.

His hands clench. "You're right. I haven't helped the Holler when it's mattered most. I'm trying to change that. Belatedly, but I'm trying. And if it's of any worth this many years too late, I've regretted refusing your offer every day I've spent alone in that Manor."

The old woman chews her cheek, looking anywhere but at him.

I give her my best smile. "What do you say? Will you help a neighbor?"

She looks me up and down. Snorts. Then faces the Warlock. "I'm still angry."

"As am I," the Warlock says. "But maybe we can be angry and kind at the same time."

Chapter Thirty-Nine

SATURDAY, JULY 2

Honey's Helpful Hint, from
Honey Frost's Southern Cookbook
for Recipes Gone Wrong:

Send the letter. Cut the cake. Pass the butter. The best things in life are shared. It takes a holler.

I bake through the night in the Apothakery's kitchen.

Generations of Frost family memories heat these ovens. It's where Momaw Frost taught my mom to be a Farewitch. For this particular recipe, this kitchen just makes sense.

I bake six mediocre cakes first, one of which I drop on the floor. There's some pillow-screaming at about three a.m. Every neighbor who contributed an ingredient gave me extra, and that generosity saves me. With the last of Gertha Fudge's pineapple, I make a seventh and final cake, full of every fervent prayer I've ever made.

When the sun rises, I escort my finished hummingbird cake to the hospital. I try to stay awake as I feed my mom a bite at a time. She chews, weakly. Smiles, weakly. Then sleeps, strongly. Carolina promises to call me when she wakes up, then orders me to go home and rest.

So I do. But I don't end up at the Apothakery.

Knight Manor's kitchen is buzzing with people.

Silas and Rett and Arna Jean. Everyone who donated an ingredient. No Gertha Fudge, but Ms. Buchanan's brought her own thin apple cake, and even the church choir is here.

At first, I assume folks came to buy something, but they're not here for the Farewitch. They're here for Marigold's daughter. No one wants to wait alone for news of their mayor.

When word gets around that folks are meeting up and dessert is involved, other neighbors arrive with more apple cakes. They plop them on top of each other, and soon we've got the makings of a proper country apple stack cake. As the layers grow, the kitchen becomes as full as I've ever seen it and Ms. Zeen ensures tea travels alongside the growing conversation. Somehow, my mom and I, the lonely Farewitches of Foxe Holler, have brought everyone together.

In the familiar warmth of the Manor's kitchen, I begin to hope that things will be okay. I got used to this place when I wasn't looking, but fell in love with it when I started. How did I ever drive away? What if I don't want to leave again?

After a while, I get overwhelmed with the crowd and head outside for air.

The Warlock stands alone on the back veranda, looking out at his gardens.

I shiver, the air cooling as late afternoon turns to evening. Maybe it's nerves. Why wasn't I scared to meet this Warlock all those months ago, and now I'm terrified to say hello?

With a steeling breath, I join him at the porch railing. "Gossip is, an anonymous donor has funded the town's plans to finally rebuild the library."

His shoulders go taut at my voice but he doesn't look over. "So I heard. Someone likely realized there's no point being the wealthiest man in the graveyard."

I try to smile, but my mind tiptoes back to my mom at the hospital. He clears his throat and my eyes latch on to his stoic profile, greedy for a distraction.

He faces me now, hip braced against the railing, and looks to the bustling kitchen. "Even once the library and church are rebuilt,

I think I'll keep the Manor open. To neighbors, visitors. The house seems tickled with all the activity."

My heart crams a hundred beats into half a second. I'm—*proud*. Teaspoon by teaspoon, the chill that followed me from the hospital melts away.

"Ms. Zeen will riot at the mess."

"It'll be good for her, too." Beyond his shoulder, fireflies come to life, skittering in the evening air.

All my nerves are frayed at this point, but I need to ask, before I lose my chance. "During all our research for Lazlo, I read up on the Language of Small Wishes. You told me it doesn't allow you to grant wishes for family and folks you live with. But that's not true, is it?"

He stiffens.

"You can't grant wishes for people you *love*."

He takes a sharp breath, and the glow from inside chases some of the shadows from his face. "For the people we love, we have to put in the work. Wishes only get a person so far."

I'm really hoping the fading evening light will hide my flushed cheeks. "When, ah . . . when did it stop working around me?"

Maybe he'll say *What do you mean?* Let us both pretend and push on with our lives. But then his full attention lands on me, eyes bright and hard, and I know none of this is going to be easy. I swallow, hoping for air, but just find fear. Hope. Both. They taste the same right now.

"When you were in the hospital . . . When you became sick, I was losing you and I'd only just found you."

I brace myself against the railing, unsteady. "That feels like ages ago."

"Feels like minutes for me. *Every* minute I spend with you feels like a new moment, like I'm learning the world for the first time."

Oh LordLordLord.

I'm not ready for this conversation. For any of this. How can I appreciate a part of my world opening up while another part is on the brink of collapse? Can't we go back to our easy repartee, the days when I was the one making *him* uncomfortable?

All I can muster is: "Thank you for letting me stay here tonight, by the way."

His brow lowers, his eyes roaming over me. I get a glimpse of the man who kissed me breathless back at the Widow Witch's cottage.

"Stay as long as you like."

My heartbeat gives a little shudder at his words, which don't sound at all as simple as *Stay as long as you like*. "You can't look at me like that."

"Like what?"

"*Like that.*"

"Elaborate, Ms. Frost."

"We can talk about this tomorrow." If tomorrow doesn't bring bad news and my shattered heart.

His jaw tenses. "Whether tomorrow or the next day, I will be unable to hide that I no longer have any ability to treat you as casually as a neighbor or colleague."

I nearly squeak. "Then why did you avoid me for a week?"

"I didn't want to reach out to you with false hope about that recipe, and . . ."

"*And?* Elaborate, Mr. Knight." I haven't been able to use his real name around him yet.

A ragged breath crawls from his chest. "And I thought you read my letter and still chose to leave."

Something unfurls within me. No wonder he didn't try to convince me to stay. He thinks that's what I wanted. "I didn't read it until yesterday."

"And?"

"*And*," I huff, "could you not have written a happy letter for once? Can you sign anything *fortunately*?"

His head tilts. "No."

Completely deadpan. Ass.

Now that same letter feels like it's burning right through the front pocket of my apron and into the cavity holding my heart. "You only gave me that letter because you thought you were going to die. Not because you might live." To further my point, I yank the letter from my front pocket and shove it in his direction. "I don't want your name like this."

A half smile. "Too late. It's yours."

I growl in frustration, burying the letter back in my pocket. "Then do it right."

His smirk returns, but it's the dangerous kind he was wearing right before he kissed me. He sticks out a hand, accepting my challenge. "Hello. My name is Verne."

I take it. "Hello, Verne," I say aloud for the first time. His grip tightens. "I'm Honey."

We shake.

"I've been thinking about you. Your name, I mean. While I'm working on a cookbook, you could write your own gardener's grimoire. *Verne's Ferns: A Guidebook to the Plants of Knight Manor for the Horticulturally Inclined.* I mean, I know you can't use your name in public, but, you know. Think about it."

He stares at me with an inscrutable expression, like he can't decide whether to laugh, kiss me, or put me to bed for the night. A part of me craves all three.

"May I show you something?" he asks abruptly.

Too focused on the static skittering across my hand, all I can do is nod and follow.

Side by side, but never touching, we round a corner into a private grove I've never seen before. It's hiding expansive flower beds, and even I can tell that whatever grows here is special. No, not flower beds. My breath hitches. The beds are full of—

"Herbs, for you," he says, watching me. "I planted this garden shortly after you arrived."

Gingerly, I step around the beds, studying the healthy greens—and the *smells*. Rosemary. Basil. Cilantro. Dill. Tarragon. Mint. Oregano. Parsley. Lavender.

Thyme. I can't escape it. I'm not sure I want to.

An entire herb garden. For a Farewitch. A garden needs someone to use it. "You planted this *months ago*?"

"Once I tasted your food."

"So my food *was* that good." *Please banter back.* He can't pick now to suffocate his sarcasm and completely flip my worldview inside out.

"*You* were that good."

All at once, dusk overtakes our little herb garden. "Verne, I don't . . ." I clear my throat, trying to thwart the rising, delicious panic in my gut. Could be another allergic reaction. "I don't think I can handle any enormous declarations at this current moment in time."

There. I've said it.

Silence tremors between us.

He shakes his head, gaze as pointed as my sharpest knife. "Sweetheart, this garden is only a *minuscule* measurement of how I feel about you."

I'm pretty sure I hiccup.

"You can't say things like that." My voice is breathless. "If we're right about what's happening to my mom, then Farewitches don't live long. I don't want you at my funeral when I'm thirty-five. Aren't you tired of living with curses?"

"You're not a curse. Quite the opposite."

I look away from those hazel eyes before I crumble or make reckless promises—

"No matter what happens tomorrow, I planted this so you would stay, Honey." His voice is low, rough, and rubs against me like a rocky creek bed under bare feet. Grounding. Persistent. "You don't have to decide now. Or ever. But you always have a place here. An open invitation."

His words about ruin me, but then he runs a thumb over my bottom lip, and *that* most assuredly ruins me.

I turn my head to leave the smallest kiss on his palm. "I prefer my invitations to arrive in spooky little black letters."

Just then, voices pour into the garden, popping the bubble around us.

Arna Jean runs into view.

"It's Carolina," she pants, catching her breath. She holds out my cell phone. Glowing and buzzing with a call. "From the hospital."

Chapter Forty
SATURDAY, JULY 9

ANOTHER WEEK LATER

Honey's Helpful Hint, from
Honey Frost's Southern Cookbook
for Recipes Gone Wrong:

Remember to be patient and kind. A little bit of thyme and honey goes a long way.

"If anyone sings 'Happy Birthday,' I will delight in removing their eyebrows."

Rett and Arna Jean immediately rub their foreheads as I place a glossy layer cake on the table in front of the Warlock.

We dragged a table outside for a picnic in the gardens, and flowers burst in color around us in the golden hour sun. The herb-scented air is almost as delicious as the food we've spread out. Benedictine and pimento cheese sandwiches, coleslaw, cornbread muffins, icebox banana pudding, ambrosia salad, and a huge pitcher of sweet tea.

At the end of the table, Governess Zeen chats with Ms. Buchanan, while Silas and Rett keep Beauregard occupied with a ball nearby. Every time the poodle bounds too close to a flower bed, the Warlock winces.

"I'm guessing the flavor is sugar?" Arna Jean asks me from her seat next to Ms. Zeen.

"A honey and thyme cake," I reply. A halo of frosted watercress leaves and thyme sprigs crown the Warlock's cake, encircling a piped *Happy Birthdays*, plural.

"I'll take a piece to Okolona on my next visit," the Warlock says.

Silas wanders over and counts the candles. No full suit today, but still a collared shirt and vest with tiny blue rosebuds. Mayor looks good on Silas Key.

"Christ. Some people really do win the gene lottery. Honey, do you realize he could legally gamble in the state of Kentucky when you were still reading Junie B. Jones—"

"That's enough," the Warlock bites.

Arna Jean cackles.

"Three weeks late, but are you ready to turn another year older, *officially*?" I ask him.

"If we must."

"We must."

"How lucky you are, then," comes a wrinkled voice.

The Warlock peers around my waist. "I see you got my invitation, Ms. Fudge."

Gertha Fudge shuffles into the garden, her cane clopping on the stone steps to the yard. "You need to fix this old shack to accommodate the elderly," she snaps. "All these old ladies going in and out, this place is like a HomeGoods. With more cobwebs. And falling hazards."

The Warlock just nods. "I'm glad you came, Gertha."

She isn't the last latecomer.

Carolina appears from the kitchen, still in scrubs. And on her arm is a thin but upright Marigold Frost.

"Hi there, my girl," my mom says, waving.

I swallow what feels like a top-shelf shot of pure sunshine. "Hi, Mom."

She's making good progress, her weak body slowly rebuilding muscle and coordination. Her hair has stayed gray, but glossy. At the first signs of improvement a week ago, she warned me not to fret over her like an anxious hen.

"Thanks for bringing her, Carolina," I say.

"You know I jump at the chance to have someone tell me how to drive."

My mom eases into the chair by Silas, who has taken a seat next to Rett. "Our Holler has more barrels of hay than people. Red lights are suggestions."

Silas pours tea for them. "I see where someone got his driving lessons from."

The Warlock scoffs. "Rude."

"Very," my mom agrees. "Considering you drive like a grandma, Silas."

"Marigold, you've just admitted to breaking the law in front of your mayor."

"Don't pull that with me, kid. You're a baby mayor right now."

"We'll add *insulted your mayor* to the list, too."

"Cake?" Rett breaks in.

My mom glances to me, to the birthday cake, and back again. She mouths: *Proud of you.* My heart melts into molten butter, a Frost favorite flavor and feeling.

The hummingbird cake jump-started her recovery. But *truly* resting, retiring from being mayor, has done the most for her so far. I'm not sure she'll regain the same energy she had before as a younger Farewitch, but she's adamant the wasting sets in when a Farewitch stops savoring her life, and I recognize a warning when I see one. I can't go back to my old habits. Not if I want to avoid flirting with some point of no return. But that's a good thing. Because for the first time in a long while, I feel . . . not simply *happy*.

I feel like me.

As everyone gathers around, the Warlock snaps. The candles spark. We sing, ignoring his protests. Rett slices the cake into neat portions and Arna Jean passes forks. The hum of pleased murmuring with full mouths returns, vibrating deep in my chest, right underneath my apron pocket where I keep both of the Warlock's letters.

I'm handing out more cake when the Warlock tugs on my apron. "Do not make me order you to sit down, Ms. Frost," he murmurs.

Caught. I can't remember if I've taken a seat yet. One of those habits to break, for sure.

Feeling bold, or maybe just at home, I perch right on top of the Warlock's knees. He's only caught off guard a moment. Then a strong palm slides across my back, and he pulls me properly onto his lap. The warmth of his body spreads like a blanket from my lower back to my shoulders. Just like that, the Warlock of Foxe Holler becomes my new favorite chair.

I should really start calling him *Verne*. When we're alone, that is.

"Thank you for the cake," he says in my ear as his fingers roam over the side buttons of my overalls. My *nice* overalls. It's a party, after all.

I lean back into his firm chest. "What did you wish for?"

"How about a bargain: I'll tell you, but only if you agree to find a mentor. You think you've seen me be difficult, but I'll mutiny if you neglect your magic."

Since making the hummingbird cake, I've only been at the Apothakery to help prep Arna Jean to take over. I'm taking a break from the shop. A real one. For now, the Warlock could use help managing his library, since he opened it to the public. Ms. Zeen has even begun tutoring kids amid the stacks. After decades of suffocation, the farmhouse feels like it's finally breathing. As for when, or if, I come back to the Apothakery . . . Haven't figured that one out yet.

Point is, I'm getting time to rest and do things I enjoy, like working on my cookbook. Time to get to know my magic, whether it's learning to better use my memory affinity as a Farewitch or exploring how I can use decay for good. I'd like to know what I'm capable of.

"Agreed. Your wish?"

His playful half smile grows serious. "Do you remember when I told you everyone tastes something different when I do magic?"

"You never told me what *you* taste."

"Honey."

My name on his lips sends a charge through my bloodstream. "Yes?"

"No, I taste honey. Ever since I began to learn magic, long before I met you."

I lean away to get a better look at him. Is he serious?

The muscles in his thighs tense under me as he pulls me farther onto his lap, closer still. His hands move lower, end up on my hips. And squeeze. Checking to make sure I'm real.

That's a feeling I could get used to.

The Manor has been so busy, we haven't gotten to spend time alone together. Every time he's looked my way over the last week, I was tempted to stuff my head in the freezer to cool off.

"I left your room empty," he says. "In case . . . Well, Ms. Zeen really doesn't need another sewing room."

Looking up at the back of the farmhouse, I feign a sigh. "Of course. And it's not like we can put all my stuff in *your* room."

His right eyebrow goes up. "Of course not. Best to keep the church-lady gossip at bay."

"Your room is probably dark and cold like those caves. Heavy bat aesthetic."

His low chuckle against my back runs up and down my spine. There aren't many things that taste as good as his laugh sounds. "Have you thought about my offer?"

You always have a place here. An open invitation.

I give a casual shrug to hide the speed of my heartbeat. "Well, I don't make birthday cakes for just anyone. But if I'm staying, I am partial to yellow kitchens."

He gives me a real, not-a-smirk smile. My heart is galloping now. Is this how all of his plants feel when he looks at them? Like they're blooming from the inside, life sprouting right from the core of their soul?

"I can make that happen. But it'll have to be done by hand. You can't wish for this one. So I'll need painting supplies. Rollers, brushes. Tarps. Overalls, even."

"Ah, you're out of luck. I bought up every pair in town already."

Verne drags a thumb across my lip, capturing some frosting. He licks the sugar from his finger. "Any other requests, Ms. Frost?"

I can think of a few. But we have time.

And the flavor of that promise is as sweet as a heaping spoonful of bright yellow honey.

Acknowledgments

As any Farewitch will tell you, it takes a coven, and the coven that spurred this book from the earth is roughly the size of Foxe Holler and just as powerful. These folks here are the reason you're holding a real book in your hands and not a sad stack of coffee-stained CVS receipts, and their dedication is the crucial ingredient to the recipe that is *The Farewitch of Foxe Holler*:

Tricia: Long before this book, you dove into my writing about the South and recognized the importance of that atmosphere as the heart of everything I write. We bonded over children's lit, but when I came to you with a hunk of an adult fantasy, you embraced this story like a neighbor you'd known your whole life. My endless thanks to you and your teams at EMLA and ACM.

Nivia: You gave this cozy fantasy a chance, and promptly went above and beyond to craft it into the story it was always trying to be. Even when we were wrestling two books into one (*promise* the next will be shorter!), you doubled the story's heart. You always saw Honey and her town, which means you saw me. The rest of the Saga team is a force of nature, and I have so much respect for these champions behind the scenes: Jéla Lewter, Ella Laytham, Lewelin Polanco, Emily Arzeno, Kimberly Goldstein, Sara Kitchen, Chloe Gray, Karintha Parker, Emma Shaw, Mabel Marte Taveras, and Yvette Grant.

Mary Kate McDevitt: This cover is everything I didn't know I wanted. You saw the soul of the book, and you gave me horseshoes, and for that I will forever be grateful.

To the Underground writing group: Back in 2019, someone

probably told me *not* to invite a group of strangers off the streets of New York to spend hours in a tiny conference room together, but I'm so glad I didn't listen, and here we are. Y'all and your creativity inspire me every day.

To the folks who have shown me nothing but generosity and kindness as this book came to life, from its first pages during workshop to editorial passes in the middle of the boonies: Darcey Steinke and Coe Booth at the New School; Sandy Coomer at Rockvale Writers' Colony in Tennessee; Melissa Helton and the Hindman Settlement School in Kentucky; and Barbara Napier and the kitchen witches working magic at Snug Hollow in Kentucky.

A love of writing always comes from a love of reading, and mine wouldn't exist without the Goshen Public Library and independent bookstores like Carmichael's in Louisville (big shout-out to Beth Bissmeyer and your team for welcoming me home as an author, not just as a reader). The other bookstores that made Honey's food come to life are Kitchen Arts and Letters, Bonnie Slotnick Cookbooks, and Joanne Hendricks' Cookbooks. A big thank-you as well to all the women whose names fill the community cookbooks from Kentucky and Appalachia.

As an only child like Honey with a small family, I must've scored the cosmic jackpot of kinship to find myself surrounded by folks who truly embody the spirit of Foxe Holler: Flynn, Jenny, Sonia, Lexi, Sydney, and Clay. First friends, first readers, first sisters, first cousins—y'all are the best soulmates I could have found. You love the good questions more than the good answers, and your hunger for life drives me to be a better human every day, on the page and off.

Mom and Dad Goff: Your love story is the reason I exist, and why I have so much to be thankful for. I write for me and the voices in my head, but I live for you.

Adam: Our love story is the reason this book exists. There would be no happy ending without you. To the Gamma Quadrant and back!

The Farewitch of Foxe Holler: Debut Author Interview

1. What was the first book that made you fall in love with the SFF genre?

Like most folks my age, I can trace my love of sci-fi and fantasy to children's literature. *The Phantom Tollbooth* by Norton Juster restructured my way of thinking about the world and space and distance. *The City of Ember* by Jeanne DuPrau was also a pivotal book for me. Lemony Snicket's A Series of Unfortunate Events saga might be more whimsically gothic than SFF, but that series is my North Star of stellar world-building. I don't often reread books, but one I consistently returned to was *The Last of the Really Great Whangdoodles* by Julie Andrews (yes, that Julie!). Ultimately, I credit the general wave of speculative fiction that overtook my childhood, from the Magic Tree House books to R. L. Stine to *Howl's Moving Castle,* to Tamora Pierce.

2. Where did the initial idea for *The Farewitch of Foxe Holler* come from and how did the story begin to take shape?

When I began brainstorming the *very* beginnings of this novel in 2019, I was writing a lot of darker Southern gothic short stories, staring down my late twenties, and thoroughly immersed in New York City with an active nine-to-five job. As you'd expect, I was thinking a lot about millennial burnout, especially for oldest and only daughters, and my own mental health. Time and making the best use of it was a constant refrain in my brain, both the force behind my creative drive and the anxiety that shadowed me at the same time. Cue the craving for something light and cozy and purely for conjuring smiles. As I drafted and revised (*and revised*) over the next couple of years, always missing the space and greenery of Kentucky, the women in my family and our Southern background were core inspirations.

3. What was the most challenging moment of writing *The Farewitch of Foxe Holler*?

Fun fact: Honey's story used to be a duology! After putting our heads together to think on what was best for the health of the book, my editor and I decided this story would be the strongest version of itself as one book, not two. Thus began the long (but needed!) journey of carving a 180K cinder block down to a respectable brick. The hardest part wasn't cutting darlings, but rather, I'd been in my own work for so long that I couldn't always see where a scene or dialogue could be cut without any harm to the story and characters. As someone who has always been an overwriter, I wanted to streamline the story, but I simply needed an extra set of eyes to help me get there.

4. Your debut is set in a small town in magic-imbued rural Kentucky. What was your approach to bringing this world to life? Is there a world-building element you're particularly proud of?

Because of my family's Appalachian roots in Kentucky and West Virginia, I wanted to prioritize the rural South that I knew, not just a small town that could theoretically exist anywhere. It was crucial to me that this story reflect the Kentucky I grew up with, the tiny hollers where you might not find *quaint and charming* but you will find big personalities and big atmosphere and big community. We grow up reading and watching content where *cozy* is synonymous with English countryside cottagecore or a New England–esque small town, so I was endlessly excited by the idea of highlighting my grandmothers' Kentucky. Bringing this world to life was always less about witches and magic and more about capturing the essence of not a *hollow* but a *holler*.

5. The characters in *The Farewitch of Foxe Holler* absolutely sing. If you had to pick, who would you say is your favorite? Who did you find the most difficult to write?

The older ladies of the Holler have a special place in my heart because they represent so much of my own grandmothers. Beulah Buchanan, Gertha Fudge, Letha Zeen—I can hear their drawls and mischievous advice and hungry gossip in my ears so clearly, it's like I'm having a conversation with my own family. They are the soul of this book in the same way women are the soul of these small towns where neighborly connection and support make up the fabric of found families. Oddly, Honey was likely the most difficult character to write for me, because in a way, we're one and the same. Reaching her voice meant exploring mine, even the more sensitive parts I wasn't always comfortable sharing. In fact, I originally wrote Honey's voice in third person. Only after I rewrote the book in first person for her did I realize, *ah*, that was the missing heart.

6. Who are some of your favorite authors and how have they influenced your writing?

Because I could write an entire novel just about my favorite authors, I'll focus on the folks whose work specifically helped me give this book a soul. Since this was my first foray into the lighter and cozy fantasy genre, I had to learn to take myself less seriously. To name just a few, the authors I clung to were Heather Fawcett, TJ Klune,

Olivia Atwater, Alix E. Harrow, Emily Tesh, Sangu Mandanna, T. Kingfisher, Diana Wynne Jones, and Christelle Dabos. Their writing and approach to story and character and craft gave me permission to be whimsical, and to embrace the idea that playful curiosity could also be sincere. A few key Kentucky authors—Lee Mandelo, Elizabeth Kilcoyne, and Silas House—taught me how to truly burrow into a place and celebrate its soul.

7. Without giving too much away, what can readers expect from you next?

We best return to Foxe Holler, shouldn't we? I hope readers love this town as I much as I do, because I'm giddy thinking about the other pockets of the Holler I've yet to share with folks. No matter what, we'll see more magic, gossipy church ladies, and really zealous descriptions of Southern food. I can't resist some of the key characters who make up the Holler, like Beulah Buchanan and the Claywells and our Kentucky fried coven of Witches. But perhaps we'll let Honey have that rest she's after, and we'll find ourselves following another young Witch learning what it means to navigate life inside the Holler but on the outside of her comfort zone. Readers can expect even more shenanigans at the intersection of *Steel Magnolias* and *Practical Magic*.

8. And, finally, if you could be one type of witch (Farewitch, Bookwitch, Hearthwitch, etc.), which would you choose?

This story began because I just wanted to be a kitchen witch. If I could cook and bake, study recipes, read cookbooks, visit farmers' markets, and taste food all day long, I would be happy. When I feel at my most relaxed and connected to myself, that's when you'll see me start cooking. My love languages are gift giving and acts of service, so naturally, my most favorite thing to do is make food for the people

I care about. I think I'd also love being a Greenwitch in another life. Growing food and understanding the earth is just another part of our relationship with food. The Warlock in this book loves his plants, and that's no coincidence. My grandmother had a truly impressive green thumb, and I grew up watching her work magic with plants, never quite able to figure out what kind of spells she was casting to be so darn good at it. When I think of her, I think of soil and flowers and the outdoors, the ingredients of one of my happy places.

About the Author

© Sidney Beal III

Ellen Pauley Goff was born and raised in the wilds of Kentucky. Her short fiction has appeared in the *Indiana Review*, *Hunger Mountain*, *F(r)iction*, and *New Millennium Writings*, among others. Her poetry can be found in the *Atlanta Review*, and her creative nonfiction in *The Inquisitive Eater* and *Karma Comes Before*. Ellen received her BA from the University of Chicago, and her MFA dual degree in fiction and writing for children and young adults from the New School. When she's not writing or reading recipes, Ellen works in publishing and international rights, and is the founder of a long-standing writing workshop and critique group in Manhattan, with the goal of providing publishing knowledge to emerging writers. *The Farewitch of Foxe Holler* is her debut novel.